SIGN OF THE WHITE RAVEN

"Thank you for your help; I will not forget it," Aleron promised.

"Think nothing of it, my friend. Now travel safe."

As Aleron turned to the gangplank, something slammed into his left shoulder, driving him to all fours, the bundle falling to the dock. Gasping to catch his breath, he looked over to see a bodkin point protruding from the front of his shoulder. He looked to his right in time to see one of Cipactli's men falling into the water, two arrows sticking from his chest.

Cipactli grabbed the bundle, hurled it onto the boat, heedless of injuring anyone aboard, and then grabbed Aleron by his good arm. "Get to the boat, now!" he shouted, as he hauled Aleron up to his feet again.

The haversack forgotten, he stumbled onto the gangplank through the fog that slowly crept into the edges of his field of vision. It was difficult to breathe, much less talk, so he simply put one foot before the other as fast as he could manage, hoping he would maintain his balance. He could feel the Kolixtlani smuggler's hands steadying him, but then suddenly falling away. He heard a splash behind him as he took the last couple of steps into the boat. He turned to see a body float past, two shafts sticking from the back of a fine silk coat.

Geldun had his shield up and his sword out, while Barathol covered behind him with his glaive in a reverse grip, over the top of Geldun's shield. Together, they shielded the other occupants as the crew scrambled to untie the boat. The lamplight from the docks allowed just enough visual warning for them to swat the shafts away. No one remained alive on the docks, as far as Aleron could see.

One of the crew shoved off from the dock with an oar, while the other two grabbed an oar each and started pulling for all they were worth. The one who pushed off dipped his oar to help steer the boat, one side or the other, as needed.

As they pulled away from the docks, Aleron allowed himself to sag against the side, his right arm hooked over the gunwale for support. He couldn't move his left arm at all without searing pain, but he was able to keep the tunnel vision at bay, just so long as he didn't move and breathed slowly.

SIGN OF THE WHITE RAVEN

Book 2 of the Chronicles of Aertu

By Julian E Benoit

THE BARDICHE PRESS

2023

This is a work of fiction. Any resemblance of characters in this work to actual persons, living or dead, is purely coincidental. Now, some of the goblins or trolls might seem remarkably familiar, as might the occasional horse's behind, but please remember, they are not anyone you know.

First, to my family. All that I do is for you.

Next, to all my readers, whose support and encouragement helped to make this second volume a reality.

And let's not forget the Puppies.

MAP OF AERTU MAIN CONTINENT

Prologue

Zorekday, Day 18, Haymaking Moon, 8765 Sudean Calendar

The Nameless One sat brooding upon his throne of black obsidian, as he did each day for over four thousand and fifteen years. The only light was not light at all, but the blue glow of elvish magic emanating from the chains and wards holding him to the throne and imprisoning him in his fortress all these millennia. Though no light penetrated his abode, he sensed each passing day with absolute clarity. The cursed elvish sorcerers assured that in the configuration of their wards.

He looked down to the bare hands at the ends of his armored forearms, the steel vambraces cleanly cut above the wrists, bare because they were absent when the elves chained him here and now regrown, sheathed in shining black reptilian scales and tipped with sharp red claws. All of his skin beneath the ancient black armor now sported the same scales, and his unblinking eyes bore blood-red irises with vertically slit pupils.

Though he had lost the power of transmutation the Allfather held, he could still slowly transform himself through red magic. The years gave him ample time to consider the form in which he would return to Aertu, and he chose one that would strike terror into the hearts of his opponents.

Soon, my son will return with Zadehmal, and my power will again be complete.

He thought back on the fateful day that brought him to his current circumstance.

I step into the light of day from my obsidian stronghold and cross the courtyard, steel-clad boots clanking upon the flagstones. The black iron gates swing open upon my command, and

I stride upon the field of battle. The armies of elves and men pushed my forces all the way back to my stronghold of Immin Bul. The ranks of goblins and trolls close behind me, and I hear the orders to march forward, bellowed by the captains. These are all the new breeds I created over the past three decades, the goblins larger and stronger, the trolls smaller and faster, and both more cunning than their predecessors. Breeding my creations to men resulted in new hybrid forms of surpassing ability. I still have use for the brute strength of the cave troll and the sheer reproductive capacity of my original goblins, but my new creations allow for more advanced tactics on the field. The halfblood sorcerers I bred from captive elves and men are interspersed throughout the formations, each with a bodyguard of trolls to shield them. This force will crush the men and elves that dare to defile my realm with their presence.

It's unfortunate that my elves are still a generation away from completion. The one-eighth goblin generation should suffice to cull the unpredictable nature of the quarter goblins I have now. The project is moving slowly because each generation is slower to reach reproductive age than the last. My son and his cohorts are just now in their teens, still children and unable to wield power. It will be at least another decade before any eighths manifest their powers. An army of elves, fighting on my behalf, would seal the outcome of this battle.

Clearing the gate, we advance at a trot. My beleaguered forces fight in disarray before the ordered formations of my enemies. Countless arrows rain down upon goblin and troll, leaving carnage and blood. There is fighting on all sides; we are surrounded, but I sense where the enemy is strongest, most likely to push through, and we move to intercept.

Clouds form, roiling angry red, as my sorcerers and I call down lightning upon our enemies. Domes of blue energy spring up to shield them as elves and halfbloods move to defend. Slivers of blue energy reach out in answer to our attack, slicing through the mass of goblins ahead, but rarely making it through to my advancing force. I sense all my sorcerers are still with me, and now I see the banners of Elvenholm and Sudea straight ahead. The strongest knot of enemy holds the biggest prize, it seems. Channels of crimson spear outward from our line, in answer to the enemy's attack, and many expendable goblins and trolls, caught in the crossfire, perish for the cause.

We will remove the head from this insufferable creature known as the "Free Peoples," and it will shrivel and die. Only then will my vision for Aertu come to fruition. The inefficiency of individuals governing their own lives will be over, replaced by my rule. Everyone will do as they should, no longer burdened with having to choose between right and wrong. Those who find themselves incapable of compliance, I will eliminate.

As we close with the enemy, the remaining goblins make way or find themselves crushed between the hammer and anvil. Some even turn on us in their desperation to survive, for my forces to cut down, as they would any obstacle. We stride over the dead and dying, goblins, trolls, elves, and men alike. Trampling boots and blood have turned the rust-red soil into crimson mud. Within moments, we are face-to-face with the massed ranks of elves and men. My great axe, Zadehmal, sings through the air, shattering armor and shields before me and swallowing the souls of all whose flesh it touches. When I gain full dominion over Aertu, all souls will join with me rather than my father, when their mortal life ends. I feel my strength grow as Zadehmal absorbs the spirits of my enemies. The carnage yields boundless amounts of the red energy of death and decay, for my sorcerers to draw upon, though I feel that many of their number have fallen by this time. Meanwhile, I feel the blue energy of life ever dwindling, curtailing the power of my opponents.

I sense victory within my grasp when I see the King of Men and the Prince of Elves converge on my position. These pitiful mortals think to defeat me with their weapons wrought of elvish magic. Aleron's greatsword and Aelwynn's halberd crackle with blue energy, infusing their bodies and causing their eyes to glow blue as well, just as my own glow with the red of death. I am death embodied, and I will add these two souls to my collection. I feel all the others writhe in agony as I shout, "Behold, Zadehmal, Cleaver of Souls and the instrument of your undoing!" I trade blows with the pair, fighting to a standstill, as the battle rages all about us, until the king lands a lucky blow to my left shin, the blade becoming jammed into the steel of my greave. The gash burns like the hottest flame, though I ignore the pain to take advantage of the king's mistake. My axe splits him from left shoulder to right hip, but wait, there is no soul to feed Zadehmal. The cursed halfblood must have known he was about to die and released his spirit into the blade. The moment of my discomfiture is enough for the elf to hack my hands off at the wrists. A scream erupts from my mouth as I witness black blood shoot from the stumps of my arms, only to be cut short by the burning blade passing through my throat, after which everything goes black.

My return to awareness finds me bound to my own throne with elvish chains that burn against my skin, even through the armor. I bask in the excruciating glow of elvish magic all around, from the wards they used to seal me within my fortress. My magic can do nothing against these wards, as I long ago gave up the ability to wield forms other than the red. I find myself regretting the decision, though the red power of death is the most powerful of all the forms, it can do nothing to dispel well-constructed wards of the other powers. Had I chosen to remain a wielder of all powers, like my siblings, I could never have risen to the strength I had just a fleeting time ago, but could I still wield the blue, I would dispel these wards in an instant. There is nothing to do now but work to regain and increase my strength. Elves and men will rue the day they thought to lock me away. Someday I will escape these bonds, there is no doubt, and that day will be one that Aertu will not soon forget.

As he sat, he thought, Zormat now sails to the frozen waste to retrieve Zadehmal. When he returns, he will use it to free me, and together we will conquer Aertu. I will not be as benevolent as I originally planned when I gain dominion over this world. The men I will enslave and the elves I will destroy, to the last child. With my son's people numbering in the millions, I have no use for them, not even as breeders.

Chapter 1

Carpathday, Day 28, Squash Moon, 8765 Sudean Calendar

Aleron awoke in the darkness of the cellar they called home for the last two days. Some light filtered between the floorboards, so he could dimly see his companions.

They managed to remain hidden whenever the tavern staff came down for supplies and nightly forays to the kitchen yielded the water necessary for their continued survival. He knew it was only a matter of time before someone discovered them, so they needed to move on soon.

He still had no inkling of even a sense for the magic he knew must be all around him, so they needed to find a way to spirit themselves out of the city without it.

In the early hours past midnight the day prior, he and Geldun ventured out into the city, while Barathol and Eilowyn stayed to guard their hiding place. They managed to find some clean men's clothing that would fit Eilowyn, left hanging on the line from the evening prior.

This morning, Geldun and Barathol prepared to find some boots that would work better than the slippers she wore from the palace. He hoped that they would find something early, so they could move out before sunrise. Every day brought them closer to discovery if they did not move.

He understood Kolixtlani fairly well, and eavesdropping on the tavern patrons revealed talk of house-to-house searches conducted by palace forces, searching for the murderers of the king. He also overheard news of Ehacatl's coronation in two more days and that the priests would sacrifice the fugitives, if captured, in his honor.

The voices upstairs were becoming fewer, and he knew the tavern would close soon. Barathol and Geldun were ready to move out, their faces freshly blackened with soot, unarmored and armed with only their long knives, for stealth.

"So, if we find boots, we head straight for the harbor and try to steal a boat?" Geldun verified.

"And, if that doesn't work out, we hole up in a warehouse or something until tomorrow night," Barathol continued.

They could not go east, toward Castia, as the Palace complex lay in that direction. The river blocked the way west, and that direction only took them to the Central Jungle, crawling with goblins and wild men. South to the dwarvish kingdom required they cross the bulk of Kolixtlan by the longest route. The fastest way out of the city of Kolixtla was north, to the harbor, and then west, by boat.

The marines had enough experience, feasibly, to pilot a small fishing vessel, and that lay at the core of their plan.

With Aleron unable to transform them, or even cast glamour over their features, there was no way for them to blend in with the local populace, so for now, darkness was their only defense.

Aleron just murmured agreement. Since the incident, the other two took the lead on most things. He seemed unable to break out of the funk he was experiencing since the magic left him. *It's like being blind,* he kept thinking to himself. *I suddenly can't see what I've been able to see plainly for over five years. I should be able to see colors all around me down here, but instead, it's just dark.*

"Snap out of it, Al," Geldun hissed. "We need you on top of things if this is going to work. Stop moping, or we'll never make it. We need you working with us, not just tagging along."

"I'll try, Gel. It's just been hard, not being able to see anything anymore."

***

Ehacatl paced the halls of the uppermost level of the royal palace, which housed the royal family. He hardly slept at all, these last two days, since the Sudeans killed his father and laid waste to the palace grounds. So many details needed attending. The king's funeral, for one, scheduled for midday tomorrow, and then his own coronation, scheduled for the next day. Repairs to the walls damaged two days ago were another priority to occupy his mind. He refused to compromise the defensibility of the palace, not in the wake of the last attack.

How the Sudeans managed to spirit such a powerful sorcerer into the heart of Kolixtla was a puzzle he intended to ferret out if it was the last thing he did. That was truly what kept him awake into the early morning.

I will avenge my father and my men who were lost. This sorcerer will not get away with what he did to my kingdom. I will pursue him and his accomplices to the end of Aertu if need be.

They found few witnesses to the incident, as all those in the courtyard perished, but a few of the kitchen staff recalled three armed men and a woman, all foreigners and light-skinned, but one. The servants attending the princess recalled nothing of the event upon waking from their stupor, as if someone had erased their memories of everything that happened.

***

The foray for boots panned out as they hoped. They actually located a cobbler's shop and found Eilowyn a pair that fit passably well. They even found her a knife for her belt. She and Aleron were fully dressed for their journey now, their faces and hands blackened like the other two. It was two or three bells before dawn, and they needed to strike out before the early-morning workers started moving about.

They exited the cellar into the alley, and Barathol whispered, "Now, we planned this out. Let's just hope we have the street layout memorized properly and nothing's changed since the map update we studied." He led the way westward and then to the north when they came to a side branch. He soot-blackened the blade of his glaive as well, to minimize their chances of detection. The others kept their weapons sheathed for now, with all shiny surfaces blackened or wrapped against glare.

"I hope this works, Barry," Eilowyn whispered. "I don't really want my heart cut out two days from now." Not waiting for a reply, she continued, "How are you doing, Aleron?"

"I'm fine, Ellie," he replied. He brought up the rear, his sharper senses and faster reflexes making him the most logical choice for that position. He wore Andhanimwhid strapped to his back. Though the sword was now dim, he was certain it was due to him losing his powers and not that it was damaged in any way. At least, he hoped that was the case.

They navigated back alleys, many times taking cover from patrols sweeping the city. At one point, as they all crouched within an alcove, a pair of foot soldiers approached their position, swords drawn. The fugitives huddled together with hoods drawn as far over their faces as possible, no one moving, and all attempting to look like bundles of merchandise. Suddenly, Barathol's glaive snapped out twice, severing the throats of the hapless soldiers. They quickly shoved the bodies into the space they had just occupied. They could do nothing about the stench of blood, though, so they put as much distance between themselves and the corpses as they could, taking a few turns they would not have chosen otherwise. Two dead bodies would certainly alert the Kolixtlanis that the Sudean fugitives were on the move. At least, it seemed so far, the Kolixtlanis didn't employ tracking hounds.

Eventually, they came to a wide avenue, running east to west. Geldun crossed first, followed by Barathol a few seconds later. They spent several minutes reconnoitering the alley and then motioned the others to cross. Eilowyn moved first, and then Aleron, with one last check of their rear guard, crossed behind her.

They found themselves in yet another dark alley, this one more squalid than the ones closer to the palace. After the storefronts lining the avenue, the remainder of the city in this direction made up the waterfront neighborhoods, a mix of warehouses, foundries, tanneries, and rude dwellings. Every city of men had such places, even Arundell, and they usually held those who performed the most menial labor, close to where their work took place. Aleron briefly wondered to himself why this was the case, when it was not so for elves and dwarves. He did not have much time to ponder such mysteries, as they quickly moved out again, picking their way around trash and debris, as well as the occasional drunkard passed out on the cobblestones.

One notable detail was the complete lack of soldiers patrolling these alleys. Apparently, this was not a part of the city where they felt particularly welcome. He hoped they did not run into any of the trouble the soldiers chose not to face.

He was quite certain that a couple of the supposed drunkards they stepped gingerly around would not have woken up if he kicked them in the ribs. He still could not see the energy of life or death, but some other sense told him they were dead.

Perhaps everyone had such a sense, or maybe his ability had not disappeared completely; that thought cheered him immensely.

Hadaras warned me about burning myself out, but I let fear and anger get the better of me. Now, because of my stupidity, we may not get through this with our lives.

Sorcerers often burned themselves out, attempting to focus too much energy at once. Often, the outcome was fatal, and equally often, the sorcerer lived, but never regained their ability. With extreme rarity, an individual recovered to some extent, but usually not to their former strength.

The smell of the sea steadily gained in intensity, telling them that their goal lay close at hand, but brightening of the eastern sky told them they were running out of time. Geldun suggested, in a low whisper, "I think we should try to break into one of these warehouses. We don't have time to make off with a boat now."

"I agree with Geldun," Eilowyn concurred. "We should find cover."

"The only problem with that is," Aleron countered, "those dead bodies we left on the other side. That will tip them off that we're moving, and they may push patrols into the waterfront."

"Al's right," Barathol agreed. "We should at least try. If we don't succeed, we can hole up somewhere closer to the water."

"Try what?" came from the darkness, in heavily accented Sudean. A man stepped forward from the doorway in which he was shadowing. He was dressed crudely, but with clothing in good repair, typical of dockworkers. He armed himself with a long, heavy bush knife. Four hulking figures materialized behind him, dressed similarly, and armed with heavy cudgels and staffs.

Aleron checked behind and saw five more of the thugs, again with staff and cudgel. *"We don't want any trouble. We're just trying to get to the harbor."*

"Ah, this one speaks Kolixtlani," the stranger announced to his companions, *"and he doesn't want trouble. I'm afraid, my friend, that you have found quite a lot of trouble, whether you sought it or not. You all need to see the boss now. You are welcome to come quietly, or we can beat you all senseless and drag you.* Several more thugs, some armed with bladed weapons now, as well as a few bowmen, joined the group, placing the companions at a distinct disadvantage, numbers-wise.

"He wants us to come with him and see his boss," Aleron told the others. "It doesn't look like we have much choice."

The others nodded in agreement, and Geldun replied, "Dead now or dead later, at least we have a chance if we pick later."

"He says we're seeing the boss, whether he has to beat us senseless, or we go willingly." He addressed the leader again, *"We'll go willingly."*

"Good choice, my friend. Now you give your weapons to my colleagues here." Two of the men stepped forward, one letting his club dangle by a loop around his wrist and the other keeping his staff in the high guard position.

"Hand over our weapons," Aleron directed. "If they wanted us dead, they would have been all over us by now." Aleron began unbuckling his sword belt. Geldun did the same, and Barathol grudgingly lowered his guard and held his glaive out to be collected.

After the thug collected all the weapons, including Andhanimwhid and Eilowyn's belt knife, the leader directed, "Follow me," and to his men, *"If they attempt to run, brain them. Now, let's go."*

They continued along the alley, toward the water, and then turned right between two warehouses. Eventually, they came upon a nondescript dwelling, in amongst the warehouses. In the dim light of pre-dawn, they saw it was a low wooden structure with walls of rough-sawn vertical boards and a widely overhanging roof of split wood shingles.

The leader opened the door, and they entered what looked like the kitchen area of a modest hovel, but no one was present cooking, as would be usual for this hour, in a working-class home. The leader knocked on an inner door, and someone answered with a low murmur. He murmured something back, and the door opened. He motioned them to follow him into a well-lit and elegantly furnished office.

Two armored guards stood to either side of an ornate wood desk, behind which sat a well-groomed Kolixtlani man, in his middle years. Three more of the men from the alley followed them into the suddenly crowded office.

The fugitives from the palace, Sir," the leader announced, before stepping to one side. One of the men from outside set down the bundle of weapons they confiscated from the group on the floor and began unwrapping and wiping off the soot they used to conceal them.

"So, my Sudean friends, it looks like I have a prize the palace will pay generously for," the man behind the desk stated, in clearly enunciated Sudean. "Why should I not turn you over and reap a rich reward? Oh, but I am remiss; allow me to introduce myself. I am Cipactli, and I own this sector of the harbor. Nothing moves here without my knowledge, not even fugitives from the crown's justice." It occurred to Aleron then that the lack of patrolling soldiers on this side of the city had less to do with fear and more to do with jurisdiction.

"We have some gold. We could pay you for our passage," Aleron offered.

"I doubt you can carry, all four of you together, the amount of gold Ehacatl would pay me for his father's murderer," Cipactli replied, chuckling, "not to mention the undying gratitude of the crown. What else can you offer, in exchange for your lives?"

It was at that point that one of the men unwrapped Andhanimwhid, exposing the glittering sapphires set in the electrum-bound hilt.

"Now what have we here? That might help sway my decision, but of course, I can just take all you have, turn you in to the authorities, and claim my reward as well. Tell me, what became of your priest who destroyed the palace courtyard?

It seems that if he were of your number, we would not be standing here together."

"He died," Geldun answered quickly. "He must have overreached or something; he fell dead right after the blast."

"I have heard of such things happening to priests when they overstep themselves. To whom does this exquisite weapon belong? The rest is all standard issue trash, next to worthless."

Aleron saw Barathol bristle at the implication that his glaive was nothing but trash. "The sword is mine, Sir, a family heirloom, of sorts."

"The palace is no great friend to me, as you may guess, so I will make you a deal. For your gold and this sword, I will put you and your friends on a boat and out of the city."

"No, Aleron!" Eilowyn exclaimed, and he saw expressions of horror forming on Geldun and Barathol's faces.

"Sir, I cannot, with good conscience, give that sword to you. It has been in my family for hundreds of years."

"Young man, Aleron, is it? Is your good conscience worth your life and the lives of your friends?"

"I'm afraid it has to be, Sir."

"All of you leave us, except Aleron here," He directed his men. *"Yes, you as well,* *he directed the two guards flanking his desk. I can take care of myself, and if he harms me, you will kill his friends. Take them and hold them in the outer room,"* he directed the leader of the men who captured them.

"Let's go," the leader told Aleron's companions, as Cipactli's men turned to exit the office.

"It's all right, go with them," Aleron told them as they looked about to protest. "He wants to speak with me alone." Apprehensive over what was to follow, he thought of how he might quietly overpower the man behind the desk, but he could think of no way that would not endanger his friends. They could play the hostage game as well as he, and he dared not risk Eilowyn's life in such a gamble.

When the door closed behind the last of them, Cipactli said. "They may not know what this sword is, but I do." At Aleron's suddenly wide-eyed expression, he continued, "The last time I saw it personally, it was stuck in the back of a throne. Were you the one to remove it?"

"I'd rather not say...When were you in Arundell?"

"I've heard that this sword will serve no other than its true master," he stated, ignoring Aleron's question and hefting the greatsword. Suddenly, he swung it in a wide overhand sweep toward Aleron, but the sword erupted in a flash of blue light, and Cipactli dropped it as if it were white hot. He uttered an exclamation under his breath that Aleron was sure wasn't in Kolixtlani and examined his singed palms. "It looks like that is indeed the case. Now, you do the same to me."

"I would rather not, Sir."

"You will, or I'll order all your friends killed. I will see this before I send you on your way. Do not worry; I will duck before you can hit me." Aleron picked up the sword, hesitantly, readied himself, and then swung at Cipactli in a wide, high, and easily dodged sideways swing. He was surprised at how deftly the Kolixtlani boss dodged the shot, regardless of how easy he made it. "No singed palms I see, should I say, Your Grace?"

"I would rather you didn't."

"Sorry, but I had to assure myself that you are worth the trouble. Let me let you in on a little secret, Aleron. I used to be a smuggler, once upon a time, and then they caught me crossing into Castia. Do you know what happens to smugglers who get caught?"

"They are either deported or brought into Castian intelligence," Aleron replied.

"Exactly, and deported smugglers are executed, so come to your own conclusions. I will do my best to see you on your way, but it needs to look believable for my men. You need to agree to give me the sword. I will find a way for you to keep it, but you need to make it look like you gave in to my demands. I will not be the man to turn the King of Sudea over to Ehacatl and his priests, but I can't speak for my men if it doesn't look right."

"Will you be able to get us to the east shore and close to the border with Castia? We are trying to get back to Arundell as quickly as possible."

"I'm afraid that won't be possible. The east shore is too heavily patrolled, as is the Castian border. I haven't been able to get a message through in over a year. I have to send messages through Sunjib now, and that's where you will need to go, as well, unless you wish to attempt the Northern Kingdom, which I also would not advise. That is too much of our country to cross undetected."

"Sunjib will take us months out of our way."

"I don't think you have much choice, my friend. To go east is to assure your capture, and south is simply not feasible. I can get you far up the west shore and upriver, close to the Sunjibi border. From there, you can make it into Waban and the coast."

"It seems like we don't have any other options, so yes, I accept your offer," Aleron conceded and added, "Thank you."

"Think nothing of it, my friend. As I said before, I hold no great love for the crown or their priests, for that matter. Let us go out and give your friends the good news. We should get you cleaned up, as well; you smell like you've been living in a cellar." Cipactli moved from behind the desk and to the door. As Aleron turned to the doorway, he happened to notice the white raven symbol painted over the door.

Chapter 2

Sildaenday, Day 29, Squash Moon, 8765 Sudean Calendar

"You will deliver this to my associate in Sunj, just as we discussed," Cipactli instructed Aleron, handing him a long bundle.

Aleron took the bundle, setting it on his shoulder, and then reached down to pick up the small haversack at his feet.

"Tell him that should settle our debt. From there, you can make your way downriver into Waban. Perhaps you can work for passage on a ship from there."

Aleron knew there was no associate in Sunj. The bundle consisted primarily of twigs from a rare and valuable shrub, known only from Kolixtlan and the Central Jungle and highly sought after by medical practitioners.

Concealed within the bundle was a certain greatsword that was supposedly still in Cipactli's storeroom. He also supplemented their food stores for the journey and provided them with a light bow to aid in their foraging. Eilowyn carried that, since she had no large blades to carry. Aleron knew her to be a passable shot and since she never trained in sword, it made for a good fit.

It was approaching the midnight bell and they were the only movement on the docks. His companions, along with three crewmen, were already aboard the twin-rigged "fishing boat" that Cipactli provided for their escape. Shallow drafted and slim, with a tall prow and stern, its design suited it for river travel as well as calm seas, perfect for a smuggler. A cloth tarp roof at the stern was the only place to store goods and equipment or to sleep, out of the weather.

"Thank you for your help; I will not forget it," Aleron promised.

"Think nothing of it, my friend. Now travel safe."

As Aleron turned to the gangplank, something slammed into his left shoulder, driving him to all fours, the bundle falling to the dock. Gasping to catch his breath, he looked over to see a bodkin point protruding from the front of his shoulder. He looked to his right in time to see one of Cipactli's men falling into the water, two arrows sticking from his chest.

Cipactli grabbed the bundle, hurled it onto the boat, heedless of injuring anyone aboard, and then grabbed Aleron by his good arm. "Get to the boat, now!" he shouted, as he hauled Aleron up to his feet again.

The haversack forgotten, he stumbled onto the gangplank through the fog that slowly crept into the edges of his field of vision. It was difficult to breathe, much less talk, so he simply put one foot before the other as fast as he could manage, hoping he would maintain his balance. He could feel the Kolixtlani smuggler's hands steadying him, but then suddenly falling away. He heard a splash behind him as he took the last couple of steps into the boat. He turned to see a body float past, two shafts sticking from the back of a fine silk coat.

Geldun had his shield up and his sword out, while Barathol covered behind him with his glaive in a reverse grip, over the top of Geldun's shield. Together, they shielded the other occupants as the crew scrambled to untie the boat. The lamplight from the docks allowed just enough visual warning for them to swat the shafts away. No one remained alive on the docks, as far as Aleron could see.

One of the crew shoved off from the dock with an oar, while the other two grabbed an oar each and started pulling for all they were worth. The one who pushed off dipped his oar to help steer the boat, one side or the other, as needed.

As they pulled away from the docks, Aleron allowed himself to sag against the side, his right arm hooked over the gunwale for support. He couldn't move his left arm at all without searing pain, but he was able to keep the tunnel vision at bay, just so long as he didn't move and breathed slowly.

As soon as the boat was out of range of the archers, Barathol dropped his glaive and picked up an oar, set it in an oarlock on the starboard side, and signaled the odd crewman to do the same on the port side. "Tend to Al now, he looks like he's fading fast." With four men pulling on the oars, the boat cut across the water, straight toward the center of the bay.

Geldun and Eilowyn moved to where Aleron hung by the gunwale, and Geldun began probing the injury as well as he could in the darkness. "Corball's balls!" he exclaimed. "It punched through his shoulder blade. Do you taste blood?" he asked.

"No," Aleron grunted. "It just hurts to breathe."

"I'll patch you up the best that I can, but I don't dare take it out yet, not until I can see." He took out a small knife and began to score around the shaft sticking out of Aleron's back.

"What can I do to help?" Eilowyn asked. She straddled Aleron's leg and held him to her, to help support his weight, while Geldun went to work, one arm holding his head to her shoulder.

"Undo his belt and then just keep doing what you're doing; this is going to get a little rough." He scored the fletched portion of the arrow and then the point end, snapping both off, leaving three finger widths of exposed shaft protruding, front and back, and then pulled the chainmail over the ends. "Now, Al, I need to get this chain shirt off you, so I can bandage you up. Try to relax, and I'll lift your arm now."

"Aarrgh," Aleron grunted in pain, as Geldun slowly pulled his arm to a hand raised position and grasped the sleeve of his chain shirt. The steady rocking of the boat on the water made the process that much more difficult.

"Let go of his side for a moment, Ellie. Al, when I let go of your hand, you need to pull it through the sleeve; got it?" He released the hand and grabbed the other side of the sleeve, as well. With a low moan and the occasional grunt, Aleron pulled his arm free of the sleeve.

Geldun gave him a few seconds to catch his breath and said, "Now we're going to get your other arm free and pull the shirt over your head." He and Eilowyn worked the other arm out of the chain shirt and pulled it over Aleron's head.

They repeated the entire process for the padded gambeson he wore beneath the chain, Aleron grunting in pain with each movement and Eilowyn doing her best to steady him.

"You're lucky it didn't puncture your lung, and I don't feel a lot of blood either. Let me get my bag so I can bind that up 'till morning."

Geldun left to retrieve his pack and, returning, opened it to retrieve dressings he kept for just such an eventuality. He wrapped each exposed end of the shaft for padding and bound them tight with a long roll of cloth, from his left shoulder to the opposite armpit. Tying that off, he used another to bind Aleron's left upper arm to his chest, fully immobilizing it. He then fashioned a cravat to support his forearm from his neck.

With Aleron's wound bound, they worked the gambeson back over his head and his good arm through the sleeve, so he would not catch a chill in the cool early morning air.

By the time Eilowyn and Geldun finished with Aleron, the others had stowed the oars, and the three Kolixtlani began unfurling the forward sail.

Barathol shifted to help, and he and Geldun picked Aleron up and carried him to the stern. Eilowyn laid out one bedroll among the stowed gear, and they laid Aleron out, propped on his right side, for comfort.

"Ellie, you should lie with him to help keep him warm," Barathol suggested. "If he goes into shock, we might not be able to bring him back. Here, let's get his legs up on this bundle." He scooped up Aleron's ankles with one burly forearm and shoved a bag under his knees.

"All right," she agreed. "Aleron, my love, I'm just going to settle in behind you. Don't worry; everything will be all right." She set herself behind him and clung tightly, while Barathol pulled another blanket over the top of both. Aleron was already asleep by the time the blanket made it to his neck, Eilowyn's face pressed into his shoulder.

The two marines settled in on either gunwale, each facing the other to see all directions, partly to spot approaching danger and partly to watch the crew. They could not guarantee their loyalty, with their boss apparently dead in the water, back at the docks. Both men had their weapons out and lying across their knees. With Aleron asleep, there was no way to communicate with the crew, other than through gestures.

The starlight was enough to see by, and one of the crew came to them and gestured to the stern, where the steering oar lay. Geldun motioned him to proceed, and the man picked his way between them, carefully, to the stern. The crew had both sails up, and a steady westward breeze had them slicing across the water faster than the Sudeans thought possible, from their initial assessment of the craft. There was nothing to do now but wait for dawn and hope the others were not planning to betray them.

✳✳✳

Ichtaca, Captain of the City Guard, addressed the young officer facing him, *"How could you let a boat shove off, Lieutenant? You were supposed to kill all the crew and apprehend the Sudeans."*

"Sir, in the darkness, the archers could not tell the Sudeans from the crew, aside from the woman. It caused them to hesitate."

"Then, your archers are idiots, Lieutenant, and that is a reflection on your leadership. In turn, it is a reflection on my leadership. Are you familiar with the old saying about excrement, Lieutenant?"

"Sir, that it rolls downhill?"

"Yes, Lieutenant, it certainly rolls downhill. That means that whatever I receive for punishment, you will get double, and I expect you to hold your men accountable as I do you."

"Yes, Sir, understood."

"Good, now get this mess cleaned up. I want the initial report on my desk by morning. Have the informant identify the bodies. Dismissed!"

He watched as the Lieutenant turned smartly and moved off to supervise the cleanup. The informant would be useful in the future. He wanted Cipactli's operation, so he didn't even ask for a reward for the information that his boss was a Castian operative, harboring Sudean fugitives. *Now, my only concern is painting this in a good light for my boss.* Failure is not well tolerated of senior Kolixtlani officers.

✳✳✳

The first rays of sun crept over the eastern horizon as the boat sped northwestward from Kolixtla. "He feels hot," Eilowyn stated, her hand on Aleron's forehead. He fidgeted restlessly in his sleep, and his face appeared flushed, even in the cool morning air. "We need to get this arrow out of him. It's making him sick."

"You're right, Ellie," Geldun replied. "Wake him up and we'll get him ready." He rummaged through his bag for more supplies, and Barathol came over to help Eilowyn.

They roused their friend, and Barathol asked, "How are you feeling, Al? You look sick."

"I just feel cold." He clung to himself and shivered, huddled in the blanket.

"You're not going to like this, but we need to get that shirt off you again, so I can get that arrow out of you," Geldun informed him.

He nodded feebly and released his grip on himself and the blanket. Eilowyn lowered the blanket from over his shoulders and then untangled the tails of his gambeson, so they could remove it. Barathol pulled it over Aleron's head, while Eilowyn steadied him. He shivered uncontrollably for a few moments as the cool air hit his fevered skin, but managed to control it after the initial shock. Geldun untied the cravat and began removing the dressing from the wound, rolling the cloth back up, to save it for later. He did not have an endless supply of dressings in his pack.

Exposing the wound revealed the problem: red streaks radiating from the puncture, a sure sign that the wound was beginning to fester. "It looks like it's festering already. I wish we could have pulled it out last night and let it bleed, but it was too risky in the dark."

One of the Kolixtlani crewmen came over to investigate, and Barathol reached for his weapon. The crewman raised up his hands, palm out, and said, *"Please, I mean you no harm. You speak our language, do you not?"* he asked of Aleron.

"I do," he replied, hoarsely.

"Tell the big one that he kept us alive, and we will do as much for you."

"He thanks you for helping them stay alive," he translated for Barathol, "and he pledges to do the same for us. *Is that all you wanted to say, friend, or is there something else?"*

"The bundle you carry for the boss, this is what it is for. Take a few twigs; no one will notice."

"That will help my sickness?"

"Yes, it is used for fevers and putrid wounds, which is why it is valued so highly. Strip some of the bark, chew it, and apply it to the wound, under the bandage. Then, chew some more for the fever. If you do, I can assure you that you will recover, but if you do not, you may die before we reach the Acatlpol."

The Acatlpol River was over three hundred leagues distant, and they would need over five days to reach it. *At least I know now that they plan to make good on their deal to carry us as far west as they can reach by boat,* Aleron thought to himself.

"He says we should use the stuff in the bundle for the wound and the fever," he said with effort, after managing a deep breath. He says I need to chew the bark for the fever and put some on the wound to keep it from festering."

He started shivering again, as another fever chill hit him. Barathol took the cue and went to find the bundle.

Geldun took position behind Aleron and said, "I'm going to pull it out from the back, Al, so I don't drag any bone chips deeper. Are you ready?"

Aleron nodded in affirmation and took a deep breath.

"Good then, Ellie, use this for the bleeding," handing her a wad of clean cloth. "It will probably bleed a little when I open the wound up again. Brace yourself, Al; on the count of three, I'll yank it out. One...two...three." He pulled sharply, and Aleron gritted his teeth as he felt the wood grate against the bone. Blood slowly oozed from both sides of the wound. Eilowyn and Geldun quickly pressed the wadded cloths to the wound, and Geldun inspected the bloody stub of the shaft and stated, "It looks clean; I won't have to go digging for any splinters. Let's get you wrapped up again."

Barathol returned with one of the twigs, shaving a long strip of silver bark with his small knife. "Here, he said to chew this, right?" he said, handing Aleron the strip. Aleron took it and fed it into his mouth, chewing as he went.

"Wait on wrapping him up, Gel. He's supposed to have this under the bandage."

Aleron finished chewing, spat the wad into his palm, and held it back to Geldun. He was already finding it easier to breathe, with the shaft removed, but a throbbing ache replaced the sharp pain he felt a moment ago, and he still felt nauseous from the fever. He had a bitter taste on the back of his throat from chewing the bark.

Barathol handed him another strip, and he repeated the process, handing the second wad of pulverized bark to Eilowyn, as Barathol handed him a third strip to continue chewing.

Geldun had Eilowyn hold both cloth pads, with the chewed bark poultices underneath, while he replaced the wrap to secure them in place.

The crewman returned, saying, *"Change the bandage twice daily and chew a little of the bark all the time; that should keep you well enough to heal. My sister is a healer; that is how I know. If we had the means, we would dry the bark and grind it to powder, for the wound and make a tea for you to sip, but for now, chewing will have to do."*

"It's good that you're not coughing any blood or bleeding much from that wound," Geldun stated. "You should heal up from the flesh wound pretty fast if it doesn't fester. The hole in your shoulder blade will take longer, though. What did he tell you?"

"He just said to change the bandage twice a day and keep chewing the bark, for my fever," Aleron replied, following with, *"Thank you for everything,"* to the crewman, who just nodded in acknowledgement.

They were about to replace the gambeson and cover him with the blanket when he suddenly broke out in a sweat. "Leave it off for a bit, my fever just broke. This stuff really works."

Eilowyn, Geldun, and Barathol set to tidying up the cargo area, from the events of the night prior. Once complete, Aleron settled in to rest again, with Eilowyn beside him.

Barathol and Geldun joined the Kolixtlani crew to allow them some rest as well. Both men knew how to sail, and hand gestures were communication enough to operate the boat.

If the wind held out and they sailed straight through, they would round the peninsula, into the Kolixtlani Sea, in another day. Their pursuit would be well behind them, and they hoped there was no way the Kolixtlani authorities could send word to other ports in time to send out interceptor ships.

"Aleron, do you suppose the Kolixtlani priests can speak over distance, like elves do?" Eilowyn asked him.

"Rare, from what Grandfather told me," he answered wearily. "Something to do with the lack of precision in red magic. Only those with extreme levels of ability can manage it. I think we killed the only one in Kolixtla likely to be that good."

"We can hope, at least. Now try to sleep, Love."

Chapter 3

Zorekday, Day 30, Squash Moon, 8765 Sudean Calendar

The last of the boats came ashore with the supplies for the journey. Two additional Arkan ships anchored offshore with Zormat's own. A small city was springing up on the shores of Mount Norwyyl, about one hundred leagues from the southern edge of the sea ice.

This was as far north as the ships were able to ply in these late winter days, due to the proliferation of sea ice. A turn of the moon later, and the overland journey could have gone entirely by dogsled, as they could have sailed leagues further north, closer to where the ice held on year-round. As it was, the local guides carried their sled dogs south to meet the Arkans in long open boats, formed of seal hide, stretched over a flexible wood frame. The locals knew how to navigate the ice-ridden waters.

The Arkans not setting up tents were assembling carts for the dog teams. They would journey more slowly overland until reaching the stable sea ice, where the dogsleds awaited them.

The efficient bustle pleased Zormat, as did the presence of the additional Arkan ships when he came to port that morning. However, the recent events in Kolixtlan troubled him. In the wake of the surprise attack, Ehacatl, barely twenty-one years of age, now held the throne of his most powerful ally among men. Now Kolixtlan had its third king since Zormat first contacted them, five short years ago.

The ancient, for men, King Quauhtli passed shortly after that meeting, succeeded by his eldest son, Achcauhtli, who reigned barely five years before the Sudean infiltrators killed him, escaping with the Princess.

Even more disturbing was the similar situation with the High Priests. Mahuizohm succeeded Itzcoatl, after the latter's unfortunate, if highly suspect, fall from one of the towers. Now, he was gone as well, and a new High Priest would rise to the position, requiring Zormat's personal grooming once again.

He could not let this disturbing information distract him from the quest at hand, not even for a moment. He refused to delay the search for Zadehmal. Zormat estimated at least three months to cross the ice and desert, but from there, no one knew for sure how long it would take to find the weapon. Men of the far north worshipped a mountain where they sensed a presence, but none knew where the actual source lay.

The expedition carried the necessary mountaineering equipment to traverse the terrain they would likely encounter, and all the Arkans were experienced climbers. Arkus, their homeland, is located at the same latitude that the expedition members now found themselves. Though the central portion of the massive caldera they called home remains warm, due to heat from below the surface, the mountains circling it are high, cold, and treacherous.

Ancient custom requires all Arkans to prove their mettle in those mountains as their rite of passage into adulthood. Zormat's generation began the tradition, and the son of the One True God and King of Arkus felt compelled to brave those peaks, prior to taking the throne, lest he lose the respect of the people he was to lead. Arkan warriors spent much of their lives in the mountains, training for the inevitable day that they would assault the dwarves in their mountain strongholds.

He turned on his heel and strode toward his command tent to meet with Karsh, his First Mate on board ship and First Councilor on land. Karsh made a capable First, moving up to the position after the killing of Malix by the Thallasians. He had, however, a disconcerting habit of questioning Zormat's decisions, which Malix never made the mistake of, nearly costing him his position on a number of occasions.

The command tent was the first set up that morning, taking precedence over all other activity. He stepped through the flap to find Karsh leaning over the map table, along with the other four members of the expedition, selected from among the Arkan forces for their mountaineering ability. The Arkans snapped to attention at the entry of their ruler.

"Sire," the First acknowledged as Zormat walked over to the table to examine the map for himself. He and Karsh studied the map many times on their journey, but planning required they refer to it again, here on the ground.

"So that everyone is familiar with the route and itinerary, how many leagues to where the sleds are located?" he inquired of Karsh.

"Your Grace, the six sleds are two hundred leagues up the coast from our current location, here," the First pointed to a pin stuck in the map. "We should be able to reach them in fourteen days' travel."

"Excellent, First, and from there, we should be able to make twenty-five leagues a day?"

"Yes, Your Grace, twenty-five, on average, and as we have discussed, it will take approximately three months to cross the sea ice and desert, into the mountains beyond." He traced a course northwest, from the coast of Norwyyl and moving parallel to the coast of a long peninsula, jutting south from the north continent.

"A week after the equinox, we should arrive here, on the coast of the continent." He pointed to a spot on the coast, nearly a thousand leagues from where they now stood. "This is the point of closest approach to the mountain the men of the north worship, and from there, we will travel fifty days overland to the base of the mountain."

"Yes, as we discussed," Zormat replied, "and there are established camps at both of these sites?"

"Yes, Sire, the native men travel there in the summer months to worship, so they maintain campsites at both locations. Due to the timing of our arrival, there should be few men yet at the coast and none when we arrive at the mountain. The only men we encounter will be at their winter hunting grounds. They tend not to venture to their place of worship until the Summer Solstice, and we will arrive over a month prior to that event."

"That is well, for us. I do not want men interfering with our search."

"Yes, Your Grace, men cannot survive long in the arid and cold conditions we will face, but we are able to."

"Are the bloodstone glyphs in order and working as expected?"

"Yes, Sire, the priests tested them in rooms shielded from access to power. They hold sufficient power to sustain one of us for months, so long as we do not draw too heavily on the power."

"That will allow us to sustain ourselves against cold and hunger in the lifeless desert," Zormat stated, mainly for the benefit of the new expedition members. All reports characterized the interior of the continent as absolutely lifeless. With no life, there was no death, hence, no red power. "A primary concern will be the extended day, coupled with intense sunlight, and the effect it will have on our power. We should plan on the short night for anything requiring power, such as melting ice for drinking. In two days, we set out for the mountain. Make sure all is in order, First."

"As you will, Your Grace," Karsh replied. The other four kept respectful silence throughout the short session. The first briefed them thoroughly, prior to Zormat entering the tent. "Are you all clear as to your instructions, and do any of you have further questions?"

"No, Sire, we are clear and ready to execute your instructions," the ranking officer of the group replied.

Dusk approached as the king stepped out of the command tent and made his way to his private tent to rest for a while. He entered through the double flap to find the space already warm from the folding charcoal brazier, though no servants awaited his arrival, as they would have in Kolixtla, that not being the Arkan way.

Kicking off his boots at the entrance, he slid his feet into the slippers, placed there for his convenience. He removed his cloak and jacket, hung them from the hooks on the tent pole, and made his way over to the rope bed. Sitting on the bed, he slid back out of the slippers and lay down flat on his back, not bothering to get under the blanket. After twenty bells on his feet, the bed felt extremely comfortable, and he was extremely tired.

A bell later, sleep still eluded him. The slow rolling of the ship he knew from months at sea was absent here on land, and no matter how fatigued he was, he always found the transition difficult. Finally, he sat back up, removed his breeches and shirt, and slipped beneath the blanket. He knew methods to stay awake for weeks, if need be, but real sleep was always the better option.

Chapter 4

Carpathday, Day 4, Harvest Moon, 8765 Sudean Calendar

Aleron felt much better five days after the arrow. The wound seemed to be healing well, so they left the dressing off last night, but he still needed the cravat to support the weight of his arm. He chewed the bark for the first two days but hadn't needed it since.

Remarkable stuff, whatever it is, he thought to himself. *It's too bad it's so hard to get at home.*

Technically, the medicine would be illegal in Sudea, as the only means to obtain it is smuggling from Kolixtlan. He felt next to useless; with only one working arm, he was little help in sailing the boat, but a crew of five was more than enough to operate day and night. He did what he could to help, now that the sickness passed, but it amounted to little.

The mouth of the Acatlpol was now in sight, as the sun crept over the eastern horizon. A look past the stern revealed sails silhouetted on that same horizon, but their pursuers were at least a half-day behind them and unlikely to be able to navigate the river. Another day's travel upriver would have them at their destination.

One of the crew informed Aleron that they had a place to conceal their vessel up a minor side branch of the river, where they could go to ground and evade detection with the locals. The same crewman revealed to him that a cult to the Allfather had a strong following in the area to which they traveled. Cipactli and most of his men belonged to the same cult, many recruited from the region the boat now approached.

Aleron filed the information for future use; a homegrown opposition movement might be a useful asset when the war escalated, as he was certain it would.

Aleron focused his gaze on the western shore, the heavily vegetated bank just gaining definition to his sharper-than-human eyesight. A steady breeze from the northeast afforded good speed for the westward-moving ship, faster than they would have managed with a straight westerly wind. The cool wind felt good on the back of his neck, and he knew he would miss it when they entered the shelter of the forest. The weather promised an unseasonably warm and humid day.

The ship took them to a more temperate region of Kolixtlan, compared to the capital and southern areas they recently left. The Acatlpol River lies at nearly the same elevation and latitude, opposite the Equator, as Arundell, so this was an early spring day for the north, still a month and a day from the northern Summer Equinox.

Once they passed the river's mouth, the tall sheltering trees would likely render the sails useless, compelling the crew to switch to oars.

$$***$$

"So the lad declared for the throne, I hear," Cladus remarked, as he settled into the rocking chair opposite the one Hadaras was about to sit in. He visited the couple every now and again, as he passed through the area.

Jessamine glided about, preparing tea and giving the males a moment of privacy before she joined them.

"And I hear that you are just who I suspected you were." If news of Aleron's claim to the throne, validated by his drawing Andhanimwhid before a multitude of witnesses, traveled like wildfire throughout the country and beyond, news of the reemergence from legend of Goromir traveled just as fast.

"Yes, he drew the sword, declared his right to the throne, and flew off in search of the Steward's daughter," Hadaras replied. "As for the second thing, you suspected?"

"I thought you seemed impossibly old and impossibly strong when we first met, so I had my suspicions then. Have you heard from him?"

"Not for about a week. What bothers me is that I can't even sense his presence anymore. It's as if he disappeared entirely."

"Yet you sensed not his death?"

"No," Jessamine interjected, "I'm certain we would have sensed his spirit passing through the veil if that was the case. He is alive…somewhere."

✳✳✳

The small "fishing boat" sailed smoothly up the mouth of the river. As luck would have it, the wind shifted to a westerly flow, funneling straight into the channel they currently plied, allowing them to continue sailing, rather than rowing against the current.

Aleron wondered about his luck; sometimes, everything seemed to come too easily, like in the fantastical stories he read as a child, where the heroes always came out on top. Sure, there were hardships and setbacks, but he and his companions could as easily be dead as escaping into the wilderness.

What if Cipactli was just a thug, like most in his position? What if the arrow hit a span further down and center? What if Bruno missed meeting the ship in Cape Town by a day or two?

Everything seemed to come together too perfectly every time, and he feared for the day that it would all come crashing down.

His shoulder loosened up considerably since the morning, so he abandoned the cravat and pitched in to help with the rigging, rather than brood on the future, but brood he did, anyway. Hadaras spoke of prophecies regarding his return to the throne, and he let slip of another one, but refused to discuss it further, no matter how hard Aleron pressed him.

"It's not time for you to know that yet," his grandfather insisted. *"If you know and understand it fully, I'm afraid you will change something to avoid it, even unintentionally,"* Hadaras explained, the last time Aleron inquired about it.

He wondered how much fate had to do with his "luck" and how much actual control he had over his own life. Once, it seemed ages ago, he pictured himself carving out his future, on his own terms, by the strength of his wits and his sword arm. Nowadays, it seemed he had little control over where his life was going, and it frustrated him.

He wouldn't trade Eilowyn for any imagined future, but he sometimes felt that her love was a matter of fate as well. *Am I just some sort of game piece of the Allfather's in an age-old competition with the Adversary? Is that all any of us are, and if so, am I integral to the overall strategy, or simply a gambit to be discarded when my usefulness is over?*

He vowed to spend some time in the royal library searching for that prophecy when they finally made it back to Arundell.

"Take it easy, Al," Geldun implored of him. "You're not fully healed, and if you reinjure that shoulder, it will take that much longer for you to heal."

"I'll be careful, Gel, but I need to start moving it sometime, don't I?"

"Moving, yes, working, not so much. Go help Eilowyn with the lighter chores instead. If you tear a muscle, it will take forever to knit, and you may never get all your strength back."

"I just want to be useful, for a change," he retorted.

"And what I'm doing isn't useful?" Eilowyn called out from the stern.

"I didn't mean it like that, Ellie!" he called back. "I meant...you know...men's work...I mean..."

"Keep digging, Al!" Barathol chided, with a low chuckle. "The hole's not quite over your head yet!"

"Just get over here and help me, Aleron, before you dig yourself any deeper," she commanded him. "Men... stiff-necked, hardheaded men," she muttered as she returned to packing their belongings for the overland journey.

Aleron succumbed to the pressure and reluctantly made his way to the stern, His friends grinning all the way. Even the Kolixtlanis gathered enough from the exchange to wear silly grins as they worked the rigging. They needed to have everything packed up and ready to go, for they needed to leave the boat as soon as they had it moored and concealed.

Sheepishly, he bent to gathering up their belongings and supplies, packing their few bags and bundles. He no longer possessed a pack of his own, so he began to fashion a bundle from his blanket so he could carry his share of the load.

After several moments of awkward silence, Eilowyn sidled up to him, draped one arm over his shoulders, and pulled him in for a kiss.

"Silly man," she whispered in his ear, as she released him to return to her work. She thought, as they worked, of the man she decided to spend the rest of her life with, however long that might prove to be. The infatuation she felt as a fourteen-year-old girl now held deeper meaning for the young woman of nineteen. She loved the intelligent and resourceful, if often rash and impulsive, man who would be king over Sudea, and she knew he loved her in return.

Now, more than ever, she knew he would do anything to protect her, with the proof of him chasing more than halfway across a continent to rescue her. For all of that, the future frightened her. As they huddled together, these many nights, he often confided in her things he told no one else, dreams he had, some verging on prophecy and none painting a happy conclusion, as in the storybooks.

Aleron was convinced that he lost his powers as punishment for his rash decisions in Kolixtla that resulted in the deaths of scores of people. His dreams told him all his abilities came from the Allfather and were not his to squander selfishly.

It could very well be that saving her was a selfish act on his part, and she suspected that Aleron believed as much. She did not believe that, but she could see fault in how he facilitated their escape. Killing the king, unintentional as it was, could do no good in smoothing relations between Sudea and Kolixtlan. Ehacatl would seek to avenge his father and his soldiers; that much was a given.

Other things he said worried her even more. He told her of old elvish prophecies that he apparently had a role in fulfilling. No one would give him the specifics, but his dreams told him he would face the Adversary one day, just as the first Aleron had. If his dreams foretold reality, they must indicate the Nameless One would someday escape the confines of his prison to walk the surface of Aertu once more.

Eilowyn looked over at her beloved as he rolled his bundle into a sort of satchel. No matter what he thought he might have to do, upon returning to Arundell, the first two things would be a coronation and a royal wedding, both firsts for Arundell in over a thousand years.

Regardless of what might come, he will be my husband when it comes about, and I will make the most of our time until then. With the bags nearly packed, they could soon settle in to wait for landfall. By midday, the twists and turns of the languid river shielded the ship from the wind, and four of the men took to the oars, with the fifth taking the steering oar.

That evening, with the boat, masts stowed and concealed in a camouflaged slip, they made their way a league inland, to the farm of a family associated with Cipactli's organization. The travelers took shelter in the barn loft. If they were found out by the authorities, the family had at least a chance to disavow knowledge of the fugitives.

"I've had worse beds," Barathol stated to whoever was listening, as he settled into a pile of straw.

"Tomorrow, you will head northwest; that direction will take you through mostly forested lands with few farms," one of the Kolixtlanis instructed. *"We will move northeast and wait until it is safe to go back to the ship. Good luck to you and may the Allfather guide your steps."*

"Thank you for all your help," Aleron replied, as he settled in beside Eilowyn.

He still knew none of the Kolixtlanis' names. They agreed that was the best course of action, so if any of the Sudeans were captured, they would not know enough to incriminate the three men.

Geldun agreed to stand the first watch as the last dregs of daylight faded, and they settled down to sleep.

Chapter 5

Sildaenday, Day 5, Harvest Moon, 8765 Sudean Calendar

Aleron awoke to the first rays of dawn seeping through the barn's shuttered windows. Eilowyn stirred beside him, and he noticed one of the Kolixtlanis up and moving already.

"We should get moving," he called out to the others.

He turned his head to see Eilowyn's green eyes open and regarding him.

"It's looking like we might actually make it, my love."

"All we have to do," he replied, "is get across the border and put as many leagues between us and Kolixtlan as we can."

"So, what are your plans for after we get back to Arundell?" she asked as she sat up, brushing the straw from her clothes.

"I'm not sure," he replied, rolling to his knees and doing the same. "My only concern has been finding you, bringing you back, and now escaping with our lives. I guess I haven't thought that far ahead. Rest, maybe?"

"That's all, rest?" she asked, in a somewhat harder tone. Aleron noticed a certain sharpness in her eyes as well.

"I said I haven't thought that far ahead. Is something wrong?"

"No, nothing is wrong. I was just…never mind…we need to get moving." She was up and heading to the ladder with her bag.

Aleron looked about as he gathered up his bundle and slung it over his good shoulder. He noticed Geldun shaking his head and chuckling to himself. Barathol leaned over to whisper something; they looked over at him, and both broke out laughing.

"What's so funny?" he demanded.

"I'll tell you later, Al," Geldun replied. "We need to talk anyway, and now is not the time or place for it. Let's get to the woods and put a few leagues between us and here first."

Two bells later, they worked their way through thick sub-tropical forest, with Barathol taking the lead and using one of Aleron's cutlasses to cut through the thorny vines that blocked their way. Geldun took up the rear, with Eilowyn and Aleron together in the middle, not talking. Aleron had Andhanimwhid strapped to his back once more, after they broke open and discarded the bundle of twigs, just a few paces into the forest. "Al, hang back for a bit," Geldun called. "I need to speak with you, if that's all right with you, Ellie."

"Go ahead, Aleron." It was the most, Eilowyn said to him for the last bell or so. Mostly, she glowered at him, when she looked at him at all, or wore a glum expression.

Gratefully, he fell back a few paces to walk beside Geldun, though he disliked leaving Eilowyn without a blade to defend her. As if to answer his concern, she drew the long knife from the sheath at her belt and held it loosely in her right hand, with surprising familiarity and ease. "What do you want to talk about? You said that this morning, too."

"Do you have any idea why you're in trouble, Al?" he murmured to avoid Eilowyn overhearing.

"No, I haven't been able to figure out what her problem is," Aleron murmured back. "She seemed fine, at first, and then did an about-face. She's given me the cold shoulder all morning."

"How long have the two of you been engaged, Al?" Geldun inquired, in the hope of Aleron reaching the conclusion on his own.

"Two years, about...What day is it today?"

"The fifth."

"Two years, today...oh Corball's balls." Though Aleron and Eilowyn had been a couple since their first meeting over five years ago, they were only officially betrothed shortly after his return and assignment to Arundell.

"Ya think she might have wanted something more than 'I guess I haven't thought that far ahead', when she asked what your plans are?"

"You mean...getting married, or something?"

"What do you think?"

After a moment's thought, he answered, "Yeah, I'm an idiot. I do plan to get married when we make it home. I just didn't realize that was what she was asking about, and I forgot our anniversary, so I'm a double idiot."

"Your words, My Friend, and I can't argue with you."

"So how do I fix it?"

"That, you're going to have to figure out on your own. I can't help you there. When was the last time you saw me with a woman for more than six months?"

"Never," Aleron answered, truthfully.

"So obviously, I'm not the relationship expert. If I find one who'll keep me more than half a year, then I'll probably go hunting for a priest to marry us on the spot. Now get your stupid carcass up there and try to make it up to her." Aleron lengthened his stride to catch up to Eilowyn again.

"What was that all about?" she asked when he came alongside.

"Me being stupid," he answered, and when she fixed her gaze upon him, continued, "Ellie, I'm sorry I didn't remember what day it is today, happy anniversary." She turned her eyes forward again and continued on, saying nothing more. "I really am sorry, Ellie; I just lost track of what day it is."

"If it was on your mind at all, these past days, you would not have let yourself forget," she replied coolly. "Five days on that boat, and what kept you so busy that you forgot?"

"I don't know; I was just preoccupied, I guess," he answered, sheepishly.

"With all your plans, for when we return?"

"You know we're getting married as soon as we get home, right?"

"To each other, or do you have someone else in mind?"

"Yes, to each other."

"How would I know that, when you have never said that?"

"I guess I assumed you knew how I feel about you, but I never did come out and say it, did I?"

"No, you did not, and when I asked you what plans you have, you essentially told me you have none."

"You're right; I should have said something before now, and I should have remembered our engagement anniversary. Is there any way I can make it up to you?"

"I just need some time, Aleron. I know you didn't mean to, but you hurt me very badly. Just give me time to get over it."

"I'm getting tired up here," Barathol called back, after another long while of hacking through vines and brush. "Do you suppose we're far enough along to stop for some breakfast?"

"I think so, Barry," Aleron replied, "What do you think, Gel?"

"We should be far enough to rest for a bit, Geldun replied. "I'm pretty hungry, right about now. I'll take a turn at the lead afterward if you like?"

"That would be wonderful," Barathol replied, letting the sword fall to his side. "My arm is about ready to fall off." He turned back and rejoined the others, handing Aleron his cutlass and driving the butt spike of his glaive into the soft loam. Aleron looked gloomily at the sap-stained blade of the sword, dug an oily cloth from his belt pouch, and proceeded to wipe the blade clean before sheathing it.

They settled down in a small circle around the glaive, facing outward, and then opened their bags to retrieve their food. They needed to remain vigilant for more than Kolixtlani pursuers in this part of the world. Hobgoblins often roam the forests of western Kolixtlan, though seldom this far north of the Iron Hills.

They dug through their packs for dried meat and fruit; a fire would wait until evening, when they had more distance between them and the river. The water filling their skins came from a small, clear stream they passed earlier that morning. It tasted fine, and Aleron hoped it was safe to drink. It was widely believed, though unproven, that even clean-seeming water was responsible for many outbreaks of disease, including the plague that killed Aleron's grandparents.

"I've had worse," Geldun commented, between mouthfuls of water to moisten the jerky he chewed. "I wonder what kind of meat this is."

"By the smell of it, I'd guess goat," Barathol offered, "or maybe, old sheep."

"Yeah, goat, most likely," Aleron agreed. Eilowyn said nothing, eating her portion in silence.

By late afternoon, the four travelers gained enough elevation to find themselves in a mixed pine forest, with far less undergrowth and vines than the bottomland they fought through most of the day, allowing them to make better time. As the shadows lengthened before them, Geldun said, "This looks like a good spot to camp for the night. What do you all think?"

"High and dry, with decent cover from the weather, if it turns bad," Aleron assessed, aloud. "It looks like a good spot to me."

They dropped their bundles to one side and proceeded to clear the stray branches and twigs from their prospective sleep area, collecting them in a pile for firewood. Next, they worked to clear pine needles and leaves well back from the fire pit area.

Geldun used the small shovel he kept strapped to his pack to dig a shallow pit, while the others cast about to gather more firewood. Several minutes later, he struck steel to flint and soon had a small fire going from tinder and small twigs. He then began snapping larger branches, adding them to the blaze.

A tripod formed of green saplings supported the cook pot, the bubbling contents of which would form a sort of stew from dried meat and vegetables.

The companions sat around the fire, waiting for the ingredients to soften to the point of edibility. "I'll take the first watch," Barathol volunteered.

"And I, the last," Geldun added. They both looked at Aleron, who sat morosely gazing into the flames, with Eilowyn seated a space apart, doing the same, with neither speaking. "Al, you have the middle watch."

"What...Oh, alright," he replied, returning to his inspection of the flames.

"No complaints?" Barathol asked, incredulous at his friend's reaction to drawing the worst shift.

"Oh, sorry, just preoccupied, I guess." He said nothing more, turning again to the flames, but Eilowyn looked over at him, with a softer expression than she had shown throughout the day, though he did not see it.

Later, after eating, as they laid out their bedding for the night around the fire, Eilowyn laid her bedroll next to Aleron's. "We're good," she stated, as he turned to face her and then threaded her arms beneath his, stepped close, and laid her head against his chest.

He, in turn, brought his face to the top of her head and wrapped his arms around her. "Thank you," he whispered into her hair, as they clung to one another.

Chapter 6

Sildaenday, Day 6, Harvest Moon, 8765 Sudean Calendar

Aleron and Eilowyn settled into their respective bedrolls after his turn at watch; she woke to accompany him for his shift, and they talked over the problems that kept them apart the previous day. With the few hours of relative privacy, they solidified a plan on marrying shortly after their return to Sudea, and both felt better for settling the matter. He lay on his right side, still favoring the left shoulder, with Eilowyn tucked in behind him, between him and the fire, and drifted off to sleep and into a dream, he dreamed many times before.

Here I am, once again, on the plain before the towering black fortress of Immin Bul. I am not myself, though still named Aleron. I see through the eyes of the first Aleron, and I can feel him here with me, as if his thoughts are my thoughts and only a thin veil separates my mind from his. The slight rise I occupy affords a good view of the battle.

Our front lines hold solid against the onslaught of goblins. The elves' longbows have eliminated most of the trolls, having targeted them from the first moments of the battle. Goblins are relatively easy opponents for a well-organized military force, as are the wild men. Neither has any grasp of large-scale military tactics, but simply throw their numbers against the opposing force, with no thought of strategy.

The Kolixtlani regulars present more of a problem, but faced with a Sunjibi shield wall, backed with the ten-foot pikes favored by westmen, they are unable to advance.

Aelwynn, resplendent in the gilded breastplate and helm of his office, directs his elvish archers, ever searching for new targets. His long halberd glows with a faint blue light, visible only to those capable of wielding the massive power within. The greatsword resting on my shoulder glows with the same radiance. I know that if Aelwynn or I draw upon the power of our weapons, the glow will be visible to all, not just sorcerers.

A rank of elvish spears backs my lines of shield and pike, inflicting the majority of casualties against the enemy line. The din of battle surrounds us with the clash of weapons, the screams and moans of the wounded and dying, but my mind is cool and detached. Connected to my leaders among the halfblood knights and seeing the whole battlefield in my mind, I sense the pendulum swing in our favor.

In the distance, the gates of Immin Bul open and another host issues forth, made up of creatures we had never before seen. Large goblins, well armored and armed, form uncharacteristically ordered ranks, while interspersed among them are clusters of what appear to be trolls, though smaller than the norm, hairless and covered instead with black reptilian scales, seemingly not armor, but their natural hide.

The column turns to me and advances, likely sensing my position as the strongest point of our line. Front and center of the new force is a figure, taller even than the trolls. Clad in gleaming black plate and mail and wielding a massive battle-axe, glowing red, the figure reeks of malevolent power.

So the Nameless God himself has decided to join the fray, with new abominations bred in the depths of Immin Bul.

The rear half of the column splits, comes alongside either flank, and then the entire formation breaks into a trot. Easily five-hundred shields across and twenty ranks deep, ten-thousand fresh enemy troops advance on my position, with alarming speed. Dark boiling clouds form overhead, from a previously clear sky, and orange-red lightning stabs down, opening gaping holes in our formation.

Elvish and halfblood sorcerers quickly raise shields of blue energy to deflect further assault from the skies, while others fling bolts of the same energy at the approaching force, slicing through shield armor and flesh. Shafts of crimson flash out in answer from the rapidly closing force, obviously issuing from the knots of trolls.

"Target the trolls," I command my sorcerers, and Aelwynn commands the same to his sorcerers and archers. The trolls must shield the enemy halfbloods. If we fail to cut down their sorcerers, we may still lose this battle, with the numbers on the field now even and the magic of death gaining every moment, as that of life dwindles.

Flights of arrows and shafts of pure blue energy converge upon pockets of trolls, but new groups move forward to take their place, scrambling over the dead bodies of their forerunners.

The goblins and few trolls left to our front finally notice the force coming up from behind, and they break and flee. Many prove to slow in their flight, cut down or trampled by the newcomers.

As our lines finally meet, the Nameless God's axe swings to and fro, taking out scores of men and elves. Raising my greatsword high in my right hand, I know it as Andhanimwhid, but here it is yet unnamed. I draw upon its immense power and send a searing bolt directly to the Adversary, but he shrugs off the attack as if it were a pebble thrown by a child.

Aelwynn has come alongside me, and I turn to meet my blood brother's eyes of the clearest blue. We nod in unison and then turn to the Adversary and sprint, screaming the battle cries of Elvenholm and Sudea. If the Crown Prince of the Elves and the King of Sudea are to die this day, we will do so as brothers, attempting to save our world from the evil of the Nameless God and his minions.

Thus, we meet the fallen god, trading blows, as our weapons afford us strength far exceeding our own unaided. We fight the Adversary to a standstill as the battle rages around us, and I sense the wailing of tormented souls captured within the enemy's fell blade. We must destroy that filthy portal to Hell as soon as we defeat our opponent and relieve him of it.

I spot a lucky opening and strike the Nameless One's greave, cleaving deeply into his shin, but my blade is jammed, in metal or bone, I cannot tell. I see the axe descending. I have no means to block, but then darkness overtakes me. I feel no pain and can see nothing. My skin is not my skin. I am trapped within something, and at first, I believe my spirit is devoured by the Nameless God's axe, but I am alone and not in torment. This place is filled with clean magic, not foul. I fear for my people, as well as the other free peoples. I may never know if we are victorious or defeated, free or enslaved. I am trapped in this place, I know not where, unable to feel any sensation.

After time interminable, I finally sense something outside of my prison. Someone reaches in for me, but who? Suddenly, joy fills me; it is my son, Beldan. I link to his mind, and I know what he knows. We are victorious, still free, but Aertu lies devastated. Tens of thousands of Sudeans dead, with hundreds of the halfblood noble caste lost in the fighting. The numbers of the elves are decimated. The Nameless God is imprisoned, defeated, but alive. Aelwynn lives, but Goromir has disappeared. I am no longer a man; I am Andhanimwhid, the Sign of the King.

The thin veil separating my being from that of the first Aleron thickens and solidifies, but a voice comes through with ice-cold clarity. "This will come to pass again, though not exactly as it was. The spiral of ages loops once again, and only you may divert its course." The voice is gone now, and once again, I am only Aleron, from the village of Swaincott.

Aleron awoke with a start, as he always did from this dream. He knew what no one knew for a thousand years, and before that, only the kings of Sudea. Andhanimwhid was Aleron, the first. He was sure of it. The dream was all too clear, and he understood its meaning after the second or third time he experienced it.

Somehow, the sword stole Aleron's spirit before Zadehmal could take it. The dream came to him shortly after he touched the sword for the first time and had recurred several times over. There were other times that he dreamed other scenes from the ancient king's life, but this was the most common one.

"Is everything alright?" Eilowyn asked, as the first light of dawn paled the eastern horizon. "You were mumbling in your sleep, and you jerked awake."

"It was the dream again," he replied, "the one where I'm the other Aleron, and he tells me it's coming around again." He told Eilowyn of this dream before, as he had others, but never related the secret involving the sword.

"Was there anything new this time?"

"No, just the same old message that the final battle will be repeated, with me facing the Adversary."

"And it still bothers you to hear that, after all this time?"

He turned over to face her, wincing when he put the weight on his injured shoulder. "Yes, it does, because it puts all the pressure on me. The dream always says that only I can change things to avoid another war like the one that killed Aleron. It scares me to think that the fate of so many people might hinge on me. I'm not that smart, and I can't figure out how I can change anything to avoid a war. If anything, I've only made things worse between Kolixtlan and Sudea."

"That may be true, my love, but I do appreciate what you did to rescue me." She leaned forward, placed a hand behind his head, and kissed him soundly on the lips.

Releasing him, but still resting her hand on his shoulder, she continued, "You are a very smart man, my love, and if the Allfather has placed his faith in you, then who are you to question Him? I have faith in you as well, dearest. What you lack is experience, not intelligence; the experience you will gain soon enough, when you return to rule Sudea. You are barely twenty, and I doubt even the Allfather expects you to save Aertu from the Adversary this very minute."

"Thank you, Ellie, for believing in me," he said, pushing himself to sit up. He observed Geldun walking the perimeter in the dim light. Porridge slowly simmered over the low fire, and the smell of the barley cooking set his stomach to grumbling. "But I feel it drawing near, whether or not I have the experience to deal with it. What if my powers never return, what then? Perhaps I made the wrong choice, and the Allfather is even now moving on with a different plan. What if there is no other plan and I just bungled things to the point of no return? I haven't the slightest idea what I could do if the Nameless one escapes his prison, much less how to keep that from happening in the first place."

"Then, why would you still be having the dreams?" she asked, as she sat up as well. "You ramble on about the hopelessness, but the dreams still come, telling you otherwise. Let's take things a day at a time, for now, and worry about all that when we get home. Your abilities will return when they are fated to return, I am certain."

"Do you believe in what the priests say about fate?"

"You, of all people, should, Aleron. You cannot escape your fate, but you can shape it by your deeds. At least that's what the priests of the Allfather tell us, and I believe. Don't you believe?"

"I do believe, Ellie. It's just that I can't see how this is part of the Allfather's plan, and my wrong decisions might leave Aertu in ruins, like the Great War, or worse, enslaved by the Adversary. You're right; we do shape our fate, but am I shaping mine in the proper direction? The Nameless God should have accompanied his brothers and sisters and left Aertu, but he chose a different fate in disobeying his father. My fate may be to oppose him, but what if my choices turn out to be as wrong as his?"

"Make the best choices you know to and trust in your faith. That's all you can do." She pulled her boots on as she replied, and it was obvious to Aleron that she was done talking about this. She began rolling up her blankets, and Aleron followed suit, pulling his own boots onto his feet.

Geldun strolled over to check on the porridge, testing a bit from the end of the stirring spoon. "Almost ready," He announced. "Now what's all this gibberish I'm hearing? We're going to make it home, rest up for a while, and then we'll save the world, end of story. You just need to get your head out of your arse for all that to happen," he finished, with a mischievous grin. As a reply, Aleron pitched a pinecone at his face. "Hey, not over the food!" he admonished as he dodged the projectile.

Barathol stirred at the commotion and clumsily rolled to his feet, just like a sleepy bear. The sight was always amusing, until one realized how dangerous a freshly roused bear could be. "I smell food; is it ready yet?"

"Almost," Geldun answered. "By the time you're dressed and packed, it will be." He was already packed, aside from the cook pot.

The others finished dressing, rolling up their bedding, and packing everything but their bowls and spoons. Each had a large bowl of the porridge, which turned out to have bits of dried peach added, and a strip of the salted meat.

Once finished, they wiped the bowls and pot out with pine needles, deposited the refuse in the fire pit, and filled it back in. After they all slung their burdens, each took a branch to sweep the pine needles and twigs back over the area they cleared for their camp. They wished to leave as little evidence of their passing as possible. It was bad enough that they needed to hack through the undergrowth for the first half of the previous day. That was akin to drawing an arrow pointing in the direction they traveled.

The pine forest allowed them to move far less obtrusively, and this morning, they planned to take advantage of the situation by taking a more northerly heading until midday, to throw off any pursuit.

They had a dual purpose in that, though it might slow their reaching the border, they would avoid crossing the main road through the region at midday. Crossing in the evening, with most travelers settled in for the night, was a much safer option. With pursuit likely days behind, their biggest risks were random patrols and other smugglers who might use this same wilderness corridor for illicit trade with Sunjib. Compared to those risks, their pursuers and roving goblins were a distant third and fourth.

By the time the sun stood straight overhead, they had crossed two valleys and a ridge, finding themselves atop another ridge, running southeast to northwest, two ridges north of where they started that morning. They minimized peril from hacking through the dense undergrowth of the valleys by the slight trail they left between those sections. Anyone following would have no idea where the group decided to turn north, unless they were exceptional trackers, or if they had hounds, and neither was likely.

They resumed their original northwest heading that would take them to the border with the least hindrance, as an early spring thunderstorm boomed overhead. They were glad for the rain, cold and uncomfortable as it was, since it worked to further mask their passage. The storm was heavy, if short-lived, soaking through their cloaks and into their clothing. Aleron, taking his turn in leading the group, could feel a small rivulet running down his spine and soaking into the back of his trousers.

As the rain tapered off, he suggested, "Let's walk ourselves dry for another bell and break for lunch."

The others voiced agreement, and they continued onward, with the storm moving off to the west and drops of water falling from the boughs, glimmering in the shafts of sunlight that managed to reach the understory. The freshness in the air from the rain was soon replaced with the steaminess that usually follows a midday shower. The wet needles underfoot made their steps particularly silent, with the chatter and activity of squirrels and birds dominating the background noise.

Once, a stag, the first stubs of this year's antlers in velvet, startled them by bursting from his place of concealment, before they overran him. Otherwise, their luck seemed to be holding, and they were alone in the forest.

Hours later, with the sun sinking below the western horizon, they concealed themselves in the tree line overlooking the road. A small patrol passed north, about two bells past, followed by a merchant train half a bell later. They had no way of knowing if the patrol might be looking for them, but it was unlikely for word to have preceded them. With the road in shadow and seeing no travelers for more than a bell, they made the dash across the open area, cleared fifty paces either side of the traveled portion. The clearing of the roadside occurred a couple years prior, and they chose an area with substantial new growth to shield their passage.

Aleron and Barathol sprinted across first, checked the other side for danger and then Eilowyn followed them across.

Geldun made one last check on their back trail before sprinting across himself.

After reforming, the group headed into the forest to find a place to camp before darkness overtook the land completely.

Chapter 7

Shilwezday, Day 8, Harvest Moon, 8765 Sudean Calendar

Eilowyn practiced with her bow, targeting an old, rotted stump against a grassy bank for a backstop. She was determined to get better after missing a shot at a large hare earlier that morning, relegating them to another meal of dried meat and fruit from their quickly dwindling supplies.

Her quiver held three types of arrows, bodkins for use against armored opponents, broadheads for large game or unarmored enemies, and small game points with steel points shaped like inverted cones, the wide, flat tip to deliver a killing shock, without going through the game. The types could be differentiated by sight, having different colored fletching, or by feel, having one, two, or three notches carved in the nocks.

She practiced with the small game tips, as she noticed that each type flew differently, and practicing with bodkins, as she had previously, would not help her to bag a rabbit. She compared their flights and determined that she needed to move her point of aim up about a handspan at the twenty-pace range she currently practiced, to hit the same spot she had with a bodkin. The flat-tipped small game arrows dropped off much more quickly than the more aerodynamic types. Though she had figured out the proper aimpoint, she was still struggling with consistency.

"You need to work on your follow-through," she heard Aleron's voice from behind her, right after she loosed her arrow. Turning to him, mildly annoyed at his unsolicited advice, her consternation dissolved at the sight of the earnest expression on his face. She knew him to be one of the least judgmental people she had ever met.

"I had the same problem in my first few years practicing with the bow, he continued. "Grandfather had the worst time with drilling it out of me. We would spend days on end focusing on nothing but archery until he was so frustrated with me that he couldn't help but move on to something else. I eventually figured it out."

She realized that her betrothed was speaking of days around a decade prior, when he spoke of his "first few years practicing," when he was likely nine to eleven years old.

"What am I doing wrong?" she asked. "What's follow-through?" She had always just shot her bow, never receiving much in the way of formal training.

"Your form is superb for target shooting, back straight, body turned to the side, bow plumb, draw hand elbow high, but you need to hold that after release. Keep the same pose until you see the arrow down-range. The slightest movement of your bow hand before the arrow is gone will throw off your shot."

"Really?" she asked, disbelief in her expression. "The arrow is off in the blink of an eye."

"Grandfather claimed he could see my bow wiggle, before the arrow was off the riser," Aleron contended. "I think that is only from his elvish vision, though I had no idea of it at the time."

"I suppose that makes sense," she conceded. "So, you just hold like you're still aiming until you see the arrow off to the target?"

"Pretty much," he agreed. "Once you get used to that, we can practice some hunting and combat stances. Positions are different, but the principles are the same."

"Show me," she demanded, holding out the bow and drawing him a bodkin, then hesitating, "I'm sorry. I nearly forgot about your hurt shoulder."

Aleron took the bow and the arrow from her and nocked the shaft to the string. "I should be all right," he replied. "It's been nine days, and this is a light bow."

Holding the shaft to the riser with his finger, he half-crouched, holding the bow at a near 45-degree angle, and loosed the arrow straight into the knot Eilowyn had been trying to hit.

"That's a hunting stance," he stated, holding his hand out for another shaft. She handed him another, and he straightened, assuming a stance midway between his hunting stance and a target stance.

"This is more of a battle stance," he continued. "It's more relaxed than target, and you can loose a lot of arrows in a hurry."

He took her arrow, plugged it next to the last one he shot, and held his hand out for another. Within six heartbeats, he launched the remainder of her dozen bodkins into a small circle about the first knot he hit.

"Let's go get the arrows, and I'll show you one more."

Returning to their shooting position, he fished an ivory ring from his pocket and slipped it onto his right thumb.

"This is a Chebek style, though it's also used across Chu, Talik, and Adar."

He turned his back to the target, placed the arrow on the right side of the bow's riser, opposite to the southern form he was using prior, twisted over his left shoulder, and loosed an arrow into the stump.

"That probably wasn't such a good idea," he said, rubbing his left shoulder. "It doesn't like bending that far yet. Anyway, that one is for shooting from horseback. It allows you to shoot directly behind you as you ride."

"Thank you, smart-ass," Eilowyn replied, like it wasn't enough for him to likely be the second-best fighter in Aertu, trained by the best to ever live. He didn't need to rub her face in it. "That should be a lesson to you about being a showoff."

"Sorry," he replied, looking abashed. "I didn't mean to be an ass."

"It's all right," Eilowyn replied, "I realize you know a lot about fighting. Just one thing…I need you to teach me how."

Right then, Geldun came stomping up to them. "What in Isselle's name do you think you're doing?" he shouted. "I told you not to risk reinjuring that shoulder, but here you are, shooting a bow!" he berated his friend.

"I'm fine, Gel. My shoulder is much better today."

"Not if you aggravate it. I saw you rubbing it after that last shot. Maybe you should stick to normal shooting, if you're going to be too dense to lay off it entirely," Geldun answered, a bit less angrily. "You are not ready to twist like that. Now go retrieve that arrow. Lunch is ready."

As they all settled in their places, Barathol stated, "I can't wait until we can get a proper dinner again. These light lunches are not the most satisfying."

"Yeah, but we don't have time for the post-dinner nap either," Aleron half agreed. "We can cover more ground eating light."

"Plus, we don't have the supplies for it," Geldun added.

"I'll hit that rabbit next time," Eilowyn interjected, taking the trend in conversation a bit personally.

"That's not what I was trying to say, Ellie," Barathol apologized. "We all miss sometimes."

"He doesn't," she countered, pointing her chin at Aleron as she said it.

"He doesn't count," Geldun explained. "Barry is talking about the rest of us, not the wizard."

Barathol and Eilowyn chuckled at the quip, while Aleron only looked embarrassed at the attention.

Following a several-minute lull in the conversation, where everyone concentrated on their food, Aleron suggested, "On the subject of moving, we ought to get this cleaned up and ourselves back on the trail."

"I suppose…" Barathol agreed, rolling ponderously to his feet.

The rest followed suit, gathered up their belongings and repacked their rucksacks, or bundle, in Aleron's case.

They set out again, this time with Geldun leading, Barathol in the rear, Eilowyn and Aleron in the middle.

"Were you asking for me to teach you to fight when Gel so rudely interrupted?" Aleron asked Eilowyn.

"Yes, I was."

"That's not usual," he replied, "for a lady to train to fight…"

"I don't care what's usual or what's proper," she responded. "I will not be the damsel in distress from those sappy romance novels my sisters like to read. If I knew how to fight, I might have been able to get away from those scoundrels who abducted me."

"That, or gotten yourself killed, or badly injured," he countered.

She glared at him, causing him to wilt slightly, before answering, "I will not be helpless any longer. You can teach me how to use a sword, and this knife, or I'll get Barry or Gel to teach me."

"All right, I'll teach you. But I'll still protect you, or die trying."

"That's fine, too. You do make a good hero for those terrible stories," she said with a grin. "If we make it home, I'm sure someone will write one about it."

"Pray to the Allfather that they don't," he replied, grinning as well.

Chapter 8

Zorekday, Day 12, Harvest Moon, 8765 Sudean Calendar

Karsh saw to the transfer of supplies from the carts to the sleds. The two arduous weeks of overland travel had weighed heavily on the dogs and drivers alike. Men and Arkans moved the food and equipment across the rocky ground to the stable sea ice, where the sleds awaited.

They would set up the tents for three days, to allow the dogs and men to recover their strength. The flinty ground wore on the animal's paws and many of them favored one or more. Often as not, the carts moved by men and Arkans pushing, as much as by the dogs pulling.

Karsh understood the issue with the dogs, but had difficulty understanding the men's weariness, since they had the advantage of boots. Arkans handled the exertion better than frail humans did, and Zormat's group could easily have continued nonstop.

Not that I'll complain about a few days of rest, he thought, but the sooner they moved, the sooner they could return with the axe, free the One True God and get on with the conquest.

Three days of rest for the sled dogs, necessary, but infuriating, Zormat surmised. They needed this mission to move forward without delay. In half a year, the entire Arkan war fleet would arrive, to coincide with the return of Zadehmal to the One True God, and the conquest of this continent would begin in earnest.

After the continent, his forces could turn their attentions to finding and subduing Elvenholm. He was certain he and his father could find the hidden path. It could not be much different from the weaves of magic that kept Arkus hidden.

Everyone knew where the homeland of the elves must lie, but none could sail to it but the elves themselves. Pilots of men had often charted courses due west on the equator, only to find themselves sailing into the Castian Sea, after months on the ocean, as if sailing directly through where Elvenholm must be. It will be interesting to unravel that particular warding. Common conception said that his father's siblings created the wards to conceal the elves from him. Zormat needed to find his way through them, lest the elves have a staging area from which to launch attacks indefinitely.

***

"Have you any word of the king, Lord Steward?" Ambassador Baruk inquired, taking his seat across from Gealton's desk.

The steward met with the Thallasian ambassador one to two times per week. He knew him to be a courageous young officer, the first of his people to venture to Sudea, suing for peace and alliance in the wake of the Arkan's appearance. The alliance proved invaluable these last five years, with the increased aggression of the Kolixtlanis and Adaris, prompted by the Arkans, he was certain.

"Unfortunately, nothing directly, Ambassador," the Steward answered.

In the weeks since Aleron departed, after declaring for the throne, word of the event spread like a grass fire at the height of summer. Eilowyn had been missing since spring, and autumn was upon them. He wished for some word, anything of the fate of his daughter. By now, everyone in Sudea who did not live under a rock knew that the throne had been reclaimed, but still no word of his daughter's fate.

"We do, however, have word of some sort of unrest in Kolixtlan. According to rumors, the king there is dead, from an attack that nearly brought down a portion of the palace. The Castian border is crawling with Kolixtlani troops, nearly stopping the flow of smugglers that the Castians rely on for intelligence."

He was sure the attack was Aleron's doing and sincerely hoped it hadn't been in retaliation for his daughter's treatment.

Baruk must have thought the same, for he asked, "The king is betrothed to your daughter, is he not? Do you suppose he struck out of revenge?"

"I hope against hope it was for her escape and not to avenge her death," Gealton replied, obvious worry in his eyes.

"Hadaras warned the lad is powerful, perhaps the most powerful halfblood in four-thousand years. I think, if vengeance were his aim, the palace would be rubble, rather than nearly toppled, as the reports state."

"That is good news, I suppose, though it wouldn't break my heart to hear he leveled the city. The blasted Kolixtlani and Adari refuse to learn from the mistakes of their forebears."

"As much as I want to see Kolixtlan fall, I would not wish it at that cost. I cannot believe the whole of the country is corrupt. They were a goodly people once, long ago, and I hope not to slaughter innocents as a means to an end. If we remove the head, perhaps the body can be salvaged."

"That is a thought," Baruk conceded. "I have given little thought to the possibility of reforming Kolixtlan or Adar. The problem is mainly with the kings, who are puppets, and the priests, holding the strings. Remove the ones pulling the strings, and the puppet collapses."

"Is that how it worked with your people?" Gealton inquired.

"More or less," he agreed. "We were pirates, way back before the war, and had no use for kings, but somehow, we let ourselves believe that we needed one. I'm sure that was the Adversary's work. With a king came the priests, and with them together came an unwinnable war."

He paused to take a sip from his wine. It was a very good vintage, and he savored it on his tongue before allowing himself to swallow. "Once the war ended, we rose up and did away with kings and priests. We went back to the way it used to be."

"You're not pirates anymore."

"No, that could only last so long before our neighbors, you included, would have done away with us. I'm a bit surprised that Castia did not move against us in those first centuries after the war. The desert and the mountains protected us, for the most part, from land invasion, so we defended our territorial waters with fierceness."

"I think the entire world was tired of war, the forces of darkness included. All sides lost dearly. I would suspect your origins in piracy led to the current organization of your government?"

"Indeed, pirates rise to power through their ability, not their birth, so a more military arrangement was inevitable, I suppose, especially considering our experience with having a king."

"We had a bit better luck with our kings when we had them. With your experience, I'm not surprised that you came up with the sort of meritocracy you did," Gealton agreed.

"It's interesting to see it on such a scale. Usually, one only sees such an arrangement amongst smaller tribes. Even the Elmenians have a hereditary aspect to the choosing of their clan chiefs. Your people don't balk under military rule?"

"Technically, we are all in the military, from the age of fourteen, Baruk explained. "If one chooses a profession requiring leadership, anyone can progress and achieve the High Admiralty."

"Those professions being the traditional combat roles, I take it?

"Usually, though, we had a Quartermaster advance to the position, in my grandfather's time."

"What of your wizard's guild? Are they a part of the military, as well?"

"They are a notable exception, but as such, they are allowed no direct political power, though they often try to influence from the sidelines."

"A safeguard to avoid ever being led by sorcerers again, I assume."

"Exactly that, they are contracted and paid for their services when needed and otherwise allowed to go about their business. We have needed them aboard our ships, since the coming of the Arkans, so the guild's coffers have been swelling more than ever these past years. I don't really care for it myself, but the measure was necessary. If we were to bring them into our military structure, we would be forced to award them rank, which we refuse to do."

"Does it concern your people at all that our new king may be the most powerful sorcerer in Aertu?"

"Even among the elves?"

"If Hadaras was correct, then yes, even among the elves."

"Well, we don't really care about anyone's politics, as long as they don't try to force them upon us. You can have who you want for a king."

"Well, it concerns me," the Steward admitted. "Plenty of the halfbloods of old turned to darkness when last the Adversary walked Aertu. If the most powerful of them does and has a claim to the throne, giving him access to our army and navy, I fear all will be lost."

"Are you truly worried that the enemy may sway him?"

"Only for the fact that he has sent no communication," he responded. "He's a fine young man, raised well, but if the Kolixtlani priests managed to capture him and discovered who he is, there is no telling what they could do to turn him."

"A valid concern, I suppose," the Ambassador agreed, "but why would you allow him the throne, if that came to pass?"

"I don't know if it is possible to turn a person against his will, or not, but it occurs to me that they could do so and release him, along with my daughter, making it look like a legitimate escape."

"Then, he could assume the throne without suspicion. I understand now."

"I'm not sure how we will be able to tell, when and if they return, but we will need to think of something to assure he is not turned to the Adversary."

"I will think on it, as well," Baruk offered, "as a friend, though I know little about such things, but for now, I must take my leave, Lord Steward. There is much I must prepare for my successor's arrival."

"Thank you, Ambassador, and once again, congratulations on your promotion to Grand Ambassador, though I am sorry to see it take you from us."

"It pains me to leave as well, but the High Admiral needs organizing the Diplomatic Corps off from his plate, and I am the most senior. Besides, I have not seen my home in five years. It is high time for me to get back."

"Best of luck with your preparations. I will see you again, before you go, so this is not yet goodbye."

"Until next time, then," Baruk said, as he took leave of the Steward, closing the dark, polished oak door as he entered the white marble corridor.

Gealton now maintained his office just off the old royal hall, rather than the one just off from the kitchens, as he did when Baruk first came to Arundell. Therefore, the ambassador had a long walk to his chambers in the diplomatic wing, with plenty of time to think on recent events.

I certainly hope the king returns before I have to leave. I would like at least an idea of what sort of man he is, before I hand over my mission. If not, my successor must know what to do if things go sour here.

After five years in the capital, Baruk had gathered eyes and ears within the palace and without. It was always easy to find some who would betray their loyalties for a little coin, often surprisingly little, especially if it seemed only a small betrayal, barely more than gossip. Baruk knew much about every noble in Arundell and several outside the city. His countrymen needed information on who was weak and strong among the powerful of Sudea.

Thallasia was committed to this alliance, but still ready to bolt like a gazelle from a pack of wolves, if the rule of Sudea went awry. Several of his personal retinue were really assassins, ready to remove anyone who threatened Thallasian interests. Fortunately, he had not needed that recourse, up to now.

Baruk did not know this Aleron from any other Sudean soldier. He had seen him, on occasion, visiting the Steward's daughter, and the name came up with some frequency, on the topic of prominent fighters gaining a reputation from the numerous skirmishes in the north.

The young man's announcement, claiming the throne, came as a surprise to everyone but Gealton in the wake of his daughter's abduction. The sudden announcement, followed by his immediate move on Kolixtlan, seemed to indicate a man of action, but hopefully not overly rash. Baruk could appreciate some rashness, considering the nature of the situation, and if the new king was as powerful a wizard as Gealton seemed to believe, he likely believed he could maintain the upper hand, even with the tiny force of two retainers.

I hope he did maintain the upper hand; otherwise, it will prove worse for the stability of this land than if he had never shown himself.

Sudea fared one thousand years without a king, under the stable hand of the stewards. To give them the king they waited a millennium for, only to take him away again, could do nothing less than demoralize the nation, just when their allies needed them strong. It might even ignite a fight for succession that would not have occurred otherwise. He hoped, for the sake of the alliance between their nations, that the king return safely.

Arriving at his quarters, he found Korella waiting for him in his sitting room. She had a key to his apartment, as they were a couple for nearly two years now. The pretty little blonde woman lounged upon his divan, two goblets of chilled white wine on the side table, condensation glistening on their surfaces.

"How is my cousin today?" she inquired, straightening, and beckoning him to sit beside her. She was the steward's second cousin, through her mother.

"Gealton is fine, though rightfully worried for his daughter's safety," he replied as he leaned his unbelted sword against the sofa, sat next to her, and accepted the goblet she handed him.

"We have reports of significant unrest in Kolixtla, serious physical damage to the palace," he continued. "We are both hoping it was from a successful rescue and not revenge on the king's part."

"We must hope for that," she concurred. "Eilowyn is a sweet girl, and it would be a tragedy if anything were to befall her.

Aleron always seemed a most agreeable boy. I wouldn't think him quick to anger, but he does love the girl, very obviously. And, he has a fearsome reputation on the battlefield."

"Love can lead one to rash actions," Baruk agreed. "On that note, are you certain you wish to accompany me back to Thallasia? Corin is a lovely city, but it is no Arundell. I'm afraid you will find only boredom there."

"Boring or not, if that is where you are, that is where I need to be, My Love," she answered, reaching an arm around his neck to pull him into a kiss.

✳✳✳

Eilowyn lunged at Aleron with the cut branch she used as a practice dagger for sparring. The thickest portion served as the hilt, with a pair of side branches forming the guard, and another foot of branch the blade. Aleron blocked her thrust with his own identical practice weapon, held in an icepick grip, pushed forward to rake the tip along her arm and into her armpit, as the momentum of her thrust carried her forward. He pivoted slightly, placed his off-hand palm against the butt of the hilt, and 'gently' shoved, careful to not actually hurt her...much. She cursed as she stumbled, nearly falling to her knees, just managing to maintain her footing.

"That was stupid," she muttered, as she spun to face him, flipping her blade into an icepick grip as well. In a real fight, that blunder would have left her with her arm laced open and the right lung punctured, ending the fight and likely her life.

"Yes," Aleron agreed, "but you are getting better. I barely dodged that thrust," he admitted.

She was learning fast. Aleron discovered her to be quick, agile, and surprisingly strong. Her offense was coming along well, but her defense lagged behind. She tended to overextend, as she had just done, leaving herself open to counterattack when her offensive moves were blocked.

Barathol and Geldun looked on with amusement, Barathol shouting, "Good going, Ellie! You almost tagged him there!"

She grinned back at the two men, nearly forgetting her embarrassment at her failure. "I'll get you eventually, Love," she told Aleron.

Chapter 9

Gurlachday, Day 19, Harvest Moon, 8765 Sudean Calendar

The rough track before them indicated that they had nearly reached the border with Sunjib. The large sign on the far side faced away from them and likely displayed a warning to anyone approaching, that they were entering Kolixtlan.

The isolated nation patrols its borders with great regularity, even the most remote parts. With no friendly borders, aside from the sixty leagues it shares with Adar, Kolixtlan considers a heavily defended border a necessity.

The nations bordering Kolixtlan share this sentiment as well, and Aleron knew there would be a similar road a couple hundred paces further, on the Sunjibi side.

Both nations maintained guard posts, strung along the border like evenly spaced beads, each about five leagues from the next. Without knowing exactly where they were, on the border, there was no way for them to know how close they might be to one, or when a patrol might pass through.

The conscripted soldiers of Kolixtlan, separated from their families for the duration of their service, stay busy by keeping the access roads clear of brush for several paces either side. It seemed safe enough, so they darted across singly, Barathol first and Aleron last, spacing their passage by a hundred count between each other.

As expected, they came upon another path, this one marked by signs in Sunjibi, warning any approaching to turn back or face prosecution. They waited again to ensure that no patrols might be near, though the repercussions from capture by a Sunjibi patrol would be slight, as they obviously were not Kolixtlani. Still, they thought it best if their passage went unnoticed until they made it further into Sunjib.

A short time later, hearing nothing but normal wildlife sounds, the group darted across in the same manner as the last time. Once regrouped, they continued northwest, toward Sunj. The ridge they followed coalesced with others into a wide plateau. The pine forest gave way to stands of mixed broadleaf trees as the soil changed from sandy to coarse and rocky.

The travelers adjusted their heading slightly to the north, in hopes of meeting the east fork of the Tonji River, which leads directly to Sunj. From Sunj, they could buy passage on a riverboat, bringing them to Wakol Bay, on the border of Waban and Kolixtlan.

It was a risky proposition, in that the last eighty-five leagues of the Tonji form the border between Waban and Kolixtlan. As long as they stuck to the west shore, they should be fine.

The only other option, to avoid the border altogether, was to make landfall early and travel one-hundred leagues overland to the coast.

Aleron mulled the choices over in his mind as they walked. They discussed them as a group several times, but as yet, they had not settled upon a decision.

The lengthening shadows told them that they should look for a place to spend the night, so they kept an eye out for a suitable spot to sleep, somewhat higher than the surrounding area, with overhead cover, in case rain moved in overnight.

A rustle from the undergrowth was all the warning they had, as a dark shape sprang from the brush to their right front. One swipe from a massive, black-scaled hand with claw-tipped fingers flung Barathol three paces back from his position, to lie stunned on the forest floor.

Geldun rushed forward to stand with Aleron and shield Eilowyn. Facing them, the half-troll towered a head taller than Aleron and roared, exposing murderously long canines. Covered in black scales, with a shock of black hair tied in a topknot, it wore a crudely stitched hide vest and short breeches, as a concession to the cold of the season.

Half-trolls go naked, often as not, in hotter climates. Fortunately for them, but not by much, it had no weapon, just claws, teeth, and easily twice the mass of either man it faced.

An armed half-troll could need an entire squad to take it down. Geldun and Aleron slashed and dodged, slowly losing ground to the creature. "Just stay behind us," Aleron directed Eilowyn. Sword slashes did little against the hard scales, and the creature deftly blocked any thrusts they attempted.

Finally, as it made a left-handed swipe that Geldun blocked with his sword braced atop his buckler, Eilowyn darted from behind the men and, with a two-handed grip, drove her long dagger into the half-troll's ribcage, all the way to the hilt.

The monster screeched and backhanded the woman, clipping her under the jaw and tumbling her into the leaf litter. It staggered back and snatched the foot-long blade out from its chest, looking as if it intended to use it against them, but dark blood flowed down its leg, from under the vest. It coughed, and blood flowed down the creature's chin, onto its chest. The half-troll's eyes rolled back into its head, and letting the dagger fall from its grip, it fell face-first at their feet, arms and legs twitching for a few moments before becoming still.

Aleron ran to Eilowyn, and Geldun rushed to check on Barathol. Barathol was just rolling to his knees, coughing, and fighting to draw a full breath. Aleron found Eilowyn face down and unconscious. He felt at her neck for a pulse and, finding one, laid his hand on her back to feel for breathing.

"She's still breathing," he called out to Geldun.

"How is Barry?"

"I'll live," Barathol answered for himself.

"I thought I might have a cracked rib, but now, I think not. Is Ellie all right? Who took the troll out?"

"She did," Geldun answered. "Stuck him with her knife, right in the heart and lungs, by the looks."

Aleron felt carefully up and down her neck and then asked, "Gel, will you check her too. I want to make sure her neck isn't broken before I move her."

"Sure thing Al," he replied, dropping down beside the unconscious woman.

Geldun took the most from their medical training in the Marines. His fingers moved first to the base of her skull and probed down her neck to between her shoulder blades. He removed her pack with care, and then he felt all the way down her spine.

"Everything seems sound; let's turn her over now." He and Aleron gingerly rolled her onto her back, revealing the spreading bruise on the left of her jaw, abraded and bleeding from the scales of the half-troll's forearm.

"Sticking a half-troll in the ribs!" Barathol said, in wonder. "Your girl has bigger stones than any of us, Al. I'll carry her out," he continued, taking a deep breath to ready himself and grimacing in pain for it.

"No, Barry, I'll carry her," Aleron asserted.

"But, what about your shoulder?"

"Probably better than your ribs, by the looks of it. I just have the knot on my shoulder blade now, and my left arm is a little weak, is all."

In reality, his shoulder throbbed from the exertion of fighting, but he would not admit to it. If anyone should carry Eilowyn, it should be him, Aleron thought.

"If one of you could get her pack, though, that would be great." He stood to straddle his betrothed, gathered her up under her armpits, and then ducked to sling her over his shoulders. Though not so much as Barathol, Aleron was still considerably stronger than the average man, halfbloods combining the strength of elves with the bulk of men. He carried the slim woman easily, despite the aching shoulder.

"Let's get a couple thousand paces between us and that thing," Geldun suggested, as he gathered up Eilowyn's pack. Barathol helped him to tie it off, so it hung on his chest, but still left his arms free to fight. They continued on their original heading, as the shadows grew longer before them. Barathol took the lead again, with Geldun at the back, walking more slowly than before, due to their injuries and extra burdens. They discussed the possibility of meeting more of the creatures but dismissed it as unlikely. They traveled far north of their usual range, and their assailant was likely a lone young male.

Little is known of half-trolls, excepting that they maintain settlements on the south slopes of the Iron Hills, and it is believed that those settlements house only one adult male, plus his harem and assorted juveniles. Solitary young males are often found outside the typical settlement zone, maintaining large home ranges, and waiting until they are strong enough to challenge a mature male for control of a harem.

Eilowyn's head lolled against Aleron's shoulder as they made their way through the forest. It was hard work, and he sweated from the exertion. As the day drew to a close, she seemed no closer to waking than she had when they started out. Aleron was beginning to worry that she might never wake from the blow she received. Finally, they reached a spot that seemed suitable for sleeping, and suitably far from the dead troll.

"This looks good," Barathol announced.

"Could you lay out her bedroll first?" Aleron requested. "I'd rather not set her in the dirt, only to move her again."

The others agreed and set their burdens down. It took a bit of doing to get Geldun loose from the doubled packs, but shortly, they had Eilowyn's blankets laid out and helped him settle her into bed. Geldun formed a pillow from a spare sack, stuffed with leaves, and used it to prop up her head.

After settling her, they went to work clearing the rest of the area, digging the fire pit, and gathering wood. Soon, they had a pot of stew simmering, and Aleron went back to Eilowyn to continue trying to wake her. After supper, he took the first shift at watch, pacing about the perimeter of their camp, while Eilowyn remained unconscious, not stirring in the slightest.

***

Hadaras, Jessamine, and Cladus entertained one another over dinner, regaling one another with tales of past adventures. Cladus traveled widely over the years, nearly as widely as Hadaras, as a bard who did not age normally needed to move around and not return to the same place too often.

Jessamine said little to add to their conversations, unless the conversation turned to Aleron or other recent events. Her memories reached back to the times before the Allfather formed Aertu, but her kind tended to stay out of the affairs of mortals, especially any affairs considered adventurous, though her relationship with Hadaras defied the typical.

Much of her knowledge was not appropriate for mortals, and if she shared some of that with the elf, it was because he was no typical mortal.

Hadaras, in turn, lived over nine millennia, two to three times the usual lifespan of an elf. Jessamine suspected with some degree of certainty that his mother was actually one of the aelir, considered a goddess among men. Though he had heard the rumors, Hadaras was not accepting of anything unusual in his parentage, knowing only that his mother disappeared when he was young, long before the first elves sailed from their homeland to the shores of the continent.

Their talk turned to their plans for tomorrow, when Hadaras and Cladus planned to travel back to Arundell. Hadaras' position as the king's military advisor hung in limbo, with Aleron yet to be crowned, but he felt the need to discuss certain matters with the Gealton. Aleron remained out of contact, and they needed to discuss the course of action for the kingdom, if he indeed failed to rescue the steward's daughter and perhaps was a captive of Kolixtlan as well.

He established contact with the elvish emissaries to Castia and Sunjib, and the Castian indicated that Kolixtlan experienced some sort of trouble in the past week, the border becoming a beehive of activity. The Sunjibi ambassador had yet to note any unusual activity on their border, but that border is much further from the capital than that with Castia.

"I think it is time for men and elves to get to sleep," Jessamine suggested. "You have an early start tomorrow, and you should get all the rest you can."

The aelient would not accompany them on their journey. Bound to this piece of land, she could only leave it for short periods. She was capable of relocating, as she had when they brought Aleron from the colony to Swaincott, but that required an extensive ritual of relocating home soil and planting an

54

offspring of the hazel tree to which she tied her life force. A nymph who loses whatever feature to which they associate, or somehow becomes permanently displaced from that feature, will not die, but will dwindle, becoming a shapeless roving spirit, until managing to resettle and reconstitute elsewhere. This process can take many lifetimes of men to accomplish.

"That sounds like a fine plan," The bard agreed, draining the last of his wine and setting his glass down. They stood and worked together to clean up the kitchen. Hadaras gestured over the plates set next to the washbasin; they crackled with blue energy, and the residues and scraps turned to fine ash.

"That's very nice, my love, but I still need to wash the plates to get the ash off," Jessamine remarked.

"And don't you dare take the seasoning off my cast-iron pots!" She poured water into those from a large kettle that boiled on the stove, leaving them to soak and bent to setting the plates, cups, and utensils in the basin, followed by a handful of powdered soap and the rest of the boiling water.

"I was only trying to help, my dearest, and get you to bed all the sooner," Hadaras retorted, with a beaming grin, as she poured the water.

She "tsked" him and flipped her long dark hair into his face, with a smirk, as she turned to replace the kettle on the stove. "Make yourself useful and pour some more water into the kettle."

"Would you like help with anything before I turn in?" Cladus inquired, with the beginnings of a smile turning the corners of his mouth.

"No, Cladus, you can go rest now. Hadaras and I can take care of the rest."

"Well then, good night and may the Allfather bless you both." He turned and walked casually to the back bedroom that used to belong to Aleron.

Jessamine and Hadaras resumed cleaning the dishes, enjoying one of their few moments of privacy since their friend arrived four days prior.

Chapter 10

Shilwezday, Day 20, Harvest Moon, 8765 Sudean Calendar

I stroll through the halls of the royal palace alone, in my favorite green silk riding dress and a cloak of matching green wool. A silver and emerald broach, in the shape of a sea turtle fastens the cloak and I have my stout brown riding boots on my feet. The strange thing is I have no recollection of plans to go riding today.

Where were all the people? No one, save me, is anywhere to be found. Even Simeon and Hans failed to show, and they usually shadow my every waking hour. I vaguely recall some unpleasant dream from the night before, of attack and kidnapping, but I find those memories fleeting at best. The amulet Aleron gave me as an engagement present lies cool and heavy against my chest. I wonder why it feels so heavy today.

My feet carry me into the great hall of the king, though I don't recall the corridor I was in leading to this place. I turn and make my way to the massive granite throne, which always seems so out of place among the soaring white arches of the great hall.

I immediately note Andhanimwhid's absence from its place in the back of the throne. How can this be? Aleron told me that he would not draw the sword again until he declared his birthright to the throne. How and why would he have done that without my knowing? Where was I and why is this place empty of people?

I spin about to survey the empty hall, but when I return to face the throne, it is not empty. The thing in the throne is not Aleron, not even human. A massive black serpent sits coiled on the seat, as thick as a strong man's leg. Unblinking eyes regard me, blood red, with vertical slit pupils, while its forked tongue smells the air. The huge snake begins uncoiling and sliding from the throne, making straight for me.

I turn about, hike up my skirts, and run, as fast as my feet can carry me, to the archway that takes me back into the corridor. I glance behind to see the black serpent, easily three paces long, gliding across the white marble floor.

Where is everyone? I need help with this thing chasing me! I sprint back up the corridor and hazard another glance backward. Nothing follows me, but I keep running, occasionally glancing back to see nothing but empty hallway, through corridors that seem both familiar and not so. I do not recall any corridor in the entire palace this long, without a single jog or turn. It seems now to go on, forever straight, and when I look back, it appears the same. It appears as a copy of any hallway in the palace, extending endlessly in either direction.

I slow to a stop; there is no pursuit from the serpent, and nothing but evenly spaced doorways on either wall or in both directions. Maybe, with no one in the halls, there are people in the rooms. Impulsively, I turn the latch of the first door I come to and push it open, finding myself looking into my father's study.

My father, Steward Gealton, seated behind the desk, looks up and exclaims, "Ellie, my dear, please come in. Have you been out riding? I thought you would be on your way to the summer house by now."

"I...I'm not sure, Father. I can't seem to find anyone else. There is a huge serpent in the King's Hall; I ran from it. Have you seen Aleron?"

His expression seems to cloud, and he replies, "I'm afraid you found him already, my dear. He often takes that form at rest, he has changed."

I notice now that my father's gorget, signifying his office as Steward of Sudea, no longer encircles his neck. In its place, a black iron collar wraps round his throat. I put a hand to my breastbone and no longer feel the amulet where it once lay. Instead, a cold iron collar encircles my neck as well.

"We have peace with Kolixtlan and Adar, finally," Gealton continued. "In fact, we have peace throughout the world, and Aleron made it all possible. He is the Hand of the One True God, after all."

I try to scream, but all that comes out is a stifled squeak, like a mouse taken by a snake. I whirl about and dart out of the room, only to find myself face to face with Aleron. My heart leaps for joy until I reach his eyes. Those beautiful silver eyes are now crimson, with the vertical pupils of a snake; they are the eyes of the serpent from the hall. This time, I manage a true scream, and I find myself sprinting down the corridor again, fleeing the monster my one true love has become.

"Ellie! Come back, my love!" He calls out to me, but I ignore him and keep running. "Come back! I command it!"

I run and run, down never-ending corridors, all the while with the beast that was Aleron calling a few paces behind, alternating between pleading, cajoling, and commanding. I simply keep running, seemingly forever, but I cannot stop, for I know that if he catches me, all will be over. I have to escape and find a means to save him from what he has become, so I keep running.

The noonday sun shone down into the clearing formed by the collapse of a single massive beech. Aleron sat beside Eilowyn, with an expression of obvious worry, brushing the stray hairs from her face and feeling her forehead for temperature. She remained unconscious, nearly a full day after the half-troll clouted her on the jaw.

The night prior, Geldun located a swelling bruise beneath her hair, likely caused by a stone when she hit the ground.

What if she never wakes up? I don't know if I can watch her fade and die like that. In fact, I know I can't.

"Ellie! Come back, My Love!" He had seen men never wake up from blows to the head. At best, they lived only a few days, wasting away from thirst, more than anything.

If she failed to wake tomorrow... He put that thought out of his mind.

She will wake; I have faith that she will. He quietly voiced a prayer to the Allfather for her recovery.

"The food is almost ready," Barathol announced. In some ways, it was good to rest from their injuries, as well as the many leagues their feet had traveled. They managed to forage, gathering some tubers and snaring two rabbits that morning, making the midday meal more interesting.

"That smells good," Geldun piped up, from casually patrolling the perimeter of their camp. "I'm famished; what are the rest of you having?"

It did smell good; Aleron had to agree, especially after the usual dry meat at midday and the tasteless stew they ate every evening. He had difficulty mustering any appetite, though, with Eilowyn lying as if dead and unable to enjoy it with him. Everything seemed dull to his senses, and his heart was heavy in his chest.

"Let's eat then," he stated, resignedly, and slowly got to his feet. So much would be easy if he hadn't stupidly burned himself out in Kolixtla. If not for that, he could have healed her injuries or fended off the troll quickly. In fact, they could be flying home right now if not for his stupidity.

He blamed himself for letting his anger take control, causing him to overreach himself, and he was sure the others did as well, even if no one said it. Now, because of him, they all have to walk halfway across Aertu if Eilowyn ever recovered enough to walk out.

As the afternoon dragged on, the men had nearly completed a travois to drag their injured friend along with them. Aleron hoped against hope that the cool spring weather would help Eilowyn hang on long enough to awaken and begin drinking and eating.

The sound of footsteps snapping trigs and rustling leaves caused the three to drop their work and scramble for their weapons, left unsheathed and close at hand. Geldun snatched up his sword and slid his arm through the straps of his buckler with practiced ease, cinching it tight with sword in hand, as he went to guard. Barathol grabbed his glaive from where he stuck the butt spike into the ground, as Aleron came up with twin cutlasses at the ready.

Whoever or whatever came towards them had no concern for staying quiet. Soon, a grizzled-looking old westman came into view, appearing to be alone. He stood a head shorter than Aleron, dressed in rough tanned leather breeches and jerkin, over stout leather boots, with a dark wool cloak pinned over one shoulder and a tall walking stick that looked to be of some sort of ironwood. His long white beard hung down to his belt, from which hung a sizable axe, and long white hair spilled over his shoulders, from under his bright red woolen stocking cap.

He took notice of the three young men, sniffed the air with his broad nose, and exclaimed, in accented Sudean, "Now what have you gone and walked into now, Bruji? Three armed men, out in the middle of the woods, not Kolixtlanis, by the look."

His heavy brows lent his face a fierce appearance, belied by his mild voice. "Now what brings you three into old Bruji's forest?"

Aleron stepped forward to speak for the three. "We mean no harm and definitely not to trespass, Sir. We are escaped from captivity in Kolixtlan and mean only to make our way to Sunj."

"Very well, very well, old Bruji doesn't mind visitors in his forest. In fact, he welcomes them. Now, if you do not mind my asking, what is that you are building?"

"We have an injured friend who we need to carry," Aleron replied.

"Oh, very well, very well; do you mind if old Bruji has a look? He knows a thing or two about healing, don't you know."

Aleron glanced at each of his friends, in turn, and Geldun said, "I can't see how it could hurt. We've done as much as I know how to do."

Barathol eyed the westman's long staff and axe suspiciously, but finally nodded in affirmation.

Aleron nodded as well and said, "Like he said, what can it hurt? Thank you for wanting to help us Sir."

"Call me Bruji, please, and think nothing of it. Bruji helps anyone who needs help out here, even the men of Kolixtlan, if they wish it. He doesn't make distinctions. Let's go see your friend, young man."

They escorted the old westman over to where Eilowyn lay, in the shade of a huge hickory. Seeing her lying there, placidly, with her auburn hair spilling loose behind her and her face marred only by the purple bruise on her jaw line, he inquired, "What a lovely young flower. What happened to her?"

"She was hit by a half-troll and hit her head on a stone, when she fell," Aleron replied, "Around midday yesterday."

"A half-troll, worse of an abomination than the original trolls. They are half westman, you know. But what's done is done, and cannot be unmade."

"She killed the beast with her knife, just before it smacked her," Barathol added, beaming with pride.

"A courageous little flower, not surprising, in the company of such men as yourselves. Has she eaten or drunk since then? Has the girl made water?" Bruji asked, slipping down beside her, feeling her head, and finding the large knot on the back.

"No and no, she hasn't woken, since it happened," Geldun stated. "We did our best to make her comfortable, but we need to move and find help now."

"Help you have found, and old Bruji will give it, like he always does."

He rose from examining her and stated, "You will bring her to old Bruji's house. It is not far, and there is room for all. There, he may be able to bring her back. She is trapped in the world of dreams now, and she will not return if her body wastes away before then."

"What do you mean by 'trapped in the world of dreams?'" Aleron demanded.

Bruji means what he says. That is why he says what he says. She is locked in a dream and can't escape. Even if old Bruji can fix her head, she may not come out of it."

"How do you know this?"

"Old Bruji could say that he has seen as much, many times in his long life, and that would be the truth, but really, old Bruji just knows these things."

"But… what can you do for her there that you can't do here?" Barathol asked, suspicious of the oldster's intentions, as were the others.

"Old Bruji lives in a sacred place, my friend. Many things are possible there that are not elsewhere. Now, you can choose to follow old Bruji, or you can let that pretty flower wilt and die on your walk to the city. It is your choice."

Aleron backed off a few steps and motioned the others back to join him. They conversed in low whispers, all the while keeping an eye on Bruji with Eilowyn.

After a short debate, they decided to accompany Bruji to his dwelling, in the barest of hope that he could help her. Otherwise, she was almost certain to die on the trip.

They finished the last touches on the travois, loaded Eilowyn, and gathered their gear. Barathol took the first shift at dragging the sled, positioning himself behind the crossed poles. He followed close behind the aged westman, with Geldun and Aleron flanking the travois, weapons drawn.

"It won't be long at all, friends. Old Bruji's house is very close." He led them slightly north of their intended path. The travois moved well across the forest floor, performing better than a wheeled cart would have in the same circumstances.

With the sun slanting low through the trees and shining golden against a mass of billowing clouds building to the east, threatening rain, they came upon a small log cabin in a large clearing. "It will be good to get out of the weather for tonight," Aleron stated, and the others agreed.

"You can drop your things here under the porch," Bruji instructed, "and bring the girl back to the spring," he continued.

"Is that the sacred place you spoke of?" Aleron inquired.

"Yes, young man, which is why old Bruji built his house here, because of the spring."

"If you don't mind me asking, Sir, why do you refer to yourself in that way, like you speak of someone else?"

"That is because old Bruji is only this body, not me. I live in this body until it is exhausted, and then I move on to a better place. Our mortal lives are just a dream, from which we all eventually wake.

Now let's go; time is wasting for this mortal life."

They dragged her around to the northwest edge of the clearing, where a clear spring erupted from the hillside. It was a beautiful spot, just inside the wood line, with early wildflowers and fruit trees in blossom.

The spring, walled in finely cut, but aged-looking, serpentine, fed a tiny stream, teeming with small fish. The remains of ancient walls surrounded on three sides, open facing the south, and covered in vines to the point of total concealment. Trees grew through portions of the old structure, but the outline remained visible. Perhaps this was a temple once, long ago.

As Barathol stepped out of the travois and retrieved his glaive, Bruji called, "Iudhael, please come forth. There is one here in need."

Through a gap in the wall that Aleron could swear had not been there before, stepped a creature from one of Aleron's dreams. Walking on two legs, with the horns and legs of a wild goat, and covered in bright golden hair, the satyr had to be the keeper of the golden pool.

Geldun and Barathol started forward, Geldun beginning to draw his sword and Barathol taking a low guard position.

"No, Barry, Gel, it's all right. He's aelient; you couldn't hurt him with those weapons if you tried. I've dreamed about him before this, and I know he means us no harm."

Everything about him was golden, including the little exposed skin of his torso and face, as well as his eyes; he literally glowed with golden light.

"Mean no harm, yes, but lending my aid remains to be seen," Iudhael stated, with the wall of vines closing behind.

"Why should I help men who destroy one another and the Allfather's creatures so readily, especially fighting men?

Oh, but this one is different!" he exclaimed, striding up to face Aleron. "This one holds the spiral of the ages in his hands. Which way will he bend it, I wonder?"

He clapped one man-like but hairy hand to Aleron's shoulder and continued, "I sense my sister's mark on him as well." Aleron felt the healing energy flow through his body, the pain leaving his shoulder, and all fatigue and hunger falling away.

"This one I heal because of what he is, and for Jessamine. I feel no obligation to any other."

Aleron started at the mention of his "cousin" but thought better of saying anything yet. His friends also reacted with quizzical expressions at her mention.

"The little flower was attacked by one of the Disobedient Son's foul creatures, fought and won, but barely. Surely, you can see it in your heart to help one so brave, with so much life ahead?" Bruji pleaded.

"She is to be my wife," Aleron added, choosing to speak now, "and I don't know how I would live without her."

"You will live, regardless," Iudhael surmised, "but I concede your thoughts and motivations might take a dark turn if you lose this one too early," he concluded.

"I would certainly prefer the spiral to reach for light over darkness. I will attempt to heal this little flower, as you say."

He moved to where Eilowyn lay still and crouched down on his goat legs, laying a hand on her forehead. She jerked, something she hadn't managed in the last day, and murmured something Aleron couldn't hear, another thing she had not done in the past day.

The aelient stood, turned, and clasped Barathol and Geldun by the shoulders, saying, "And, your friends, for good measure. I'm feeling magnanimous tonight."

The men felt the weeks' worth of hurt and weariness fall from their bodies before the golden being released them.

"Thank you," they both said, nearly in unison.

"No need to thank me, it is what I do. Now the girl, she was in a dangerous place, and she has left it now for the normal dreams of her kind, but I cannot say how she will fare upon waking. I know not what she experienced in the world of real dreams."

Ending on that statement, Iudhael turned and strode back through the gap in the wall that hadn't been there a moment before.

"Where did he go?" Geldun asked no one in particular, stepping up and examining the wall that Iudhael casually strolled through. The vines concealed solid stone, and he could see undisturbed forest over the wall's top.

"There are more planes of existence than what you can see with mortal eyes, my young friend," Bruji answered, "like the world of dreams where our little flower was trapped for a time.

You have been there many times yourself, Aleron, haven't you? I could see that you knew my old friend for who he is, as soon as you laid eyes on him."

"Yes, Bruji, I know him from my own dreams." The reminder made him think to reach for the magic lost to him for weeks past, but he met with only disappointment. That aspect of the world was still dead to him.

"Perhaps you will know old Bruji in time. He spends considerable time there as well."

"Perhaps," Aleron answered, gazing upon the elderly westman, remembering Hadaras' old friend Morguilis, wondering what Bruji truly was.

"Should we wake Eilowyn now?"

"Old Bruji would say to wait until she does on her own. She will survive the night, with the healing she received, and wake as if from a normal night's sleep.

Let us bring her to my house now." Without further discussion, Aleron stepped into the travois and gently picked up the poles to rest on his now fully mended shoulders.

Inside Bruji's cozy log house, a fire already crackled in the small fireplace. The men all wondered to themselves how the westman managed the trick, with all of them outside.

They gently laid Eilowyn on one of the narrow pallets, piled with furs and wool blankets, to one side of the fireplace. The other being the obvious choice for Aleron to sleep, close to his betrothed. The strangeness of it all nearly overwhelmed the three men, seeing the cabin ready for guests, as if Bruji knew he would have guests that night.

After settling Eilowyn under the blankets, Aleron asked, "Is old Bruji a sorcerer?"

"Old Bruji is many things," the westman replied, with a chuckle, "but a sorcerer, he is not. You might call old Bruji a priest, but that may not be accurate either."

"If old Bruji is a priest, is he a priest of the Allfather, or does he serve some other god?" The other men followed the conversation in silence, a nervous look in their eyes.

"Old Bruji serves no one, particularly not those called "Gods" by others, but he helps all who ask his help. You might say he has connections to the one you call Allfather."

That night, with Barathol and Geldun settled into the small loft for the night, Aleron drifted off to sleep, feeling safer than he had in many weeks.

Bruji sat in a sturdy rocking chair, next to the fire, puffing on a long-stemmed pipe and seeming to stare off into the distance.

Aleron's dreams that night revolved around him and Eilowyn strolling through an ancient forest, always with a white raven wheeling overhead. It was a portent, but what did it mean? Aleron's sleeping mind contemplated the question through the night.

Chapter 11

Corballday, Day 21, Harvest Moon, 8765 Sudean Calendar

"I had a very disturbing dream," Eilowyn answered Bruji. After waking, they apprised her of the events since their encounter with the half-troll and made the necessary introductions.

"I ran endlessly through the halls of the palace, until a…a satyr, a golden satyr, appeared before me, pulled me through a side door and into a pleasant dream of a beautiful fountain, in a temple of polished serpentine."

"That was Iudhael, who healed you and pulled you from the world of dreams, my flower." Bruji seemed to refuse calling her by her name, preferring the pet name he adopted for her when he first saw her.

She blushed a bit, though it was not the first time he used it addressing her.

"The world of dreams can show what is, what was, and what may yet come to be, but never what will definitely come. The spiral of the ages is not carved in stone; rather, it is as a growing vine. None can know for sure where it will turn, not even the one you call Allfather. What was it that you ran from?"

"I would rather not say, Bruji," she replied, glancing at Aleron with a look mixed between apprehension and relief. She was glad that what she saw in the dream would not definitely come to pass, but frightened that it could.

"Very well, my flower, Bruji will not press you to go back there. Keep in mind, though, having entered that plane of existence once, you may find yourself there again. Know that you can always choose to step back out again. Keep that in your thoughts always, lest you be trapped there again."

"Who is Iudhael?" she inquired after her savior's identity.

"He is an aelient, whom I saw in one of my first dreams," Aleron answered, before the westman could reply with one of his cryptic explanations.

"He carries the magic of healing."

"And he lives in the world of dreams, like many of his kind, rarely appearing in the mortal world," Bruji added.

"Bruji thinks you very lucky he deigned to heed my request and come to your aid. He cares little for men in this age."

"I am certainly glad that he did, as I am that you did. Thank you again, Bruji."

"Think nothing of it, little flower. Old Bruji helps all who need his help. Now, I suppose you will be wanting away soon now that you are healed and rested?"

"I think so," Aleron answered. "The sooner we move out, the sooner may we gain passage back to Sudea."

Geldun and Barathol passed the time tossing dice off to the side, both sitting on the pallet Aleron slept on the night before. They all had a good breakfast of oat porridge, sweetened with honey and an odd spice that blended well with the sweetness. To Aleron, the spice appeared to be dried red bark, of some sort, left to boil in the water and fished out at the end of the cooking. It filled the cabin with a pungently sweet scent.

"We thank you again for all of your help. I owe you more than you know."

"The only payment old Bruji requests is that you keep to the path of light. You hold the fate of this age in your hands, young Aleron, King of Sudea."

Aleron's eyes grew wide, as did Eilowyn's. Barathol and Geldun stopped their gaming to look up, in alarm.

"Don't be alarmed, young friends, who else could you be, escaping across the border as you did? I told you old Bruji spends time in the world of dreams. Are you truly that surprised that he knows you for who you are?"

"No, not surprised, really, only startled," Aleron admitted.

"Are you truly certain that there is nothing more old Bruji can do for you, before you leave this sacred place?" He looked expectantly back and forth between Aleron and Eilowyn.

"Just how sacred is this site?" Eilowyn asked.

"Aside from Iudhael's spring, which was here first, this is the site of an ancient temple, from the earliest days of Sunjib, consecrated to the Allfather. This place remains consecrated to this day, even if the ruins of the temple have long since crumbled to dust. That is why old Bruji chooses to live here, and no creation of the Adversary dares enter."

"You are a priest of the Allfather, aren't you?" Eilowyn asked.

"Of a sort," Bruji admitted, "of a sort, old Bruji is." He grinned, ever so slightly, and Eilowyn turned to face Aleron, with a smile of her own just touching the corners of her mouth and her eyes sparkling.

"And certain things can only happen on consecrated ground, with a priest in attendance, right Bruji?" she verified, still looking straight at Aleron.

A guffaw from the pallet revealed the others understood the exchange, the men grinning like fools, their game forgotten.

"Are you trying to say…I mean…you're saying we should…" finding it difficult to form the words, even harder with everyone in the room grinning and snickering, "get married now?"

"Why, of course, I will marry you now, my love, and thank you so much for offering." She started giggling then.

Bruji and the two other men joined in, and soon everyone was chuckling at the confused look on Aleron's face.

"Right now, this morning?"

"Why not now? We won't be home for many months yet."

"But what about your family and the people? They will expect a public wedding."

"We can have one of those, no, we surely will have one of those, when we return. In the meantime, I want to be married to the man I love. Is that a problem?"

"I don't know; I guess not," Aleron responded, "but what if something happens to me? You'll be a widow then."

"Really, Aleron, is that your excuse? I'm about to be insulted."

The others continued to look amused as the couple bickered.

"All right, all right, you just surprised me. Of course, I would love to marry you today, rather than later."

"Excellent!" Bruji exclaimed. "It has been ages since Bruji performed a wedding ceremony, indeed, it has been quite literally ages."

"We have no rings, though. I'll have to buy us some… when we get to a town," Aleron said.

"Let old Bruji check; he has various trinkets lying about the house." The aged westman began rummaging through the assorted bowls and jars on his windowsill and counter, soon returning with two gleaming rings of white gold.

He went to Eilowyn first. "Let us see if these fits, little flower." He tried the smaller ring on the third finger of her left hand, and it fit snugly enough to stay on, but not too tight, in other words, perfectly.

Eilowyn held it up to admire it on her hand for a moment, then, reluctantly, slid it off and handed it back to Bruji.

He came to Aleron next, who held up his left hand for the same test. Bruji slid the larger band onto Aleron's third finger, and he saw that the wide band was worked with ravens wheeling in flight, perfectly matching the smaller band in Bruji's other hand.

"Perfect fit, again," the westman stated.

Aleron wondered at this "coincidence," as he often did about his luck lately.

The ceremony took place in the meadow, below Iudhael's spring and next to the stream that flowed forth.

Eilowyn wore a wreath of white wildflowers upon her brow, woven by Bruji on the walk from the cottage. He claimed them an appropriate adornment for the lovely flower that she was.

With the sun halfway to zenith in the eastern sky, Aleron and Eilowyn faced south, with Barathol and Geldun to either side and Bruji facing them to their front.

"Do you Aleron, pledge to take this woman, Eilowyn, to be your wife, to protect her and serve her, for all the days you live upon Aertu and for all of eternity beyond?" The ancient looking westman asked, in the traditional manner of Sudean marriage vows.

"Yes, thusly I pledge my life and eternal spirit," Aleron answered, in the same tradition, attempting to maintain a serious expression, but not quite managing to conceal the happiness he felt.

"Do you, Eilowyn, pledge to take this man, Aleron, to be your husband, to comfort and serve him, for all the days you live upon Aertu and for all of eternity beyond?"

"Yes, thusly I pledge my life and eternal spirit," Eilowyn answered, her smile radiant with joy.

They turned to one another and extended their right hands, palms down, she placing hers atop his. Bruji took a long strip of cloth and snugly wrapped it six times around their hands, fastening it with a neat square knot on top.

"In the name of the one called Allfather, let this binding signify this man and this woman, bound to one another, in life and in spirit, for all of eternity."

Each of them held the ring of the other, between thumb and forefinger of their left hands, for the next step of the ceremony.

"Let these rings of precious gold act as a visible sign, for all to see, of the never-ending nature of time and their commitment to one another, for all of eternity."

Shakily, they placed the ring on the other's finger, simultaneously, as the ritual required.

"Now, under the eyes of the Allfather, I name this once separate man and woman married, sealed to one another and their children to come, for all of eternity."

Barathol whooped as Aleron gathered Eilowyn, now his wife, to him and bent down to kiss her. She gazed up at him, and their lips met, for the first time as husband and wife.

Geldun waited until they released to sweep in and hug them both. "Congratulations, Ellie, Al, this all seems very right. I am happy for you."

"First one out of circulation!" Barathol exclaimed as he moved in for his hug, engulfing them in his massive embrace.

"He better have been out of circulation for the last five years," Eilowyn replied, with a glint in her eye, but still gazing adoringly at her husband's strong, chiseled face. He no longer was the smooth-faced teenager with the wondering eyes she met all those years ago. Before her stood a strong, hard man, with gray eyes, at once stern as steel or warm and gentle, depending on what was required of him.

As he looked down at her face, the face of a beautiful and stately woman, he thought back on the pretty, young girl he saw at the market on his first day in the city. That girl had been experienced and crafty, even then, from growing up at court. Now, her intelligence shone through those bright emerald eyes, and he knew he had better craft an effective retort to Barathol's wisecrack.

"I never go past the common room, as these two fools can attest."

"Definitely the truth," Geldun acceded, while cuffing Barathol in the ribs.

"Thank you for letting old Bruji be a part of this day," the westman said, moving in for his hug as well, his eyes twinkling below heavy brows and bushy eyebrows.

"Can I persuade you gentlefolk to hold off one more day, to celebrate with old Bruji?"

"I don't see why not," Eilowyn answered, "Aleron?"

"Yes, we will stay," Aleron agreed. "Do you two have any objections?" The other men agreed, emphatically so, when Bruji mentioned an aged oaken cask of dark ale he intended to broach for the occasion.

"Excellent! Let me fetch a ham from the smokehouse then." The old westman's face, remarkably animated, despite the heavy features and expansive beard, shone with unadulterated joy as he stomped off to the smokehouse.

It occurred to Barathol that he hadn't noticed a smokehouse before, but there it stood, fifty paces from the back door of the house, with a lean-to sheltering a good supply of split hardwood.

The dark ale they sipped tasted heavy of oak and fragrant, bitter hops. It was an excellent example of Sunjibi Bitter, perhaps the best Geldun ever had.

Barathol sat snoozing in a sturdy chair, near the fire, his belly full from the excellent wild boar ham with carrots and parsnips they enjoyed for the wedding feast.

Eilowyn and Aleron reclined against some pillows, she in front of him, leaning against his chest on the pallet he slept on the night before, listening to Bruji recount some of the history of the place.

He revealed the healing spring to be the ultimate headwater of the Tonji River, so following the stream would eventually lead to Sunj.

Bruji told of days when a large city thrived, just a few leagues northwest, where several smaller streams merge to form a swift-flowing river. Capar, the name of the ancient city, was a rival of Sunj in the days before the kingdom united, and had wealth enough to build many grand temples. This area was an important grain-producing region in the days before the Great War.

After the turning of Kolixtlan to the Adversary, goblins and other foul creatures overran the region, and then, in the fighting that preceded the Last Battle, enemy forces razed Capar and the surrounding villages, exterminating most of the population.

Though the creatures of the adversary are unable to cross onto consecrated ground, consecration does nothing to stop men. Kolixtlani and Adari troops tore down the grand temples and executed the priests before Sunjibi warriors pushed them back across the border.

After the war, the land remained under Sunjibi control, the city of Capar all but forgotten, but few Sunjibi ever came to settle the new territory, so it returned to wilderness.

"You tell the story as if you were there yourself, Bruji," Eilowyn observed.

"It does seem that way, sometimes it seems that old Bruji was there in person. Now old Bruji sits here, alone with the memories, usually. Remember, the world of dreams can show you what once was. Old Bruji has seen Capar and the grand temples, in all their splendor. You have yourself seen the Last Battle, have you not, Aleron?"

Aleron started at the question, wondering how the old westman could know about his dreams. After a moment, he answered, "Yes, but through another's eyes, it seemed, not like other dreams, where I am myself."

"That often happens in dreams of things past, more so than other dreams. Do you not understand how old Bruji knows?"

"I understand," Aleron replied, thinking back to the carnage he witnessed through the other Aleron's eyes. He understood the pain on the old westman's face, and he hoped he would never witness such devastation in his lifetime.

Later that evening, after finishing off what was left of the ham, along with some sort of sweet orange tuber the Sudeans did not recognize, they settled into their beds. The newly wedded couple moved their pallets together for the night, while Geldun and Barathol returned to the loft, and Bruji took his place in the rocker, gazing into the fire.

"Good night, my young friends, may you sleep well and wake refreshed," Bruji said, as they settled in.

Aleron wondered how the aged westman managed to sleep like that. He also wondered when he and his new bride would truly share a wedding bed, since common decency precluded that in their current situation.

Chapter 12

Carpathday, Day 22, Harvest Moon, 8765 Sudean Calendar

The morning broke clear and cool. The four companions set out on the trail, with the sun rising over the treetops to their backs. They followed the stream as it ran along the wood line, intending to follow it to the Tonji and eventually to Sunj.

As they left that morning, Bruji had brief words of wisdom and a stout hug for each of them, in turn.

When it came to Eilowyn's turn, he said, "Lovely flower, I have seen you destined to bring the world much joy, or much sorrow, depending on what you choose to hold dear. Choose wisely."

Finally, he came to Aleron and foretold, "Young king, you have the power in your hands to heal Aertu or to destroy it. The spiral of time circles ever round and outward. It does not repeat itself, but it does pass through regions of similarity. This age is a critical one, and your choices will warp its path, for good or ill. In time, you may regain what you lost, but not until you prove yourself worthy and in need. That I see clearly.

Good luck to you, Aleron," he concluded, wrapping his arms tightly around the young man and patting his back.

"Thank you for everything, Bruji," Aleron said. "You saved Eilowyn. I'm sure that without you, she would have died."

"Old Bruji helps who need help, without reservation. That is his nature," the old westman replied, patting Aleron on the back again.

"Be safe, all of you."

"I'm going to miss the old man," Barathol admitted, from the front. He turned to look over his shoulder, back at the house, and stopped so abruptly that the others almost ran into him. He turned his body around and just stared back the way they had come. The others turned to see what had their friend gawking.

"It's gone," Geldun said softly. The clearing was empty. The ancient walls of Iudhael's temple remained, covered in vines, along with a few scattered stones from the grand temple that once stood in the clearing. There seemed to be a trace outline of the cabin's foundation, a faint rectangular depression, barely visible through the new spring grasses, just poking through last year's brown thatch.

"Well, my stomach feels like that breakfast was real," Barathol asserted, "so that wasn't just a dream."

"Especially considering that I'm awake, walking, and Aleron has a real haversack again," Eilowyn pointed out.

"And look at this." She held up her left hand with its new addition of a gold wedding band.

Aleron held up his left hand to look at the gold band with its wheeling raven pattern, running his thumb across it, as if to verify the realness of it.

"It was real, as real as anything ever was. Maybe Bruji is aelient, like Iudhael," he surmised, after a brief pause. "Some of them still care about the lives of mortals."

"That's odd," Geldun stated. "This is really far inland for a gull," he said, pointing to the sky. The others looked up to see the white bird soaring high above them.

That is no gull, Aleron thought to himself. His halfblood eyes, sharper than any human's, clearly saw the outline of the bird. *Old Bruji, what is this supposed to mean?*

We are married. Eilowyn resolved. *The words were spoken on consecrated ground, according to tradition. He is my husband, for all of eternity.*

By late afternoon, they covered nearly ten leagues from the old temple site. The land sloped gently to the northwest, toward the distant river. The terrain became more difficult here, large boulders strewn about, some with oddly squared or cylindrical shapes.

The stream they followed had become a rushing torrent, as other tributaries joined to form the beginnings of a river. Earlier, they crossed the stream to the northeast side, knowing that more and larger channels were likely to join it from the Iron Hills to the southwest. They were glad of their choice, seeing just such a stream intersecting the one they followed, a hundred paces ahead.

"This is the place," Geldun observed. "This must be Capar that old Bruji spoke about. This is the perfect place for grain mills, and all these stones must be the ruins. Anyplace else and they would have been scavenged for new buildings, but the westmen never came back here."

"I think you must be right," Eilowyn agreed. "I don't like it here. I almost feel like they are still here, somehow."

"A whole lot of murder happened here," Barathol added. "I can feel it somehow. I can't explain how, but I can just feel it."

"I learned about Capar from my grandfather's history books," Aleron related.

"An army of goblins and trolls overran the city after a short siege. Over seven-hundred thousand died here, five-hundred thousand in that one day. The priests followed and sacrificed over two-hundred thousand captives, over the next week, mostly women and children, according to the historian who wrote it. The entire countryside was razed. I don't blame the westmen for never coming back."

"We won't be camping here," Barathol decided.

"If ever there was a place to harbor ghosts, this is the place. Let's hook north a bell or so before sunset and find a nice place in the woods to camp, with no loose stones."

"I'm with you, Brother," Geldun approved. "I don't need any shades stepping on me in my bedroll."

"Absolutely, we camp in the woods, well away from this place. This is not a good place, and sometimes, the dead don't want to return to the Allfather. Sometimes, they have unfinished business," Aleron acceded to his friend's wishes.

"I'm not going to argue," Eilowyn stated, "This place is just plain eerie, but do you all really believe in ghosts?"

"Yes!" all three men replied, in near unison.

"But those are children's tales," the woman countered, "meant to keep the little ones in their beds at night, or to stay out of places they shouldn't be."

"When your bunkmate comes into the hold and climbs into his rack, after you saw his head leave his body that morning, and you watched him burn on the pyre that evening, you believe in ghosts," Barathol related, without a hint of emotion in his tone.

"We've all seen things, Ellie, men walking through the camp at night, which look like friends you lost, others taking up sentry duty and then disappearing, just before the real guards show up for duty," Geldun added.

"Grandfather told me it happens, Ellie," Aleron corroborated, "and I have heard too many accounts, like seeing men walk up on the perimeter that the living remembers killing on the field themselves. Battlefields always carry tales of ghosts. I think they get confused for a time, finding their way back home, and if home isn't with the Allfather, I don't think they hurry on their way either."

"Enough said, now you have me believing you, too. Can we split north now?"

"I don't see why not," Aleron conceded. "What do you two think? We could head north now, get clear of the ruins, and then hook west."

The others agreed, all of them wanting to place distance between them and the ruins.

Two bells later, they came upon an area, relatively free of underbrush, with a clear area for a fire pit. Towering hickory and oak provided an overhanging canopy for the campers. They had walked a league and a half north, to get well clear of the ruins, and then another league west, to regain lost ground.

Aleron bent to digging the fire pit and setting the tripod for cooking, while Eilowyn worked to clear loose twigs from their sleeping area. The other men scouted the area for potential danger and to secure enough dry firewood for the night. Aleron started the initial cook fire with the twigs his wife gathered and set to preparing the stew. They still had fresh ham from the night before, so tonight, the stew would be better than most nights.

Aleron lay curled on his side, with his new bride nestled in front of him, his arms around her. Andhanimwhid formed a lump behind his shoulder, as it always did at night. He drifted off to sleep and into another real dream.

I walk the destruction of a once beautiful city, reviling at the stench of death around me. The perfumed scarf wrapped around my mouth and nose does little to cut the smell. Carrion flies buzz in huge swarms, and in some places, I hear the maggots moving through the masses of bodies.

Kangal, king of Sunjib, walks beside me this day, through the ruins of his city's one-time rival. Stately Capar, jewel among the cities of the westmen, is no longer, its people slaughtered.

Kangal's army, from the west, was too late to save the city, but managed to hold the Nameless One's forces from penetrating further than the outskirts of Capar.

My forces, along with Mittean heavy cavalry, arrived days later to assist in driving the dark minions of the Adversary back across the borders of Kolixtlan and the Central Jungle. Someday, we will drive their master from Aertu altogether and exterminate his creatures.

I often wonder at the Allfather's intentions in letting that one live, or at least not driving him off and ridding the world of his abominations. The story of creation relates the creator's unwillingness to exterminate that which his rebellious child created, stating that what is made cannot be unmade. I do not understand the precept.

The dwarves recount their origins here, in the nearby Iron Hills, and speak of beasts from that time that no longer roam anywhere on Aertu. Obviously, some things have been unmade. Perhaps, the Allfather could not bring himself to exterminate a race of creatures by his own hand, but would not the hand of mankind be considered a natural turn of events? Regardless of the right or wrong of it, I will kill them all, given the chance. How could that be a mistake?

Men and westmen labor together to clean up this tragic scene. Too many bodies to burn, so mass graves are the only solution.

It is obvious that the priests of Kolixtlan had a hand in the destruction here. All the buildings are leveled, more than could be accomplished by siege engines in an entire year. Literally tens of thousands lay piled in heaps, with their chests split open and the hearts torn out. The priests drank deeply of the red power of death and chaos.

Oddly enough, the blue energy of life is plentiful here, days after the massacre. Maggots and flies are life, like any other life. We ordered each of the mass graves piled high with rubble to form huge cairns. When finished, they will circle the city in a ring nearly a league around. Lovely Capar will become a gigantic cemetery, with a desolate, ruined center.

I watch as a wagon loaded with corpses rumbles slowly by, pulled by a pair of the packhorses we brought with us. Mainly women and children in that load, disgusting!

The priests will die like the goblins and trolls when we conquer Kolixtlan. I will execute anyone caught wielding the red. This madness has to stop. If it means razing Kolixtlan, Adar, and the jungle of every living person, I will do it to rid the world of the Nameless One's taint.

Aleron woke from the dream with a start, eyes wide open and staring at the stars shining brightly through the forest canopy. The reassuring scent of the fire fought to replace the stink of death still in his nostrils.

That can't be right, he thought. *The first Aleron wanted to exterminate the Kolixtlani, Adari, and even the jungle men?*

Those were surely the memories of the old king, coming through the sword. They often did that when he slept with the weapon, coming through in his dreams. How could he have meant those things? Those were as evil of thoughts as any Aleron had encountered.

Maybe that is why he had to die. The desperation he felt after four years of constant warfare, coupled with the anger and pain from witnessing the atrocities committed by the Adversary, must have driven him to such unsavory ideas. The king's thoughts, in his last months, had taken such a dark turn that defeat of the Nameless One's forces may not have yielded a better world, if he had lived through it.

In many of his visions from his ancestor's later life, Aleron felt an underlying current of tyrannical thought. Aleron suspected that exterminating even the creatures of the Adversary would be an affront to the Allfather. Had he not forbidden the aelir to do so when they first discovered the transgression? The creation story of the elves said as much, and the aelir taught them that story.

Aleron roused himself, careful not to disturb Eilowyn, as he slid from under the blankets. He pulled his boots on and folded the extra blanket over his bride to keep her warm in his absence. After slipping into his gambeson and mail hauberk, he belted on his swords and dagger. It was nearly time for his shift, so he might as well relieve Barathol early.

He took a second glance at Andhanimwhid, where it lay next to Eilowyn, and decided to take it with him. He drew it, setting the scabbard against the bags and brought it to the fire, where Barathol crouched, adding a few sticks to maintain the coals until morning.

Grandfather forged this blade over four thousand years ago. The watered steel blade looked odd, reflecting the orange light of the fire. It usually glowed blue when he held it, and he never appreciated the fine pattern formed by the thousands of layers in the blade.

"Do you want to turn in a little early?" he asked his friend.

"I won't argue, if that's what you're asking," Barathol replied. "You gonna take to actually using that thing, instead of just carrying it around?"

"I think I need to get used to it, much as I prefer two swords."

"We'll have to revise our tactics, with two great weapons and one sword and shield fighter."

"I wouldn't worry about that, Barry; I'll still carry the cutlasses when we move. This is for after we get home. We won't be fighting together as a team, once I take the crown, not like before."

"It'll be hard to see those days go, but there's no way around it, I guess. Well, I'm going to take advantage of this extra sleep. See you in the morning."

Aleron watched him go to his bed and then began his walk of the camp perimeter, with the greatsword resting on his shoulder. Arriving back at the fire, he tossed a couple more pieces on and looked at the sword again. Setting it point first on the ground, the pommel was even with his collar. Atop the four-foot blade, long steel quillons curved downward, backed by a foot-long hilt, with a heavy teardrop pommel, all wrapped in brown leather.

Aleron untied the leather wrap and unwound the strips to reveal the hilt, bound in twisted electrum wire and the pommel of solid electrum, set with sapphires and blue quartz. The pommel used to glow incandescent when he grasped the hilt, but now, the stones just reflected the firelight. He tossed the leather strips into the fire, watching them flare brightly, in odd colors from the salts in the leather.

The time for hiding is over.

Chapter 13

Carpathday, Day 28, Storm Moon, 8765 Sudean Calendar

The Tonji River flowed wide and swift out of the canyon it cut from the high plateau and onto the bottomlands surrounding Sunj. The air grew steadily warmer as Aleron and his three companions made their way down the trail, turning from the northeast canyon wall to follow the cliffs bounding the northern edge of the Capar Plateau.

The elevation afforded them a good view of Sunj, nestled in the fork where the Harede River joined the Tonji from the south. Farther to the north, the mid-morning sun shone on the southern edge of the vast grassland that covered north Sunjib and all of Waban, a sea of bright green, in contrast to the greenish brown of the mostly leafless forests to the south.

It should have been too far to see, even with their elevation, but much of Sunjib consists of a deep basin, surrounded by high ground on all sides. Some natural philosophers believe it once was a massive lake, drained by the Kanjes and Tonji Rivers, and that eventually, canyons cut deeply enough to drain the lake completely.

The Kanjes forms a deep gorge, all along the border with Mittea, crossed in only four places, by massive stone bridges of dwarvish make. Much of the settled portion of Sunjib lies only a few hundred feet above sea level, while the surrounding hills and plateaus average about a thousand feet above the sea.

They left the towering forests of the plateau and around them, tough evergreens and tufted grasses, new growth peeking through the old, clung to the cracks in the rock, while over a thousand feet below, the trees at the base of the plateau showed deep green, with tinges of red, likely oaks, but too distant to tell.

A short distance from the boulder-strewn base, a checkerboard pattern of fields, pastures, and coppiced woodlots stretched for hundreds of leagues around the city. The well-manured pastures, dotted black and white with sheep and cattle, gleamed like emeralds in the morning sun alongside fields showing the dark brown of freshly turned soil.

Small brown thrushes and black-headed gray finches flitted among the branches of the stunted trees, searching for insects or seed left over from winter.

It took them six weeks to reach this point, and it appeared, with luck, that they might reach the city by sundown. Tomorrow, they could locate the embassy and arrange for passage back to Arundell. Tonight, all any of them wanted was a bath and some fresh clothes.

Aleron wondered if they would find any clothing to fit them in the Westlands. Geldun might be of a height to find something, but Barathol and he were taller, by far, than any westman. None of them, aside from Barathol, was near the breadth of a westman, so if Geldun found anything of the proper length, it would likely fit like a tent. Eilowyn would be easier if they located dresses, not yet hemmed to length.

He put those concerns to the back of his mind and concentrated on the trail ahead. Once, this path was the main route between Capar and Sunj, but that was thousands of years ago. Much of its former width was no longer, due to rockslides, often only wide enough to pass safely single file, and in many places, obscured altogether. They had reached one such place, having to pick their way carefully over boulders, lest they fall hundreds of feet, to the next place the trail crossed the cliff face. Had they traveled another two days west, they would have found an established road coming from the mines of the Iron Hills.

After the tumbled landscape at the base of the plateau, they found wide level roads, passing through an area of scattered farm complexes and large gristmills, lining the river on both sides. Sunj is located to take perfect advantage of the fast-moving currents of the Tonji and Harede Rivers, as they rush out of the highlands. A profusion of gristmills lines the Tonji, for the plentiful grain of the region, while the Harede also supports a number of hammer mills, to process the iron transported from the blast furnaces of the Iron Hills. Sunjib and its western neighbor, Mittea, are major producers of steel and other metals for the Westlands.

They were walking north, along a well-maintained road, surrounded by fields, with the occasional field worker stopping to stare at the outlanders. A cloud of dust ahead warned of the patrol of Sunjibi cavalry that rode up and stopped them, suspicious of the ragged group of armed foreigners approaching the city from such an improbable direction.

The officer especially, a lieutenant by the blue crest on his helm and gold scrollwork on his shoulder pauldrons, eyed the jeweled hilt of Andhanimwhid above Aleron's right shoulder with a look of recognition in his eyes.

"Who leads this band and what business have you in the kingdom of Sunjib?" he asked, choosing to speak in Sudean and not offering to identify himself first. Four archers fanned out to the sides to cover them.

"We have journeyed long, after escaping captivity in Kolixtlan," Aleron answered truthfully. "I am Aleron, and I lead this group. We wish to go to the Sudean consulate in the city, so that we may arrange passage back to our own country."

"You seem particularly well armed for escapees."

"We were aided in our escape by some not loyal to the rulers of Kolixtlan, who managed to return to us our arms and armor."

"Traitors are everywhere, I suppose. Smugglers?" When Aleron nodded in affirmation, he continued. "We must search your bags to assure you are not carrying anything for the smuggler who aided you. If you would please disarm and set your baggage down, we can get on with the process."

Aleron conferred briefly with the others before drawing the greatsword and standing it point-first in the ground. He wouldn't have done that to a normal sword, but Andhanimwhid was virtually indestructible. Barathol leaned his glaive to lock against the quillons, and Geldun wedged the hilt of his long sword between the two to form a lopsided tripod. Aleron unsheathed his cutlasses, leaned them against the stacked weapons while Eilowyn leaned her bow with them, unbuckling the quiver and placing it alongside.

They set their packs down in a row, and as they backed away, the Sunjibi said, "knives and daggers too."

They drew their smaller blades and set them beside the stacked weapons, Geldun taking one from each boot as well as the one from his belt, to the bemusement of the westmen.

The officer signaled behind him, and two of the lancers dismounted, leaving their long spears socketed in the tube hanging in front of the stirrup from the saddle. Each wore a long straight sword, on a baldric and belt, looking heavy enough for a bastard sword, but hilted for a single hand. The tips of the scabbards nearly trailed on the ground as the pair walked up to the packs.

They rummaged through each bag thoroughly, but politely, not setting any items in the dirt of the roadway, instead, stacking them on a pack not being searched. They concluded their inspection, each stating something to the officer, in Sunjibi.

Aleron understood little of the language, but he did recognize the word for "clean."

The leader replied, and the westmen returned to their saddles. "My soldiers have verified you carry no contraband into Sunjib. Would you gentlefolk care for an escort to the consulate?"

"That will not be necessary, Sir," Aleron replied. "I'm sure you have more important business, and I do not wish to take up more of your time."

"As you wish, gentlefolk, good day to you and safe journeying. I advise that you reach the consulate without delay. I believe they may be expecting you," he said, somewhat cryptically.

At his signal, the troops split and rode around the travelers, off in the direction from which the four companions came. Likely, they would ask questions of those out along the route to ascertain what direction Aleron and his companions came from. Fortunately, they had no lie to become caught in, and farmers working in the fields would answer that they came directly from the south.

With the sun still high in the western sky, they found a massive stone bridge crossing the Tonji, bringing them onto the same side as the city. It would still take the rest of the afternoon to reach the south gate.

The sound of steel-shod hooves clattered on the stone of the bridge, causing the travelers to glance behind them after crossing. The same patrol that searched them earlier was returning to the city.

"Good day, gentlefolk," the lieutenant greeted them, "I will announce your approach to the gatekeepers, so you may avoid another search. We are unused to foreigners entering the south gate." The Sunjibi patrol passed them by, raising a cloud of dust as they continued to the city.

With the sun low in the western sky, they entered the south foregate district, one of three, a chaotic arrangement of dwellings, shops, and taverns, catering to residents and businesses unable to afford or fit inside the walls of the city.

Narrow lanes, some looking like a cart would scrape both sides in passing, met the road at odd angles. The buildings here were of wood, for the most part, some of the better specimens three stories tall, and some of the worst single-story, ramshackle affairs, with little division between the extremes. Often, the shanties seemed to have sprung up in the spaces between the nicer buildings.

The foregates had their own docks, independent of the city docks, and it was rumored that more than twice the commerce ran through the three sprawling boroughs than through the city proper. This was the place with the best prices for everything, but finding an inn where a foreigner wouldn't be clubbed, or drugged, and robbed might be a problem.

"We should go into the city first, since the gate guards are expecting us and find an inn first," Aleron suggested, "but we should come back here tomorrow to buy clothes and supplies."

"Maybe we could stop for a drink or two," Barathol offered. "I haven't had good ale in six weeks, not since Bruji's place, and I'm not even sure that was real."

"Any ale at all," Geldun corrected him, "but maybe, we should wait 'till we get to a good inn."

Near-naked, dirty children ran about, yelling and squealing, dodging around carts, horses, and the legs of those on foot. They looked to be playing, but there was likely just as much thieving going on. Most of those going about their business did so in rough woolens, but a scattering of fine coats and dresses of wool and silk dotted the crowd.

"I'd prefer not to get stabbed today. It hurt enough last time, so I think I'll pass."

"I think not, Barry," Eilowyn added. "I may not look like a lady, at the moment, but I am one, and these are no places for one," she finished, gesturing at the couple of taverns close at hand, both of which already had drunken patrons stumbling out, with the sun at least a full bell from setting.

Three armed Sudeans, in chain mail, escorting a young woman in boy's clothes, drew plenty of eyes as they proceeded toward the gate. The faces of the westmen, with their beetle brows, made every look seem cross, though most were likely only curious. A westman, gazing at you intently, can cause you to reassess yourself to find what fault you are under scrutiny for.

Most adult males wore full beards, cut square at the bottom and with the upper lip shaved, in the Sunjibi fashion. Many had their beards bound with crossed lacing as well.

The females had no discernible chins, as well as brows and noses nearly as prominent as the males. Stocky of build, like the males, none would be considered beautiful in the lands of men.

They continued on, soon reaching the south gate. The two guards on duty looked them up and down for a moment and then waved them through. The lieutenant appeared to be good for his word. They were equipped in similar manner to the cavalrymen they encountered earlier, though with more extensive plate and heavily decorated.

"Do either of you speak Sudean?" Aleron asked. The languages of the Westlands were some of the few in which he had little to no proficiency.

"Aye," the slightly shorter of the two answered, with a thick accent, "What might you gentlefolk be in need for?"

"Could you please direct us to a reputable inn?"

"Certainly, Sir," the guard answered. "You will not be able to read the sign, but the Ox and Boar be only two streets down, on the ...right," he said, getting it wrong and gesturing with his left hand. "It be the best on this side of the city. The Golden Stork be even better, but it be up by the northeast gate, a long way on foot."

"Thank you very much, Sir. I'm sure that the Ox and Boar will do just fine, for our purposes."

They entered the city, and after two blocks, they saw a sign to their left, depicting an ox and a boar, facing each other, with indiscernible Sunjibi script below.

"This looks to be the place," Geldun said. "Shall we get settled in? I'm starving."

"Let's go then," Eilowyn agreed. "I'm starving too."

She led the way into a common room with a respectable crowd already gathered, the sun only just setting. The clientele appeared to be middle-class merchants, for the most part, with a smattering of finer clothing indicating a few higher-class, or at least wealthier patrons.

Several of the patrons appeared to be Talik and Chebek merchants, curiously far from home. Taliks, Chebeks, and Adari looked little different physically, but could usually be differentiated by style of dress. The Taliks wore short, tight-waisted coats over baggy trousers and tall riding boots, while the Chebek tended towards voluminous cloaks over snug wool shirts, the trousers and boots similar to Talik dress. Chebeks of rank also wear a gold or silver torque, denoting their standing in society. Several of the men in the common room wore silver torques, indicating commoners of high standing in the Merchant's Guild.

The innkeeper bustled up to them, a wide white apron covering her expansive bosom and midriff.

"You do be Sudeans, I wager?" an easy enough guess, considering their complexions. "Will ye gentlefolk be needin' rooms, or just supper? Her red hair, gathered in a bun, showed streaks of white, and her face held a jovial expression, despite her westman features. Bright blue eyes twinkled below heavy lids.

"We are looking for both, please, Mistress," Eilowyn answered. "Would you have two rooms, next to each other, one for my husband and me and one with two beds, for our friends? Oh, and do you have bathtubs? We have been on the road, nigh on two months."

"We nay have tubs for the rooms, dear, but we do be havin' baths, free of charge. They be on the first floor and be most busy in the early morn. Ye should be findin' them most empty in the evenin'.

We do be havin' just the sort of rooms ye be lookin' for, two bedrooms off a sittin' room, on the first floor, to boot. It be meant for families, really, but works as well for married folk with singles. The price be two silver a night for that one, and for an extra four pennies, we can have a dressing robe and towel for each of ye."

"That sounds most reasonable, Mistress...?"

"Canja, dear," she replied. "Now will ye be payin' up front, or when ye go?"

"Up front is fine, for the first night, at least, right Aleron?" She glanced up at him, and he nodded, undoing his coin purse. He still had all the money her father sent to him.

"We are unsure how many nights we will be staying, though."

"That be quite all right, dear; ye can just settle up at the end." After Aleron handed her two silver and four copper, she continued, "Ye can bring your things to the room and be lockin' them up," handing them two padlock keys, "and we can be havin' the rest ready in half a bell. Would ye be likin' some supper now?"

The men voiced their agreement, and Eilowyn said, "Yes, that sounds wonderful. We'll put our things up and be right out, Mistress Canja."

Supper consisted of a well-seasoned smoked brisket, sides of parsnips and carrots, with a pitcher of dark ale to wash it down. They all ate ravenously, this being the first good meal since leaving Bruji, six weeks prior.

Barathol drew a few sidelong stares from the other patrons, with his massive, tattooed arms exposed by his sleeveless tunic. "You do be a strappin' one for a southerner," Canja remarked, patting his shoulder as she came to check on them. She was a dutiful hostess, making her rounds among the patrons.

"Is there anything you be lacking, gentlefolk?"

"I wouldn't mind some more water," Eilowyn offered. "The food is just wonderful, Mistress, thank you."

"Ye be very welcome. I'll be makin' sure the server be getting' ye that water, dear." She bustled off to take care of her request and those of other patrons.

This bath is simply exquisite, Eilowyn thought, as she reclined in the stone pool. A constant flow of hot water streamed through, the slight sulfur smell indicating a hot spring as the source.

Her clothing lay folded on the bench, behind her, along with a large fluffy cotton towel and a thick cotton robe. She didn't wish to wear the robe against her unwashed skin, so she came to the bath in her dirty clothes. She planned to wash her undergarments in the room and hang them to dry overnight.

Aleron will just have to deal with me having no bedclothes tonight, she thought, smiling, *but I'm in no rush to finish this bath.*

She settled further, just her face out of the water. The men would be doing the same, taking turns to watch the doors to the baths until they all could return to the rooms together, meaning she had time for a good soaking.

Chapter 14

Sildaenday, Day 29, Storm Moon, 8765 Sudean Calendar

Aleron woke to a faint scraping sound in the darkness. The first story windows, little more than arrow slits, let in faint light from the street, adding to that of the lantern on the table in the corner, dimmed for the night.

Immediately alert, he looked to the door and thought he saw a knife blade wiggling between two boards. Someone was trying to lift the bar securing the door.

He quietly slid from beneath the blankets, leaving Eilowyn curled up asleep, and padded to the foot of the bed, where his sword belt hung. Silently as possible, he slid first one, then the other, cutlass from their scabbards and crept to stand to the side of the doorjamb. Naked, his undergarments drying on a line, he stood pressed up to the wall, left sword at low guard, right sword high and ready to strike.

The bar lifted, and there was a brief pause, the knife blade remaining to hold up the bar. The door swung slowly open, and the first thing through the opening was a saber, glinting softly in the dim light, as a man slowly inched into the opening.

As soon as a hand appeared, Aleron chopped, and it came off at the wrist, sword clattering against the boards. He immediately stabbed with the left and was met with a gurgling sound, as his sword ripped through the man's throat.

Pushing through to the common area, he shook the dead man off his sword and confronted two more assailants, each armed with saber and dagger. The clash of steel on steel rang through the room.

Eilowyn screamed, "Aleron, what's happening?"

"Close the door and bar it!" he shouted back, as he held off the pair, guarding the door and trying to keep them both to his front. She tried to comply, but something blocked the door. Looking down, she winced at the sight of the severed hand, still gripping the saber hilt. She bent down, snatched it out of the way, and slammed the door closed, beating the bar down against the wedged knife.

The door to the other room slammed open, and the man to Aleron's right found himself skewered on Barathol's glaive. Geldun came right behind, slashing that one across the throat. Both entered the room, naked as Aleron was. He turned his full attention on the opponent to his left, who glanced once behind, to the outer door, just in time to see Barathol's blade, before it split his skull.

The three of them stood panting, naked as the day they were born, gripping their weapons. The outer door was closed and barred, the intruders not wishing to be surprised from the rear, and an open door would arouse suspicion if the innkeeper happened by.

"That was unexpected," Geldun remarked, wiping his blade on the dead man's pant leg.

Barathol trimmed the wick of the lantern, left burning low for the night, to afford more light, before he did the same for his blade. All three intruders wore the garb of Talik merchants.

"My guess is Adaris, posing as Taliks and looking for us."

"I wonder how they got to us so quickly," Barathol questioned. "It would have taken weeks to get here from Adar."

Aleron finished wiping the second of his blades and offered, "The priests. If Grandfather and I can communicate over distance, so can they.

They likely got word as soon as we escaped, and it was obvious where we were heading. We're probably just lucky they had no priest in the locality where we crossed the border."

"By the light of the Allfather, what a mess!" Eilowyn interjected after she opened the door and took in the scene, dressed in her robe and slippers.

"Get some clothes on, for Korelle's sake!" she added, looking suddenly at the ceiling.

Barathol and Geldun started at her sudden appearance and then darted back to their room. Aleron strolled past her, both swords in his right hand, giving her a peck on the cheek and a smack on the rump as he passed by to their room.

Loud banging came from the outer door, accompanied by the voice of Mistress Canja. "What be all the racket ye boys be makin', two bells before the dawn?" Eilowyn, forced to step over a body and avoid the pooling blood, opened the door for Canja. "Great bells of Capar, what be happenin' here? Where be your menfolk?"

"They are making themselves decent, Mistress. These ruffians broke into our rooms, and the men had to fight them naked," she answered.

"We'll be out in a moment, Mistress Canja," Aleron called from the bedroom. "I'm almost dressed now."

His undergarments were still damp from washing, but at least they were clean. He had rinsed the blood off his feet and wherever else he found it before slipping them on. Dressing quickly, he buckled his sword belt but left the greatsword in the tall wardrobe.

"Here I am," he announced, stepping into the common area, to see Canja and a young westman, who looked to be her son, hefting a large cudgel, filling the doorway.

"You can get dressed now, Ellie. I'll take care of this."

"If you'll please excuse me, Mistress, I will be back in a moment."

"Yes, of course, dear, do be getting' some clothes on, while I be speakin' to your menfolk."

The other men emerged from their room, tightening their belts and smoothing their tunics.

"Now do ye be mindin' tellin' me what it is be goin' on here? Those do be some merchants we be takin' in, shortly after we be takin' you in."

"We're pretty sure they weren't merchants, Mistress, nor were they Taliks," Aleron explained. "We think they were Adari assassins, or at least kidnappers, likely hired by Kolixtlan."

"Why do ye be havin' Adar and Kolixtlan after ye?"

"You should probably send for the city guard, if you haven't already, and I'm sorry to bring this trouble upon your establishment, Mistress."

She whispered something to the young westman, and he hurried off.

Aleron continued, "We rescued Lady Eilowyn from the Kolixtlanis and caused a bit of damage on the way out. We escaped across Capar, making our way here. I hoped to have a chance to procure some acceptable attire for the lady before presenting ourselves to the consulate, but I fear we must go there, straightaway. I didn't expect to find our enemies already waiting for us in Sunj."

"This will have to do, I suppose," Eilowyn announced, stepping out in a slightly rumpled gown of sea green silk, in a Kolixtlani cut, with elaborate gold embroidery about the collar and down the sleeves.

"I packed it as carefully as I could, but I couldn't fit the full shift that goes underneath, better than boy clothes though."

"Ye do be the ones them rumors been about. I thought ye might be, but I do be tryin' to stay out of my patron's business, Your Grace. But if I may, do ye two be married, really?"

"Yes, we are married, Mistress Canja," Eilowyn reassured her. "Why do you ask?"

"Well, My Lady," she abandoned familiarity at the revelation of Eilowyn's standing, "the rumors be sayin' that the new king be gone to Kolixtlan to free his betrothed, not his wife."

"We found a priest on the way, Mistress. We've been married six weeks now."

"Wherever did ye be findin' a priest up in Capar? There be no temples there."

Before Aleron could say anything to stop her, Eilowyn replied, "His name was Bruji, and he married us on the site of an old temple, at the source of the Tonji River."

Mistress Canja's eyes widened at the name, and she made a sign to the Allfather, meant to ward off evil.

"Is that name significant, Mistress?" Aleron asked gently, remembering well the strange occurrences at the old temple.

"Folks be talkin' of meeting Old Bruji, up on in Capar; they be sayin' it for longer than any can be rememberin', hundreds of years. Some be sayin' he was High Priest of the Grand Temple before the Great War. You be married by a priest, is true, but he be the ghost of a priest."

"Well, the rings he gave us seem real enough," Aleron stated, holding up the golden ring that hadn't left his finger for six weeks. Eilowyn held up her own ring, looked at the wheeling raven pattern, and then moved closer to her husband, linking her arm in his.

"And the food was real enough, too," Barathol added. "We had leftover ham for our trip."

"The watch be here, Your Grace," Canja announced, as her son came to the door, with two lightly armored westmen, wearing the green surcoats of the city watch, in tow.

Next came the detailed explanation of the early morning events, with Mistress Canja acting as translator, since neither watchman spoke any appreciable amount of Sudean.

The outer door showed signs of forced entry, and that, along with the knife still jammed in the bedroom door and the dead men obviously armed, made their story more than believable.

Eventually, satisfied with their explanations, the watchman in charge directed Canja to tell them, "For the safety of ye folk, they wish you to be accompanyin' them to their post, with your belongings, then they be sendin' to ye consulate."

"Mistress Canja, will you accept some compensation for the trouble we have brought upon you and your establishment?" Aleron asked, as he took her hand and pressed two gold pieces into her palm.

"That be enough to rent these rooms for a week, Your Grace. It be too much."

"Call me Aleron. We're friends now, and I don't believe you will be able to rent these for a few days, not without some serious cleaning, so please accept this along with our gratitude."

"Well, I suppose it be rude to refuse the goodwill of a king," she reluctantly admitted, pocketing the coins.

"I be thinkin' ye be like the kings of old, a fightin' man of honor first. May the light of the Allfather shine upon ye and your lady always, King Aleron and ye good men as well."

"My thanks to you, Mistress Canja, and may the light of the Allfather be with you and yours as well.

After a brief discussion, the companions retreated into their bedrooms to pack the remainder of their gear. Wearing their armor was easier than carrying it, so the men donned their padded gambesons and mail hauberks, with only their light helms in their packs. Aleron had Andhanimwhid strapped to his back, as usual, the jeweled hilt standing over his right shoulder, as they followed the watchmen down the street, in the growing light of dawn.

The waiting area of the south command post for the city watch was austere, with only a couple benches along the wall and a small table with two benches, mainly for watchmen to take their meals, two of which were doing just that. A small counter for the duty sergeant sat just inside the entrance, with a latched gate to restrict entry.

Aleron and his companions sat upon the benches, their belts and weapons hanging from and leaning against racks caged off behind the sergeant's station.

The Captain of the Watch had his office in the back of the building. He informed them upon their arrival that word was sent to the consulate on their behalf. All there was to do now was wait.

After nearly three bells of their arrival, the outer door opened, and one of the guards stationed outside shouted something into the building. The door to the captain's office swung open suddenly, and he stepped into the room as a tall man with iron gray hair and beard entered, with two marines in full dress uniform right behind.

The man wore a coat of fine blue wool, with the four-pointed star of Sudea embroidered on the left breast and a gold chain of office hanging across the front.

The captain exclaimed, "My Lord Consul, what a pleasure it is that you came in person! You honor us with your presence."

"Uncle Damian!" Eilowyn shouted, startling everyone, as she jumped up and ran to the door. "I can't believe it's you!"

The sergeant quickly unlatched the gate, allowing Damian and his escort entry.

"Lady Eilowyn, it is my eyes that are unbelieving!" the consul exclaimed, in turn. "We feared you were lost."

She reached him and wrapped her arms around him, staring up at his face and his clear blue eyes.

"I thought you were still in Chu," she continued.

"I arrived here just two months ago, my dear," he explained, smoothing her hair as he returned her hug.

Aleron recognized the name as that of her mother's eldest brother, Lord of House Astor.

"Now, what of your companions? Sergeant Jorik?"

"They be the lads, My Lord; I couldn't forget that bunch from Swaincott."

They recognized him as one of their class from training. Jorik was a quick pupil, and everyone knew he would rise quickly. Consulate Guard was a sought-after position, sure to propel one's career.

"Hey Jorik," Geldun greeted their old friend. "Looks like you're moving up in the world."

Jorik just smiled, with a slight nod.

"Uncle," she began, waving them forward, "This is my husband, Aleron, and his companions, Geldun and Barathol."

Damian released his niece and bent to one knee, bowing his head as Aleron approached. The two Marines followed suit. "Your Grace, it is my honor to serve...Husband?" He looked back up at Eilowyn suddenly.

She giggled, placed her hand on Aleron's shoulder, and said, "Yes, Uncle Damian, we found a priest along the way. We didn't know we would survive our journey, and I wanted to be married to the one I love if we did not."

"Rise, Lord Damian, please," Aleron commanded, not comfortable yet with displays of subservience.

"I would not have you bow to me before I wear the crown." He stretched out his hand to the lord, and Damian took it, rising to his feet.

"I hear that you were attacked, just this morning?" he inquired, already getting down to business.

"Yes, Uncle, Aleron heard them breaking into our rooms. He and his companions dispatched three assassins."

"Assassins, or kidnappers, were not sure which," Aleron elaborated. "Unfortunately, they were in no condition to question. They dressed as Talik merchants, but we suspect they were really Adari."

"Yes, Adari spies are always making their way into the Westlands, posing as Talik or Chebek. We've uncovered a fair amount lately, much more than in the past.

If you please, Your Grace, I have a carriage outside and an armed escort to bring you all safely to the consulate," and to the Captain of the Watch, "The Kingdom of Sudea thanks you, Sir, for your assistance in recovering our Liege and his queen. The goodwill of Sunjib will not be soon forgotten."

"The honor was all ours, My Lord. The ties between our realms stretch back before the Great War; may they always hold strong."

The men went to retrieve their weapons, the sergeant unlocking the cage for them.

As Aleron returned, with Andhanimwhid on his back, Lord Damian said, "My entire life, I have seen only that hilt, rising above the throne. May I see Andhanimwhid unsheathed, Your Grace?"

Aleron grasped the hilt and felt a familiar tingle as his skin contacted the sword. To his wonderment, as he twirled the sword point down in front of him, the sapphires glowed with a faint blue light, for the first time in nearly two months.

He cast out, trying to sense for power, but found nothing else. He felt a pang of disappointment, but at least it was a start; he felt hope return, that his abilities might heal with time.

"I dreamed that I would see this in my lifetime, but I always pushed that hope down, thinking it mere fancy," Damian confessed. "Now I see renewed hope for the future, by the Light."

"There will be darkness before the light, I fear that is why I was brought here, in these times," Aleron replied, solemnly. "Let us hope the light reigns in victory."

"He always talks crazy when he holds that sword," Barathol commented drily to Jorik and his companion. "Becomes a regular orator."

Aleron looked ever so slightly annoyed at his friend's comment, as he resheathed the sword, but smiled as his hand came away.

I do change whenever I grab it, he admitted to himself.

Chapter 15

Sildaenday, Day 29, Storm Moon, 8765 Sudean Calendar

"It would be unwise for you to attempt finding passage through Waban," Damian asserted, as they discussed their next step over breakfast.

"Kolixtlan and Adar have the Wabani inlet effectively blockaded, and control of the lower Tonji river changes hands on a near-daily basis. The situation would force you to travel overland, much of the way to Wadj and sailing out of Wakol Bay is out of the question. Your party would need to travel far to the north coast, to sail out safely. With that in mind, it is better for you to journey to Mich and sail out from there. It is roughly the same distance overland, with twelve-hundred leagues less coastline to circumnavigate."

"That's certainly a blow to our plans of making the majority of the journey by water," Aleron replied.

"I know it to be around nine-thousand leagues from here to Arundell, by river and sea. With good winds, we could make that in four months. With over six-hundred-sixty leagues overland to Mich and five-thousand leagues, by sea, that would take us at least six months."

Geldun made a low whistle at the revelation, but otherwise did not interrupt.

"Unfortunately, it cannot be helped. Nothing is sailing out of Wadj these days, and I would not send you into the jaws of the enemy so soon after recovering you. Unfortunately, as well, we have no faster way to send word of your well-being back to the capital than the route you are taking."

"Is there an elvish emissary in Sunj?" Aleron asked.

"Yes, there is, as a matter of fact," Damian answered. "Why do you ask?"

"Please ask the elvish representatives to send word to their counterparts in Arundell, or directly to Lord Hadaras, if they can. They have much faster methods than ground messenger," Aleron explained.

"Ah, yes, I had heard that elves may be able to talk over distance, using sorcery. I hadn't thought of that before. I will do so straightaway, Your Grace."

Damian hesitated for a moment before continuing. "Rumor has it that you are something of a sorcerer yourself, Your Grace."

"Was something of a sorcerer," Aleron corrected him. "I was injured in some manner when we escaped the palace in Kolixtla. I've been unable to wield magic since," he completed, lips turning to a sullen frown. Eilowyn patted his arm before taking his hand in hers, and his smile returned when he glanced at her.

"He crushed their garrison, breached the outer walls, and nearly toppled the northwest tower, is what he did, My Lord," Barathol expounded. "Probably lucky he didn't incinerate himself in the process.

I've never seen so much damage done in so short a time, and I've seen my share of fighting. He was knocked out cold after the blast."

"Thank you, Barry, but that's enough about my stupidity. I overextended myself and paid the price for it." He explained further, "I was warned that you could burn yourself out by drawing too much power at once, even kill yourself, but I let my anger overtake my judgment. I don't know if I'll ever heal from this, but at least it taught me a lesson."

"Your Grace," Damian said, "That is a lesson anyone who holds any sort of power must learn. At least you learned now, and not at the cost of your followers' lives. That is a difficult debt to ever pay off, when your folly costs the lives of those who believe in you."

He was referring to an incident from early in his military career, with many lives lost. Aleron was familiar with the story and did not ask the consul to elaborate, discreetly wiggling his head in the negative to answer a curious look from Barathol.

Attempting to turn the conversation to a lighter note, Geldun offered, "My Lord, you have to hear about your niece killing a half-troll, with nothing but her knife." Damian's eyebrows raised, and he looked across the table at Eilowyn, now blushing furiously and glaring at Geldun. Barathol's eyes lit up, and Aleron couldn't repress a grin at her discomfiture.

"It wasn't that big a deal," she protested. "The blasted thing knocked me out for a full day, for his trouble."

"Oh, my little Ellie!" Damian exclaimed. "I will definitely need to hear that story, in its unabridged entirety, my dear girl."

Aleron had learned, in short order, that Eilowyn was among Lord Damian's favorite nieces and nephews, and he was her favorite uncle, as well. This would be an entertaining discussion.

"But first, why don't we start closer to the beginning, with how you escaped Kolixtlan and made your way here. Then you can place Ellie's daring exploits in their proper frame of reference. Feadra, bring us another pot of hot tea and more biscuits, please."

The pretty black-haired serving girl waiting on them stepped from her place against the wall, answering, "Yes, Milord, right away," before hurrying off to the kitchens.

Geldun tracked the willowy girl across the room, only to find Eilowyn glaring across the table at him when his eyes returned. He gave her a surprised look, implying his total innocence, to which she merely snorted and turned her attention back to her uncle.

"Way to be obvious, Gel," Barathol muttered into his ear."

"My Lady," Geldun intoned, "Though pleasant to look upon, the lady's beauty holds not a candle to the radiance of your own."

You're not fooling anyone, Gel," Aleron stated. Damian chuckled at the exchange, while Eilowyn simply glared at Geldun again.

"Please go ahead and begin," Damian requested. I will try to not interrupt."

Eilowyn briefly recounted her capture and journey to Kolixtla, explaining their plans to marry her to Ehacatl, to form a tie to House Arundell.

Aleron grew stony at her description of the massacre of her entourage. He had friends among them. He, in turn, related their flight from Cape Town and the events surrounding their visit to Arundell.

Damian interrupted once, unable to contain his disbelieving wonderment, at the part of transforming their party into ravens and actually flying. Otherwise, he listened intently, sometimes raising his eyebrows at some of the more dubious events, such as using their abilities, as dogs, to track two foreigners in Kolixtla, by their smell differing from the local populace.

The others interjected, periodically, as he recounted their escape from the palace, especially the portion after he lost consciousness.

He interrupted again, quite interested in the prospect of dissidents in western Kolixtlan.

A look of concern crossed the Consul's face when they described, in great detail, the attack of the half-troll and the grave injury his niece sustained. His look of interest, mixed with a tinge of disbelief, heightened when they told him of their healing at the hand of Iudhael and the disappearance of Bruji's dwelling.

Finishing off with the relatively uneventful journey to Sunjib, but capped by the attack that morning, they awaited his full response.

Both he and Eilowyn said nothing of the strange prophetic dreams they both experienced. Those not speaking busied themselves with nibbling on the biscuits Feadra brought them and sipping tea from the fine porcelain cups. Aleron finally grabbed a biscuit for himself and found his tea had grown tepid.

"Well, that was truly a remarkable tale you craft," Damian remarked. "I would normally have difficulty believing a fair bit of it if you hadn't journeyed from Arundell to Kolixtla at impossible speed. I knew from recent messages, the date you left the capital, and there is no possible way you could be here yet, even had you bypassed Kolixtla.

News of the destruction there only just reached Sunj days ago, that carried by men on horseback, traveling established roads. You must have traveled two-hundred miles a day to cover that distance in the time that you did, so I have no choice but to believe your fanciful tale.

How is it that I have never heard of elves or halfbloods with this ability?"

My grandfather told me that my abilities are unprecedented," Aleron explained.

"Elves can only use blue magic, but halfbloods can choose blue or red magic. They always assumed only those turned to darkness chose red, but the Thallasians disproved that when their wizard's guild came to light, a few years ago. It seems to be difficult for a halfblood to transition between red and blue, so they usually choose to master only one color."

Damian nodded, somewhat familiar with the information Aleron gave him so far.

"There are two other colors of magic, green and yellow, available only to the aelient. Iudhael used yellow magic to heal us at the site of his old temple, and others use green magic to make things grow.

I was able to wield them, as well. That's what I used to age the guards and the high priest, so we could overpower them and escape to find Ellie. I could easily switch between the four primary colors and combine them to make new colors.

Grandfather thinks only the aelir had that ability; he says he never witnessed the aelient use but one color at a time, though they can use any color they choose.

I found that if I combined all the colors, it makes white magic. With white magic, I could change one thing into something else, and that's what I used to change us into ravens or dogs.

Grandfather says he doesn't remember even the aelir doing that, but he thinks they may have been capable and hid it well, or that it was forbidden by the Allfather for them to use it."

"Your grandfather being Goromir, he would have personal recollection of when the aelir walked among us," Damian said.

"These are odd days indeed, when darkness gains in power, and figures from legend openly walk the face of Aertu. Even the aelient are considered myth by most, but you have talked with one, or maybe two, in the last months."

"Maybe three," Aleron confessed, "If you count Jessamine, who helped raise me. She's really a nymph as it turns out, but we don't really know what Bruji was."

"Jessie's a nymph," Geldun blurted out. I don't believe it, but it's hard to believe old Hadaras is really Goromir and nine thousand at that."

"Do you remember how she seemed to have eyes in the back of her head, and she could hear and smell better than a treeing hound?" Aleron asked him.

"It's because she does, and she can. I didn't find out she's not my cousin until a couple years ago."

"I heard that Hadaras hid your identity from you," Damian said. "When did you find out who you are?"

"A little over five years ago, on the day I met Ellie." He glanced at her fondly, and she placed her hand in his on the table.

"She took me to look at the sword, and I touched it. Fortunately, nobody saw but her, her father, her bodyguards, and my grandfather. Ellie's father managed to cover it up, so we could leave quietly."

"Gealton always was a shrewd one. It was probably best for you to remain hidden a bit longer, while you were still young. So you just went and joined the Marines a couple of years later?"

"It's what the three of us always wanted to do," he explained, "and I thought I'd enjoy as much anonymity as I could, until I absolutely had to claim the throne."

"I see that Hadaras trained you well. It's unusual for a sixteen-year-old boy NOT to run off at the mouth, but you held your secret for five years, and I believe you would have for longer, had not Ellie been abducted. Am I right?"

"I was prepared to, but my gut told me the time was right."

"I believe your gut told you true," Damian agreed,

"There is much darkness afoot in recent days, goblins, and trolls on the move, along with these Arkans, from Zorek only knows where, children of the Nameless One himself, so I've heard.

The people need a symbol to forge their resolve anew, on the eve of what looks to be another Great War. Now, the only trick is to get you back to those same people, Your Grace."

"That would be best, Uncle," Eilowyn agreed.

"Good, it will likely take a few days to gather all that is needed to escort you to Mich, and I'm certain the king has heard and will want to meet with you today, so we need to get you all some decent clothes.

Might I assume you would appreciate a couple nights of comfort before you get back on the road?"

They all voiced their agreement, and Damian led them off to find their rooms in the wing for visiting dignitaries.

Chapter 16

Sildaenday, Day 29, Storm Moon, 8765 Sudean Calendar

"Good news, finally," Hadaras announced as he stepped into Gealton's office. "Eilowyn and Aleron are safe in Sunj."

The Steward jumped up from behind his desk, scattering papers as he pushed off. "Really, when did you find out?"

"Just now, the elvish consul contacted me on behalf of Consul Damian, your brother-in-law.

Apparently, Aleron injured himself in some way that precludes him from communicating with me, as the elves do. Otherwise, the whole party is healthy and safe.

They came into the city last night, taking rooms at an inn, but were attacked in the night by Adaris, posing as Talik merchants."

"They were attacked, but not harmed?" Gealton asked, concern for his daughter replacing the look of joy his face held moments before."

"Yes, around the third bell of this morning," Hadaras replied.

"According to the report, the boys killed three armed assailants who broke into the room.

They were dressed as Taliks, but Damian claims that Adari spies have been infiltrating Sunjib in increasing numbers, posing as Talik or Chebek merchants.

The boys are quite capable, so they escaped harm. He also verified that Aleron killed King Achcauhtli during their escape from Kolixtla, and smugglers aided them in leaving the city.

Oh, there is one more item in the report that might interest you."

"What would that be?"

"Eilowyn and Aleron are now married." He paused to allow the information to sink in for a few moments.

The Steward's expression contorted from consternation to happiness and back. "How?" was all he said in reply, steadying himself with a palm on his desk.

"They found a westman priest, living among the ruins of an old temple, in Capar, apparently."

"Well, that's all fine and good, but there will be another ceremony, here in the palace, a real one that befits their station. The people of Sudea deserve nothing less."

"I don't think anyone will argue that point."

"How long before they arrive back in Arundell?"

"The Consul estimates six to seven months, going by way of Mittea, to the seaport. The way through Waban would be faster, but there is too much trouble along the border of Kolixtlan, along with the blockade of the inlet, for them to take that route."

"Then let's hope my daughter doesn't arrive to her wedding, six months pregnant."

Hadaras chuckled at the response, "We can always hope," he replied.

"We need your boy to return as quickly as possible. The way things are heating up, all over the continent, I have little doubt that open war is close upon us."

"I agree; the massing of goblins in the wilderness along the Blue Mountains is most troubling," Hadaras stated.

"This is the first time, in thousands of years, that they have grouped under a single leader and openly held territory within Sudea, Ebareiza, and the Southern Kingdom.

This new king of theirs, Xarch, must be a formidable foe to unite the tribes, as he has done. If I know anything about goblins, he would have needed to kill most of his rivals to achieve that.

My contacts in the colonies tell me that wild men and hobgoblins press the border like no time in living memory, and our living memories go back far."

Gealton answered with, "Yes, and the latest reports from the Westlands speak of increasing and deeper raids into the Iron Hills and beyond. Mittea and Sunjib have skirmished with hobgoblins and half-trolls, all the way to the north foothills, nearly into the settled regions."

"The forces of darkness are moving again, my friend, as hasn't been seen in over four-thousand years."

***

Following their breakfast with the consul, he went off to the elvish consulate to send word to Arundell, while Aleron and his party went off in search of the resident seamstress.

Attendants collected their armor, weapons, and gear from them that morning, destined for the armory, for mending, sharpening, and polishing, all but Andhanimwhid, which Aleron still carried, across his back.

The power-forged weapon, now over four-thousand years old, required no sharpening or polish, though Aleron intended to make a personal visit to the armory to have the scabbard and harness looked after.

At the seamstress's shop, Geldun and Barathol had a relatively simple time of it, though Barathol required some alterations to his uniforms to account for his larger-than-average stature.

Most clothing that he could fit over his shoulders required taking in at the waist.

Geldun, being of average build for a marine, could fit in clothing straight off the rack.

The old Sunjibi woman had two younger assistants working at the sewing tables, but took all measurements herself, marking the fabric with a piece of chalk or pinning it into place, as she went.

The assistants operated curious machines, run by a foot treadle that sewed the seams for them, as they ran the cloth beneath a plunging needle.

"Ah, Your Highness, you be noticing my sewing machines. Dwarvish make, they be and blessed clever contraptions too."

Latka, the seamstress, was all business; though she spoke Sudean well, she lacked Canja's outgoing personality and said little, aside from directing them, in the way of small talk.

Though the staff remained thoroughly professional, the younger women looked with obvious interest when Barathol stepped from behind the screen, wearing nothing but short pants. Dressed, most assumed he had a bit of extra padding; shirtless, that illusion was destroyed, as he was nothing but hard muscle.

She outfitted each in new dress uniforms, of deep red, with gold piping on the trousers and gold scrollwork at the cuffs and collars, signifying the rank of captain, at Aleron's direction. "What's that all about?" Geldun asked, after Aleron specified the rank. "We're not captains."

"You don't think that the personal advisors to the king would be a couple of corporals, now do you? Congratulations, Captain Geldun of Swaincott and Captain Barathol of Swaincott."

Their dumfounded expressions made him smile. He and Eilowyn discussed this earlier, and she weighed in on the historical precedents surrounding commoners brought into close confidence with past kings.

"Eventually, we'll need to raise you to the nobility," she chimed in, "so you should probably start thinking of crests for your houses, something with cows, plows, and beer mugs, perhaps? I don't think anyone has used that yet."

Aleron nearly doubled over laughing at her jest, especially after Barathol replied, "Definitely beer mugs. I don't know about the cows and plows though."

Geldun just snorted derisively and went on with the fitting. They received one uniform, fitted properly for that day, and another set aside for alterations, to be picked up in two days. The seamstress also measured them for two new sets of combat uniforms, in subdued green and brown, for the upcoming journey. Somehow, she even found new dress boots for them, but needed to take down their sizes for traveling boots.

Latka measured Aleron for the same combat uniforms as the other men. He had no interest in standing out when they traveled across the Westlands.

When it came to his dress clothes, however, his choices were somewhat different from those of his friends. No marine officer's uniform for him, Eilowyn made sure Latka knew cuts and colors that would be expected of the King of Sudea.

After she finished with him, he wore midnight blue trousers, piped with stripes of royal purple, bordered in gold. Tall black dress boots rose to his knees, polished to a mirror shine, and causing the trousers to balloon out of the tops. Over a crisp white shirt, rode a coat identical to the one Damian wore, of a slightly lighter blue than the trousers, with the star of Sudea emblazoned on the left breast.

"This will have to do," Eilowyn conceded, "until we can have the proper embroidery applied. I'm not even sure what that might be yet, but this one signifies a high lord, so let's see what we can find to set it apart."

She and Latka decided on the same purple cloth used for the piping of the trousers, double thick and fashioned into a wide baldric and belt. Made to cross his right shoulder and bordered in gold ribbon, it fastened at his left hip.

"There now," she said, admiring their handiwork. "You look positively noble, for a change."

Aleron turned to the tall stand mirror and commented, "I look like a peacock."

"And you sound like a jackass. Don't be an ungrateful lout."

"My apologies, Mistress Latka, I'm just not used to seeing myself dressed up."

"Oh, I be getting' that all the time from ye fightin' men, the first time I be putting them in their best dress when they come here. Ye'll be getting' used to it soon enough."

"I like it just fine," Geldun stated. "I always pictured myself in something like this. Why don't you check out how it looks with your sword? I think that's what it's missing." He snatched Andhanimwhid from where it leaned against the coat rack and stepped up behind Aleron, holding the sword where it would normally ride, hilt over his right shoulder.

"That does look better," Aleron agreed. "Hold it there, but watch out that I don't cut you, pulling it out." The scabbard was open on its left side, two thirds of the way down, to free the four-foot blade when he drew it. A strong steel spring held the top of the scabbard snugly around the blade for travel. He reached behind and drew the blade, in one fluid motion, spinning it to rest point down before him.

Latka gasped and took a half step back, not for fear of the weapon, but at the sight of the stones glowing softly, of their own light. "It do be true," she said under her breath.

"Now, you surely do look like a peacock," Eilowyn observed, as Aleron struck a heroic pose with the sword, "and a jackass, all at once."

Barathol coughed at the jibe, grinning at the pair.

"But it still needs something," Aleron concluded. "A baldric doesn't look right, without a sword hanging from it, but you can't do that with a greatsword."

"Let me be getting' some measurements off that sword," Latka insisted. "I do be going to the leather shop to get this baldric in purple dyed leather. Harld can be makin' it to accommodate ye sword there, and ye can be hangin' a seax or somethin' like, where the sword be normally set."

"I like that idea," Aleron agreed. "Thank you, Mistress Latka." He took the scabbard from Geldun and handed it to her. She took some measurements from the scabbard, jotting them down in a small notebook, and then took more measurements from the baldric Aleron wore.

"Now, if you gentlemen will excuse me, it is my turn." Eilowyn asserted. "Why don't you go check on your weapons at the armory while you wait? I should need only a couple bells to get this straight, and then we can go for our mid-day meal.

"That will be a late mid-day meal," Barathol mumbled, as they left the shop, "since it's already mid-day. That took forever."

"We were there about three bells and got three uniforms fitted. That's not bad at all," Geldun retorted.

"Well, two uniforms and whatever that is that Al is wearing.

Those machines they got are amazing. Back home, we'd still be in our dirty old clothes, waiting at least a day for the first fitting and a week for all the clothes we have on order."

"Thanks for the vote of confidence on my new look," Aleron said, punching Geldun in the shoulder. "Let's go get our gear, so these uniforms don't look so empty."

They entered the armory to see a pair of apprentices working on their chainmail, snipping and removing damaged links, in preparation for repair.

As they passed one of the tables, Aleron noticed the separate bowls of solid and split links, along with one of tiny triangular rivets, to close the split links. He did not envy them their task. Making and repairing chainmail is a meticulous task, akin to knitting and requiring the riveting of half of the tiny links, smaller than the width of his pinky finger. It could be worse, he thought; their mail was four in one chain. He had seen six in one chain, intended for heavy cavalry, and wondered how anyone riveted the tightly woven links.

"What can I be doin' for ye gentlefolk?" the armorer asked. "My name be Tejain." He was a solid, middle-aged westman, with bright red hair and blue eyes. The rigors of his profession obvious; his sleeveless tunic revealed rope-muscled arms, rivaling Barathol's own in thickness, and the leather apron did nothing to conceal his expansive chest.

"We came to see if our weapons are ready," Geldun replied.

"Ye be the ones comin' in the mornin'?"

"Yes, that was us," Barathol answered.

"As ye can see, the lads be still workin' on the mail, but we got ye weaponry shined up for ye. They be over there on the rack." He pointed to the wall to his right.

"Our thanks, Master," Aleron said. "Let's go get our gear, lads."

It felt good to him to buckle his sword belt over the ridiculous purple belt of the baldric. Twin cutlasses now hung at his hips, with a long knife just behind the one on his right. He decided to unhitch that cutlass and place it back on the rack. Twin swords worked for going into battle, but proved unwieldy indoors.

Geldun belted on the long sword and dagger he preferred, drawing the blades, each in turn, to check the honing and polish. "Excellent job," he complimented the smiths.

"That's not likely to work, for carrying around the consulate, Barry." Barathol had a pair of long daggers affixed to his belt and held his newly sharpened glaive. "We need to find you a wear-about sword."

"I hate swords."

"But they are needed for a dress uniform. Two little knives look plain silly on someone your size."

"Master," Aleron called out, "Might there be a loaner sword, my friend can borrow, for a few days?"

The armorers ended up outfitting him with a decent standard-issue long sword, leaving his glaive and the extra dagger in the rack.

They stayed around for a few more minutes, inspecting the progress on their armor and looking over the weapons stored in the armory, before leaving to explore more of the consulate.

By the time they returned to Mistress Latka's shop, they had found the kitchens and main dining room, where they each grabbed a muffin and some tea to hold them over until Eilowyn finished, as well as the barracks rooms where the consulate guards stayed. Jorik was not present, but they managed to chat with a few off-duty marines after they got over the shock of their new king stepping into their living area.

Inside the seamstress's shop, Eilowyn wore a long-sleeved gown of dark green silk, with a boned corset of deep green, nearly black velvet, revealing the curves she had hidden under men's clothing for months.

The light flowing dress she brought from Kolixtlan, though attractive, did nothing to accentuate her beauty like the one she now wore.

"What do you think, My Love?" she asked, as she twirled in the center of the floor. The light fabric of the skirts swirled up to show pale green petticoats and low boots of fine goatskin, dyed the same color as the corset. The low sweep of the neckline revealed a conservative amount of cleavage, with her silver and blue quartz amulet centered at the top. The color of the dress accented her bright green eyes, while setting off her auburn hair beautifully, with a pair of silver hoop earrings completing the ensemble.

"Simply beautiful, my dearest, lovely as ever."

She giggled, like the young girl he met so many years before. "To think, Latka had this on the rack, in this house full of men, and it only needed a little hemming. It's as if I were meant to find it here."

"I'm sure you were, my love," he told her, as he strode forward to scoop her up in his arms and spin her around once, before setting her down and kissing her softly on the lips. The men accompanying him turned to look at the walls, uncomfortably, while Latka and her assistants grinned openly at the display of affection.

"Your Highness," Latka called to get his attention, first waiting for them to finish the kiss. "Ye must promise me to not be rumplin' Her Highness too much, before the day be out," she stated, with feigned reproach. "I did be puttin' a lot of work in them pleats."

Aleron laughed as Eilowyn buried her face in his chest, gripping him tightly. "I give you my word, Mistress, to do no more rumpling than is absolutely necessary." As they made their goodbyes, Latka assured them that the rest of their clothing would be ready for pick up in two to three days.

They left, in search of Damian and finding him in his office, asked if he would care to join them for a meal.

"Your Grace," the Consul responded, upon seeing them. "You certainly managed to snare the most beautiful of the steward's daughters, you did.

You look absolutely radiant, my dear, and I see that you have our new liege decked out properly. You make a striking couple.

We will have to come up with something for the coat, though. The cuffs and collar say High Lord. I'm not sure what is appropriate for the king.

Alas, I have already dined," finally answering the initial question. "I will send to the kitchens for some food, and I will sit with you in the dining room, if you wish."

"That will be wonderful, Uncle Damian," Eilowyn answered.

"And I have given some thought to the matter of Aleron's decoration. I consulted with Latka, and his second coat will have something more fitting. We thought that since my husband is, in fact, the High Lord of Sudea, the pattern is appropriate, but she will apply it on a royal purple background, edged in gold, like the baldric."

"That does sound reasonable."

"We also considered a coat of all purple..."

"I will not be dressed to look like a giant grape!" Aleron interrupted her.

"But we decided it better to retain the colors of the Sudean flag, on the coat," she completed the sentence, with a glare at her mate.

"Let us retire to the dining room and relax," Damian offered, "so we may continue our conversation in comfort."

Chapter 17

Corballday, Day 3, Falling Leaves Moon, 8765 Sudean Calendar

"It has been a very long time, Jessamine, even for our kind," Iudhael stated, after materializing in the yard, where she tended the fruit trees, gathering the last of the season's apples.

"Indeed, it has, Iudhael. You have traveled far, along the dream paths, to find me here. To what do I owe the pleasure of your visit?"

"Alas, I cannot stay for long. Being away from my place of anchor weakens me, on this plane, but I encountered a young halfblood, a very significant person, I believe. His name is Aleron, and he bore your signature, as well as others of our kind. Do you know him?"

"Others, you say? Come and sit, please, and tell me what you found. I helped to raise the boy, but I know of no others of our kind that would have had any significant contact with him."

"Perhaps, I should be more specific, sister," he said, following her to a bench, alongside a fallow flowerbed, "The other signatures I sensed were of his blood. You say you spent much time with him; did you not sense them?"

"I have little skill with yellow, as you well know, brother. My strength has always been with the green."

"Ah, yes, I shouldn't assume that what is natural for me would be so for you. Let me tell you what I delved of him. He came seeking healing for a woman companion, but he had a half-healed arrow wound on himself that I healed. His father was definitely a man, quite ordinary, but his mother is a different story."

"She was an elf, daughter of Goromir, a name you should recall, but go on."

"That explains the hint of aelir I sensed, faintly in the background. Goromir's mother was Iselle, was she not?"

"There was always suspicion of such. Though I was never a witness, many claim that Iselle was never present in Elvenholm when the queen, Chaldee, was present. Iselle only appeared after the queen departed Cyte, for her "sabbaticals" in the wilderness. It was never more than a theory, but if you sensed aelir ancestry in his grandson, it lends much credence to the theory."

"Much stronger than that was the aelient I sensed. Aleron is fully one quarter of our blood, and I was able to sense the identity clearly. His grandmother is Jacanda."

"Jacanda, are you sure? She was of the third that went over to her father's side."

"I knew Jacanda well before the split. It is definitely her, daughter of Iselle and the one who will not be named."

Jessamine paused for a few moments. "She must have posed as his wife, Quiana, and bore his daughter, Audina," she concluded. "That is perverse; if his mother was Iselle, then she is technically Goromir's half-sister, aelient or not, and she must have known who he was, to have done this. He was hiding his identity, but not from his wives or children."

"I agree, sister, that she must have some ulterior motive for her action, though she may not have known of their shared parentage."

"The suspicion was common enough, among us at least, that she likely suspected, but didn't care.

So, Aleron is one quarter aelient, and through that and his grandfather, three eighths aelir, with one quarter of his ancestry likely from Iselle," Jessamine calculated.

"And, as he is also great-grandson of the Adversary as well, that last eighth aelir of him," Iudhael added.

"That may explain some of the power he manifested, but not entirely. If Goromir is fully one-half aelir, he still only possessed the normal abilities of an elf, only more powerful than most, and he has lived much longer than any.

Audina had only average ability to handle magic, despite being a three-quarters aelir and two-thirds of that aelient."

"When I met the halfblood, I sensed that he was one who bends the pattern of time and space, by his very presence. However, when I healed him, I sensed his abilities locked behind a barricade of his own building. I dared not touch it, for fear of what it might unleash.

I have seen before when a mind constructs such a barrier, it has its reasons. Often, it is to stem off outright madness or extreme pain. It is usually best to leave it in place, especially if very fresh like this one was. What was exceptional about the boy's power?"

"Hadaras, I mean Goromir, Hadaras is the name he goes by, in these times; he told me that Aleron is unable to communicate across distance, but he did turn up among the westmen, a few days ago.

Before whatever happened to cause him to erect the block you speak of, Aleron possessed very unique abilities. He could wield all colors of magic, with equal efficacy."

"That is unheard of, outside of the aelir," Iudhael said thoughtfully, "Even among us, we seldom have real strength in more than one of the powers, though we can wield all. Elves were only given blue, and for some odd reason, halfbloods can use red, as well as blue, but no other colors."

"On top of that, he can blend colors. He discovered white magic and has used it on multiple occasions."

"That was forbidden for our parents even, though they were capable of it. Why would a mere halfblood have such ability, and why would our grandfather permit it to happen?"

"I believe we are entering into a new age, my brother, and I cannot say what our grandfather intends for the boy, but the instructions came to him in the world of dreams. As well, the white raven appeared to him, in the waking world, telling him to mix the magic, as he saw in his dreams."

"Grandfather himself, then? This boy of yours must have some high purpose, if our grandfather willed these abilities on him."

"Are you familiar with the Eltheri Prophesy?"

"I pay little attention to the predictions of mortals, Jessamine, but if it helps to illuminate this puzzle…"

"It was recorded from an elvish oracle, while our parents still taught the elves, and all on this continent lived in savagery, save the dwarves. It was forgotten for thousands of years until Goromir discovered it in the archives during the war. She recited:

Darkness shall envelope the world, and the mighty shall fall to contain the nameless shadow.

Though the light shall seem victorious, it is but the start of the waning.

The tree appears dead; yet one branch lives on, hidden among the weeds, and the fruit of the living branch shall be chosen above all others, when the nameless shadow shall walk the world again.

The chosen will carry my power and might and shall be the only hope against the nameless shadow.

Should the shadow consume the fruit of the living branch, all is lost, but the chosen may turn the darkness to light."

"Well, that seems very straightforward, in hindsight," Iudhael observed, "though at the time, they knew not that the one who will not be named would return. I take it that the halfblood is the fruit and the chosen?"

"I assume so, but the last line is troubling, and I wonder what the last part means."

"I have some thoughts on that last line, though I have only now heard the prophecy for the first time. It seems possible that if the halfblood shares the blood of the Adversary and Jacanda, then they will have a means to control him, through that blood," Iudhael surmised.

"Yes, that was likely Jacanda's plan. She must have found out that Goromir watched over the line of the Sudean kings. If she had the control of blood over Audina, she might have influenced her to marry Aleron's father and bear a halfblood heir to the throne, in fulfillment of that prophecy. But what of the second part?" she asked. "How could Aleron turn darkness to light?"

"I wonder if the servants of the Adversary are aware of the old prophecy. Perhaps the control of blood can go either way."

✳✳✳

Barathol checked his saddle girth one last time. He wasn't much of a rider, compared to Geldun and Aleron, or even Eilowyn, for that matter.

Marines are not cavalry troops, and most of his experience with horses had them hitched to a plow or wagon.

Geldun's father bred horses, and he used to race them for fun when they were youngsters.

Aleron was taught to be a soldier since he was a young boy, with riding lessons an integral part of that training, while Eilowyn was a noble lady, and riding went with that territory.

Barathol could stay in the saddle without much difficulty but fighting from horseback was out of the question. He did not know how to steer a trained warhorse with just his knees, freeing his hands to fight. Considering he would spend the next few months in the saddle, he thought he might find the time to learn. It did nothing for his confidence that, due to his weight, they gave him the largest horse in the group, a brown stallion named Grimbal, who stood seventeen hands at the withers. The stable master told him that fighting with a glaive, from that height, would give him a considerable advantage, but to make use of it, required he have two hands free.

Today was the Feast of Andulle the Huntress, and back in Arundell, there would be festivities, archery contests, as well as tests of strength and tournaments, because it always landed on Corballday, the day of Corball the Warrior, consort of Andulle. Instead of feasting and fighting, they were heading out on the road, once again, and Barathol was dreading it.

The others busied themselves in readying their own mounts, with the help of the stable hands. Two additional marines were to accompany them, for added protection and to lead the horses back to Sunj, as well as a translator.

Barathol had yet to see the translator, but he expected a westman who knew Sudean and Mittean. He did not expect the woman who strolled up behind him as he checked the girth strap one last time.

He didn't hear her approach and spun about in surprise at the tap on his shoulder, right hand grasping the hilt of his dagger, left hand shoving outward. The left hand encountered something soft, and when his eyes came about, he saw it planted firmly on the ample bosom of a tall and quite pretty woman.

"Well, sir, that is quite forward of you," she said, backing half a step to break contact, and smiling mischievously, "but don't you think we should introduce ourselves properly first?"

Barathol dropped the hand and stammered an apology, or at least attempted to. "I…bu…I mean…sorry, you startled me. I didn't mean to touch you there!" he said, his face flushing with embarrassment, despite its dark complexion.

She stood near to his height, with pale, reddish gold hair and clear blue eyes. Her strong angular features, with a nose a bit too proud, might have marred her attractiveness to some, but Barathol thought she might be the most beautiful woman he ever laid eyes upon. Tall, well-worn riding boots, snug brown trousers, and a dark green tailed coat did nothing to conceal an athletic, yet still voluptuous figure.

"I'm Anjani," she said, holding out her hand in greeting, "your translator, and you are?"

"Barathol," he answered, regaining his composure and grasping her hand.

Seeing his exposed forearm, she stepped in and patting him on the arm and shoulder, continuing, "Well now, I thought you all padding when I walked up, but you've nearly no padding at all. Are you half westman too?"

"No, not at all…Too? You're half westman?"

"Yes, my mother is Mittean, and my father was a traveling bard from Sudea, who doesn't know I exist, if he still lives. My stepfather is Sunjibi and brought us here when I was five."

"You speak Sudean very well; no accent to speak of," Barathol complimented her.

"I've been working in the consulate since I was twelve, so, eight years now. I think already speaking two languages helped me to pick up yours, without the usual impediment Sunjibis have with it. But, if ye be wantin' me to be talkin' more like them, I can be accommodatin' to ye."

"That's quite all right. So you'll be coming with us to Mich?"

"Yes, I will, so I need to speak with the leader of your party, unless that is you."

"No, not me, you need to speak with Aleron, the tall one with the moustache over there, with the little red-haired woman." As she started to go, Barathol asked, "So, are you leaving a husband or boyfriend behind on this trip?"

She turned her head back to him and smiled knowingly. "No," was all she said, as she moved off toward Aleron.

"Wait up, I'll introduce you," he called, trotting up beside her.

"Thank you, Barathol, you're such a gentleman."

"I wouldn't go that far," Geldun countered, while having to look up to meet the statuesque woman's eyes.

"Stow it, Gel," was all Barathol had to say, but punched him in the arm, for good measure.

Geldun followed along, rubbing his shoulder, but wanting to see what this was about. "

Aleron, I'd like to introduce you to our interpreter, Anjani. Anjani, this is Aleron and Eilowyn."

"Pleased to meet you, Highnesses," she greeted them while genuflecting.

"Pleased to meet you, as well, Anjani. You came with the highest recommendation of Consul Damian," Aleron replied, "and thank you for the courtesy, but that won't be necessary from here out."

"Yes, my uncle said you are the most fluent in Sudean and Mittean that he has in his employ," Eilowyn added.

"Why, thank you, Highnesses, I hope to live up to your expectations, and I must thank Lord Damian for his excellent recommendation when I next see him."

"So," Eilowyn began, "you look Sudean, but you speak with an odd accent, if you don't mind my saying. How did you come to speak Sunjibi and Mittean? Were you raised here?"

"I don't mind you saying, Your Highness. As I told Barathol, I am Mittean, with a Sunjibi stepfather. I only learned Sudean, from working in the consulate these last eight years."

"But you do look Sudean," Aleron stated. "So your father was…"

112

"My father is…or was a Sudean bard. I never knew him, and he had no idea I was born."

"Do you know his name, by chance?" Aleron inquired, suddenly curious. "I happen to know a bard who traveled the Westlands."

"Cladus, that was his name," Anjani answered. "It's not likely the same man you know, but I do hope to find him some day. Not for any nefarious purpose, mind you. I bear him no ill will, and neither did my mum. I just think that I would like to meet him, to see what he is like, if he still lives."

"Well, he does, the last time I knew, which was about a year ago. Unless there were two bards named Cladus roaming the Westlands twenty or so years ago, then I do know your father. He is a good friend of my grandfather."

"Really!" Anjani exclaimed, excitedly. "Then he is a good man? I always hoped he was."

"Yes, he is a very good man, and he will likely be very upset to learn that you grew up without him knowing. He is not the type to abandon his own."

"Oh, good, I always pictured him so. Mum always spoke of him fondly, at least when Dad wasn't about."

"There is something else you should probably know," Aleron continued, hesitating slightly. "You are one quarter elvish. Your father is a halfblood and close to two hundred years old."

Shocked silence followed his statement, as Anjani worked to process that revelation.

Barathol thought for a moment and said, "That probably explains why you're so tall and why you hardly have any Westman looks about you. It makes sense now; elvish comes through pretty strong. Just look at poor Al here; still can't grow a beard to save his life."

Anjani looked to him, with a puzzled expression, breaking out of the daze she momentarily entered, and laughed. "This one always knows just what to say, doesn't he?" she said, facetiously.

"No, not ever really," Geldun offered his opinion. "I'm Geldun, by the way," he introduced himself, holding out his hand. "Al, Barry, and I grew up together and served in the Marines together, back before Al was a "His Highness," or "His Grace," or anything."

"Well met, Geldun," she reached to grab his hand. "That was a much more cordial greeting than the groping I received from Barathol."

Everyone turned to look at Barathol, and turning red again, he stated emphatically, "That was an accident! You surprised me, and I didn't mean to grab there."

She released Geldun's hand and leaned into Barathol's ear, whispering, "Maybe next time, you will mean to." Barathol's eyes widened in surprise, while she said, loud enough for the others to hear, "I must be seeing to my mount, gentlefolk, if you will excuse me."

"Of course," Aleron replied. "We will all gather, before we set out, to discuss the route and schedule. She turned to go and smacked Barathol on the behind, as she sauntered off. Barathol stared after her, dumfounded, while Geldun watched her retreat appreciatively. Barathol noticed where Geldun was staring and punched him in the arm again.

"Looks like this will be an interesting journey, my love," Eilowyn stated, smiling mischievously while hooking her arm through Aleron's.

"Oh, look, Uncle Damian is here to see us off."

She led Aleron to where the consul and two marines waited.

Chapter 18

Zorekday, Day 6, Falling Leaves Moon, 8765 Sudean Calendar

Hadaras sat with Cladus in the room the bard rented over the Golden Dragon. He offered to find him rooms at the palace, but Cladus declined the offer, preferring the atmosphere of the city's common rooms, where he could gather the latest news and make some coin in the process.

It was mid-afternoon, essentially mid-morning for Cladus, who stayed out most of the night and woke at noon. Hadaras had just finished recounting some of the revelations Jessamine shared with him, from her conversation with Iudhael.

"So what you are telling me is that you were married to a dark aelient for over thirty years, and you did not know it?" Cladus asked, incredulous. "You never even suspected?"

"No, I did not," Hadaras replied. "Quiana seemed to me like any other elf. I find it very hard to believe, even now, but Jessamine's brother claims to sense a distinct imprint of an aelient on Aleron's blood, through his mother, to the point of knowing her identity." He pointedly left out the revelations concerning his own parentage. Hadaras trusted Cladus and Gealton more than he trusted any men on Aertu, but he hadn't the time to fully process this new verification of the ancient rumors of his parentage, and was unwilling to share it with anyone yet.

"The yellow allows him to see to that level of detail?"

"Apparently so, but I have no basis to verify the claim, though I have no reason to disbelieve Iudhael. She must have transformed herself completely for the duration of the time we spent together. It could not have been a simple glamour, such as Jessamine uses. I'm not sure how she could have done what she did without white magic, and I have never heard of aelient color blending. I'm sure the aelir could do it, but did not, for some reason. Jessamine assures me that she never heard of one of her kind having the mastery of all four colors necessary for white magic use."

"There are, however, several stories of aelir doing just that and mating with mortals, what of this Zormat, of the Arkans, who claims to be son of the Nameless One himself?" Cladus pointedly avoided mention of the one story involving the elves and a very powerful sorcerer.

Hadaras felt the point of his friend's inquiry poking too close to a sensitive subject. He had heard the rumor himself, it being difficult to avoid, over the course of nine millennia, but had always dismissed it as an unfounded rumor.

He betrayed nothing in his face or gestures about how close the inquiry came to his personal secret and continued, "That is interesting, because no one ever witnessed the Adversary use anything but red magic, though he must have been capable of using the other three and perhaps blending. In addition, he was far more powerful in red than he had any right to be, hinting that he gave up the other colors to concentrate his strength there.

He must have fathered the Arkan before he gave up the other colors, as far as I can see."

"But is there a way to transform, using just red? I have never heard of one."

"I don't believe so," Hadaras replied, glad to leave the subject of aelir and demigods, "but one can alter things, to some extent, beyond a simple glamour.

A dark aelient possessed an acquaintance of mine once. This one decided to forgo a physical body entirely and inhabit the body of her host. She made some subtle changes that drastically increased my friend's natural lifespan, but not to the point of changing what he actually was."

"Did you manage to banish the demon, and did he retain the long lifespan, if you did?"

"Yes, and yes, this particular person will likely live as long as an elf now, and there is no trace of the demon that inhabited him."

"Where did the she demon end up? From what I understand, an ephemeral will jump from one host to another, given the chance."

"She now inhabits a small crystal prison, at the bottom of an extremely deep and abandoned mine shaft, buried beneath a thousand feet of rubble, among other things."

"Oh, a spirit trap, you know how to build those? Well, I suppose you would, and you had the dwarves bury it in the roots of a mountain, how quaint. There's no danger the dwarves won't accidentally dig her up again?"

"Not likely, they don't tend to go digging in their refuse pits, though, they will have to dig a new one a couple hundred years early, because of all the stone we put over the top."

"Cladus laughed gleefully, slapping his knee. "You put her in the bottom of a dwarvish cesspit!"

"And buried her under a thousand feet of useless rubble and slag, plus whatever they have deposited on top of that, since the deed was done," Hadaras added, with a grin.

"It occurs to me," Cladus suddenly sobered, "If an aelient can give up its body, to become a demon that possesses mortals, and even alter them, to an extent, could this Jacanda have simply possessed your wife, before and while she bore your daughter? Could she have altered your wife in some way, to make their blood the same?"

"Those questions deserve looking into, my friend. It may have begun with a simple act of possession, but given enough time, Jacanda may have merged with Quiana so seamlessly that they became one person.

It's possible that an aelient could use that method to become one of a mortal race. That is likely the end result that my friend's demon intended for him, a seamless melding of their beings, with his will reduced to nothing but a deep memory."

"Jacanda could have done the opposite with your wife, merging, but concealing herself within the layers of your wife's being, while at the same time, usurping her legacy in her progeny. Did Quiana use magic?"

"Not often, or strongly, but all elves do, to some extent. She always wielded blue, in my experience, and any use of red would have immediately raised alarms, so Jacanda must have buried herself very deeply."

"Well, we have an idea of how it could have worked, and I have never heard of a demon reconstituting a body from scratch. They always possess others, as far as I know. So, if this is true, what does it mean for Aleron, our new king?"

"Iudhael and Jessamine suspect that the bond of blood may give Jacanda and the Adversary a means to control Aleron. It is likely that Jacanda influenced Audina to marry Valgier, Aleron's father. The Eltheri Prophecy has another implication, though."

"That the chosen may turn the dark to light?" Cladus deduced.

"So you're familiar with it. Yes, Iudhael believes that the bond of blood may work in both directions," Hadaras answered, "And with the unconventional abilities Aleron was granted, I suspect that may be the Allfather's intent."

"A risky gambit, for all of us," the bard concluded. "On one side, a mortal with the powers of the aelir and ties of blood to the Adversary could possibly turn the darkness against itself, but another possibility is that same mortal, in the pocket of the Adversary, could be used against us."

"I just wish that I could communicate with him. Iudhael said Aleron erected some sort of mental block, which shields his powers from his own use. I believe he overextended himself and likely nearly killed himself. Something in his unconscious cut him off to protect himself, I would guess. Now, he will need to find his way around the blockage his own mind created. The aelir dared not try to remove it, for fear of what lay beyond."

"He will not have the strength to face the Nameless One without his abilities, and he will need time to train those abilities. So far, he has mostly been muddling around and experimenting, has he not?"

"Yes, I encouraged it, in fact, so that he could grow familiar with his powers and perhaps make a few discoveries before training for arcane combat. He did have a few interesting findings, especially in shape-shifting, with white magic.

But yes, he needs training on shielding himself and fighting. We can teach him about blue, and he could use that knowledge to extrapolate for the other colors. I noticed problems in his use of other colors, of them bleeding into him, as he wields them.

For example, he cannot heal you with yellow without healing himself, which is not any real problem. However, he cannot promote growth with green magic, without aging himself, which is a serious problem.

We never notice a problem wielding blue, because blue is the magic of life, which we generate from our very being alive. It makes me think that prolonged use of red may make one more chaotic and violent, or even more deathlike."

"He needs to overcome his affliction, or it is all moot."

"Indeed, it is," Hadaras agreed.

✳✳✳

Shaggat looked to the elf for further guidance. She did not look like Zormat; she was not an Arkan, but her red irises indicated she was not completely elf either.

He supposed she was beautiful, in the manner of elves, with her pale white skin, delicate features, and golden-brown hair, cascading to the small of her back.

Her filmy gown of fine red silk was nearly transparent, leaving little to the imagination and thoroughly incongruous to the cool temperatures of the Iron Hills.

The impressive display of red magic she used to announce her arrival was also inconsistent with her elvish appearance.

"I say again that I bring you instructions from the Master himself, not his son, the Arkan called Zormat. I also am the child of the Master, born eons before even the first elf walked this world. I inhabit this body because it suits my purposes, and I will abandon it when it wears out or no longer suits me.

You may call me Jacanda, and you will obey me or be destroyed."

She had already incinerated two half-trolls that charged her, after she appeared from nowhere into the center of the clearing, so Shaggat believed that part and her words reverberated with truth within his skull, just as those of Zormat had, years before.

Shaggat dropped to one knee and bowed his head in supplication. "We are yours to command, Lady Jacanda."

He led a sizeable force of ten-thousand hobgoblins, half-trolls, and jungle men encamped along the border with Sunjib, in one of two passes that allowed easy passage through the Iron Hills. They had spent many months conducting forays into northern foothills and beyond, testing the enemy's defenses and raiding for supplies and fresh meat.

Westman was a bit stringy, compared to other man-meat, but good enough. Their sheep and goats were delicious, however.

"I accept your service, Shaggat," using his name, though he never gave it, and that was another reason to believe her claims.

"I need you to collect a certain individual for me. He is of great importance to the Master, and I must bring him to Immin Bul. He is of our blood and no harm must come to him, but his companions are of no concern to me. Those, you may eat, for all I care."

"You are most generous, Lady Jacanda. We will find this one that you desire; we need but know him."

"That, I will grant you now," she projected the image of the man she sought into the minds of all those around her, along with the thought, *His name is Aleron, and he is blood of my blood, and so of the Master's blood. Take him alive and kill the others.*

She had a good mental image of him, gleaned from the minds of the Kolixtlanis who saw him escape, as well as from the Adari kidnappers, before they failed in their task.

Her grandson was a dangerous man, and she supposed she could thank Hadaras' influence in raising him.

It would have been much better if that arrogant Kolixtlani assassin hadn't botched his assignment eighteen years ago. Then, she and those loyal to the Master could have raised the boy with full knowledge of his birthright and placed him upon the throne at just the right moment.

The fact that the assault led to her daughter's death did not upset Jacanda, but the mote of being that was still Quiana grieved. Jacanda was upset at the assassin's failure, and the fact that Hadaras covered their tracks so thoroughly that none found the heir before he managed to claim the throne on his own volition.

She threw down a set of manacles that seemed to glow with a strange inner light, one cuff blue and the other red.

"When you have him, bind him with these, then bring him back to this very spot and wait for me. He may bear a long sword; take that and bring it here as well. I will know when you arrive, and I will come."

With that statement, she disappeared from Shaggat's view. To those behind her, she appeared to step through a hole in the air, revealing a courtyard paved in white marble and surrounded by tall white columns, before closing up behind her passage and revealing only Shaggat there, on one knee, looking bewildered.

Chapter 19

Zorekday, Day 6, Falling Leaves Moon, 8765 Sudean Calendar

It was his third day in the saddle, and Barathol's backside felt no better than it had at the end of the first. His glaive rode in the socket to the front of his right knee, where a lance would normally ride, and on his left hip, he wore the Sunjibi long seax he purchased at the market the day before they left.

He liked the heft and handling of the single-edged sword. The blade was as long as his arm and hilted for two hands, the sharpened edge nearly straight, with a slight downward turn towards the tip. He found it a more suitable sidearm to his taste than a standard long sword.

They rode among open pasturelands, distant groups of cattle or horses dotting the landscape, hoping to save some time by cutting a corner from the road. Well-worn tracks indicated that this was a common practice and that they were on the right path.

"Squeeze with your left knee, like I showed you," Anjani directed him.

The reins lay slack on the saddle, while their horses walked at an easy pace. He spent most of his time practicing how to ride with his hands free for fighting. His mount sidled gradually to the right.

"Good, now really prod him."

He pushed harder and more abruptly, and the horse turned sharply right.

"Now bring him back."

He repeated the move with his right knee, and the horse returned to their original direction of travel.

"Now, bring him to a trot."

He was a little apprehensive about this one, having nearly fallen off the last time he tried. After a few moments' hesitation, he prodded with his heels, and the beast broke into a quick trot, with Barathol managing to keep his hips relatively level this time.

"How do I make it slow down?" he asked, as they caught up to the head of the formation. This was the most success he had, to this point, in controlling the horse without reins, and he had no idea how to stop the horse without them. Until now, his concentration had been on moving forward, not slowing or stopping.

"Squeeze with both knees, but not too hard."

He complied, but did squeeze too hard, and Grimbal stopped suddenly, nearly pitching Barathol over the horse's neck.

Anjani laughed aloud and said, "Not too hard, or you'll pitch right over his head."

"Thanks for the timely advice," he said, sarcastically. They were right alongside Aleron, Eilowyn, and Harm, one of the marines sent to accompany them, who was leading the train of packhorses.

Aleron looked over, to see what they wanted, but Barathol just called out, embarrassed, "Just practicing my horsemanship."

That satisfied Aleron, who grinned and waved back. They slowed their mounts to fall back alongside the string of packhorses carrying their tents, food, clothing, and extra equipment.

Aleron, mounted on a tall gray stallion, wore the same combat uniform and armor as the other marines. He had Andhanimwhid lashed to the saddle and wore a standard-issue long sword.

In contrast to Geldun, Harm, and the other marine, Elrud, he wore a small horse archer's shield, this one of Talik make, instead of a large lancer's shield, though he still carried a lance to his right front. A cased Talik horse bow and a quiver, bristling with arrows, also adorned his saddle.

Eilowyn, on her medium-sized bay gelding, wore a fine wool dress of deep green, with the skirts divided for riding and snug brown leggings. She carried a sinew-backed yew longbow, cased on the saddle, with a full quiver as well. It was not as handy on horseback as a Talik bow, but it was next to impossible to find her a horse bow in a weight she could draw, at least in Sunj. She proved deadly accurate with it, though, and the sinew backing allowed stringing it for long periods without it weakening.

Barathol saw threatening clouds to the north and hoped that the bow cases were waterproof. No matter how well greased, a sinew bow was difficult to keep working in the rain.

Geldun watched from his position at the back of the pack train. *There is definitely something going on with those two,* he thought, as he watched Anjani and Barathol, with just a twinge of jealousy. He pushed the thought down, striving to be happy for his friend.

It was rare that Barathol found a woman with whom he related better than awkwardly, and this one was definitely not a frail one. Honestly, Geldun couldn't think of a better match for his brash, unpolished bear of a friend.

What made him jealous was not Anjani in particular, but the fact that he would have no female companionship for the trip. He did manage to steal some kisses, with the pretty little serving girl at the consulate, but there was no way to take Feadra with him and away from her parents, both high-ranking employees of the kingdom. Geldun would just have to resign himself to a long and boring series of days spent riding and watching, followed by as many days on board a ship.

At least he was not alone in his suffering; Elrud, guarding the right flank and Harm, leading the pack train, were in the same boat as he. There was little watching to do, out here in the open spaces, but a lot of time for thinking.

He broke out of his reverie at the sound of rapidly approaching hoof beats, from behind. He whirled his mount around, half drawing his sword, only to see a fair-skinned, dark-haired woman riding hard, her dun mare lathered.

"I'm sick of pouring swivin tea, Geldun! I'm coming with you." Feadra's young face held a determined set. The others noticed the commotion in the back, and the entire procession halted.

Geldun looked over his shoulder and called out, "Al, I think we have a situation that needs your attention!"

He turned back to Feadra, and she smiled at him. He smiled back, not knowing whether to be happy or terrified.

"Feadra, how did you get here?" Geldun asked.

Aleron and Eilowyn were making their way to them from the front of the train.

"Your horse is exhausted," he added.

"I left half a day behind you and followed your tracks," she stated, as if the answer was painfully obvious.

"All right, let me rephrase that. Why are you here?"

"Feadra, from the consulate?" Eilowyn questioned, recognizing the girl, as she rode up. "What are you doing here?"

"Your Highness," She said, bobbing her head in deference, "I needed to get out of that god-forsaken city, where nobody speaks Sudean, and all I do is wait on Damian and his guests."

"But what of your parents?" Eilowyn inquired. "Did they let you leave?"

"I didn't ask for their permission. I left them a note, so they wouldn't be worried that I just disappeared."

"I'm sure that they are worried, nonetheless."

"Maybe so, but I'm finished with worrying about what they think. Besides, I like him," she said, motioning to Geldun, "and he'll get away from me and never come back, if I don't come with you."

Geldun looked down, uncomfortable with the entire situation, and Aleron, who had said nothing up to this point, glanced at him coolly and stated, "We will have to cut the guards loose and escort you back to your parents. I see no other recourse."

"Your Grace," Feadra addressed him, standing in her stirrups and awkwardly bowing from her saddle. "As my king, I respect your wishes, but I am seventeen, nearly eighteen, and by the law of Sudea, I can choose for myself. I will not be herded back to a place that makes me consider hanging myself by the neck every day. I hate my life there, and I will not be driven back to it."

Taken aback somewhat by her forceful assertion, Aleron asked, "What makes you think we will take you with us then?"

"You do not have to, Your Grace. I have saved enough of my own money to pay my passage. I have supplies for my journey. I will make my own way there, if necessary, but I would prefer to travel with your group, if you'll have me. This is my own horse, and I will sell it in Mich for the additional money or supplies."

"Not if you ride it to death, you won't," Geldun interjected.

Feadra looked at him crossly, for a moment, and then her expression warmed, as if amused by his consternation.

"My love, won't you please fall back to confer with me on this matter?" Eilowyn asked Aleron, as she guided her mount around the others, to move a distance away from Geldun and Feadra. Aleron nodded and moved to follow.

"You don't seem happy to see me," Feadra accused Geldun, after the king and queen moved out of earshot. "I thought you might miss me, but you're acting very rude. Did I make a mistake in thinking you cared about me?"

"Yes, I mean no, I mean…I do care about you, and I did miss you," he stated in a hushed voice, looking sidelong at his companions in earshot. "This is just kind of awkward, but I am happy to see you. I like you, and I wanted to take you with me, but I didn't see that as a possibility."

"Will you talk to them for me? I won't go back there, and I mean it. I will run from those guards if I have to."

"Of course I will, Feadra. Aleron is a reasonable man, and I'm sure I can convince him."

Aleron and Eilowyn returned shortly, and Eilowyn announced, before Geldun had a chance to say anything, "I am currently without a lady in waiting." Aleron thought coldly of what happened to the last person to bear that title, but remained silent. "If you would care to take the position, I will take you into my employ, from this day forward."

"My Queen, I would be honored to accept such an esteemed position." She bowed again from her saddle.

"At the first town, we will send a message back to your parents and Lord Damian, regarding our decision. What is your family's standing, Feadra?"

"We are a side branch of a minor noble house, Your Grace, House Galan."

"Good," Eilowyn said in a businesslike tone. "There will be no need to raise you to the nobility in order for you to hold the position.

Captain Geldun, Lady Feadra is your charge now, and you will keep her safe and see to her needs."

"Yes, My Queen, absolutely," Geldun replied, squelching a grin. Aleron favored him with a smirk as he and his queen rode back to the front of the train.

As they passed, Barathol asked, "Isn't that the little serving girl from the...?"

"Yes," Aleron cut him off and stopped briefly to explain the proceedings to his friend.

"We should walk the horses for a while," Geldun suggested, dismounting with practiced ease and offering Feadra a hand to climb from the saddle.

She ignored his offer of assistance and swung out of her saddle with the same practiced ease.

"I'm sorry, Ginny, for riding you so hard," she said, patting the beast on the neck. "You know I love you."

"We'll be stopping to water the horses in a bit. She should cool down before she drinks anyway."

"Of course, you are right, my Captain and protector," she replied, with a mischievous grin and a wink.

Geldun began to think she might be more of a handful than he bargained for. A quick-witted and adventurous young woman, who seemed quite capable and resourceful, replaced the demure serving girl he met just a few days ago.

That evening found them still far from any sizeable town, forcing them to make camp in the pastureland. Everyone helped to set up the camp, though Harm and Elrud objected at first, when Aleron and Eilowyn pitched in.

Aleron's answer was, "We don't have enough hands on this journey for any of them to be idle. I was a marine, just like you, for five years, before I claimed the throne, and we spent the last two months on the run, camping nearly every night of it. I would rather finish this early, so we can all relax."

That ended their protests, and they soon had four compact circular tents set up around a central fire pit, each just large enough for two people and their gear.

Originally, Anjani was to have her own tent, but with the addition of Feadra, she now had a tent-mate. She knew the girl and how she felt about living and working at the consulate, so she voiced no objection to sharing her quarters.

A folding steel tripod supported a large copper kettle, in which they set water to boil. They had brought with them a large supply of dried soup mixes, based on par-boiled then dried grains, with dried meat and vegetables. That was to be their primary nutrition on the road, plus whatever fresh food they could acquire at farms and small villages along the way.

If they came to a place with a sizeable enough inn for the eight of them, they would take rooms for the night and eat a couple good meals in the common room.

Fuel for the fire turned out to be a bit of a problem in the largely denuded region they traversed. They gathered what wood they found as they traveled, placing it in baskets strapped to the sides of the packhorses, for that purpose, but a good share of what they were forced to burn was dried dung, which wasn't as dry as they would have liked it, this early in the summer.

The fire was smoky and put out little heat before the outer layers dried out. Everyone found something to do away from the smoke, until it finally caught well and started burning with a bright orange flame.

"Day two of cooking on poo," Geldun quipped, as he brought the sack of soup mix to dump into the pot. A few snickered at his joke as they pulled their chairs to the fire, to enjoy an evening meal together.

Geldun found himself sitting on one of the fuel-gathering baskets after giving up his chair to Feadra.

"I'll be buying another of those folding chairs, the next time we pass through a town."

"I dunno, the dung basket seems appropriate to me," Barathol taunted.

"Thanks, Barry, very funny, maybe you should get your own comedy show when we get back home," Geldun replied. "You might draw a huge crowd of two, maybe three."

"Quit trying to impress the ladies with your witticisms," Eilowyn interjected.

"I don't want this to devolve into a fistfight. You might spill the soup, and I'm hungry."

Chapter 20

Zorekday, Day 12, Ice Moon, 8765 Sudean Calendar

They left the native men and their dogs on the ice of an ancient river that brought them deep into the frozen desert of the northern continent. That was one week ago, and in another two weeks, the men of the north would arrive in droves to worship the power they sensed here.

Zormat sensed the essence of his father, the One True God, close at hand. He laughed to himself at the absurdity of their worshipping his father's essence on the longest day of the year. The winter solstice, longest night of the year, would be the appropriate time to worship the One True God, whose power was greatest in darkness.

Men are ignorant of the true nature of the world, he reflected. *True worshippers would have built a great temple here and kept it manned, regardless of the bitter winter conditions. Sacrifices could fuel the red magic needed for priests to survive the winter.* The point was moot, though, as they would be leaving with the focal point of their worship, long before the solstice.

Three hard days of hiking and climbing brought them to the cave they now faced. Someone sealed the opening with precisely cut blocks of stone, the weathering of four thousand years' worth of blowing sand leaving the cracks between blocks barely discernible.

When Zormat probed the barrier, he met with a backlash of blue elvish magic. The wards proved to be incredibly strong and intricate, and Zormat spent many hours probing the wards and pondering how they might defeat them and extract Zadehmal. He believed he found a weak point in the spell that he could exploit with a focused concentration of power.

He gathered Karsh, his Second, and the other Arkans.

"I have located what I believe is a weak point in the structure of the warding spell. If we can destroy that portion, it will act as if removing a keystone, and the ward will unravel from there. We will link together, so that you may lend me additional strength. Are you all ready?"

Karsh and the others signaled affirmation, and the five Arkans linked their minds to Zormat and began channeling their power to him. Zormat gathered the red energy into his core, feeling almost as if he would burn away, from inside out, and focused on the knot of blue energy that seemed to bind the entire ward together.

He thought it interesting that he could visualize the elvish magic so vividly. He was always able to see blue magic clearly, but his teachers warned him never to attempt its use. He released a blast of energy that sheared the knot free of the weave, and he watched as the elvish magic unraveled, retracting onto itself, before dissipating entirely.

His second move was to blast the stonework from the entrance of the cave, before releasing the energy and breaking the bond. Red magic was in short supply in this cold, lifeless desert, and it wouldn't do to waste it. Oddly enough, he sensed a fair amount of blue energy in the vicinity, seeming to emanate from some of the rocks themselves. Something grew beneath the surface of the outwardly lifeless, translucent stone, thriving in the copious sunlight.

Zormat stepped over the rubble, followed by his companions, to peer into the darkened cave and realized it was not a cave at all, but a perfectly round tube, melted straight into the side of the mountain. He had seen lava tubes before, but this was too uniform to be one. A very powerful sorcerer drilled this with magic.

"Torches," he commanded to the Arkans behind him.

Moments later, a sputtering torch was in his hand, and he entered the tunnel. Four of his companions followed him inside, leaving one to stand guard. The curved floor of the tunnel necessitated they travel single file, Karsh directly behind, followed by the three remaining mountaineers. The tunnel sloped gently upwards, and as they proceeded, the temperature dropped rapidly. The stone around them acted to buffer the extremes of temperature found at this high latitude, retaining a deep chill, reminiscent of early spring.

The tunnel took them several hundred paces before opening to a small circular domed chamber. At the center of the chamber lay a large bronze chest, coated in the brown oxide of four-thousand years. Yet another ward blanketed the chest, like a dense net, anchoring to the stone of the floor.

Zormat fully expected this contingency and once again, probed the intricately woven spell for weakness. He found no weakness that he could exploit through brute application of red magic. He probed further, to no avail.

Here was the true ward securing Zadehmal; he could find no way through it.

I see no way to break this with the power available to me. I can see the precise weave, outlined in blue elvish magic. If only I could reach in and unravel it.

He reached, tentatively, for the blue power and found, to his surprise, that he could manipulate it and no harm came to him.

Karsh and the others saw this and backed away, fearing this new revelation. Blue magic was supposed to be anathema to Arkans, yet their leader was manipulating it with impunity.

It is remarkably precise, though obviously not as powerful as my native red. If I simply work backward, from this point... He picked apart what he believed to be the outermost portion of the spell, careful not to let it unravel uncontrollably. He could tell that by the structure of the spell, one mistake would unleash a backlash, potentially killing everyone in the chamber. Several long moments passed, as he slowly peeled back the layers of the defensive ward.

Finally, he reached a critical junction and directed his companions, "Pick up the chest and remove it from the chamber."

Karsh and the three soldiers each hesitantly grasped one of the four handles and lifted the trunk from its spot on the floor. Carefully avoiding the warding itself, they carried the trunk to the side and then out into the tunnel.

"Keep going; I will release the spell when you have moved out of range."

He waited a few moments and then slowly backed into the entrance of the tunnel. Simultaneously raising a shield of crimson power, he released the ward of elvish magic. A blinding flash of blue energy filled the chamber, buffeting and nearly destroying the shield Zormat held. He let the shield drop and blinked rapidly, attempting to clear the spots from his vision. When he could see again, the elvish ward was again intact, guarding an empty space.

I may not have been able to destroy it, but I defeated it.

With a deep sense of pride, he turned on his heel and followed his companions down the tunnel. He soon caught up with the other Arkans, and they walked together out into the light of day.

After setting down the chest, Karsh spoke up, "My Liege, if I may ask a question?"

"Of course you may, Karsh," he answered, knowing what the question would concern.

"How did you do…what we witnessed in the chamber? How was it possible?"

"I am not certain," Zormat replied.

He cast out his senses and drew the blue energy to him from the surrounding rocks. Soon, he held a glowing blue orb of raw elvish magic in his palm. The feeling was exhilarating, in a different way than when he handled red.

"I seem to be coming to no harm. Perhaps our teachers were mistaken about the blue's effect on us. It would make sense, considering our elvish ancestry, that we could wield both forms, just as the human halfbloods are said to be capable."

"Yes, Your Grace," Karsh agreed. "It makes sense, but it is difficult to believe, even before my own eyes."

"Can you see the latent blue energy in the surrounding rocks, particularly some of the ones in direct sunlight?"

"Yes, Your Grace, I can see it easily. It is more plentiful than the red."

"And the rest of you, can you sense it as well?" The four soldiers voiced affirmation that they could.

"Second, as I release this power, I want you to take it from me. If you succeed, pass it to the next and so forth, until all have handled it."

Karsh held out his hand and drew the orb onto his own palm. He stared with wonder as he held the alien power and felt its energy course through his being. Reluctantly, he passed it to the next soldier, and they repeated the performance four times.

The last soldier looked up from the orb to meet Zormat's gaze, with a questioning look in his eyes. "Your Grace, what should I do with it now?"

"Attempt something simple with it, a simple act, nothing requiring a spell." The Arkan thought for a moment and looked at the energy filling his cupped left hand. Pointing with his right, he directed a thin blue beam at a nearby boulder, and the orb vanished from his palm. The stone split down the center, with a resounding crack, falling into two halves. When they moved closer to investigate, they saw a layer of green, just below the porous outer surface of the translucent rock. Some sort of tiny plants grew inside, even in this most inhospitable of environments.

The soldier seemed amazed at what he had done. "Your Grace, I have never felt such precise control before, though I could have vaporized the rock with less of the red, I could never cut this cleanly."

"I agree, soldier," Zormat replied. "This new development raises many possibilities. Such precision and efficiency," he emphasized the words, sacred concepts among Arkans, "might prove very useful in our struggles to come.

I must discuss the matter with my Father when we free him."

He encouraged all of them to experiment with drawing in the blue energy and direct it outward.

Karsh even managed a simple spell that, when tied off, left two stones spinning about one another, in a figure eight pattern, a half pace above the ground. The effect would eventually wind down over time, as the energy dissipated, but they were convinced that if the spell were set to draw power from the outside, it would operate as long as sufficient life existed nearby.

Zormat left them to their practice and went back to the chest. Kneeling, he undid the latches and lifted the heavy bronze lid. The hinges screamed in protest, and the sound brought the other Arkans around to see.

Inside, lay a massive battle-axe, designed for wielding one-handed, but by a much larger being. It was nearly as long as an Arkan was tall. Its black blade shone with a faint red glow, even against the intense sunlight, like steel cooling from the forge.

The Arkan king so wanted to touch the artifact, but dared not, lest the temptation to wield the power within overcome him. Instead, he closed the lid and refastened the latches. "We have what we came for. Let us move out now."

Zormat and his Second took the lead, while the four soldiers followed behind with the chest. They moved slowly over the treacherous terrain, having to lower the chest, slung from ropes, at several points.

After countless bells, the sun disappeared behind the tall peaks to the north, indicating late night. They halted often to rest, eschewing sleep. The twilight afforded enough light to see, especially for the Arkans, whose night vision was nearly as sharp as a goblin's.

The sun did not actually set this far to the north at the height of summer, and its light reflected off many of the peaks around them.

They intended to maintain this pace until they reached the sleds in two days. They could take the necessary sleep on the sleds, where the well-rested men and dogs would take over the brunt of the effort.

He had to admit that he was somewhat impressed by the sheer stamina of the sled drivers and their animals, covering as much ground in a day as a rider pushing his horse to near death. They performed at that level, day after day, the men spending half of the time running behind the sled to relieve the strain on the animals.

On their way to the mountains, he and his Arkans spent much of the journey jogging alongside, to speed the journey by reducing the weight of the sleds, but even their endurance eventually failed, forcing them to ride periodically.

The grueling pace continued, with the sun peeking out to the northeast, through a saddle between two peaks, indicating that their journey had ground into the next morning. They moved onward and downward, ignoring the fatigue that plagued their bodies.

Zormat had no doubts about their success. *We are Arkans, and Arkans can handle physical discomfort. Where we come from, we learn to handle it, or we die trying.*

None of them noticed the elf, clothed in white, standing high above them on the snowpack of the mountain they had recently penetrated.

Good, little brother, you have done well, Jacanda thought.

Of course, she could take Zadehmal to Immin Bul directly, through the pathways of dreaming, but hurrying this process would not be conducive to her plans, pieces of which she put into play centuries ago. A major piece to the puzzle now made his way across the Westlands, and these mortals must do the legwork for themselves.

The apparent emotional barrier to Aleron's use of magic troubled her, but for now, it worked to her advantage. She turned from them, opened a gateway, and stepped back into her palace in the world of dreams.

All was as she had left it in her study, thousands of writings lining the shelves, some little more than ledgers, but dating from the dawn of recorded history. She loved her books and would have liked to spend some time reading, but now was an age for action. The reading would have to wait.

First, she needed to check on her servants, give them direction and reassurance of her continued presence, as she had been absent many days. Then, she would find her errant grandson in the Westlands and arrange for his passage to her abode.

Chapter 21

Corballday, Day 15, Ice Moon, 8765 Sudean Calendar

Shaggat pressed his body to the ground, concealed behind the tall grass and shrubby growth of the roadside. He and the twenty-one hobgoblins accompanying him were smeared head to toe with mud from the nearby riverbank. He brought two half-trolls with him as well, similarly camouflaged. This gave him twelve fighters on each side of the road, spread out evenly for thirty-three paces. He positioned himself in the middle of the southern squad, where he could direct the entire group.

When the group of riders he watched passed to the center, he sprang the trap. Shouting in the language of his people, he commanded, *"Archers up...and volley."*

Six archers stood and loosed their first volley at the hapless humans. *"Spears forward,"* he commanded next, and he, with the other nine hobgoblins and two half-trolls, sprang up, rushing the humans, with spears raised to charge. He placed the half-trolls at opposite ends of the two squads, so that they would cap either end of the trap.

He heard the screams of horses, as well as women and the shouted curses of men, as the arrows rained down among the riders. One horse reared, an arrow in its flank, throwing the rider to the ground. The rider rolled clumsily to his feet, improbably still holding his glaive. He glanced behind himself, turned to hack through the rope of the rearmost packhorse that foundered, with an arrow in its neck, and shouted something at the others. The huge man then charged Shaggat's line, roaring like a wild beast.

133

A tall man, with yellow-brown hair and moustache, mounted on a gray horse and wielding a greatsword with one hand, charged the half-troll. He dodged the half-troll's spear and coming around his offside in a sweeping arc, took the half-troll's head from its shoulders. Motioning and shouting, he seemed to direct the three women, one slumped in her saddle, and the remaining packhorses to rush to the bridge.

The huge, glaive-wielding man had already killed one of Shaggat's hobgoblins and now engaged two more, in a duel of spear against glaive.

The man on the gray horse wheeled around, sheathing his blade, and lifted a bow from a saddle case.

Shaggat recognized him then, pointed to him, and screamed, *"That is him, on the gray horse! Take him and forget the others!"*

The man began shooting the hobgoblin archers, alternating between the north and south groups. A hobgoblin dropped every time the man shot.

The remaining archers concentrated their efforts on the gray horse, trying to avoid hitting the man they were charged to capture, but not harm. Soon, the animal went down, bristling with arrows.

The man jumped free of the beast and its churning limbs. He resumed shooting as soon as his feet touched the ground, taking out two more archers and one of the spear-wielding hobgoblins that broke from the fighting to charge him.

Shaggat charged him as well, as two human riders came about to attack the archers. Another of the men was unhorsed and, limping as he ran, attempted to chase down the hobgoblins that broke from the fighting.

Shaggat's quarry shouted something at the men and the limping swordsman, and the glaive wielder hesitated. He shouted louder, and the still mounted men, just finished with the archers, rode off in pursuit of the women.

The two men on foot turned in time to see the remaining half-troll barreling up on them, without its spear. The one with the glaive managed to hit it once across the ribs but didn't cut deeply, and the half-troll slapped them both to the sides, where they lay stunned.

The hobgoblins parted for the charging half-troll, and the man dropped his bow, reaching for the sword on his back. The half-troll was too fast and took the man in the midsection, hoisting him onto its shoulder.

"To the boats!" Shaggat ordered, and they all ran in pursuit of the speeding half-troll.

He had only five remaining hobgoblins, plus the half-troll and himself, losing seventeen to only five men, and the bastard before him was responsible for at least six, one of them a half-troll.

He wanted to skin the worthless halfblood alive and then roast him slowly, but Jacanda was quite specific, and he did not wish to incur her wrath.

Hopefully, she won't mind this, he thought, as he brought a club down on the struggling man's head. The man's body went limp, and they continued running south, to where they moored the boats.

Two half-trolls apiece manned the three longboats they stole upriver. They modified the seats so that the brutes could sit in the center of the boats and pull both oars.

"Into the first boat with him," he directed the half-troll, and to the others, he said, *"You five, into the second boat. Half-trolls in the third boat, abandon it, and one of you come to each of the first two boats. We are all that is left."*

He sprang into the first boat, followed by one of the half-trolls from the third boat. The vessel rocked dangerously as the massive creature clambered aboard.

Shaggat moved to the unconscious man in the middle of the boat and checked his breathing. It was slow and even, as if he were merely sleeping.

Relieved for himself, that he caused no lasting damage, he proceeded to disarm the man, strip his armor, and then bound him, hand to foot, behind his back, with rope he placed in the boats for that very purpose.

The manacles Jacanda provided fell into the river, upstream, when one of the clumsy brutes nearly capsized the boat. He hoped that it would not prove to be a problem.

The half-trolls had shoved off and were rowing against the languid current of the river. He expected no downriver traffic since they captured all the towns and garrisons along this stretch of water. The former inhabitants of those settlements, those still living, were on their way across the hills to Shaggat's encampment in the pass. They would be useful as slaves and food, in the coming months, what with war brewing.

Aleron's last words, "Get the women to safety! They want me, get to the women, now!" rang in Geldun's ears as he thundered across the bridge, Harm close on his heels. He glanced back to see Barathol and Elrud prone in the weeds, and the half-troll carrying Aleron south, with half a dozen hobgoblins tight on its heels. He needed to check on them quickly and go back for the other two. An additional worry was the sight of Feadra, slumped over and clinging to the saddle as the women rushed off. The entire altercation lasted only three or four minutes, but resulted in Aleron captured, three of his friends injured, and the ground littered with dead hobgoblins.

Eilowyn steadied Feadra in the saddle, while Anjani inspected her wound. A bodkin passed through her lower chest, at an angle, the point just protruding from her skin, next to her spine. She tore the fabric from both sides to better expose the wound and saw tiny bubbles in the blood that oozed from the front side of the wound.

"This doesn't look good. If we pull the arrow, she will have a sucking chest wound, and I have no idea how much she is bleeding inside."

She looked at Feadra's face and said, "Her color looks good still, so I don't think she's bleeding too badly."

They all looked up as Geldun and Harm rode up. "They caught Al and carried him south!" he announced, "and Barry and Elrud are down.

"What, why aren't you going after him?" Eilowyn shouted. "You have to go get him!"

"He ordered us to go after you, Ellie. When I looked back, the half-troll was charging to the riverbank, with Al on his shoulder and all the hobgoblins behind it. The last thing he said was, 'They want me,' and then to protect you. I think he was worried they were after you, too, but it looks like they all ran south."

"This is terrible, Geldun. I...I don't know what to do." Tears began running down her cheeks. "They have Aleron, and they're going to kill him, but Feadra's hurt and Barry..."

That brought Geldun's mind back to Feadra, leaning against a weeping Eilowyn, looking pale and sick, with an arrow sticking from her chest.

"I don't think they are going to kill him. They wanted him for something, and they didn't care about the rest of us. Once they had him, they ran. We'll get him back, Ellie; I promise we'll get him back.

Harm and Anjani, go back to check on Barry and Elrud. I think they were just knocked out. I'll stay here to patch up Feadra."

"At once, Sir," Harm replied, wheeling his horse about and riding for the bridge. Anjani followed, wearing the frightened and worried expression she had since Geldun arrived, without Barathol. She hadn't uttered a word, which said volumes for the usually effervescent translator.

"I'd rather take her from your side, Ellie. Do you think you can hold onto your saddle for a moment, my love?"

Feadra nodded, her face brightening a little, through her pain, at the term of endearment from Geldun. She straightened in the saddle and held tight to the pommel, while Eilowyn released her hold on the bridle and stepped her mare to the side, to allow Geldun in.

He moved beside Feadra and put one hand under her leg and the other on her back. "Now lean to me, put your arm around my neck, and take your feet out of the stirrups."

The young woman complied, gasping in pain, as she leaned over to Geldun, and he gently eased her out of the saddle and into his arms.

"Ellie, can you please snatch off my cloak and lay it down somewhere?"

Eilowyn had dismounted and was tying the reins of the three horses together, so they would not bolt. She hurried over and undid the clasp on Geldun's cloak.

"I keep telling you, that's Queen Eilowyn," Feadra admonished him, as she buried her face in his shoulder, muffling her voice.

Geldun smiled grimly at her attempt to make a joke and followed Eilowyn as she situated the cloak in a spot nearby, where the wind lay the grass down flat.

"Will she be all right, Gel?" Eilowyn asked, as she kneeled at an edge of the cloak.

Geldun set Feadra down, gently, on her side, with her head in Eilowyn's lap, and replied, "Of course she will. I've treated this type of wound before. Wait here while I get my kit."

He ran back to his horse and grabbed his medical kit from the saddlebag. Stopping at a flat stone, he dug out a tin cup, set it on the sun-warmed rock, and dumped some finely ground herbs into it, followed by a bit of water from his flask. Finishing that, he ran back to the women and set down his bag, as he kneeled in front of Feadra.

Producing a small knife, he scored the fletched end of the arrow shaft, close to the skin, and snapped the back half of the shaft away.

"I need to get this clothing away from you, so I can wrap your ribs." Without waiting for a reply, he unbuttoned the front of her short jacket and pulled her left arm from the sleeve.

At least she's wearing coat and breeches. If it were a dress, I'd probably have to cut it off her.

He did the same for the shirt and then untucked the light undershirt, hiking it up to expose the wound. He threaded a wide strip of cloth from the kit, under her ribs, and then drew out two circles of thin oiled leather, placing them on her hip.

He went back for the cup he left steeping on the warm stone. Using a small spoon, he fished some of the herb mixture out of the cup and plastered it onto the smooth sides of the oiled leather disks and a bit at the entrance wound, coating the stub of the arrow shaft.

"You're very lucky it missed your heart and didn't seem to damage your lungs either, else you'd be coughing up blood.

Here, Ellie," he said, holding one of the leather pieces, atop a piece of wadded cloth. He had the other in his left hand. "Put that leather down over the stub, press it down over the hole as soon as I pull the arrow, and don't let up.

Feadra, I need you to roll forward a little so I can get a good angle on it. This is going to hurt, so brace yourself. Take a deep breath, and when I say, 'push,' breathe out as hard as you can.

Are you ready, Ellie?"

"Ready when you are," She replied.

He braced his knee against her back to steady her, grasped the bodkin point in a firm grip, and waited for her inhalation.

"Push," he directed, and then yanked the shaft through, slapping the leather over the wound.

Feadra grunted in pain as she exhaled, and Eilowyn could feel air bubble out from under the patch. Geldun brought the two ends of the cloth strip around her chest, Eilowyn carefully working her hand from beneath it, without dislodging the patch. She then reached over to steady the patch on Feadra's back, so that Geldun could tie the dressing off snugly, but not so tight as to keep her from breathing.

"Thanks for the help, Ellie. That's much easier, with two sets of hands.

Feadra, I need you to sit up now, so I can finish the dressing. Do you think you can manage that, right now?"

"I think so," she whimpered. "The pain isn't so bad now."

He helped her to sit up and said, with no small amount of embarrassment, "Unfortunately, you need to take off the undershirt too, for me to finish the dressing."

"This is an odd time to be trying to look at my goodies," She replied, with a pained grin.

Geldun blushed but was glad that she seemed in good spirits.

Eilowyn helped her with her shirt, as he took a longer roll of cloth from his kit. He unrolled it fully, got behind her, and passed it around her front, linking the ends, before tucking one end under the first dressing. He drew the tails up and passed them over either side of her neck. Moving to the front, he tried hard to avoid looking at her 'goodies,' as he passed the tails between them and once again, tucked an end under the chest wrap, before tying them together.

"There," he said, pointedly looking her straight in the eyes. "That will keep it from sliding down." He reached over to the cup, swirled it a few times, and handed it to her.

"Here, swirl this around, and swallow it all down. It will hold off fever and numb the pain some. Do you want a clean shirt?"

"Yes, please, my dear, and thank you for saving me." Her dark eyes smoldered as she spoke the words.

"I...'ll be right back." He sprang to his feet and walked to the remaining packhorses. Fortunately, the one with her things was a survivor of the attack. He rummaged through her pack until he found a fresh undershirt and shirt for her.

"I've never seen Gel act that...awkwardly around a woman," Eilowyn commented to Feadra, in a low voice. "He's usually quite smooth with the girls. I think he's taken with you."

"Well, that is all part of my fiendish plan, Your Grace.

Korelle's bilge water, this tastes awful! What's in this stuff? Did he actually put bilge water in it?"

"I think it's mostly that bark we got in Kolixtlan. I know Geldun saved a fair amount and ground it up once it dried."

Eilowyn looked at the dregs in the cup. "It looks like there's a couple other things, as well, but you'll have to ask him if you really want to know. He's a pretty fair battlefield medic, or so the lads say."

Her eyes took on a distant look as the statement reminded her of Aleron. Geldun returned with the clothing, handed it to Eilowyn, and busied himself with cleaning and repacking his medical supplies, while she helped Feadra to dress.

Harm and Anjani returned with Barathol and Elrud, as Geldun finished securing his gear. He noticed Elrud rode Harm's horse, with Harm and Barathol afoot. Barathol led his horse, which favored its left rear quarter.

As they drew closer, he saw the spreading bruise on Barathol's face, creeping from beneath his beard, and Elrud sported a black eye, nearly swollen shut. He pulled the kit back from where he tied it to his saddle and started walking back to where Feadra and Eilowyn sat upon his cloak.

At least she's dressed now, Geldun thought, relieved. She looked fondly at him as he approached, and Eilowyn looked worried.

"You look pretty good for just having an arrow through your chest," Barathol said to Feadra. A couple of the lighter bags were slung over Grimbal's saddle, and the horse had fresh blood trailing down its left flank. The other two horses dangled with a collection of bags and saddles.

"Why, thank you, Barathol," Feadra replied. "Whatever Geldun gave me took most of the pain away, but I'm getting sleepy now."

"Powdered opium and valerian root, along with that bark we picked up in Kolixtlan," Geldun answered. "You two look pretty rough."

"Yeah, we got swatted by that half-troll, and I think Elrud broke his leg when his horse went down. You'll want to check him out next.

Aside from mine, these horses have just a few scratches, but we lost Aleron's, Elrud's, and a packhorse. We got as much of the gear that wasn't ruined and the saddles. You'll need to buy a few horses and supplies, but at least you won't have to spend the money for saddles. What condition are these horses?"

"I haven't had a chance to check them over yet. What do you mean "we" will have to buy horses?"

"I'm taking Harm to go after Aleron," Barathol answered. "You need to get the women to the port."

"But you can't go without me! You'll need as much help as you can get."

"Think about it, Gel. You're the only trained medic in the group, and you have a girlfriend with an arrow wound to the chest and a marine with a broken leg that you still need to set.

He might be able to fight from horseback, but he'll be useless on foot. Anjani wanted to come too, but her job is to be an interpreter, and you'll need her to buy supplies and such, plus, she can fight in a pinch.

Al's last order was to protect the women. We don't have time to wait around; I'll check over the horses while you look at Elrud, and then we're going."

"Well, I don't have to like it," Geldun replied. Let me look at your face first, you big oaf." He reached up to press on Barathol's bruised cheekbone. "Does that hurt?"

"A little."

"Can you move your jaw all right?"

Barathol opened and closed his mouth, working his jaw about as he did. "Seems fine."

"Good, nothing's broken then. I'll get to work on Elrud."

"Harm's going to need his horse back, and I need a fresh horse. Grimbal's not carrying anything heavy for a good week. I had to yank an arrow out of his rear end, and let's hope it doesn't fester."

"You can take Acton. Just swap our bags over. Anjani and I will just have to walk to the next town.

Just find his sorry arse and bring him back. All right?"

Barathol checked over the remaining horses, while Geldun set and splinted Elrud's leg; he had a broken fibula.

Harm and Anjani worked quickly to move the gear among the horses, while Eilowyn settled Feadra down to rest as comfortably as she could manage.

Within half a bell, Barathol and Harm were ready to leave.

"The rest of the horses look fine," Barathol reported. "Those hobgoblins couldn't aim to save their own lives.

Don't worry, Ellie; we'll get him back, if it's the last thing we do."

"Thank you, Barry; I know you'll do your best," Eilowyn replied. She was crying again, as she hugged the two men, each in turn.

"Take care of yourselves, my brothers," Geldun added, moving forward to grasp forearms and embrace the men.

"If it looks hopeless, don't go getting yourselves killed for no good reason."

Anjani strode up to Barathol, hugged him fiercely, and kissed him hard on the lips.

"Come back to me, you big oaf. I'll wait for you in Mich. You'll find me at the consulate there, and then I'm coming to Arundell with you. Please don't make me wait too long."

She released him and turned to hug Harm. "Be careful out there, my friend, and try to keep your captain from doing anything too stupid." She stressed the word "too."

The men mounted their horses and galloped off to the south, upriver.

"Well, I guess we should set up camp here," Geldun decided.

"Those two are in no condition to move, just yet."

Chapter 22

Corballday, Day 15, Ice Moon, 8765 Sudean Calendar

The riders slowed their horses to a canter, as the horses had galloped for quite some time. They still had no glimpse of the hobgoblins, after half a bell's riding.

"You're sure they took to the river, Harm?"

"Absolutely, Captain. They jumped over the bank, just around the bend from the road. Remember, we saw the boat moored there? They must have abandoned it since we killed two thirds of them."

"Then how, in Zorek's name, are they outpacing us, rowing against the current?" Barathol knew it was a gamble to ride up the west side of the river, when he last saw Aleron's abductors on the east side, but Harm was certain they took to the river and there was the abandoned boat, as further evidence. This side had a road, at least, whereas on the other side, they would have to navigate the forest.

"My guess is that we didn't see all their trolls," Harm answered.

"I bet you those half-trolls could row that fast, if you had enough of them and kept the whip to them."

Eventually, after another half bell, they slowed their mounts to a walk. The lathered horses needed some rest to cool down. Riding them to death would do them no good.

Barathol was frustrated with their lack of progress, but neither was rushing a good option. Galloping up in a rush would likely force the hobgoblins to the opposite bank, and the further from the bridge they traveled, the less likely it would be for them to catch up.

The river here was wide, with steep banks and deep, making it difficult to find a place to cross.

∗∗∗

Shaggat felt uneasy about leaving the men alive. He saw only two men moving and the few women, but the two other men were likely only stunned, rather than dead. If he hadn't lost so many of his people in the skirmish, he would have stayed to clean things up.

"Pull harder!" he yelled at the half-trolls. They were dim-witted, but strong, and they understood enough language to be useful. After all, they would never have taken the Sudean, without the help of the half-troll.

They were putting good distance between themselves and the bridge, while the men tended their wounded, he was sure.

The men still had horses, though, and horses could move faster than boats rowing against the current. The captive still slept as if dead, and he wanted the man to awake before they resumed foot travel.

Shaggat's fears were realized when his rearmost half-troll dropped the oars, gurgling and clutching at an arrow in its throat.

"Grab the oars and pull!" he screamed at the other half-troll crouching in the rear of the boat.

The west bank of the river was clear for a stretch, and a man walked his horse at a casual pace, rapidly shooting arrows at the boats.

He had no remaining archers to answer the threat, so he needed to get out of range.

"To the east bank!" he commanded, as he narrowly dodged an arrow.

Looking to the front of the boat, he saw the half-troll that carried the captive slumped, an arrow protruding from its forehead. In the second boat, another half-troll and two more hobgoblins were down. He lost the rear half-troll a moment later, leaving him only the forward one, pulling the oars, the captive, and himself.

He ducked another arrow as the boats angled toward the east bank. Another half-troll tumbled into the water from the second boat, and he saw only one hobgoblin moving, as well. The boats ground into the muddy riverbank, and Shaggat shouted, *"Get him to the bank, now!"*

The half-troll leapt to the center of the boat, grasped the captive by his clothing, and hurled him, like a sack of grain, over the top of the bank.

One, then two arrows sprouted from the half-troll's back as it finished the toss, and it toppled, headfirst into the mud.

Shaggat leapt from the boat and scrambled over the bank, an arrow narrowly missing him. He spun about on his stomach to take in the scene on the river. All in the second boat were down, some moving feebly, but most lying still, as arrows continued to fall, finding any bodies still moving.

The horseman raised his bow, and an arrow whistled past Shaggat's ear, sending him scrambling backwards. It was just he and the captive now, so he crawled to him, through the brush, and placed himself behind the bound man, using him as a shield.

Grabbing the man's tunic with both hands, he pushed with his feet to drag them further into the wood line, out of range of the archer on the far bank.

"So now what, Captain?" Harm inquired, holding Aleron's horsebow.

"I missed one of them, and they managed to get the king over the bank. We have to get across the river somehow, and that will put us a day behind."

"You did well, Harm," Barathol replied. "All the half-trolls went down, and that will slow them down. We should head upriver, find a place to cross and head them off, but first, we need to get to those boats."

"Why is that? We can't use them to cross the horses."

"Aleron's sword is in that boat, if I'm not mistaken, and I don't think he would approve of us leaving it behind."

"Andhanimwhid. I understand now.

The bridge is a long way off now, but I have some rope hanging off my saddle. I don't have any sort of grappling hook, though. How about you?"

"No, but we can come up with something."

What they came up with was a medium stone at the end of the rope, with a stout forked branch lashed to it, to act as hooks. They tied the end of the rope to a tree and then coiled the rope carefully on the bank. First, Harm and Barathol took several turns swinging the rope over their heads and missing the boat by a sizeable margin each time.

Barathol got fed up with this and began throwing the grapple like a shot-put, coming closer and making good contact on the third toss. They assumed Aleron's things would be in the first boat and were not proven wrong. As they hauled the boat across the river, they caught glimpses of Aleron's armor and weapons, among the dead troll bodies. "Plug some more arrows in those bodies," Barathol directed, as they tied off the boat. "I'd just as soon not be surprised down there. As a matter of fact, shoot 'em in the face."

"Right away, Sir," Harm replied, grinning. "Shoot 'em in the face!" was a common refrain among the marine archers when they prepared for battle.

He took careful aim from the bank and put an arrow in the eye socket of the two half-trolls on their backs. For the one slumped forward, he placed a shaft behind its ear. None so much as twitched.

"Keep one nocked and cover me," Barathol said, while sliding down the bank. He vaulted into the boat and began gathering Aleron's weapons, the greatsword first among them, and throwing them onto the bank. With no small effort, he wrenched the chain shirt from beneath a dead half-troll and flung it onto the bank, as well. He jumped out of the boat, tied its own mooring rope off on an exposed root, and then unhooked their rope, untying the makeshift grappling hook. Using the rope for support, he climbed the bank and untied it from the tree.

"Why did you bother to tie the boat off?" Harm asked, as Barathol coiled the rope.

"It's a good boat, and somebody might be able to use it. Be a shame to let it go over the falls."

"Not sure I'd want it, all covered in troll blood and shit."

"Plenty of soap and a scrub brush, followed by a new coat of paint, and I'd take it."

He hung the rope on Harm's saddle and proceeded to tuck Aleron's greatsword beneath a strap at the back of his own saddle. Harm cased the bow, replaced the quiver to his saddle, and fastened Aleron's longsword to his saddle.

The dagger was conspicuously missing from the arms recovered from the boat.

"Here, Master Sergeant, you have more use for this than me," he said, handing Harm the Talik shield, designed for use with the bow.

"I'm a sergeant, Sir, not a master sergeant," Harm contradicted, as he took the shield."

"By Corball's balls, if Al can promote me from corporal to captain, I can bloody well use my authority to promote you to master sergeant.

You're good in a pinch, and I intend to keep you around when this is all over, that is, if you are willing."

"Sounds good to me, Sir.

It looks like we got everything. I think that hobgoblin lifted the king's dagger, though. We didn't give him time for the rest. Otherwise, hardly a miss but I missed that slippery little mud sucker twice," he said, shaking his head while rubbing a shoulder, sore from the exertion of working the heavy horn and sinew recurve bow.

"Don't worry about it. That was some fine shooting. I don't think you get to be a leader among the hobgoblins by being slow or stupid."

"I should have gotten him first. Once he knew what was happening, he was too quick."

"Like I said, you did well. Now let's ride upriver and find a place to cross." They mounted up and continued up the road at a canter.

✳✳✳

The captive began to stir. Shaggat sat against a tree, watching him with hooded eyes. He bound the man with hands tied to his waist and feet still tied together. A short section of rope anchored him to a tree.

Lying on his side, among the moldered leaf litter of last season, the man's eyes opened, immediately meeting Shaggat's gaze. The look of confusion only lasted a moment, replaced by one hard as steel.

He spouted a stream of gibberish at Shaggat and then pressed his lips to a thin line, a look of obvious hatred on his face.

"Shaggat hurt no," he said to the captive, pointing to himself upon saying his own name and then to the man, for the other words.

He knew very few words in this man's language, though he had a fair grasp of Kolixtlani after five years collaborating with them.

He stood, using his spear for support, and motioned with his other hand for the prisoner to stand. The man seemed not to understand, so he motioned with the spear this time and remembered the word, "Up!"

He understood that and rolled to his front, slid his knees under, and rose to his feet.

With the man on his feet, Shaggat moved to untie the end of the rope from the tree. Finished, he moved just close enough to saw through the single loop of rope that held the man's feet. He was not stupid enough to put himself within kicking range of this prisoner.

The man jumped back and aimed a kick at him anyway, but Shaggat was too quick, snapped the rope around the offending leg, and yanked up and back, causing the man to fall to his back. He drove forward with his spear, pressing it hard under the man's chin, as a warning.

Backing off, he snapped the rope from around the leg and said, "Up!" again.

The man complied, and Shaggat motioned to the south with his spear and a motion of his chin.

He seemed to understand and turned to start walking down a narrow path between the trees, paralleling the river. Shaggat's wood sense said beasts frequented this path more than people did, but it would serve his purposes for the time being.

Suddenly it occurred to him, Kolixtlani is a language of men, and maybe this man knows at least some.

"If you give me no more trouble, you will come to no harm," he said, in Kolixtlani, to the man in front of him. The captive slowed a bit, turning to see Shaggat.

"So, you speak some Kolixtlani," Aleron said to his hobgoblin captor. *"I guess I shouldn't be surprised. The goblins back home speak Sudean."*

"It is useful to know the tongues of your neighbors," Shaggat replied.

"I agree. I saw you leading those who captured me. I gather that you are a leader among your people?"

"I am the highest among equals."

"Interesting concept," Aleron admitted, partly to make the time pass faster, but mostly to put his captor at ease and to gather as much information as he could.

"What does that mean, exactly?"

"It means that, unlike you men, anyone among us may rise to a high place."

"There are some groups of men who do the same. We do not all have kings. How did you ascend to be the highest?"

"I started as a warrior and rose to chief of my village by killing the old chief," he stated, with obvious pride, *"and I kept my place, against all who came against me."*

Pausing for a moment to collect his thoughts, he continued, *"Then, one day, the Son of the True God came to me and charged me, Shaggat, to gather the tribes, and I did. Long years it took, but I succeeded. I even allied with the dim-witted half-trolls and brought them into my army.*

"Impressive," Aleron remarked, in flattery, though he was in fact somewhat impressed. This one was not the stupid brute he expected.

"You are a very important person, Shaggat. Why did you come after me yourself? Why not send someone less important?"

Shaggat felt some apprehension at the slip that let his name be known, but put it aside. He did not believe in any name magic superstition, at least not when it came to common people, Gods, perhaps, but not common folk.

"The task was too important to be trusted to an underling. The Lady was very clear on that. You are to be brought to her unscathed, and my underlings, unsupervised, may have taken that to mean alive but not necessarily in possession of your arms and legs, or all of your skin."

"If I may be so bold as to ask," Aleron began, as he crouched to avoid some low-hanging branches, *"what lady is this who wants me unharmed?"*

"The elf, Lady Jacanda," Shaggat replied, *"your grandmother, so she says. She claims you are very important but brought up by the wrong people."*

Aleron remained silent for a time, as they walked, processing the information. He hoped to lower the hobgoblin's guard with casual conversation, but his captor's spear remained poised to strike.

"My grandmother was not called Jacanda. Her name was Quiana."

"I know just what I was told, man. She came through a hole in the air and killed with red magic, but she was an elf. She said your name, Aleron, and said I must bring you to her, unharmed. That is all I know, and I don't care to know anything different."

Stepping through a hole in the air sounded reminiscent of what Iudhael did at the old temple.

Dark aelient, it has to be, Aleron thought. That could be the only explanation for what Shaggat described. It was no surprise that the enemy might know his name by now, so that knowledge meant nothing to prove the grandmother claim.

"I will have to meet the one who would make such a claim to me."

"Do not worry," the hobgoblin replied. *"You will definitely meet the Lady."*

They continued their trek through the forest, Shaggat never once slipping in his vigilance, regardless of Aleron's attempts at disarming conversation. Soon, the last rays of the sun fell behind the trees on the west bank, and the long shadows of great oaks and beeches faded into dim twilight. Sounds of night creatures replaced the buzzing and chirping sounds of day, while the soft breeze settled to stillness.

As darkness descended, Shaggat had no trouble, but Aleron began stumbling over roots and rocks, dropping to his knees on numerous occasions. He remembered that men have nearly no night vision.

"It looks like we must stop for the night. Your eyes fail you in the dark." He did not wish to stop and give the pursuit time to catch up, but there looked to be little choice in the matter.

"That would be good for me. May I have some water?"

This thing is constantly thirsty, Shaggat thought, as he moved to the man's front with a water skin, as he had several times that day. He even let him kneel in a stream to drink his fill, a bit before nightfall.

Relieving himself was another matter, with hands bound behind him. The hobgoblin dared not untie him, lest the man fight his way free and run, but after the first time helping him to perform the deed, Shaggat simply left the man's fly untied and his male parts dangling out.

Hobgoblins have no natural sense of modesty, so Shaggat did not understand why his captive seemed so embarrassed by the situation and left it as it was. He found them a decently comfortable spot, beneath a large beech, and tied the rope off to a low-hanging limb.

Shaggat settled back against another trunk to watch his captive. He could go several days on end with no sleep, and he always felt more awake in the night.

Aleron settled down on the deep carpet of leaves, on his side, facing the hobgoblin. He had no reason to trust the creature, but he did trust that it meant to bring him to its destination and not to kill him in his sleep.

Shaggat's eyes glowed a dim red in the faint starlight, watching Aleron as he drifted off to sleep.

Chapter 23

Carpathday, Day 16, Ice Moon, 8765 Sudean Calendar

Already riding when the first rays of dawn broke through the rustling canopy overhead, Barathol and Harm continued their search for a crossing point. Soon, the golden orb rose above the trees, visible through the gap left above the river.

The warm sunlight felt good on Barathol's face.

Instead of finding a ford, the prospects looked worse, the further south they moved. As the land rose, approaching the Iron Hills, the river narrowed, becoming deeper, with a faster current. He was losing hope that they would ever find a proper fording spot, but turning back for the bridge, after traveling ten leagues upriver, would put him a solid two days behind Aleron and his captor.

While it is all well and good, when mounted, to overtake someone on foot, you cannot gallop a horse for twenty leagues, which was how much distance they would have to travel, if they turned back, to get to the opposite side of the river from where they were. At that point, Aleron and the hobgoblin could be another two days and twenty leagues ahead.

As it turns out, a man on foot can cover about the same distance in a day, as one who is mounted. Numerous accounts supported the ability of Elmenian highlanders to outdistance mounted armies, back in the days that Sudea employed their forces. The main difference is that the horseman can carry more amenities and has the advantage when there is need for speed over a short distance. Therefore, short of riding their mounts to death, it could take weeks to catch up with their quarry.

Another bridge would be a great idea, he thought sourly, to himself.

"Don't these people ever need to get across this bloody river?" he asked no one in particular.

Since Harm was the only one around to answer, he assumed the question was for him. "Not so much here, as this road leads directly into the mining country. There's another road that goes west to east, up in the foothills, so there has to be a bridge up there, but that's several weeks' travel. This is mostly unsettled forest through here and for a good way east."

✳✳✳

Aleron began his second day of walking in the twilight before dawn, with barely enough light to avoid tripping over the rocks and roots in his path. His wrists chafed and bled from the coarse ropes that bound them, and he was especially uncomfortable with his private parts dangling outside his trousers. However, the alternative, Shaggat assisting him every time he needed to make water, held no more appeal.

"How long will I be bound this way, Shaggat? We could move faster if I could use my hands a bit."

"You think me stupid, man? If I untie you, you will run, and then Jacanda will skin me alive and shrink my head. I think that I would rather not have that done, so you will stay tied. Had your followers not killed the rest of my people, you would be moving more comfortably, but what is done, cannot be undone."

The hobgoblin's last turn of phrase rang with familiarity in Aleron's mind, but he couldn't place it.

"I can assure you that I will not attempt to escape. I wish to meet the one who would call herself my grandmother. I will not attempt to flee if you untie me. I give you my word."

"Unfortunately, I have no reason to trust your word." In fact, Shaggat did feel somewhat sorry for the man, trussed up like this, and led to whatever fate the Lady had in store for him. Better a quick death in battle than this, but nothing he could do would change the situation. With no one to cover him, he dared not untie the bonds and retie them into a position more convenient to his captive.

Surprising to Shaggat was the fact that he was beginning to enjoy the man's company. Intelligent conversation is a rare thing among hobgoblins, and Shaggat's frequent interaction with men and Arkans had gotten him used to it.

Shaggat was right, Aleron begrudgingly admitted. He felt no obligation to keep his word to a creature of the Adversary and planned to break away at the first opportunity.

Some misgivings clouded his thoughts on the subject. Shaggat was not at all what he expected from a hobgoblin. Expecting a savage brute, he found the hobgoblin quick-witted and intelligent, with as good command as he of Kolixtlani, a foreign language to both.

He felt that somehow, breaking his word to Shaggat would leave as black a mark on his honor as if he did the same to a man or elf. Granted, their ways were somewhat savage, rising to and holding position like wild pack animals, but such behavior was not unheard of in the history of men.

***

Geldun checked the rabbits, one simmering in the pot, and two more spitted over the fire. Eilowyn and Anjani made productive time hunting in the early morning. They all breakfasted on boiled porridge that morning, but Feadra had little appetite, consuming only a few bites before concentrating on the bark tea he prepared for her. He left out the opium powder, wanting her appetite to return, so she was in more pain than during the night. If the pain became too bad for her, he may have to reintroduce the opium, but that would cause her to sleep the day away. He hoped that lightly salted broth and well-boiled meat might go down better than porridge, and what she did manage to eat would pack more nutrition than boiled oats.

They set up only two tents last night. Eilowyn invited the other women into her tent for company, and Geldun shared a tent with the injured marine.

Though the next town was only a half-day travel, the group would go nowhere today. They could not move Feadra, for fear of worsening any internal bleeding she might be experiencing or loosening the patches that sealed off her chest cavity.

She had no fever that morning, so the wondrous bark from Kolixtlan was doing its part and, for the moment, he didn't worry about the wounds festering. Tomorrow, he would remove the patches and check the wounds for signs of pollution. By then, they should have sealed up.

In the meantime, the concoction acted as a sort of glue, due to the gelatinous nature of the powdered bark. Elrud, as well, would benefit from a day with his swollen leg propped up. A half-day in the saddle would likely bring the swelling to dangerous levels.

Both the wounded relaxed in the shade of their tents, and he planned to check on them as soon as the food finished cooking.

They broke into a clearing, around midday, stepping into bright sunlight. The clearing was the result of recent logging, the first sign of activity Aleron had seen in two days of walking, with brush piled into neat stacks, the forest floor churned by hooves, boots, and logs. A crude track, deeply rutted from log skidding, exited the south side of the clearing, leading back into the forest.

Aleron's spirits brightened, as this obviously meant a settlement of some type and possibly aid in his escape. Shaggat knew this place, and he knew what his captive was likely thinking. He would find no aid ahead. All inhabitants of the logging camp and the village that supported it were now marching to his encampment in the Iron Hills.

Shaggat and Aleron both halted in surprise at the appearance of a figure on the far side of the clearing.

Jacanda stepped into the air, coming down softly in her fine kidskin slippers, onto the rough ground. She glided toward the halted pair, coming to the center of the clearing, where she stopped.

"Come to me, Aleron," she commanded, and then to Shaggat, in his native tongue, *"Bring him to me, loyal servant Shaggat."*

Shaggat moved to prod Aleron with the butt of his spear, but Aleron walked forward on his own accord.

When they stopped before her, she remarked, *"I instructed you to bring him unharmed, but he appears battered and attired in a humiliating fashion, Shaggat. Where are the manacles I gave you?"*

"My Lady, it could not be helped. They fought fiercely, and only I escaped alive with your prize. I dared not untie his bonds, me alone, for fear of his escaping.

The manacles fell into the river, My Lady, and we were unable to recover them."

"I suppose that is understandable, though I cannot imagine how you could have blundered so badly, against such a small group, with the force you brought against them.

As for the manacles, you are lucky something blocks his powers. This man is a potent sorcerer."

"My Lady, I am deeply shamed at my incompetence. This one alone defeated a half-troll and six of my archers in the first moments of the battle."

"I see," Jacanda said. In fact, she had seen all of it, from a distance. She thought it important that these mortals complete without assistance the task she set upon them. It would instill pride of accomplishment among the force and help to avoid any expectation that their betters should assist them in the mundane tasks of war.

Unfortunately, current events required she abandon that plan and claim her prize, before the approaching men took it from her.

"What say you, Aleron, my grandson? It appears that my husband taught you well in the ways of war."

Aleron wanted to be obstinate and refuse to answer, but something about this elf compelled him to answer, just as he felt compelled to come when she called him. He did his best to answer obstinately.

"My grandmother's name was Quiana, and I heard Shaggat refer to you as Jacanda. Who are you really?"

"Quiana is the name a part of me once used, the lesser part of me that provided this mortal body. I hold her memories, but the essence of her personality long since passed from this plane."

Aleron knew at once what stood before him. The strange, beautiful, but red-eyed elf was a demon, possessing his grandmother's body and devouring her spirit in the process. "You killed my grandmother and possessed her body, demon," Aleron accused her.

"That may be true, in a sense, young man, but I am in truth your grandmother. Goromir never knew Quiana before our beings melded, only me pretending to still be her.

My preparation for you began many years before Goromir and I ever met. The one who was Quiana had long since departed.

Now come with me, Aleron. You really have no choice but to obey me."

She opened a hole in the air that revealed the courtyard of a fine marble palace.

"What of me, Lady Jacanda, your loyal servant, Shaggat?"

"You have served me well, Shaggat, but where we go, you may not follow. You must make your way, as best you can, back to your people in the hills."

With that, she gestured for Aleron to precede her into the dream world.

Shaggat released the rope when it came taut in his hand, and Aleron stepped out of the world.

"Fare thee well, Shaggat, First Among Equals. I thank you for your assistance."

She stepped through the opening, and it snapped shut behind her, leaving the hobgoblin to stare into the clearing like an idiot before collecting himself and moving onward.

Shaggat was upset that he would return to his camp without the captive or any of his people to corroborate his story. He wondered whether any would believe him, and what his standing would be upon his return. He would likely face numerous challengers for his position.

He still possessed the man's dagger, the jeweled and gilded hilt jutting above his belt, but that was little in the way of proof. Why had Jacanda veered from the original plan?

As he approached the exit from the clearing, it occurred to him why she had done it, and he took to the forest, instead of the track. He found a rough-barked cherry and began to shimmy up the trunk, aiming for the sheltering branches, several body lengths above his head. Hobgoblins may not be able to climb as well as goblins, but they can climb well, nonetheless.

He was halfway up the tree when he heard the voice below him. He looked down to see a man with bow raised, and arrow nocked. He attempted to circle the tree, putting it between himself and the archer, as he climbed, but the man simply circled the tree with him. The forest was too open here to hinder the man's movements. The man said something that Shaggat could not understand, so he continued to scramble around the trunk with the archer following.

"I can play this game all day," Harm said as he followed the hobgoblin around the tree.

"We would rather take you alive, but I'll kill you if need be."

He let fly an arrow, hitting just above the hobgoblin's head, immediately nocking another arrow. The creature began slowly descending, looking in all directions, likely for an escape route.

When it came within a length of the ground, seeming poised to jump, Barathol burst from behind a stand of young trees, leapt to grab a leg, pulling the hobgoblin to the mossy ground, and climbing atop the struggling creature. It kicked and scratched at him with its claw-like nails, snarling like a beast while its nails slid harmlessly over boiled leather and rings of blackened steel.

Barathol snatched the dagger from its belt and tossed it aside, careful to keep his face out of range of the claws. He carried no blades himself, planning already to wrestle the hobgoblin into submission, and soon flipped the small but strong opponent onto its front. He used the advantage of his size and weight to immobilize the creature and laced his gloved and mailed forearm under its chin.

He set the chokehold, closing off the windpipe and blood flow, waiting for his opponent to cease moving, and then holding a moment longer before releasing his grip. Careful to maintain control, he sat up, looked for the rise and fall of its chest, to assure it was still alive, and said to Harm, "Bring the rope, and let's bind up the little stinker. Get his ankles first, just in case he comes to."

"Right away, Sir," Harm replied, unhitching a coil of rope from his belt and leaning the bow against the tree. He knelt to tie the hobgoblin's ankles together and then drew his knife to cut the rope. "I hate to cut this, but I didn't bring any short lengths." Cutting it, he moved to the front and bound the creature's wrists, leaving a length to fasten around the hobgoblin's waist.

Only then did Barathol get up from the captive and helped complete the bindings.

"Gag him with the rope. I don't need him biting me or the horse if he comes to."

Harm gagged the hobgoblin as Barathol went to retrieve his weapons from behind the trees. He snatched the dagger sheath from the creature's belt and moved to retrieve the king's dagger.

"He had the dagger, all right," he commented, sheathing it and tucking it into his own belt.

Barathol returned, wearing his sword belt and carrying his glaive now. He stuck the glaive's butt spike into the ground and picked up the trussed hobgoblin, slinging it over a shoulder. Grabbing the glaive, he headed to where they hitched the horses, Harm following behind.

This one was some sort of leader to the hobgoblins and trolls. He was going back with them to Arundell, where they could pry any useful information out of him.

There was no sign of Aleron, so he might have escaped, or he was dead somewhere in the forest. Maybe this creature understood some Sudean and would have answers, but that would have to wait until it woke up.

Barathol flung the hobgoblin over the back of his saddle and said, "Harm, tie him off nice and snug-like. I want to go back and scout that clearing for any sign of Aleron. The moss is pretty delicate. It should be easy enough to track anyone through there."

He walked back to the cherry and backtracked the hobgoblin from that point. As he expected, the passing footprints were easily visible in the moist mossy earth, despite the bare feet of the one who left them. The tracks became more difficult to follow, but still discernible, when he entered the clearing. At the center of the clearing, he came upon a second set of tracks, along with the first. He could easily make out the imprint of a boot heel, here and there.

Following the tracks back, he saw that there were only the two sets of footprints and they led to the center of the clearing, with no sign of struggle or of the booted feet doubling back on the trail. Barathol returned to the spot where he found the booted prints to examine the area more closely. There, he noticed the booted prints veered slightly off the path of the barefoot prints, before ending suddenly.

It was then that he noticed what could have been the faint imprints of yet a third set of tracks. He circled the area, in a slowly widening spiral, but found no sign of what could be Aleron's footprints anywhere but where they accompanied the hobgoblin's trail. He did come across more traces of the third set, seeming to lead to a different spot on the edge of the clearing than the hobgoblin's prints.

He followed these back to the edge of the clearing, where they also ended suddenly.

Returning to the horses, he said to Harm, "Aleron was here, back in the clearing. I found his tracks."

"Was here?" Harm replied, the question obvious in his tone. "Where is the king now?"

"I don't know. His tracks just ended. They were there with the hobgoblin's tracks, and then they just veered off and ended. I found a third set of tracks that led from that spot to a place on the edge of the clearing, where they just ended too. I can't make any sense of it."

"Magic?" Harm offered.

"That's the only thing that makes any sense to me, unless something big enough to carry him flew off with him, but there's the third set of tracks too."

"Have you ever heard of anyone disappearing into thin air? I never heard of wizards doing that in any of the stories I know."

"Not from a wizard, but I have seen it done. Al couldn't do that sort of thing, and he could do some crazy things. What I saw was an aelient just step in and out of an opening in the air."

"You saw an aelient? I thought those were just some sort of bedtime tale, for children, to keep them from wandering the woods by themselves."

"They are real," Barathol assured him. "We met one by the name of Iudhael, back on the Capar Plateau. He stepped right out of an old stone wall and healed Ellie from a blow to the head that she got from a half-troll we ran amok with. Then he healed Al for an arrow wound and my cracked ribs before he walked straight through the wall again."

"Do you think one of them took him?"

"I can't think of anything else that it could be, and where they go, we have no way to follow. I think we need to get back to the others."

"Which side of the river?"

"We'll cross the bridge and take the road. That will be faster, and I saw no sign of Al going back the way he came. Let's saddle up."

Mounted, Barathol's mount laden with an extra body, they made their way at an easy pace south to the bridge. Neither man spoke much, their disappointment in not finding Aleron obvious in their demeanors.

Chapter 24

Carpathday, Day 16, Ice Moon, 8765 Sudean Calendar

"Poor boy, you look all a mess," Jacanda observed. "Turn around, please." Aleron complied, hesitantly. A fine thread of red power sliced through the blood and sweat-soaked rope holding his wrists. The first thing he did, once the ropes fell away and his hands were free, was to lace his fly before turning back to Jacanda, inspecting his raw, bloodied wrists as he did.

"It's unfortunate that you were injured in coming to me, but I suppose Shaggat had little choice. Two dozen should have been a sufficient force to subdue your group and take you, but alas, the training of our forces has been lax in the absence of the Master, all these millennia."

Aleron gave her no reply, only looking at her warily and taking in his surroundings. Everything around was built of polished white marble, from the flagstones on which he stood to the tall columns, supporting second and third stories, providing a covered retreat from the open courtyard. The courtyard opened out to a panoramic view of a wide forested valley, the thread of a river glittering like silver below. He appeared to be on a high ridge, overlooking a tropical landscape.

The central jungle, perhaps? He guessed.

"Give me your hands, Grandson," she instructed him, and once again, he felt some sort of compulsion to obey.

He held out his hands, and she stepped forward to take his into her own.

"I am less practiced in this form than others, but I should be able to mend the mild injuries you have sustained."

Aleron thought he could make out a faint glow of yellow in her hands, but he could not see the threads of power as he once had. The chafed wounds at his wrists knitted into new skin, and he felt his raw, blistered feet mend as well. Soon, all of his aches and pains receded to nothingness.

"There now, doesn't that feel better?

You must have some questions, my boy. Are you not curious about this place?"

"I would like to know where I am, and that is all," Aleron replied curtly. "Is this the central jungle?"

"In a way, yes, but no, at the same time. What you see in the distance is the jungle, but this palace does not exist in your world. This place is an offshoot of the world of dreams, subject to my will and open to me alone. It is a refuge of sorts."

"This is the world of dreams, and I'm here, in my body, not just my mind? I assume that I cannot walk off into the jungle, though I can see it right there before me. Is there some sort of a wall?"

"This is a bubble, so to speak, superimposed upon your waking world. If you were to walk away, you would find yourself walking right back to this place. You may wander freely, but you will always come back here, Aleron.

I can enter and leave, at will, but for mortals, like yourself, I must bring you here. We are not visible to those on the outside. Anyone walking this ridge simply strolls through this spot, seeing nothing but forest."

"How did you come to build this place?" Aleron inquired, his curiosity piqued, despite the animosity he felt for this being. She may have healed his wounds from captivity, but she was the one responsible for that captivity.

"I simply imagined it, Aleron, and it became so. The magic you know is not needed here in the dream world. I know that you have walked this realm in your sleep. Know you, that one can control and shape the world of dreams to one's liking. Anyone capable of walking this realm has that ability, regardless of any magical talent they may possess."

"Everyone dreams, do they not?"

"Yes, boy, but most dream only in their own heads. Only a very few mortals ever enter the dream realm itself and experience true dreams. Most have no idea that they are anywhere but their own dreams and are unintentionally reshaping the dream world around them. Those who do realize what they do can create pockets like this one, but only the aelient can bring our physical bodies into this realm.

You, Grandson, are one of those whose spirit readily enters, and I wager you have seen events from the past, as well as things that may yet come to pass. Am I correct?"

Aleron declined to comment, and she continued. "I know that I am right, for I have seen you there. You must have training, so you may control your gift and avoid the dangers of that realm. Here I am in control, but out in the dream world, the dreams of others may swallow you. If your spirit fails to return from the world of dreams, your body will wither and die."

"It occurs to me," Aleron said, "that if you can will anything you wish in this place, you could have willed my wounds to heal. Why did you use yellow magic to heal me?"

"A very good question, boy, Jacanda replied.

"The problem with the dream world is that things made from will here do not persist in the waking world. Time does not flow here, as it does in the waking world, either. If I healed your wounds by my will, when you returned to your world, they would return with you.

Now, I could will you clean, but I believe you could use a real bath."

She clapped her hands together, and two attendants appeared from behind the columns. He turned to face them, and they stopped before him, eyes lowered.

"Who are they?" Aleron asked. He was beyond worrying that Jacanda meant him any immediate harm, but he could only guess as to her ultimate intentions. The attendants were a pair of small, dark-skinned young women, clad in diaphanous white silk that concealed very little of what lay beneath. They looked Kolixtlani, but smaller and darker than usual.

"The girls are gifts, from my worshippers in the surrounding lands. I accept only the most beautiful of their young to my service. With me, they will never grow old, fade, or die.

Isha here," she pointed to the one on Aleron's left, "came to me over three hundred years ago by your reckoning on the outside, and Liril has been with me for over one hundred years. They know Sudean and will assist you with any needs you may have. I will see you after you are properly cleaned, dressed, and rested."

"Today, or tomorrow, Lady?" Aleron asked.

"I suppose it will seem like tomorrow to you," she replied, "and you must learn to call me Grandmother."

She turned from him and strolled into the columns, disappearing into her palace, leaving Aleron alone with the attendants.

"Come with us, My Lord," the one he thought he remembered as Isha said, turning in unison with the other and walking to the south wing. Aleron had little choice but to follow, or be left standing by himself.

He followed behind the women, trying not to look down at their shapely figures, barely concealed by the sheer silk of their gowns. Fortunately, their straight black hair hung well below their waists, so he found them less distracting if he hung back a bit.

Passing between the columns, he looked up to see a ceiling of solid marble slabs, ten feet wide and fifteen deep, supported at the outside corners by the massive pillars. From the courtyard, he saw they were at least two feet thick.

The women opened a set of great gilded doors, tall and wide enough to drive a covered cart through, motioning Aleron to enter ahead of them. The doors opened into a spacious hallway lined with golden sconces that burned with an unnaturally clean white flame. There appeared to be an intersection with another corridor ahead. He could see several doorways, all gilded as the entry doors were. The attendants closed the doors behind him and proceeded to lead him down the intersecting corridor to the left.

Entering the baths, Aleron spied three large steaming rectangular pools, set into the floor, with steps leading downward, into the water. Aleron's face went beet-red at the sight of a half-dozen more dark-skinned maidens bathing in the pools, or sitting along the edges, dangling their feet, none of them wearing a stitch of clothing. He attempted to look every place but the pools, but it was difficult to do that and follow his guides at the same time.

Isha announced, "This is our honored guest, Lord Aleron, grandson to the Mistress Jacanda."

He received a hail of greetings as Isha and Liril untied the drawstring cords that held their robes at the collar and let them drop over their shoulders, wiggling their hips free of the silk.

"We must disrobe you now, My Lord Aleron," Liril stated.

When Aleron failed to make eye contact, instead staring over the top of her head, she asked, "Does our appearance displease you so that you cannot bear to look upon us?"

"It is said that elves and Sudean men hate the very sight of the forest people, Liril, and he is both," Isha stated, with a hint of contempt in her tone. Gone was the subservient air she held in the presence of her mistress.

He looked down far enough to meet Liril's eyes, the irises such a dark brown as to be nearly black, concealing the pupils, set in a near-perfect face and framed by a cascade of jet-black hair. He noted in his peripheral vision that all eyes in the room were upon him.

"It is not that," he stated, ashamedly. "You are all so very beautiful, and I surely do not hate the very sight of you.

It is just not the custom of my people for men and women to be naked in the presence of one another. I am simply embarrassed."

"There is no need to be embarrassed, Lord Aleron," Liril stated. "We are the ones naked, and we are not embarrassed of our bodies."

Aleron blushed again at the reminder, and the women occupying the room returned to their conversations in a language Aleron didn't recognize, but assumed was of the central jungle.

Isha continued, "If you wish to be embarrassed for your own body, you will have that opportunity shortly. We must get you out of these filthy clothes and scrub you down. You smell worse than a wet dog. Now sit down, so we can get those boots off you."

He sat upon a bench, as she directed, and she pulled his boots off, while Liril began on the laces of his shirt. After Liril pulled the shirt over his head, he stood, barefoot and clad in only breeches. Isha went to work on those laces and in a moment, he stood there as naked as the rest of them.

"Now you can be embarrassed, My Lord. Please follow us."

He followed the women, stepping down into the steaming water. He closed his eyes and plunged his head under, came back up, and slicked back his hair.

The women began working him over with soap and rough sponges that looked made from some sort of large, dried seedpod. He noticed the soapy water flowing to an outlet at one end of the pool, fresh hot water replacing it from behind him. "Crouch down so that we can wash your hair," Isha instructed him. After half a bell of scrubbing, with an embarrassing period of having to climb steps for them to scrub his lower half, they allowed him to lounge upon a submerged bench, soaking with water up to his chin.

Isha and Liril swam while he lounged, and he was becoming used to the scenery. It seemed as many women entered, disrobing to bathe, as those who dressed and departed.

"How is it that you know my language and speak it so well?" Aleron inquired of his companions.

Isha answered him, saying, "Our mistress gifts us with language when we come into her service, and we practice them among ourselves. New girls may speak only one language at a time until they master the accent and move through all the languages, until their training is completed.

We must be prepared to serve whatever guests our mistress brings to the house."

"You learn all the languages?"

"Yes, we learn Kolixtlani Adari and Thallasian first, followed by Arkan, which is similar to our native tongue and that of the goblins and trolls. Then we learn Elvish, Sudean, Coptian, Castian, Dwarvish, Chuan, Talik, Chebek, and several other tongues, spoken by a very few, like the seal hunters of the north. Chuan is the most difficult to get right, out of all of them."

"So, you all learn every language spoken on Aertu?"

"Not so much learn the language, as learn how to speak it. Mistress Jacanda places complete knowledge of each tongue in our minds. We simply learn how to form the words properly."

"That's amazing, nonetheless, to know every language. Does your mistress have many guests?"

"Only occasionally do we have guests," Liril answered this time, "usually very important people in their own lands. We see to their every need during their stay with us."

She emphasized the word "every," leveling her gaze on him, with an expression both mischievous and hungry at the same time.

Aleron found himself blushing again, and she giggled at his discomfort. He had to remember that, due to the nature of this place, these seemingly young women were old and experienced beyond their outward appearance.

"What do you do here to pass the time, when there are no guests or when your mistress is away?"

"We do this, practice speaking in other tongues, read, gather food from the gardens and orchards, and other things our mistress requires of us. If she ever leaves us, I am not aware of it."

Aleron was beginning to suspect something about this bubble of the dream world and how it functioned. He asked again whether Jacanda never left, and both women affirmed this fact to him, saying she was always in residence.

He knew that Hadaras and Quiana lived together for over thirty years, and he believed in his gut that Jacanda spoke true, about her and Quiana being one and the same. If true, time must stop here whenever Jacanda departs for the world outside. The fact that no one aged in this place pointed to time not being of the same nature as on the outside.

"Isha, how long have you been here?"

"By my reckoning, I should be a grandmother, five or six times over, but here I am, a young woman still. This is a wonderful place to live. No bad weather ever touches us; the gardens and orchards bear year-round, never needing tending. They just bear on their own."

"Are you the eldest here, Isha?"

"Yes, but it was not always so. I was not the first of my mistress' servants. There were many before me."

"No one ages here. Where did the others go?"

"Most women eventually tire of the long life here and wish to return to the land of our people, grow old, and pass. They begin to miss never having a husband and family. Our mistress graciously returns those to our people to live out their lives.

I came to this place after one such returned to our village and chose me as a suitable replacement. Those who return from Mistress Jacanda's service hold great standing among our people, and never want for anything for the remainder of their lives."

"Your mistress sounds very kind and generous. At first, I believed you were slaves of some sort."

"Oh no, Lord Aleron, not slaves at all," Liril interjected.

"It is a great honor to be chosen for service to Mistress Jacanda. All who are here came willingly, and we can return to our people whenever we wish. All she requires is a replacement."

She lounged across the pool from him with her arms across the ledge to keep her head above the water, occasionally pushing herself higher to afford him a better view. Aleron pointedly maintained eye contact at those points, but he couldn't help his peripheral vision, and Liril knew it.

After the bath and a light meal, dressed in fresh silk breeches and shirt, with supple leather thonged sandals on his feet, he had free range to wander the palace and surrounding grounds. True to Jacanda's word, every time he walked away from the palace and into the surrounding forest, he somehow turned around and walked straight back onto the palace grounds. After a few tries, he tired of the game and returned to his rooms, finding Isha and Liril waiting for him with his supper.

"Did you have a pleasant walk, Lord Aleron?" Isha inquired as he entered. They were back in the filmy white robes and sat to either side of the table they set for him.

"Your evening meal awaits. Would you care for any entertainment after your meal? We all dance and play instruments, and many of the women are unoccupied at the moment."

"I think I will be going straight to bed after supper," Aleron replied. "I have had a long couple of days."

Liril looked pleased at his decision, and Aleron became wary as he sat down to eat.

Chapter 25

Zorekday, Day 18, Ice Moon, 8765 Sudean Calendar

Shaggat knew now that the men had no intention to kill him. They arrived midday yesterday, at the encampment of the men left behind, near the site of the ambush. A man and a woman sustained injuries in the attack, and one man and two women stayed behind to tend the wounded.

The tall, yellow-haired woman spoke a little Kolixtlani, not as well as their leader, but better than the men who captured him. He learned from her that they intended to take him to the Sudean officials in the Westland kingdom of Mittea, and perhaps all the way to Sudea itself.

His captors treated him well, not running him too hard and feeding him when they stopped to eat. He wished he thought to bind Aleron in the manner the men tied him, allowing him to eat, drink, and relieve himself, without assistance.

On the subject of their leader, Shaggat felt no qualms about telling the woman about Jacanda taking Aleron. He hoped they believed his story rather than thinking he killed the man and disposed of the body.

Just finishing their morning meal, his captors were busy breaking down the camp in preparation to move, all but the smallest of the men, the quick, yellow-haired one that Shaggat witnessed cut down a fair number of his fighters, before peeling off to protect the women. That one stayed to watch over him.

He and the wounded woman had some sort of attachment; he was certain of that.

The man watched Shaggat suspiciously, while the hobgoblin sat cross-legged on the ground, tied to a small tree.

Geldun watched the hobgoblin; Shaggat was what he called himself, according to Anjani. He wondered at the information the Westland woman extracted from the creature. It certainly agreed with the evidence Barathol gathered near where they caught the thing. Apparently, some dark aelient claiming to be his grandmother took him through a gateway to somewhere else.

Jacanda was not a name familiar to him. He couldn't remember the names Aleron gave for his grandparents, aside from Hadaras, but he was sure none of them was that. It was difficult to surprise him about his old friend, however, especially after learning that he was king and Hadaras was really Goromir, from the old stories.

Why shouldn't his grandmother be some wood spirit too? he asked himself. *His cousin Jessie is one of them.*

Geldun was not aware of Jessamine's true relationship with Hadaras. He only knew her as Aleron's cousin, who he only recently learned was aelient. He saw Iudhael walk through an old stone wall, into what looked like a different world, so the hobgoblin's story was plausible to him. He and Barathol were witnessing things they never would have believed, just a year ago.

It looked like the camp was packed, and Harm was coming to retrieve the prisoner. He untied the hobgoblin, and the two of them escorted him to the horses. Shaggat would have to walk the rest of the way to the town, but then again, so would one of the men. Barathol's horse was healing from its wound yet, unable to carry more than light baggage.

They agreed that Geldun would be the first to walk, guarding the hobgoblin afoot, with its lead rope tied off to Harm's saddle. He would have preferred riding along with Feadra to this, but the other women had her well in hand, and he would get to that when Barathol relieved him in a couple bells. The girl was healing well from the arrow wound, but she would have two nice scars to remember it by. This would be a hard day of riding for her, but he was certain she was well enough for it.

With the sun sinking low on the western horizon to their left, the line of horses and riders came to the gates of the walled town of Koln, situated at the joining of the Lesser and Greater Kanjes Rivers. A cloud of mist rose to the north, behind the town, as the waters of the Lesser Kanjes plunged five hundred feet to meet the Greater Kanjes, at the bottom of the canyon that separated Sunjib from Mittea.

Eilowyn and Barathol led the group, with Anjani, for her translating skills.

"This is Eilowyn, Queen of Sudea, and her retainers," Anjani announced in Sunjibi to the gatekeepers.

"She has been a month on the road and seeks lodging for her group, but first, she must speak to the garrison commander concerning an attack at the river.

We also have a prisoner to house, temporarily," she explained further.

"Bring Shaggat forward, please," she called back in Sudean.

Geldun rode forward, with Harm on foot, prodding the hobgoblin forward. The guards' eyes widened at the sight of the little monster. One of them yelled to the guard shack, and moments later, a young runner came out to the gate. The guard instructed the boy to bring a representative from the garrison, and more guards to escort the prisoner.

"We have two wounded in the attack, and we would like to get them settled into rooms as soon as is practical. May some of our number enter the village to get our rooms settled?"

"That won't be a problem, My Lady," the lead guard replied, *"but the goblin stays outside, for now."*

"Thank you Sir and you may call me Anjani; my family is common," she said, with a warm smile, answered in kind, by the guard.

"He says we may bring our wounded people through, to get settled in the rooms, while we wait for the garrison with the prisoner.

"Gel, why don't you give the stinker to me?" Barathol offered. "We have the guards here, and you and Harm can go settle Elrud and your girl in. I'll watch the hobgoblin and stay with Eilowyn and Anjani."

"But shouldn't the smartest one stay with Ellie?" Geldun quipped.

"I suppose," Barathol conceded, scratching at his beard, with a thoughtful expression.

"That would be a good idea, but I really think Harm should go with you. I've got Anji, in any case," he finished, grinning.

"Fine, be that way," Geldun answered, with feigned affront in his voice, but grinning all the same.

"I'll go get Feadra settled in her bed. She's exhausted."

"The staff of the Pipe and Mug speak passable Sudean," Anjani informed them.

"It caters to foreign merchants and dignitaries, so you won't find a better place to stay in Koln.

"Follow this street one block down and then left, for two blocks. The sign is in Sudean, Mittean, and Sunjibi, so you should not have any trouble finding it."

"Thanks, Anji," Geldun replied as he handed Shaggat's leash over to Barathol, who tied it to the pommel of his own saddle, Harm covering the transfer, with his sword drawn.

"Anji, tell the archers on the wall to shoot him if he tries to run."

Barathol nodded in agreement.

Anjani relayed the message to the Sunjibis and then said, in Kolixtlani, *"Shaggat, the men on the wall will shoot you if you try to escape."*

"I would expect nothing different," Shaggat replied, smiling, revealing his long canine teeth.

Geldun, Feadra, and Elrud proceeded through the gate, on horseback, with Harm on foot, leading the packhorses. In short order, they found the inn.

"Wait here a moment, while I go speak with the publicans," Geldun instructed, handing his reins off to Harm, before dismounting.

He had a bag of coin from Eilowyn to use for their lodging. He entered the inn, and after several long moments returned with two stable boys and a large westman to help with the baggage.

Geldun helped Elrud and Feadra dismount and led them to the door, while Harm and the men hitched the animals to the railing before going to work on the baggage.

Geldun returned, after seating the two injured companions in the common room, and pressed a silver coin each, into the palms of the two stable boys. Their eyes lit up at the generous tip, and they bent to the work with increased vigor.

He handed a gold piece to the older westman and asked, "Am I right in assuming that our saddles and camp gear can be safely stored at the stables?"

"Of course ye may, Me Lord," the stocky westman replied.

"We be havin' a good stout shed for that there purpose." He turned to the boys and instructed them on where they would store everything, before reaching down and slinging the two heaviest bags onto his shoulders and leading them into the building.

Harm and Geldun followed, with two more bags each, made their way up the stairs and down the hallway, to the set of rooms they rented.

Eilowyn wished for adjoining rooms, and they had coin aplenty, so Geldun rented them a dignitary's suite, much like the rooms they rented in Sunj, but larger, each bedroom having three beds.

The larger bedroom had a double bed, intended for a married couple, with single beds for two retainers or children.

The common area was spacious, with a couch, several comfortable chairs, and an area to heat water for tea.

"Ye say that ye be havin' four men in ye party, so I'll be bringin' a cot up for the extra one."

"That won't be necessary, Sir," Geldun informed him.

"One of us will stand guard, so we won't need a seventh bed."

"Suit yeself, Me Lord. I'll be getting right back with the last of ye bags," he said, as he left the room.

Harm followed, and they soon returned with the rest of the baggage. The westman handed him keys to the room, and, making his goodbyes, left them to arrange the bags.

"Let's get down to the common room and see what the others are up to," Geldun suggested, after they situated the bags in the rooms.

Eilowyn saw a small contingent of armed westmen approaching the gate, the foremost of them, with three red plumes sticking up from his helm and a bright red cape, gracing his shoulders. "Who is that?" she asked Anjani.

"It looks like the garrison commander himself will grace us with his presence," she answered. The gate guards snapped to attention and saluted when their commander approached.

"Queen Eilowyn," the officer greeted her in barely accented Sudean.

"I apologize for keeping you waiting. The messenger said you have important news for me and a rather unusual prisoner."

He looked over at the hobgoblin on the end of the lead Barathol held. He was tall for a westman, with the full stockiness of his race, making him a truly massive figure, on par with Barathol. His curly blond hair hung below the edges of his helm, and he kept his brownish beard trimmed neat and close.

"We were led to believe that the king would arrive with you, My Queen."

"King Aleron was abducted by a force led by that one," she informed him, pointing at Shaggat.

Captain Barathol and one of his men killed the rest of the party and captured their leader here, but the hobgoblin had already handed my husband over to his leader.

There are other things that we should discuss, as well, in a less public forum, if you do not mind, Commander...?"

"Delfane, My Queen," he said, in answer to her questioning tone.

"Of course, we will escort you to the garrison and get this beast into the stockade.

Open the gate for our guests," he ordered, and the gatekeepers hopped to obey.

"Were there not four more in your party?" he inquired, as they filed through the gate.

"Yes, Commander Delfane, they proceeded to the inn to arrange our lodging. Two of our party were wounded in the attack, and we wished to get them rest as soon as possible."

"Are their wounds serious? I could send a physician to see them if you wish."

"Perhaps for the marine, with a broken leg, in case it is not set properly. My handmaiden is recovering well from an arrow wound. I do not think she requires further attention. Our medic, Captain Geldun, is very capable; otherwise, she might have died."

"That is good news," Delfane replied. "I will send our physician over in the morning. Will you be staying with us long?"

"A few days, I think, we need to make our way to the coast and return to Sudea, at the earliest opportunity."

Delfane took Eilowyn's reins in hand, taking the lead, with Anjani and Barathol behind. The soldiers formed a guard around the three riders, the hobgoblin, and their commander, as they started back to the garrison.

Passersby gawked at the procession; most recognized the commander, but the hobgoblin was the one garnering the most attention.

They arrived at the blockhouse, hitched the horses, and entered, while the guards split off to inter the prisoner in the stockade.

They built this one along the same lines as the one in Sunj; Sunjibis build all their public buildings along fairly standard lines.

In Delfane's office, they set to explaining the events at the bridge and the day after.

"The village was completely empty?" he asked Barathol to verify, after he explained what they found at the next river crossing, to the south.

"Aside from the dead, yes," Barathol answered.

"There weren't many of them either, so I assume they took the bulk of the citizens away alive. There were charred bones in the fire pits as well, I'm sorry to report."

"That sounds about right for hobgoblins and trolls," the commander commented.

"They take captives for slaves and eat the dead. We have dealt with their incursions these last few years, but this is much further north than we have seen. If they made it downriver with a force large enough to take a village of four hundred, this is by far the largest incursion yet.

I will send reconnaissance upriver to assess the extent of the damage, but I fear that I already know what I will find.

So, you captured the hobgoblin near the village; why did you take him, rather than kill him?"

"We determined him leader of the group that attacked us, and we wanted to find out what he did with Aleron, mostly," Barathol replied, "but also, he might have useful information on organization and numbers."

"Were you able to garner any information from the beast?"

"Some, Anjani was able to speak with him. He wasn't very forthcoming with his troop numbers, but he must have had a large force to take that village away like that. His story about Aleron's whereabouts matched what I saw at the capture site. I think Anjani could tell you more."

"You speak the black tongue?" Delfane directed to Anjani.

"No, My Lord, the hobgoblin speaks Kolixtlani, probably better than I do. He refused to answer any questions on how many hobgoblins and trolls are in the Iron Hills.

With the king, he was very forthcoming. I feel that he believes he has nothing to lose in giving that information. He claims to have undertaken the expedition at the command of a dark aelient and that he handed the king over to that same person."

"A dark aelient, like from a bedtime story? That is difficult to believe."

"Shaggat, the hobgoblin that is, described an elvish lady, who wields red magic and travels through holes in the air. He claimed she took Aleron through one such hole."

"I have met two aelient," Barathol interjected, "so I can say for certain that they are not just stories and one of them traveled in the same fashion, through some sort of magical gateway."

"I see," Delfane answered, pondering for a moment before speaking again.

"I have no reason to disbelieve you, Captain Barathol. What evidence did you uncover at the site where you captured the hobgoblin, and what do you intend to do with the creature?"

"I found the tracks of a booted man, along with the hobgoblin's footprints. They veered off suddenly and just ended, while Shaggat's tracks continued to where we found him. There was a third set of tracks that began from nothing and ended at the same spot that Aleron's prints stopped. They were small and faint, like you might expect from a small woman.

As for the hobgoblin, we want to bring him to our consulate in Mich, to question him further, and possibly to Arundell."

"That does point to the veracity of the creature's story," the Sunjibi commander concluded.

"He has little to lose giving you that information if his mission is complete.

I would appreciate the opportunity to question him myself before you continue on your journey. I believe time may be short, to counter another attack from the hills, and we have use for every bit of intelligence we can get our hands on."

"There won't be any torture, will there?" Eilowyn demanded.

"I cannot abide torture, even for one such as him."

"Fear not, My Queen; torture does little but force the recipient to confess to precisely what the torturer wishes to hear. We have better methods than that now. Certain drugs make the tongue much more pliant, and the right wording of a question, combined with the drugs, will extract the truth over the lies.

Your interpreter could learn the method of wording the questions quite easily, and I'm afraid we would need her assistance, as none of my staff is fluent in Kolixtlani."

"I can agree to that," Eilowyn stated.

"Are you interested in assisting, Anjani?"

"I am at your service, My Queen, and as a loyal subject of Sunjib, it is my duty to assist."

"Excellent," Delfane exclaimed.

"Might we get started by the ninth bell tomorrow morning?"

"That will be fine, My Lord," Anjani agreed.

"I believed we have covered enough for one evening, and I am sure that you would all like to get some rest, in a real bed," the commander stated.

"Two of my men will escort you to your lodgings." He rose to escort them out, and they all followed suit. Outside the blockhouse, they exchanged courtesies before Eilowyn's party, accompanied by two stout guardsmen, were on their way to the inn.

Entering the common room, their companions greeted them with raised mugs from a large rectangular table of polished oak.

Barathol saw that Geldun was nearly through his mug and wondered if that was his friend's first, or second, or third, even.

"How many is that, Gel?" he inquired.

"It's only my second, Barry, if you're worried about the guard shifts. I've been nursing them along, waiting for you to get here to catch up.

Have a seat, everyone. The white flagon is wine, and the brown one is beer, possibly the best I've ever had on my lips. You'll have to ask Fea about the wine. There's bread and butter on the table, and a smoked brisket with roasted parsnips waiting on the warming hearth, so sit yourselves down; I'm starving."

The remaining companions sat at the table, snagged bread, and poured drinks, as a serving boy carried a steaming platter of food to the table.

Things are looking up, Barathol thought as he carved off chunks of meat for everyone.

Chapter 26

Zorekday, Day 12, Allfather's Moon, 8766 Sudean Calendar

Eilowyn stood upon the docks of Mich, watching the sailors haul their baggage up the gangplank of the Sudean carrack, with Feadra, Harm, and the two Sunjibi guardsmen that accompanied them from Koln.

Anjani, Geldun, and Barathol were off selling the horses and should return within a bell.

The crew already interred Shaggat in the brig. He was one of the reasons they chose a warship, rather than a more comfortable merchant-class ship. Aside from the clear advantage of greater speed, it had a solid brig, with marines guarding it.

Delfane's method of using drugs for questioning had proven fruitful, with the hobgoblin revealing the presence of a force, ten thousand strong, poised for invasion on Sunjib's southern border.

Apparently, Shaggat was their overall leader, but another would likely replace him when he failed to return from his mission to capture Aleron.

They agreed that Anjani should stay on, as she was the only one with a reasonable grasp of Kolixtlani, and she had a working relationship with the hobgoblin.

Delfane sent messages, by carrier pigeon, to Sunj and several other garrisons, advising them of the situation in the Iron Hills. He expected the king to order a counterattack, to disperse the forces gathering against them.

Eilowyn also sent a message for her uncle, Consul Damian, informing him that Anjani, Feadra, Elrud, and Harm were well and had entered into her service.

"It looks like things are well in hand here, My Queen," Harm stated. He had already said his goodbyes to the three off at the horse market.

"May I have your leave to depart?"

His plan was to return to Koln, pick up Elrud, whose leg should have mended by then, and return to catch a later ship.

Both men, promoted by Barathol and Geldun, would serve as aides to the new captains in their positions as advisors to the king, provided they ever found said king.

"Certainly, you may, Master Sergeant Harm," she replied.

"We should be perfectly safe here, with all these sailors and marines. I look forward to seeing you and Master Sergeant Elrud in Arundell when you return."

"And I you, My Queen," he replied, bowing deeply.

"Lady Feadra," he addressed her, with a shallow bow, "fare thee well."

Both women answered with solemn nods before Harm turned on his heel and headed for the end of the dock, the Sunjibi guardsmen closing in behind him.

Geldun, Barathol, and Anjani returned from the market, Geldun with a fat bag of coin fastened to his belt.

"We got good prices on the horses," Geldun reported, "four gold pieces for the saddle horses, five for Barathol's and two gold each, for the pack animals, twenty-seven gold, overall."

"That's good news, Captain Geldun. Hold onto that, and we will divide up the money after we get underway. I believe it's time for us to board."

She turned and headed for the gangplank, the sailors who had just erected the rope railings for the queen's benefit standing at attention to either side. She led the way up the plank, followed by Feadra, Anjani, Geldun, and Barathol bringing up the rear. The sailors gathered the railings and posts as the party ascended.

The ship's captain, Aelfied, waited at the top of the gangplank.

"My Queen, it is a great honor to have you aboard," he announced, bowing low.

"May I escort you to your cabin, Your Grace, and would you be pleased to dine at my table tonight?"

She returned the bow with a respectful nod.

"Both would be wonderful, Captain Aelfied. I would see my party housed and look forward to speaking with you over dinner."

The captain led the way to a set of top deck cabins at the stern, under the aft castle, the location of his own quarters. Beside the captain and first mate's cabin was a large cabin, reserved for important passengers.

"Will this suffice for your needs and those of your ladies, Your Grace?" he asked, as he opened the door to a sumptuously furnished cabin, with a double bed, two single beds, and a separate alcove for one's ablutions and other business.

"If not, may I offer my own cabin? I would only require a few moments to move my things."

"This will be more than adequate, Captain Aelfied. Where will my two captains be staying?"

"There are open billets with my officers, Your Grace, one deck below.

If you lads know your way about a carrack, you'll find your bags down there, and I'll be expecting you at my table as well."

"Yes, Sir," Geldun replied, "We know our way about a carrack. What time should we arrive for supper, Sir?"

"Seventh bell after noon," he replied. "Now, if you would excuse me, Your Grace, I must see us off."

"You are excused, Captain, and thank you for your hospitality."

"Think nothing of it, My Queen," he answered, flourishing a bow, as he departed.

It should be noted that Geldun's and Barathol's deference to the ship's captain was due to a navy captain's rank being the equivalent to that of a marine colonel, as well as to his supreme authority by Sudean law over all things onboard when underway, exceeding that of even the king and queen.

Geldun and Barathol set to helping the women secure their things in the cabin. Spacious and well-appointed for a ship, with everything secured to the floor or stowed in cabinets with stout doors and latches.

"Make sure you always put things away when you finish with them, and make sure you latch the doors and drawers," Barathol instructed.

"If we hit rough seas, a flying bottle could kill you."

"Understood, Barry," Eilowyn replied, "I've been at sea a few times, have you, Ladies?"

"I was so little, I hardly remember leaving Arundell," Feadra replied, while Anjani shook her head to indicate that she had not.

"It's very sound advice," Eilowyn continued.

"I once received a black eye from a hairbrush I'd forgotten on top of my trunk. I was oh so presentable when we arrived at the Castian court," she finished, with a giggle.

After the men departed, she sat upon the bed, her thoughts turning morose. *Aleron, where are you? You have to come back to me and come back to me, as you were.*

She lived in fear of her husband returning with the dark taint of the Adversary upon him.

Feadra noticed her change of mood and sat upon the bed, beside Eilowyn, while Anjani lay flat across her bed, eyes closed and boots dangling over the edge.

She placed a hand on Eilowyn's shoulder and asked, "Thinking about Aleron?"

"Yes, Fea, I just hope he's alright."

"He will come back to you, Ellie. He has to," she told her, in an attempt to comfort.

"He's smart and resourceful. He'll find a way to escape."

"I hope so, Fea, I certainly hope so."

✳✳✳

Jacanda lounged in her sitting room upon a red upholstered divan, facing Aleron, who sat upright in an identical seat opposite her. She was once again attempting to convince him of the merits of the Adversary's plans for Aertu.

"Surely you see the benefit of a world without injustice. Every man is equal in the eyes of my father, and none would seek to gain advantage over another. The need to choose between right and wrong would no longer exist, and all would live in harmony."

"What would happen if one were to try to do wrong to another or try to gain advantage over another?" he asked, not for the first time.

"My father will take the inclination to do wrong from the hearts of all."

"You mean we will all be slaves, without the free will to choose between right and wrong. What is life, without the freedom to make choices?"

He estimated that he had spent about a month in Jacanda's palace. Every evening, he fended off the advances of Liril and Isha, only to find them snuggled in next to him each morning. He made sure to sleep in his short breeches, with the drawstring knotted tightly, which was an inconvenience first thing in the morning.

They knew he was married, but they didn't seem to care, saying that his wife did not exist in this place, just as he ceased to exist in the waking world.

"You still refuse to understand, but you will eventually. My father will impress the truth upon you, if all else fails, when you meet him."

Aleron dreaded meeting his great-grandfather. He was now convinced that Jacanda was indeed his grandmother. She had a strange power over him that he could not understand.

She explained it as a natural compulsion, stemming from their shared blood.

"Today, we will focus our efforts on something else," she continued.

"We will attempt to remove the blockage you erected in your mind. You must be able to wield your powers if you are to be any use to our cause.

First, you must place these upon your wrists." She leaned forward and held out two silver bracelets.

"I wouldn't want you to attempt something unwise when your ability is restored."

One bracelet, studded with blue quartz, and the other with bloodstone, Aleron knew them to be power traps. Wearing them, he would be unable to wield red or blue and, by inference, any combinations requiring them, to include white. He took them from her, clasping one and then the other upon his wrists, an idea forming in his mind.

"Why would you expect me to do something foolish, grandmother?" he asked, innocently.

The first thought was simply to kill her. If she even knew he could wield green and yellow, she must not suspect he could use them as a weapon, but a powerful bolt of yellow can blast a hole as well as blue.

He discarded this plan, for fear of what Jacanda's death might bring to pass in this world of her making. If she died, one of two things would most likely occur: either time here would stop, essentially trapping him here for eternity, or her bubble would cease to exist.

If the second were to occur, Aleron feared that he and all the women would also cease to exist. It was too risky to hope that they would all be deposited on this ridge in the waking world.

"You are who you are," Jacanda replied, wryly, "and you are definitely your grandfather's spawn.

He was rash and impulsive for an elf, even at nine thousand years of age. You would think that such time would temper rashness and impatience, but to him it was as nothing."

"I never knew him as such. I believe he just thinks faster than anyone else, elves included."

"There is some merit to that belief, Grandson," she conceded, rising up from the divan. "Now, I need you to lie back and relax. You must freely allow me into your mind, and I will attempt to dismantle the wall you have erected there."

Aleron did as she instructed, lying flat upon the cushion. She moved behind him, placing her hands on either side of his head.

He felt her enter his mind, feeling between the layers, and he followed along. He sensed some amusement, on her part, at some of the thoughts that flowed to the surface, and he feared that she might uncover his secrets.

He attempted to banish the thoughts recently brewing, focusing instead on thoughts of the nude women in his bed that morning, which led to thoughts of Eilowyn, and how angry she would be to learn he had nude women in his bed every morning. He decided he would leave that part of the story out of any retellings.

Eventually, deep within, they came upon what appeared as a mirror, reflecting back at them, and allowing no further movement.

This is where my ability lies, and I've walled it off somehow.

Yes, Grandson, you are correct, and now we must break it down.

Aleron could feel her moving, attempting to find the edges of the barrier. He followed along with her, trying to see for himself what she looked for.

It is like a sphere of polished steel, no edges to be found. You made this, Grandson, to protect yourself from something. Perhaps you have the key to dispel it.

They could not truly see the shape of the barrier if it had a shape at all. It appeared that way to the mind's eye, completely sealing off a portion of Aleron's being from the outside.

Aleron thought back to the escape from Kolixtlan. He remembered the fear as the masses of soldiers surrounded them in the palace courtyard, followed by intense rage at the ones who would harm Eilowyn and his friends. Drinking the power from Andhanimwhid, he absorbed all the red power the priests threw at him. With so much power coursing through him, both red and blue, he felt as if his mind would burn away to a cinder.

I see it now, how it built itself as I collected and focused the energy. I can find the edge now.

It wasn't so much an edge as a spot where the sphere sealed itself closed. The structure formed to shield the rest of his mind from the immense power he wielded on that day. He could now see the path it scorched through an unimportant portion of his mind, claiming it for its own. The pathway led directly to the point that allowed him to release the energy before sealing off completely.

I think you can unravel the shield from this point.

You wield red and blue together, like the aelir, Jacanda spoke in his mind, her tone both fearful and awed.

How is that possible?

I do not know; it just is, he replied, feeling her confidence resurface with the reassurance of the bracelets on his wrists.

He found the point where his unconscious mind tied off the shield and focused on it, to mark it for her.

Here it is, but I don't know the first thing of how to untie this.

I will take it from here. Just relax now and let me do the rest.

He let his mind go, trying to think of nothing, and soon felt an odd tug, not really a physical sensation but something deeper. Immediately, he felt an awareness of forces that he hadn't perceived in months, colors that he needed no eyes to see, pulsing and vibrating from the land, air, and living things nearby. The awareness grew stronger and clearer as she unraveled the shield further.

It is done; you may rise now, Grandson. She released his head and returned to her divan to sit.

"Can you feel the magic around you now?"

"Yes, Grandmother, I can see clearly again," he answered, sitting upright again.

"Thank you for healing me. Something occurred to me, and I have a question if you do not mind, Grandmother."

"Of course not, my boy, go ahead and ask." She was confident that in his gratitude, he would become more pliable to her persuasion to choose the path of truth.

"I was wondering, how is it that magic works here, if this is a separate place from the waking world?"

"This is but another level of existence from the waking world, where the force of will exerts a greater power than magic, but here is still a part of Aertu, so magic exists just as in the waking world. Do you understand now?"

"I believe I am beginning to. Thank you for all you have taught me."

"There is still much to teach you, Grandson, before you leave this place."

"Then...I am truly sorry for this."

In a flash of golden energy, the bracelets disintegrated in a shower of sparks. Aleron dared not leave the bloodstone and blue quartz intact, to sap his power from him, and a byproduct of the destruction was the release of the substantial energy trapped within the devices.

He raised a shield of blue magic around himself and drew red and green into his body.

Jacanda countered with a bolt of red, harmlessly absorbed by the shield, which he used to channel the energy to himself.

He projected a bolt of false yellow, a combination of green and red, into Jacanda before she thought to raise a shield of her own, and she collapsed upon the divan.

He dropped his shield and stepped over to the aelient-elf who was his grandmother. Her eyes were open, staring at nothing. He laid her out comfortably on the couch, placing a pillow beneath her neck, checked her for a pulse and breathing, of which there was none, and closed her eyes for her. She was not dead, yet she did not live either.

False yellow magic causes a sort of lifeless stasis that can go on indefinitely, holding the body of a living thing in precisely the same state as when the magic is applied.

Aleron's gamble had paid off. By not killing Jacanda, her bubble of the dream world continued on, as it normally did with its mistress in residence. Time did not stop, and the bubble did not disappear.

Aleron left the sitting room to explore Jacanda's quarters more fully. He had never before been past the sitting and dining rooms. He found a sumptuously appointed bedroom, as he expected, as well as additional sitting rooms, dining areas, and a luxurious private bath.

The next door he opened held what he hoped to find. It was an expansive library, thousands of books, scrolls, and tablets lined the shelves. By their appearance, many had to be centuries, even millennia old.

There, at the center of the room, stood a raised pedestal, surmounted by a polished crystal dome. He had seen this crystal in one of his dreams, years ago now. In his dream, the crystal showed him distant places, and he hoped that this one was of the same sort.

He stepped over to the pedestal and gazed into the crystal, seeing only his distorted reflection staring back at him. He focused on thoughts of home, and a vision of the farmyard swam into view. He seemed high above, but as he focused on a single spot, it zoomed into view, as if he floated just a few feet above the ground.

He thought of his grandfather, and the scene flickered to one of Hadaras, walking the gardens of the palace at Arundell.

So, I can use this to locate people, as well as see places I know from memory. Grandfather is in the capital, as well. I wonder where Cladus is.

An image materialized, of the bard playing in a common room that Aleron recognized from Arundell.

So, he's in Arundell as well. Anjani might find that interesting.

He bent his thoughts to Eilowyn, hoping that perhaps she had yet to leave the Westlands. The image that swam into focus showed that not to be the case. She stood upon the deck of a Sudean carrack, under full sail and leaving Mich.

He planned to attempt willing his way out of this place, back to a place of his choosing in the waking world. He held reservations, however, about trying to step out onto a moving ship. Most likely, he would open a hole where he saw the ship and step out over open ocean, in the wake of the ship's passage.

He thought for a moment of going straight to Arundell and waiting for Eilowyn and the others, but that could take months, provided he could figure out how to move there. Even if he did find his way out, he wasn't sure he could come back to this place again, and he didn't want to waste the trip.

Returning to Arundell would have its advantages, but he wanted to return to Eilowyn more than anything else. Another thought occurred to him. Carracks from Mich make a stopover at Wynn in the elvish colonies, and he could find a stationary spot near Wynn. He would wait for them there and bring them to Arundell if he could learn to move back and forth at will.

He tried to think of a particular place in Wynn, where he visited over five years before. There was the plaza in front of the royal library, where he spent much of his time when he was there. The vision floated into view of the courtyard, a few elves entering and leaving the library, with a scattering of others wandering the grounds. He took a good look at the scene, focusing on a quiet spot with no foot traffic, in a back garden area, and memorized every detail.

He turned away from the pedestal and imagined the spot before him, envisioning the scene opening up before him, through a hole in the air. Nothing happened. He turned back to the crystal dome and brought forth the image again, rotating his view to see it from all angles. He concentrated, envisioning himself stepping into the scene, and again, nothing happened.

Aleron sat down in an ornate mahogany armchair, with the ubiquitous red upholstery, to think.

What did she say about moving between worlds? I thought that I understood, but I guess I really didn't."

He remembered Jacanda speaking of using her personal realm as a staging point to move wherever she wished on Aertu. She told him that in the world of dreams, one had to travel great distances to move from one place to another, distances corresponding to distances on land in the waking world. One could move at great speed through the dream world if one possessed the skills, but travel still required time and effort.

She also told him that, as time did not work in the normal way in the world of dreams, the transport might seem instantaneous to those in the waking world but seem like months to the traveler. The saving grace was that nothing ages in the world of dreams any faster than if it remained in the waking world. The traveler would not seem any older for having spent what seemed to be months moving across that alien landscape.

There has to be a way out of here. I just need to figure it out.

The only other recourse he could conceive was killing Jacanda, in the hopes that it would simply destroy her private world, deposit him on this ridgeline in the waking world, and not simply destroy him, in the process.

Chapter 27

Gurlachday, Day 13, Allfather's Moon, 8766 Sudean Calendar

Spending the night in Jacanda's chambers was uncomfortable at best. Aleron spent most of the previous day, and into the night, poring through the library, looking for any clues on how to work the translation from here to the waking world.

He found texts in dozens of languages, only a few of which he could read. He located a couple entries that discussed the world of dreams, with theories on its nature or what it represented. One spoke of methods for attaining a trance state to enter the dimension purposely, but none spoke of physically entering the realm. Human and elvish writers seemed to consider it an entirely spiritual realm, apparently having no knowledge of its ability to harbor flesh and blood denizens, so there was no help from that angle.

He slept fitfully on his divan, across from the inert Jacanda, dreaming incoherent dreams that seemed to fly from his mind as soon as he woke. He hoped for revelation, through his dreams, but that never came when bidden. He roused himself to try the method outlined in the one text, but the meditation technique proved difficult to master, likely requiring weeks of practice.

Pacing about the sitting room, racking his brain for a solution, he realized he was hungry and thirsty. He went to the table and attempted to will food to appear as he had seen Jacanda do, but to no avail. After a few tries, he gave up and used white magic to transform a large volume of air into a loaf of fresh bread, a hunk of soft cheese, and a tall glass of cool water.

"That's more like it," he said to no one in particular, before tearing into the food.

Wondering why the force of his will seemed unable to accomplish anything as he washed down some bread with a large gulp of water, it suddenly occurred to him. Jacanda built this tiny world as an offshoot of the world of dreams, a bubble where only her will held sway. If she had built it any other way, her servants would be capable of exerting their will upon her creation. Her will was supreme here, and she would not have needed to write down the key to manipulating her own realm. The key was within the aelient's mind, and he needed to find a way to extract it.

Aleron went to Jacanda and knelt beside her prone form. Placing his hand upon her forehead, he began delving her mind, much as she had done to him the day prior.

The first thing he encountered on the surface of her thoughts was the shock and horror at what she suddenly realized he was capable. The thought seemed frozen, like a painting, crystallized in time. He delved deeper, looking for a clue to how she manipulated this place.

Many of the thoughts and memories he encountered were nearly incomprehensible. He witnessed her and others of her kind, still in their spirit forms, inhabiting vast expanses of darkness punctuated by impossibly bright stars. The great and terrible spirit forms of their parents, the aelir, were second only to the Allfather, all-powerful creator of this universe.

He saw the creation of Aertu and the rebellion of the Adversary against his Father and siblings.

Aleron caught glimpses of Aertu, through countless ages, even before the arrival of elves and men, when gigantic lizards ruled the land and skies, with sharks the size of brigantines, plying the ocean depths.

Finally, he located her memory of building this place where she now had him trapped. He studied each movement in incredible detail, understanding how each piece worked together. What might seem simple to an aelient was mind-boggling to a man, even a halfblood with aelient ancestry.

He knelt for several bells, working to comprehend the complexity of this construct, until he felt it could be his own. He saw exactly how she opened holes into the waking world, at any place of her choosing, and how she opened them back to her base of operations. Now, he truly felt as if he could do it himself.

Aleron stood and looked into his grandmother's placid face. He believed that since he cast no particular spell, to place her in this stasis, the magic would eventually dissipate. He was unsure if she would wake or simply die when the magic wore off.

He decided that he really did not wish for her to die. She really was a kindly mistress to her servants, without the seething evil he expected to find at her core. Ambivalence he found aplenty, but was not Iudhael ambivalent to the plight of mortals, though he was an untainted aelient?

He found the dark stain of the compulsion her father, the Nameless One, placed upon her being through the ties of blood. Her memories revealed that his children, to the last, followed him into rebellion, while many other aelient followed of their own free will. He learned that the compulsion of blood produces an inexorable force to obey among those of her kind.

He had a bit of the same in his own mind, but his mortal blood thinned it to a manageable level, though he always found it difficult to disobey his grandfather and, more recently, Jacanda, his grandmother.

He also found, in his delving, the core being of Quiana, the mortal aspect of his grandmother, even more reason for him not to wish her dead.

He took the time to weave a complex ward of false yellow, precisely held in place by ribbons of blue and protected from intrusion by massive charges of red magic. This ward would hold her in stasis for an indefinite time, feeding automatically upon the local energies, and if the false yellow did dwindle, a charge of green energy would revive Jacanda, rather than let her fade and expire.

He made the protective wards easily breakable from the inside, but practically impregnable from the outside.

He left her there so protected and returned to the crystal dome in the library.

He pulled up the vision of the courtyard at Wynn, looked again for the least trafficked spot, and turned away from the crystal. With little effort on his part, he opened a hole and stepped into the already warm tropical air of the courtyard. He closed the portal behind him and looked about for any witnesses to his sudden arrival.

He was happy to notice that his clothing traveled with him, apparently not wrought in the dream world. Satisfied that he was still alone, he opened another portal to return him to Jacanda's library and stepped back through.

Relieved that he finally deciphered the method of departing and reentering the dream world, at least this isolated bubble, he returned to the crystal and brought up an image of Hadaras, in his rooms at the palace, enjoying his breakfast.

Hadaras paused from his breakfast; he felt a presence that he had not felt in many months. Aleron was alive, somewhere in the world, with his powers restored.

The last news from the elvish consul in Mich was not promising. Apparently, a dark aelient, claiming to be Jacanda, abducted Aleron, pulling him from the waking world. Until that point, he could sense that Aleron was alive somewhere, but they could not communicate, not since the altercation in Kolixtla.

For the past month, he felt no sense of Aleron whatsoever and greatly feared for his life, until the recent news from Mich. Now, for a brief moment, he sensed his grandson, in possession of all his usual faculties, and then he was gone again. It did give the old elf hope, and he returned to his breakfast, a bit more cheerful than before.

As if in answer to the questions swirling through Hadaras' mind, a hole opened in the wall, looking into what appeared to be a well-stocked library. Aleron stepped through the hole into Hadaras' apartments and simply said, "Good morning, Grandfather. How have you been?" before plopping down in a chair across the table from Hadaras, the portal closing behind him.

"What's it been, seven months now?"

"Thereabouts," Hadaras replied, standing up from the table and coming around to Aleron's side. He moved a bit cautiously at first, as if wondering whether it was real, and then faster as his excitement grew.

"Now get your duff out of that chair so I can hug you properly, you unruly lout!"

Laughing, Aleron sprang up and held his arms out to embrace his grandfather. "I was wondering if I could get your goat by that."

"You mean, to come waltzing in through a portal after seven months gone like you just left yesterday and hopping through holes in the air is as natural as walking?"

"Exactly that, Grandfather," he replied, laughing again. Hadaras was squeezing him tightly, and Aleron returned the hug, just as hard.

"I guess I have some things to explain, and I definitely have something to show you."

"Explain away, my boy." Hadaras released him and gestured to the chair. "Would you like me to send for some more breakfast? You look thin as a rail."

"Thank you, but I just ate something. Also, I would as soon my presence was not widely known as of yet. I have some unfinished business I need to attend to."

"Going off to find your wife?"

"Yes, sort of, I know right where she is, but I don't think I can get to her very easily."

"Why is that? Is there something wrong? I just received word from Mich that she would be on her way aboard one of our warships."

"That is precisely the problem," Aleron revealed.

"She is safe aboard a carrack, moving under full sail. I think that if I try to travel to it, I'll most likely miss the ship and step into the Western Ocean."

"Good point, that is," his grandfather conceded.

"Now, I think you should explain this traveling to me. Where have you been this last month?

I know most of the rest of the story from speaking with the consuls in Sunj and Mich, but you can fill me in on more of the details later. I think your most recent adventure might be the most pressing issue at the moment."

Aleron told him the whole story, from the day traveling with the hobgoblin onward. Hadaras was interested and a bit concerned by his description of Shaggat's intelligence.

"Yes, he was fluent in Kolixtlani, and it was his idea to use it. He was a lot smarter than I was expecting. I honestly don't think they are that different from jungle men." Aleron continued on to the meeting with Jacanda, and her convincing him of the truth in her claim to his ancestry.

"What makes you so certain?" Hadaras inquired.

"She had a strange power of persuasion over me, like I just wanted to obey her, but it wasn't so complete that I couldn't resist or ignore it. It was more like the influence you have over me. She told me it was the ties of blood, demanding obedience. Later, I saw it for myself, in her mind and memories."

"I have heard of the influence of blood from Iudhael, via a conversation he had with Jessamine," Hadaras offered.

"He said he sensed Jacanda in your ancestry when he healed you."

"Apparently, it's a powerful force among the aelient, but it seems diluted in me. All of the Adversary's aelient children followed him into rebellion, because of it; otherwise, some would have stayed with the light."

He continued on, telling Hadaras of the instruction she gave him on navigating the world of dreams, and of her arguments for the righteousness of the Adversary's cause.

"That does concur with my determination of his intentions in ages past," Hadaras agreed.

"His intention was always to take away the free will of the people, removing the burden of choice between wrong and right. It seems that true evil is actually the absence of wrong and right."

"It sounded like nothing short of slavery, no matter how sweet she tried to make it sound."

"So, how did you manage to regain your abilities and escape? You must be getting to that fairly soon, I hope."

Aleron caught a small glimpse of his grandfather's impatience, to which Jacanda referred. It was decidedly not elflike, he agreed.

"Well, she actually healed me," he began and recounted the course of events that led to his healing and Jacanda's imprisonment.

"Even when she saw you could wield blue and red in combination, she never expected you could do damage with the other colors, a major error on her part."

"Yeah, I'm glad that's all she saw. If she saw what I did to the Kolixtlani High Priest, I'm sure she would have stopped right there."

"Oh, and what was that?" Hadaras asked, suddenly even more curious, if that was possible.

"He had me shielded from red and blue, as well," Aleron explained, "so I used green magic to age him and his soldiers to debility, before I probed his mind for Ellie's whereabouts."

"I thought you had a certain air of maturity about you. Some of it bled off into you, didn't it?"

"Barry said I looked fifty when it was done, but I managed to heal myself back to looking about thirty. That's about as much as I can do, short of transforming myself back to twenty. I had to do the same after I set up Jacanda's wards. That green magic can be potent stuff."

"Yes, without it, nothing would age, but then nothing would grow or mature either. It's a two-sided coin of sorts. After that, you travelled to Wynn?"

"Not as simple as that, I'm afraid," he began.

"I found a device in her study that allows me to look anywhere in the world. It seems able to focus on a person or place from my memory. That's how I found you here, eating breakfast. Then I needed to find my way out of her private bubble of the dream world, which wasn't as simple as I thought it might be."

"Had she not yet taught you all you needed to know to open the pathways?"

"I thought so, at first, but as it turned out, here abode is tuned to her will alone. I think it protects her from outside intrusion and keeps her servants from altering anything."

"How did you find your way out then?"

"I had to go into her mind and see how she built it. Only then could I manipulate the fabric of what she built and find my way out. Would you like to take a look?"

"I would love to," Hadaras answered, "and I just so happen to be free right now."

"Let's go then. I think you'll find her library particularly interesting."

Aleron stood up and went to the clear area, where he opened a new portal back to Jacanda's sitting room. He stepped through, on his guard lest one of the servants managed to find a way into her mistress' quarters, or if Jacanda somehow managed to foil the spells that bound her.

Hadaras followed him in and walked straight to the recumbent form on the divan.

"It is her. By all the gods, it's her. She died some five-hundred years ago, leaving me alone to raise Audina, and now here she lies. I placed her body in the pyre myself. She must have somehow feigned death and escaped the flames."

"I think she was worried about maintaining the ruse any longer than she had to," Aleron offered what he knew from the little she had revealed of her relationship with Hadaras.

"She must have opened a portal to escape the fire. How old was my mother when she left?"

"Audina was nineteen or twenty as I recall, just a half-grown child when her mother left us. She cried for weeks, but then suddenly, she was happy again.

Jessie thinks Jacanda somehow influenced your mother into marrying your father to produce an heir."

"Jacanda spoke as if I was part of some great plan, years in the making," Aleron shared.

"She claimed that she took over grandmother's body, years before you met her. When I looked into her mind, I found only a tiny core of the person that rightfully belongs in that body. I'm not sure how much of the original person is left in there, but I don't think it's enough to run the show, if you know what I mean."

"It looks as if I was truly married to a dark aelient, for over thirty years and never knew it," Hadaras admitted.

"I wonder how she managed to hide it so well. I never saw her use anything but blue magic in all those years."

"She never gave up the other colors, like many did, to grow stronger in the red. She healed me with yellow after she took me from Shaggat.

I also don't believe she is particularly evil, so that may have made it easier for her to pass as an elf," Aleron offered his opinion.

"Not particularly evil? That's odd to claim of a dark aelient."

"From what I saw in her mind, none of the Nameless One's children really had any choice but to follow him. There seemed to be some sort of compulsion built into her mind, and when I followed along as she healed me, I saw that I have a bit of the same thing, only not as strong. I honestly don't believe she would have chosen her path without the compulsion."

"She is a fervent proponent of the Adversary's plan, is she not?" Hadaras countered.

"I suppose...She does seem to be a firm believer."

"Evil can be a subtle thing, as we just discussed. It doesn't necessarily need to involve cruelty, just disregard for the freedom of others. Jacanda cared nothing for Quiana's rights or freedom when she possessed her body and destroyed her mind."

"I understand," Aleron replied, "but the Adversary cared nothing for Jacanda's freedom, or that of her brothers and sisters, when he took them all with him. They should have been only a seventh, or so, of all the aelient.

I worry more about the roughly one-fifth of them that went over of their own accord."

"Why do those worry you more than the others?" Hadaras wanted to know.

"Jacanda doesn't delight in pain or cruelty, but I wonder about the ones who chose freely. I seem to remember from my lessons that many of the dark aelient were well known for their cruelty. She seemed to genuinely care about her servants, if only as one cares about a favored pet, but she cared nonetheless."

"I suppose you may have a point, Aleron, but I still contend they are simply different faces of evil, but still all evil in the end.

Now, you said you had something to show me, and I doubt it was Jacanda lying in state. Nicely crafted wards by the way. I can only see the blue portions clearly, but I can sense the other parts dimly, and it's an ingenious blend of all the powers."

"Thank you, Grandfather, coming from you, that means a lot to me. I wanted to show you the library. I think you'll be impressed." He led the way into the library, with its thickly stacked shelves, the center of the room clear but for the pedestal and domed crystal.

Hadaras gawked at the sheer compilation of literature arrayed before him. He made a beeline to the section containing mostly clay and stone tablets.

Pulling one from the shelf to examine, he exclaimed, "This is ancient Castian, over eight thousand years old. I haven't seen anything like this in thousands of years."

He replaced it, pulled a large scroll from the next cubby over, and unrolled it. "I believe this is an original copy of the treaty, establishing the independence of Sudea from the king of Elvenholm. How, I wonder, is all of this so well preserved? Parchment crumbles after a couple centuries."

"Nothing ages here, Grandfather, not even the people serving Jacanda. Come here and look," he called from the crystal dome.

Hadaras replaced the scroll and joined his grandson.

Aleron thought of Isha, and a scene formed on the surface of the crystal. Unfortunately, the scene that formed was of the baths.

"Umm…I focused on the person I was looking for, not the place she's in."

A dozen or so dark-skinned, nude, and very pretty women swam, soaked, or lounged about the chamber.

"I see, you had it rough for the last month," Hadaras joked.

"Why was it you wanted me to see this, aside from the aesthetic virtues?"

"Isha there," he said, pointing to one particular woman, sitting with her feet dangling into the steaming water, "is over three hundred years old, and she still looks eighteen, like when she arrived here."

"So, as long as Jacanda remains here, all this remains preserved forever?"

"I believe so, but if she dies, I'm not sure what will happen to it all. All this might just cease to exist, or maybe, the things she took from the waking world would remain on a hilltop in the jungle.

Another possibility is time will just stop here in this bubble. I figured out that's what happens when she leaves here. The servants have no recollection of her ever leaving the premises, so I believe time stops for them until she returns."

Incidentally, it appeared that some of the servants conversed in whispers off to the sides, with worried expressions. They likely wondered why their mistress remained locked up in her quarters for the last day, sending for nothing.

"Well, we probably should be getting back to the palace before I'm missed," Hadaras said.

"Alright," Aleron agreed.

He turned, opened a portal back to Hadaras' apartments, and they stepped into the waking world in Arundell.

Chapter 28

Shilwezday, Day 14, Allfather's Moon, 8766 Sudean Calendar

Sea spray passed over the bow of the carrack, as the ship plied south, sails angled to the strong southeasterly wind.

Eilowyn stood atop the forecastle with Feadra beside her, watching whitecaps break before them. The sun shone dull red, as it crept up from the hazy eastern horizon, promising foul weather in the near future. She could see the thin dark line of the Mittean coast, to the left, with the peaks of the Iron Hills rising to the southeast.

"Worrying about Aleron again?" Feadra asked.

"Is it that obvious, Fea? How is Anji doing? I went out before she woke."

"Still sick to her bed, with a chamber pot strapped down next to it, just in case."

"I can't think she would have anything left to throw up, after yesterday."

After the wind picked up and the seas turned choppy, around midday yesterday, Anjani's mild nausea turned to full-blown seasickness. She spent most of yesterday afternoon with her head over the railing.

"Nice job of changing the subject," Feadra said. "There's not much I can do for her. Is there anything I can do for you?"

"Unless you can bring my husband back from where that hag took him, I'm afraid not," Eilowyn replied. "Have you seen the men this morning?"

"Not as of yet, I assume they're breakfasting with the other officers. On that note, I believe our food should be coming to the room any time now. Would you care for some breakfast?"

"I suppose so. The ship won't get there any faster, just because I want it to."

She turned and walked to the ladder at the rear of the forecastle, Feadra close behind, both of them careful to avoid the sailors working the rigging. The men worked day and night, making the best speed possible to their next port of call.

She had never been to Wynn, capital of the colonies, and she looked forward to seeing it.

I would much rather see it with Aleron, she thought, as she made her way down the ladder.

It was tricky business, with the heavy skirts and petticoats appropriate to her position. Once again, she envied Anjani of her prerogative to wear men's clothing for travel.

The higher your rank, the fewer choices you get. At least, I still have sturdy boots under the petticoats, she conceded, descending the ladder.

She looked up and saw that Feadra was having a harder time with the ladder rungs, in the light shoes more appropriate for the outfit.

"You might want to dig out your riding boots," she advised the younger woman, as she completed her descent, wincing from the pressure of the rungs through the thin soles.

"I think you're right," Feadra agreed.

"I'll be getting to that, right after we eat."

"Ugh, what a smell," Eilowyn exclaimed as they entered their quarters and noted the sharp contrast of the sick smell after the fresh sea air.

"Do you mind if I open a couple windows?"

"Sorry," Anjani croaked from the bed.

"Please do, I think I could use some fresh air."

"I've got it," Feadra volunteered, before Eilowyn could get to the shutters. She bustled about, opening all the shutters and propping the door, allowing a fresh breeze to permeate the cabin.

A pair of sailors came up from below decks, with two covered trays, and seeing the door open, one asked, "Your Grace, may we enter?"

"Yes, you may," Eilowyn answered, and the men entered, setting the trays into indentations in the sideboard and locking them down with the attached bails.

"Would you care for us to serve you, Your Grace?" the sailor asked.

"That will not be necessary, Sir; my lady in waiting and I are capable. Thank you for the offer, but you may be excused."

"As you wish, Your Grace," the sailor replied, bowing low and leaving the cabin, his counterpart mirroring his movements.

Feadra lifted the heavy lid from one tray and hung it from the hooks provided over the sideboard, revealing a steaming heap of sliced ham, peeled boiled eggs, and fresh biscuits. The other held a kettle of tea, honey, cups, dishes, and silverware.

Anjani saw the food and rolled over, burying her head in the covers.

"Would you like me to serve you, My Queen?"

"Don't be silly; I'll get my own," Eilowyn replied, "but you will do well as a lady in waiting when we get back to the capital."

She strolled over, grabbed a plate, and served herself, set down her plate, and poured a cup of tea, adding no honey.

"I don't think Anji will be joining us," Feadra said as she loaded her plate.

She followed Eilowyn to the table, and they set their plates and cups into the indentations provided to keep them from sliding in rough seas.

"Do you think we'll arrive in Wynn before the month is out?" she asked, as she took her seat.

"I don't see why not, if these winds hold out. When we get there, I'll contact the Governor and send a message to my father, informing him of our progress. Hopefully, they will have some word of Aleron by then."

✳✳✳

"I have an idea of how I can reach Eilowyn and the rest of the party before they reach Wynn. Then, I should be able to return within the day," Aleron explained to Gealton and Hadaras, in Hadaras' apartments. "I wish I could have caught up with Cladus. I have a bit of a surprise for him."

"What sort of surprise would that be?" his grandfather inquired. Hadaras told him earlier that Anjani and Shaggat were among the party journeying to Arundell.

"I think I should save this one for him, Grandfather. I think you'll both be pleasantly surprised," he finished, cryptically, with a sly grin.

"The sooner you bring my Ellie back to me, the happier I will be," Gealton stated. "It's been nearly a year since I've seen my little girl."

"She's not a little girl anymore, Lord Steward," Aleron said. "She's seen things no decent lady should ever have to see and more of the world than most see in a lifetime. In all that, she never faltered or gave up hope. Did I tell you how she killed a half-troll, with just a knife?"

"I realize she must have grown up with the trials she's faced. I'll try to remember that, when I see her again, and I'll try to remember that she is now your queen, My King, but try to understand that I am also a father, who was robbed of his youngest daughter, then still a girl, nearly a year ago. Try to forgive me if I act that part at first sight of her.

Now, what's this about the half-troll? I heard she was injured, not that she fought it directly."

"I understand, Gealton," Aleron assured him and then went into recounting the assault upon them in Capar and Eilowyn's courageous action that ended the fight.

Upon completing their conversation, Aleron rose, turned to the clear portion of wall, and opened a portal back to Jacanda's library. At the crystal dome, he brought forth an image of Eilowyn, walking the deck of the carrack, accompanied by Barathol, Geldun, and Feadra.

***

Barathol thought his eyes were playing tricks on him. As he looked off in the direction the ship traveled, he thought he saw a spot of darkness against the cloud-streaked blue sky. He blinked, and the spot was gone, so he put it out of his mind, for the moment.

A short time later, one of the sailors shouted, "A raven! There's a raven in the rigging!"

"You're crazy, or you been drinkin' on the job!" another sailor shouted back.

"We're too far offshore for ravens and…Zorek's bloody trident! There's a raven in the rigging!"

Geldun and Barathol both snapped their eyes to the rigging, looking for the object of the sailors' attention.

Hey lads, did you miss me?

"Aleron!" Geldun shouted as the raven deftly circled to the deck, in the brisk wind.

Eilowyn stood, momentarily frozen in shock, with the massive black bird alighting on the planks.

Feadra stood, looking confused at the whole exchange.

The raven dissolved into a shimmering whiteness, quickly growing to man-sized and fading to reveal Aleron, in fine red silks and thonged leather sandals, working to gain his footing on the shifting deck. He stepped over to Eilowyn and grabbed her up off her feet, swinging her in a circle.

"I missed you so much, my love," he whispered to her, setting her down before kissing her softly on the lips.

"I missed you, too, darling," she whispered back when he released the kiss.

"I barely slept this last month, worrying for you."

"No more worrying, Ellie, I'm taking us home now. I need to see the Captain," he announced.

"Where are Anji and Shaggat? I heard they were with you, as well."

The sailors on deck just gaped at the spectacle, some making signs against evil.

Barathol noticed and shouted, "Men, I give you your king, Aleron the Second, Lord over all of Sudea, halfblood, and one of the greatest sorcerers on Aertu."

Recovering from their initial shock, the men, singly and in groups, dropped to one knee and placed forehead to fist, in the traditional gesture of fealty to the king.

"Rise, sailors! I accept your fealty!" Aleron called out to them.

"Return to your duties. I'm a marine, and I know these ships don't sail themselves."

"We have some things of yours that I'm sure you'll be happy to see again," Geldun informed him.

"Would you like to get out of those prissy clothes?"

"Happily," Aleron agreed, "but after I see the Captain.

I want to speak to Anjani and Shaggat before too long."

"Anjani is seasick as can be," Barathol informed him, "and Shaggat is in the brig."

"Are they treating him well?" Aleron asked.

"I don't want him mistreated or otherwise abused.

Sorry to hear Anji is sick, but we'll get her off this ship before long."

"Why do you care about the hobgoblin?" Eilowyn asked. "He tried to kill us and took you captive."

"He treated me as well as he could have, given the circumstances," Aleron replied.

"He was given a mission that he could hardly refuse, lest he lose all he worked his entire life to achieve. I'm afraid he has lost that anyway, with your capturing him. I think his presence can work in our favor if we treat him fairly."

Captain Aelfied now strode across the deck, towards the group. He went directly to Aleron, bowed low, and said, "Your Grace, the men brought word to me just now of your...unconventional arrival."

Aleron returned the bow, stating, "Rise, Captain; I apologize for my method of arrival. I think it may have shocked the men, but I had no other options at my disposal.

I do need to discuss some details with you if you don't mind."

"Of course, My King," Aelfied replied.

"We can retire to the conference table in my quarters. Please follow me."

He led the way to the aftcastle, opening the door to his quarters and waving them inside, with a flourish. The front room, dominated by a large oval table of polished teak, was obviously the conference room, with doors to the captain and first mate's private rooms at the rear of the chamber.

"Please, have a seat, everyone," he invited, closing the door and checking the shutters to make certain they were secure before seating himself.

"So, how may I be of assistance, Your Grace?"

"No questions as to proving my identity?" Aleron asked.

"Your Grace, the stories have been circulating, over half a year now, of a tall, fair-haired lad, drawing the sword, proclaiming himself king, and then turning himself into a raven, to fly to Kolixtla. Then there's the rumor of him nearly knocking the palace down to rescue the Steward's daughter.

When the men started babbling about a raven landing on the deck, turning into a man, and that man claiming to be the king, it wasn't hard to put two and two together. Plus, the queen and her captains seem to know you, if all the hugging and kissing is any indication."

"Fair enough, Captain...?"

"Aelfied, Your Grace."

"Thank you, Captain Aelfied. I was wondering if you could afford to drop anchor."

"For my king, I can afford anything, but may I ask why?"

"The being who took me taught me a way to travel between distant points, through a sort of portal. The reason I arrived in the form I did is that there is no way to open a portal onto a moving ship. I had to open one near the ship and fly to it. If the ship were relatively stationary, I could take myself and all of your guests directly to Arundell, saving them a four-month journey."

"Well, with all the other strange things going about lately, that doesn't seem any stranger than anything else. We'll move to shallower water, cut sail, and drop anchor.

Is there anything else you require, Your Grace?"

"Only my regular gear, whatever didn't get lost in the attack, especially some decent boots. I feel like some sort of fop in this getup."

"We have all your things, except what you had on your back," Geldun offered, "so we might have to scrounge a gambeson to go under your chain, and we recovered all your weapons," placing emphasis on "all."

"We have your good clothes as well," Eilowyn stated sharply. "I don't see why we have to return to Arundell dressed for the road."

"There's the issue of Harm and Elrud," brought up Barathol. "We promoted them to serve as our seconds, but Elrud is laid up in Koln, with a broke leg, and Harm is on the road to go get him."

"I'll tell you what, Ellie, we bring you all to Arundell, with all the bags, and then I take one of the lads to collect Harm and Elrud. After that, I can clean up and change into something presentable. Will that work?"

"I suppose so," she replied, patting him on the back of the hand, "though I don't much care to let you out of my sight right now. You can't seem to stay out of trouble."

"Me! It seems this whole thing started with you needing rescuing."

"If that's all settled and if you'll excuse me, I can get to mooring this beast of a ship," Aelfied proclaimed, rising from his chair.

"Just let yourselves out when you're ready. This should only take a couple bells."

He left the cabin, grabbing a rolled-up chart on the way out, and went to the quarterdeck.

"If you ladies would care to get ready to appear at court, I will go change into something more appropriate," Aleron suggested.

Just over a bell later, the group gathered on the main deck, with all their baggage. Anjani sat upon a trunk, barely managing to remain upright. The return to solid land couldn't come quickly enough for her.

Only Aleron and Geldun wore their mail, deciding that Barathol would stay to settle Anjani into some quarters and make sure Shaggat was properly housed.

"I need to go speak with Shaggat now," Aleron proclaimed. "Who wants to take me down there?"

"I'll go," Geldun volunteered.

Barathol was busy, acting as a backrest for his ailing lady, combing his fingers through her hair, to relax her.

They climbed below decks, and Geldun led the way to the brig. The marine sergeant allowed them through the outer gate to the cells, which would have two guards on duty. One marine corporal was in evidence as they arrived at Shaggat's cell, the only one currently occupied.

"Hello, Shaggat," he greeted the hobgoblin, in Kolixtlani.

"Have you been treated well?"

"Good morning, Aleron," the creature replied, in Sudean. "I well. It good see you."

"You speak Sudean now?"

"Only small bit. Anjani and guards teach me. Better switch Kolixtlani. *My words are still limited in your language, but I am learning.*

Your people have treated me well, but the Sunjibis did drug me to get information out of me."

"*Better than torturing it out of you, I wager,*" Aleron replied.

"*Agreed, but the end result is worse. I would have held out under torture. It is a point of honor, among my people, to die well, under duress.*

Now, I am a traitor to my people and my army. Sunjib knows where all my forces are massed and will attack in force, I am certain.

I can never return to my people now. You may as well kill me."

"*I will do nothing of the sort, Shaggat.*"

He noticed scabbed-over chafing on the hobgoblin's wrists, ankles, and neck, as well as what looked like a swelling under his eye.

"He looks a little beat up, Gel. What happened?"

"He didn't give much trouble until it came time to board the ship. Then he caused so much ruckus that they had to thump him and put full shackles on him. He ranted for a full day before we convinced him to come to the door, so we could unlock them."

"*Afraid of the ship?*" Aleron asked.

"*No, I was afraid of the ocean,*" Shaggat replied. "*There is a difference.*"

Aleron laughed.

"*Hold your hand out to me, so I can help you.*"

At Shaggat's worried look, he continued, "*I give you my word that I will not harm you in any way.*"

The hobgoblin hesitantly extended one hand through the bars, and Aleron grasped it in his own hand. The yellow magic flowed from Aleron into Shaggat, causing his body to glow incandescent for a brief moment before snatching his hand away.

Eyes wide, he felt to his wrists, seeing the old scabs slough on contact, revealing the new skin beneath them.

"*How are you using magic so? You could have escaped me if you were a sorcerer.*"

"*I was afflicted with a sort of hurt that robbed me of my powers. The Lady Jacanda cured me of it.*"

"*And then, you defeated her and escaped?*"

"*Essentially, yes, but I did not kill her. She is my grandmother, after all.*"

"I have heard that men are sentimental about such things. Poor choice, on her part, to heal you of what made you controllable," Shaggat remarked.

"Poor choice indeed," Aleron agreed.

"We are leaving the boat to go straight to Arundell, my capital. I would like you to accompany us, or would you prefer to stay on the ship for four more moons?"

"How will you go straight to your home from here?"

"We go through Jacanda's lair."

"Then I cannot accompany you. The Lady said that such as I cannot go where she goes. That is how I was left to be captured by your companions."

"I think she was wrong. It may be, for pure goblins, but your folk are different. Give me your hand again; I would like to check something. Do you trust me?"

"As much as I can trust any man." He thrust out his semi-clawed hand and held it steady.

Aleron grasped the hand again and probed the nature of the hobgoblin with blue magic. What he felt was little different from a man, dwarf, or elf. The contrast was like that of a halfblood to a pure man or elf. Shaggat felt like a man, with a hint of something else, something dark, but still mostly man-like. He imagined that a goblin or troll would feel entirely alien and dark.

"I am certain that there is enough man in your blood that you can pass through her realm," he assured Shaggat.

"I suppose it's worth a try. I think I would rather be struck dead than spend four more moons in this floating box."

"Guards!" Aleron called. "The hobgoblin will be moved to the main deck to accompany us. Please treat him gently and do not over-tighten the shackles. On that note, wrists behind the back only; I do not wish to see anything around his neck, and he will need to step high, so no leg irons."

"Yes, Your Grace," the guard on duty concurred. "Will you be waiting, or shall we bring him to you?" A second guard came running from wherever he was taking his break.

"We will wait," Aleron replied.

"I think there will be less trouble that way."

"Shaggat, the guard will come in with shackles. I ordered him not to hurt you. Will you cooperate?"

"Yes," the hobgoblin replied.

"I want to get off this boat."

"Then turn around and put your hands behind you, and we'll get on with this."

He shouldn't give you any trouble now, Corporal," Aleron assured the guard.

The private that came to assist cocked a crossbow, loaded a broadhead bolt, and covered the corporal as he unlocked the cell door.

Shaggat obediently held his hands behind his back, allowing the guard to shackle his wrists.

No longer needed to guard nonexistent prisoners, the marines led the way out of the brig, their sergeant joining them and the hobgoblin, after relocking the outer gate. Aleron and Geldun brought up the rear, and the entourage made their way to the main deck.

Chapter 29

Shilwezday, Day 14, Allfather's Moon, 8766 Sudean Calendar

Aleron and Geldun stood upon the open road, two days ride east of Mich. Lake Kamig, Mich's great freshwater harbor, spread out past the horizon to the south. A dust plume revealed the approach of a rider, hidden from view by a slight rise. A few moments later, the horseman appeared. Aleron's sharp vision revealed the rider as a Sudean marine, lance in socket, dressed in subdued brown and green, with blackened chain and helm.

"That must be Harm," Aleron said, "unless there are other marines trouncing about Mittea."

"Nothing to do, but wait for him to get here then," Geldun replied.

Harm slowed his horse, from a canter to a walk, as he approached the armored men standing in the road, and took up his lance, couching it under his arm. It looked like Sudean armor, but what were marines doing here and where were their horses?

When he caught sight of the sapphire studded pommel, over the taller man's shoulder, he goaded his mount to a trot and replaced the lance in its socket.

"Your Grace!" he exclaimed.

"Captain! How did you get here?"

He appeared utterly confused by their appearance, which was understandable. He dismounted and stepped up to the men.

"I'm glad to see you managed to escape, Your Grace, but how did the two of you get here? I just saw Captain Geldun on a ship out of Mich, two days ago."

"It might be easier to show you, rather than tell you the whole long story," Aleron answered. "We can't bring the horse, though, so we'll just have to let it loose."

"If you say so, Your Grace, what about the gear and saddle?"

"That can come," Geldun replied, "but I'm not sure about the lance, Aleron?"

"That might be a little long for Hadaras' apartments," Aleron observed.

"I think we should leave it here. Lances are easy to come by."

Harm continued to look confused as they worked together to pile his bags and saddle on the roadside.

Aleron stepped to one side and opened a doorway into Jacanda's library.

Harm stood, dumfounded, as Geldun picked up the first of the bags and headed for the opening.

"Don't just stand there, catching flies; grab a bag," Geldun chided him.

With the saddle and all the bags piled to one side, in the library, Aleron looked to the crystal, to find Elrud. He found him sitting in the open courtyard of the inn, leg propped on another chair, sipping beer.

"He looks pretty comfortable," he commented.

"I wonder how much he'll appreciate us bothering him."

"He can drink beer in Arundell," Harm retorted.

"Granted, it won't be as good beer, but he'll have to make do."

"Shall we go?" Geldun asked.

Chuckling, Aleron stepped to an open space and opened a portal to the courtyard where Elrud lounged.

Beer sloshed out of Elrud's mug as he sat up in surprise, seeing three men in marine battle dress step out of the wall.

"Your Grace!" he shouted, recognizing Aleron.

"Is it truly you?"

"Relax, Elrud, yes, it's me. We've come to take you back to Arundell."

"Well, that's good news. I'm in danger of becoming a drunk, stuck here in Koln, with a bum leg."

"Let's get you out of here then," Geldun said.

"I'm sure there's some desk work I can put you on for the next couple weeks. After that, there will be training to build your strength back."

"Sounds good, Sir, let me get my things." He drained the rest of his mug and stood, using a crutch for support, and led the way back to the inn.

Within a bell's time, the four men stood in Hadaras' apartments, with the master sergeants' baggage and saddles. Hadaras, Gealton, and the palace concierge were there as well, the concierge directing porters on delivering the baggage.

"Indeed, Your Grace," the concierge explained, "the queen and her handmaiden are installed in the royal family quarters. We began cleaning and renovating just after you declared for the throne. Your bags were moved there as well, Your Grace."

"And the others, where will they be staying? I want my advisors close," Aleron declared.

"The captains and their aides are in apartments adjacent to the royal quarters, as is the Sunjibi interpreter in your party."

"Good, good, I was hoping the arrangements would keep us close together. What of the prisoner, the hobgoblin, Shaggat?"

The concierge said nothing, looking to Gealton, as if to affirm that prisoners were no concern of his.

The Steward took over. "You specified that he be treated well, Your Grace, so we placed him in the upper level of the prison block, not the dungeons. Are you familiar with the location?"

"Yes, I'm familiar. Thank you, Lord Steward. I'll be calling on him a bit later today. I think he will be useful to us, and he has nothing left with his own people.

Grandfather, is there any way to rope Cladus into dinner tonight? There is that surprise I have for him."

"I think a summons from the king should be enough," Hadaras said, "and I think he'll be wanting to see you anyway.

I'll go to his room at the Dragon this afternoon. Sixth bell past noon?"

"That sounds like a good time, will you join us, Gealton...Lord Steward, I mean?" Aleron looked to the concierge, not knowing him, or how he felt of over-familiarity between nobles and officials.

"Um...I don't believe I caught your name yet, Mr..."

"Joffe, Your Grace," the concierge replied.

"Joffe, my name is Aleron, and in private, I expect everyone in this room to call me that, or Al, even. I grew up in the country and joined the Marines, with Geldun here and Barathol, whom you met earlier.

I'm not used to all this 'Your Grace,' bowing and scraping and such. I'll do my best in public to put on the show people expect, but not in private chambers. I'll call everyone by their first names, excepting my grandfather, because he is, and I call him "Grandfather". Are you alright with that, Joffe?"

"Absolutely, Sire, it will be as you say."

"Then call me 'Aleron,' not 'Sire,' please."

"Of course, Si…" He looked to Gealton again, an almost pleading look in his eyes, but the steward only grinned, knowing what a stickler Joffe was for protocol. "Aleron," he finally spat out.

"Good, now if you'll show us to our rooms, I could stand to get into something a bit less martial and more comfortable, but I suppose Ellie will dress me like some prize peacock again instead.

I'll be back shortly, Grandfather. Will you be here, or do you have other business this afternoon?"

"If we're not here, we'll be in Gealton's office, or about the palace offices somewhere. I presume you want to release the news of your return now?"

"If it hasn't gone out already, you mean? Yes, make it official.

I should probably catch up on what's going on in the world, and there is another pressing issue we need to discuss. I'll see you in a bit then.

Lead on, Joffe."

The concierge led the way down the corridors, toward the royal quarters.

Aleron directed, "Please take me to my officer's rooms first, Joffe, so I know where to find them and then to mine, please."

"As you wish…Aleron."

By mid-afternoon, Aleron had lunch, a bath with Eilowyn, which was quite enjoyable, and a long snuggling nap in the most comfortable bed he'd ever slept in, even as a guest of the Steward when still courting his daughter.

After their nap, Eilowyn dressed him in the purple-trimmed lord's coat she had made in Sunj, with dark blue trousers because he couldn't abide the purple ones she tried to foist on him.

Andhanimwhid rode in the new scabbard and harness of purple dyed leather, forming a belt and baldric in royal purple. A pair of long, heavy daggers rode where his cutlasses used to reside.

"I miss my cutlasses," he admitted.

"I never was much for the greatsword."

"Well, now you're the king, my love," Eilowyn said, stretching up to kiss him, before stepping back to admire her handiwork, "and the king of Sudea carries a greatsword."

"Do you want to come with me, to see Hadaras and your father?" he asked.

"No, I visited for a while, while you were getting the others.

My sister, Majori, is on her way from the other side of the city. We're taking Feadra and shopping for the wedding today. We have to take care of that soon before the rumors start flying about us living out of wedlock."

"That's swivin garbage! We're married, and if any blasted fool says otherwise, I'll have their hide!"

"No need for profanity, my love. It doesn't suit you and never has.

Gossip and rumors happen, and you can't go about stringing people up over them. Someone is bound to think we faked our marriage for our own convenience. We need the big public spectacle, and we need it soon.

By the way, speaking of public spectacle, you never told me about calling lightning in the throne room and swearing to the people to get their queen back. That was very romantic, almost epic."

"Well, you know me, always the romantic one," he said, with a laugh.

"Right, that's you for sure," she agreed, before slapping him on the behind.

"Now get to work; you have kingly things to attend to."

In the Steward's office, Aleron received the latest news on Kolixtlani incursions into Sunjib, Waban, and Castia.

"The situation has heated up considerably since your flight from Kolixtla," Gealton reported.

"The Elvish Colony and Mittea both report an increase in attacks from the central jungle, while Sultea is currently still unaffected by the conflict, aside from the obstruction of trade with the northeastern nations.

Adar is pushing against Talik and interfering with Chebek shipping as well, but not to the same extent as Kolixtlan. We believe the new king is in a vengeful mindset, following your killing of his father.

The Arkan presence seems to have diminished as of late. The Wabani blockade is composed entirely of Kolixtlani and Adari ships, with none of the strange ships associated with the dark elves.

The lack of foreign advisors to rein him in may be contributing to Ehacatl's aggression. He is in danger of spending his combat resources too early and finding himself spread thin when the real conflict begins."

"That's good for us, at least," Aleron said, "and I think I know why the Arkans are missing. They all went north."

"North, what news do you have of Arkans moving north?" Hadaras asked.

Aleron answered, "That is the issue that I mentioned earlier. Jacanda told me that Zormat had just retrieved Zadehmal from wherever you locked it away. We have about three months before he makes it back to Kolixtlan, and then he'll be off to Immin Bul to free the Adversary."

"Very grave news indeed," Gealton stated. "With his weapon of power, he alone was nearly invincible, and now he has had four millennia to brood on things."

"That might explain the blockade of the Wabani inlet," Hadaras surmised.

"The extra resources they poured into the operation this summer were likely aimed at keeping the path from Norwyyl to Kolixtlan open for Zormat's passage."

Gealton added, "It would take longer than three months to mobilize enough ships to break that blockade.

I would guess, as well, that the massing goblins and trolls in the Iron Hills are meant to guard against any Sunjibi and Mittean incursions into the central jungle."

"That's the likely motive," Hadaras agreed.

"What about the dwarves?" Aleron asked. "Have they seen higher activity than usual?"

"Some, but not a great deal," Hadaras said.

"I don't believe the enemy sees them as a threat. They defend their territory fiercely, but seldom venture far afield. In the last war, they held the line against crossing the Blue Mountains, but they did not march with us to Immin Bul."

"I have a feeling that may have to change, for us to have a hope of reaching Immin Bul before Zormat arrives with the axe."

"That may be, but the likelihood of them mobilizing is low.

I'm thinking that even if he breaks free, his forces are not what they were four thousand years ago. Then, the hobgoblins and half-trolls he brought against us formed up with military precision and had good armor and weapons. Adar is at a similar strength as then, which is low, but Kolixtlan is far weaker than they were then, and we have Thallasia now."

"Our strength is lower, as well, Grandfather. What of Ebareiza and Elmenia, territories once ours, that broke away in the decline? Can we call upon the desert folk any longer? They never attempted to break free of Sudea, but when was the last time they sent recruits or sat a representative among the Council of Lords?

Meanwhile, the dwarves have multiplied in their mountains, developing machines and keeping to themselves. Do you suppose some of their machines might be built for war? I don't think we should count the dwarves out. We should be trying to bring them out of their hiding."

"The lad is right, old friend," Gealton said.

"We don't have an army of halfblood knights, with weapons forged of magic. We have but one halfblood king and one magic sword. We may still be the most powerful kingdom on Aertu, but our power is not what it was."

"I think we must face the likely possibility that the Adversary will free himself and regain Zadehmal," Hadaras declared.

"If he does, he will not strike at once. It will take years to rebuild his armies. We will have as many years to rebuild our own strength.

I will send a detailed description of our current situation to the Governor at Wynn, and he will relay the same to the king at Cyte. We will need elves in large numbers to reinforce our ranks. There are few sorcerers left among men.

The weapons we used in the Great War would not have decomposed. I am sure that many of them are adorning the walls or locked in the armories of the great houses. We should bring them out of storage and train in their use. Even a non-sorcerer will gain advantage in the wielding of such a weapon, fully charged with magic."

"How many generals and admirals are in residence?" Aleron asked.

"Five, I believe," Gealton answered.

"Please let them know that in two days' time, we will meet over lunch to discuss our way forward."

"As you wish, Aleron, I will send the word out today."

"Thank you. Now, if you'll excuse me, I want to visit Shaggat while I have the opportunity."

"I think your boy has grown up, Hadaras," Gealton commented, after Aleron left the room.

"We have a king for certain now, and I believe the generals will be in for a shock."

"I agree with your observation. He is not the same lad he was seven months ago, and the generals and admirals will learn that quickly."

Chapter 30

Shilwezday, Day 14, Allfather's Moon, 8766 Sudean Calendar

Aleron left the office and made his way through the palace to the east doors, facing the prison block. Men and women of all stations bowed, bobbed, and curtsied as he strode past.

The winter sun had already dipped below the roofline of the palace, bathing the courtyard in shadow as he stepped onto the freshly shoveled lane. He shivered despite the long wool undergarments and his coat. *Suddenly switching from summer to winter, inside of one day, is a shock to the system.*

As he arrived at the gate to the prison, the guards, a corporal and a private, snapped to attention. Apparently, his description circulated among the guards and staff because all recognized him wherever he went.

"Your Grace," the corporal greeted him. "We were told to expect you this afternoon. The Sergeant of the Guard will be along momentarily to escort you to the hobgoblin prisoner, Sire."

"Thank you, Corporal, Private. You may stand at your ease, and I will await the sergeant."

The sergeant came shortly, along with two guards and a young captain, as well.

"Your Grace, I am Captain Lemael, warden of the prison block, at your service."

The sergeant and the pair of prison guards had the grizzled look of old veterans, in stark contrast to the fresh face of the warden. Aleron would have bet that Lemael was no more than a year senior to himself.

Truth be told, Aleron looked older than his twenty years, partly because of green magic, but mostly it was the look in his eyes, they having seen wonders and horrors enough for a lifetime already.

Seeing those eyes, the warden and guards looked to him with a measure of true respect. The hard man before them was not what they expected of their youthful king.

"Thank you, Captain Lemael. Please take me to the hobgoblin if you don't mind."

"Right away, Sire. Open the gate, men."

The guards complied, and soon Aleron strode across the no-man's-land between the wall and the building, flanked by the guards, with the captain directing them from a position immediately to Aleron's left, the guards and the old master sergeant bringing up the rear.

"If I may ask, Sire," the captain began, "what is the importance of this prisoner? We were given strict instructions from the Steward to treat him as well as a noble prisoner of war."

"Basically, that is what he is, Captain. Shaggat was the high chieftain of his people and leader of their army. Aside from the fact that hobgoblins have no hereditary rank, he was essentially their king. I consider him an enemy prisoner of war, and he will be treated as such."

"Understood, Your Grace, but aren't goblins little more than beasts?"

"The 'beast' of which you speak, Captain Lemael, treated me mercifully while I was his captive, and I will do the same for him. He is fluent in Kolixtlani and picking up Sudean quite rapidly. From our conversations, I think he's more intelligent than many a man I've known. That is not what I would consider a beast."

"Point well taken, Sire." Lemael wasn't stupid and realized he was treading on potentially thin ice.

"He is on the top level, Your Grace." He said little more, as they climbed three flights of stairs, to the third and highest floor, aside from the guard towers that stood two stories higher than the roof.

"Here is his cell, Your Grace."

A sturdy chair was set before the door, for Aleron's convenience.

"Why does he not have a chair in his cell?" Aleron inquired.

"Sire, we don't normally provide loose furniture to the prisoners, lest they use them as weapons," Lemael informed him.

"Understandable, Captain, but I think, in this case, we will make an exception."

The only furnishings in the cell were an iron bed frame, bolted securely to the wall, and a stone writing shelf, set into the actual blocks of the wall, beside the bed.

"Shaggat, if I have them bring you a chair, can I have your word that you won't try to club them with it?" he asked in Kolixtlani.

Shaggat rose from the mattress at Aleron's arrival and stood at the barred door of his cell.

"You have my word, as a warrior, but it is not needed. We don't normally sit in chairs where I come from."

"Yes, but it will make it easier for us to converse if we sit at the same level. I will be having Anjani come often to work on your Sudean, as well."

"Very well, have them bring it if you wish. I promise not to club them with it."

"He gives his word, as a warrior, that he will not attempt any mischief with the chair if you bring it. On second thought, this will be faster.

Shaggat, my friend, please step back from the door."

He concentrated on the memory of the sturdy wooden chair from his room in Swaincott. The warden and guards felt air rush past them as a bright white haze coalesced into a sturdy wooden chair, inside the cell. Afterwards, they only blinked, shook their heads a bit, and said nothing. Shaggat blinked as well, equally dumfounded.

Aleron experienced a certain wonder, making things of wood, because he realized that everything in the wood was already present in the air. He could sense the different components of air and could make a steel sword from it, by converting some of those components into iron, while the one derived of charcoal was already present in the air, oddly enough.

Wood was mostly that same component as charcoal, with the other components of air, linked in intricate patterns.

When he wielded white magic, a portion of his mind, working high above his conscious self, processed these patterns and built what he wished.

"W...will that be all, Sire?" Captain Lemael asked, he and his guards obviously shaken. Perhaps they hadn't believed the tales of their new king being a sorcerer as well.

"Yes, that will be all, thank you. I will send for you when I am finished."

He pulled the chair to face the door and sat.

Shaggat approached the chair carefully, touched it, feeling for its realness, and then suddenly a thoughtful expression crossed his features.

He sat down and said, *"The Lady had no idea what a wasp's nest she was opening, thinking it honeycomb,"* laughing softly as he finished.

"No, I think not," Aleron agreed.

"How are you doing up here? Are they treating you well?"

"Yes, they are treating me well, better than I would have expected for a prisoner. You called me "friend" earlier; did you mean that?"

An idea was beginning to form in Shaggat's mind, but he was wont to share it with anyone yet.

"I did, Shaggat. I would consider you a friend, despite the circumstances."

"I feel the same about you, for some strange reason."

"Would you like to return to your home, Shaggat? I could get you back there, you know, and I see no point in holding you here any longer."

"No, I think not. When the Sunjibis attack, they will know where the information came from. If I alone return, they will brand me a traitor, and they will kill me, likely in a most unpleasant manner.

Anyhow, I would like to share something with you."

"What is that?"

"I feel differently somehow than I did before we came through the Lady's place. I cannot quite single out what it is, but I feel somehow lighter. I can't explain it any other way.

"That is interesting. Would you mind if I checked you again, as I did before we crossed over?"

"It failed to harm me in any way the last time. Besides, I believe you could turn me into a pigeon from where you sit, so go ahead and check, I suppose."

He extended a hand through the bars.

Aleron took his hand and felt for the hobgoblin's essence with feelers of blue energy. After a few moments, he released Shaggat's hand, just thinking for a while, before commenting.

"You are different, but not elementally so. I still sense part man and part something else that must be goblin, but the darkness I sensed in the background is no longer there. That must be the part that cannot enter the world of dreams. Were you a full-blooded goblin, it would likely kill you to pass through."

"So, the man blood in us allows us to pass through this world of dreams, but it strips something from us? I did feel a sort of wrenching sensation when I passed into the Lady's abode. She lives in this place you call the world of dreams?"

"That would seem to be the case," Aleron agreed, *"but I'm not sure what we should make of it yet. Give me some time to think on it.*

Lady Jacanda built a sort of bubble, out of the world of dreams, where only her will held sway, but it is still the same sort of place. The true world of dreams overlays our entire world, or so she told me. Now, if you do not wish to return to your people, what do you wish of me?"

"Of that I am unsure, friend. I also need some time to think on things. My thoughts seem to come much more clearly this last day, so we shall see what I arrive at.

***

As the guests arrived for the evening dinner, in the private royal dining room adjacent to the royal quarters, Aleron asked Cladus to join him in a private sitting room. He asked Eilowyn to keep an eye out for Anjani and to send her in, without Barathol.

"Why all the secrecy?" Hadaras asked Eilowyn after they disappeared into the sitting room.

"He said he had a surprise for Cladus but never let on what it could be."

"I don't think this surprise is meant for a public venue," she answered.

"This is more of a private thing, unless he wants to share it with everyone."

Cladus sat in a cushioned chair, with a cup of mulled wine, his multicolored striped cloak still on his shoulders, and his zither propped against the chair.

"So, to what do I owe your summons from a lucrative night of singing, playing, and storytelling? I understand we haven't seen each other in quite some time, but why the private audience?"

Aleron took a seat across from him, with his own steaming cup. A small fire crackled in the fireplace between them, and heavy curtains kept wintery drafts from penetrating.

"I have a bit of a surprise for you, but I'm not sure how you will take it. I thought we should have a bit of privacy."

A soft knock interrupted their conversation.

"Enter," Aleron called out.

Anjani entered and closed the door behind her. The tall blond woman looked quite different than Aleron was used to seeing her, in a low-cut gown of sky blue, rather than trousers, boots, and jacket.

Standing and taking her hand, he turned to the bard and said, "Cladus, may I present to you, Anjani, daughter of Sheana, our translator from Sunjib."

"Pleased to make your acquaintance, young lady," Cladus said, as he stood and flourished a bow.

"You know, I knew someone in Mittea by the name of Sheana, about twenty years…" He failed to complete the sentence, as the light of realization woke in his eyes.

"I was born in Mittea…Father," she replied, tears beginning to well in her eyes.

Aleron released her hand and stepped back.

"Daughter…I have a daughter?" He choked out the last word as his own tears came to the surface.

"I never knew…If I had…"

"I should probably step out now," Aleron offered.

"There's mulled wine on the table, Anji. Feel free to help yourself."

Getting no response from either, he crept through the door and closed it softly behind him.

All those Aleron and Eilowyn asked to dinner that evening, excepting the two in the sitting room, took seats at the table. The royal couple sat at the head, with Gealton and Eilowyn's sister Majori to Eilowyn's left, her husband absent on business at their country estate. Hadaras sat to Aleron's right, with two empty spaces for Cladus and Anjani between him and Barathol. Geldun and Feadra rounded out the opposite side, next to Majori, while Elrud and Harm sat at the end opposite the king and queen.

"It is good to see you again, Aleron," Majori said.

"Thank you for bringing our sister home. Mother should be back in three weeks, and our brother Hameln should be along in a couple weeks, well before the wedding. He always idolized you; you know."

Majori, the second of Gealton's children, resided in Arundell, wife to Lord Anderly of House Bertome, one of Sudea's most influential houses.

Incidentally, her brother-in-law was the one that Aleron kicked in the ribs at the market, the day he first saw Eilowyn.

Can't pick family, Aleron thought, as he was reminded of the relatedness that would result from the wedding.

"It's good to see you again, Majori, and I look forward to seeing Hameln again."

Hameln, just eighteen, stationed in the East Marches bordering Coptia and the Green Mountain dwarvish kingdom for the past two years, was fortuitously already on his way back to Arundell, in the process of reassignment to the Northwest Garrison.

Aleron rather liked Eilowyn's younger brother, who always looked up to him, as a marine and notorious fighter. It would be good to see him again.

He liked Majori a bit less, her being quite critical of her sister's choice of mate, due to his perceived station prior to claiming the throne.

The door to the sitting room opened, just as the servants were bringing in the first course of roasted partridges. Cladus and Anjani came out, arm in arm.

"Gentlefolk," Cladus called out, in his best oratory tone, "may I present my daughter, Anjani, delivered to me after years of separation?"

He wiped one last tear from his eye. Anjani's eyes were puffy and red from crying, and she just sniffed, smiling radiantly.

Majori sniffed as well, with disdain rather than sympathy, earning a nudge and quick glare from her father.

Hadaras gestured to the empty seats beside him, and Cladus led his daughter to their places.

She leaned down to hug Barathol and plant a kiss on his cheek before taking the chair her father held for her.

"I see my girl has taken to taming bears," Cladus joked, slapping Barathol on the shoulder.

"Not sure if she'll manage to tame that one, Cladus," Aleron commented, as the bard took his seat, "but best of luck trying."

"Barry doesn't need taming," Geldun said.

"Docile as a new lamb, that one is."

That comment drew laughs from many around the table.

"That's enough of that, pretty boy," Barathol growled.

"Why don't we get to supper? I'm half-starved, and those partridges smell delicious."

The evening progressed amiably, most of the conversation revolving around the high points of their adventures since Eilowyn disappeared.

Majori looked skeptical at first, but with so many corroborating the stories, her father's, most of all, her skepticism turned to enthusiasm. She especially liked Eilowyn's account of her long journey and captivity in Kolixtla.

"My brave little sister," she exclaimed, "kidnapped and courted by the Crown Prince of Kolixtlan, and then rescued by the king of Sudea and his hearty band. It's a tale fit for a story book!"

"Indeed it is, My Lady," Cladus replied, "and it will be one, some day, when I settle down to write it. How about "The Exploits of the Halfblood King" or something such?"

"Don't forget about the 'Hearty Band,'" Geldun said, eliciting more laughter.

"Or the damsel in distress, trapped in her high tower," added Eilowyn.

Cladus brought out his zither and a flute to play and sing for the group, after they finished the main courses. Overall, it was turning into quite a lovely evening, until the serving woman screamed.

Aleron looked up in time to see the bolt loose from the crossbow in a serving man's hands. He must have hidden it under the cover of the cart they brought in to clear the dishes and platters.

The bolt disintegrated in a flash of blue flame, while twin bolts of purple slammed the attacker into the wall, crumbling the thick plaster. A collar of blue radiance held the man by the neck.

Cladus dropped his instrument and deployed both of his wicked knives, all while conjuring and maintaining the collar.

Aleron stepped over the chair he knocked over while standing to deliver the blow that threw the attacker into the wall.

Hadaras rose gracefully from his seat. He was the one to react first and incinerate the arrow.

The other men in the room advanced and surrounded the servant, knives and daggers drawn, as none wore swords at the table, though the seaxes Cladus and Barathol preferred were very nearly swords.

Aleron addressed the serving woman who screamed.

"Thank you for the timely warning, Ma'am. Please notify the guards to come straightaway."

The woman bobbed a curtsy and ran up the hallway. Aleron turned his attention to the man pinned to the wall. Cladus had added several strands of support, pinning his arms and legs, not allowing the man to strangle.

"This was a suicide mission on his part, don't you think?"

"Considering the group he chose to attack, probably so," Gealton agreed.

"It's been many a year since an assassin made his way into the palace."

"I don't think this one expected to face three sorcerers," Barathol said.

"If the girl hadn't screamed, he may well have been successful," Hadaras commented.

"All of our guards were down, here in perceived safety."

"The mess will have to wait," Gealton stated.

"I am about to order all servants from the palace tonight. We will need to re-vet all employees. The cooks will be the first, of course, but things may get a bit rank here, as the process will take days."

"He doesn't look too good, boss," Geldun observed. The attacker was leaking clear pinkish fluid from his nose and seemed to drift in and out of consciousness.

Aleron stepped forward and placed his hand on the man's head for a moment. A flash of yellow engulfed the assassin, and his eyes snapped open in shock as he drew in a rasping breath.

"There, all healed up if a bit roughly.

You would have died here on this wall if I hadn't healed you. Tomorrow, I will ask you some questions. If you answer me truthfully, I will have you executed quickly and humanely. If you resist, I will pick your mind to pieces and leave you a live drooling idiot. I've done it before, and I didn't enjoy it, but it's your choice.

Guards, place this man in irons and toss him into the lowest dungeon you have. I will deal with him tomorrow."

"Right away, Your Grace," the first guard responded, "but if I may make a suggestion, the first level down is the coldest. It gets a bit warmer in the bottom tier."

"Very well, the coldest dungeon you have."

"We'll search the rest of the level with Harm, in case there's more hiding in here," Geldun offered, Barathol and Harm adding their agreement.

"I may have this damn crutch, but I can still look around," Elrud added.

"Don't count me out just yet."

"Good," Aleron agreed. "We can use all the help we can get, Elrud. Those of us with the ability can send out our feelers just in case eyes and ears miss something. Do you mind, Cladus, Grandfather?"

"Not at all," Cladus stated, with Hadaras nodding in concurrence.

"Now, do you think I was too harsh with the assassin? Any of you, please tell me if you think I was. I do not want to rule by my temper or be ruled by it."

"Aleron, my boy," Gealton replied, "many a ruler would have ordered the man beheaded, or just killed him outright. He is destined for the executioner's block regardless. I think you did well."

Eilowyn spoke, "I think you want a formal trial, my love. The evidence is overwhelming, but it will make you look just, rather than simply vengeful."

"Your bride makes a good point," Hadaras agreed.

"A formal trial is not required, as you are the king, but it will look better on you to air the accusations in public, giving the man an opportunity to defend himself before passing judgment."

"That does sound better, Aleron agreed.

"Thank you, Ellie."

"Elrud," Aleron called out, before the man left to help search.

"Please come here. It appears I have forgotten to do something in all the confusion these last several days."

"Yes, Your Grace," the marine replied, limping up to the king. "What would you like?"

Aleron reached up and put his hand on the man's shoulder. A flood of yellow energy poured into the injured man, invisible to any not gifted with the ability for magic.

"How does your leg feel now?"

Elrud shifted his weight to the formerly injured limb and replied in amazement, "It's even better than before I broke it!

Thank you, Your Grace," he added, before hurrying off to assist in the search for any other enemies who may have infiltrated the palace.

"Lady Majori, it looks like you will leave tonight with tall tales of your own to tell," Cladus said.

"I do believe you're correct, my good bard," a still wide-eyed Majori agreed.

"It will only get worse as you associate with these characters," Cladus went on.

"The pattern of time twists about them like a choke vine."

She nodded in agreement before asking one of the now numerous guards to send for her escort back to her mansion.

Chapter 31

Corballday, Day 15, Allfather's Moon, 8766 Sudean Calendar

"I'm going to talk to the assassin this morning," Aleron told Eilowyn, over a simple breakfast of sausage, biscuits, and dried fruits. With all the palace staff ejected, short of the most senior, it had been up to the concierge to meet the needs of the palace residents with only palace guards to fill the role of servants.

The morning was clear and cold outside their window, the sun almost too bright, reflecting off the thin covering of snow. Snow never lasted long in Arundell, not as it did in the highlands surrounding it, but recent weather had turned exceptionally cold, even for the first month of the year.

"It looks cold out there," Eilowyn commented.

"I hardly remember it ever being this cold in the city. Make sure you dress warmly."

"Don't worry about me. I'll be fine," he assured her.

"Are you going out with your sister today?"

"Yes, Majori and I are going out shopping for the wedding again. Fea asked to spend some time with Gel today, so we're going without her."

"I want you to see the watch captain and take some extra guards along today. After what happened last night, we can't be too careful."

"Who are you taking with you, my love?"

"Barry and Anji will come with me, along with two extra guards. Anji is coming to speak with Shaggat, and Barry is coming to watch my back."

"I suppose that will be enough. Place your plates on the cart when you finish. I'll bring it out to the hall later."

They had to do things a bit differently, with all the palace servants sent home. Everyone, including the king and queen, needed to pick up after themselves, with only soldiers to manage the upkeep of the place.

Aleron donned his coat and buckled on his belt and baldric.

"I'm heading out now, dear. Have a good day at the market."

"Good luck with your inquiry, my love. I hope you aren't forced to do something you don't want to do."

Barathol and Anjani waited for him outside the royal quarters, with the two additional palace guards. "Ready to go?" Barathol asked.

"Ready when you are," Aleron replied.

The prisoner waited for him in the questioning room, still in irons, with wrists locked to the table and ankles to the floor. The heavy oak table was bolted to the floor, as well, making it highly unlikely for a prisoner to cause much mischief.

The guards walked in first, taking positions on either side of the door, followed by Barathol, with his glaive, taking a position in the far corner, behind and to the left of the prisoner. Two prison guards remained outside the door, ready to take the prisoner back to the dungeon, after the king departed.

Aleron walked in and took his seat across from the assassin, on his narrow stool. The warden informed him that the prisoner had yet to sleep, being questioned throughout the night, but revealing nothing.

Aleron noticed a medallion on a leather cord, hanging from the man's neck. It looked to be enameled silver, depicting a white raven, on a blue background.

Religious? Odd trait for an assassin, he thought.

"I'll keep this simple. Why did you attempt to kill me last night?" Aleron asked.

"Because you are an abomination," the prisoner answered, as if it were a matter of fact.

"Funny, I don't feel particularly abominable. Who sent you?"

"Wouldn't you like to know that? I tell you nothing! I will go before the headsman regardless, so why should I tell you anything?"

"I will get the information from you, regardless. Oh, and you don't rate the headsman's axe, as it turns out. Traitors and assassins are hung from the neck in Sudea. Now, explain to me why I am an abomination."

"You need to ask that, sorcerer? You halfbloods are all abominations. The Allfather never meant men to wield magic. If he had, he would have made us so."

"I think I'm beginning to understand," Aleron said.

Religious, indeed, he thought.

"You believe halfbloods are unnatural and shouldn't exist at all, much less as your king."

"You do understand, filthy wizard," the assassin replied.

"Did you act alone, or are there others who feel as you do and helped you?"

"There are many others who feel as I do, and there's nothing you can do to me that will make me betray them."

"The smart answer would have been that you worked alone, but I wouldn't have believed you anyway. I will root out your co-conspirators, and they will follow you to the gallows. All of you will receive fair trials, of course, though I am not required to give you one, having witnessed your crime myself, but you will have one."

"I will not tell who the others are, and I don't believe your rubbish about reading my thoughts."

"Are you so sure of that?" Aleron spoke directly into the man's mind.

"I can peel your memories back like the layers of an onion and see all your deepest and darkest thoughts. That would be a shame, though, because it will leave you as a drooling idiot, and I can't, in good conscience, send one such as that to the gallows. I do so want to see you dangle from that rope, so be reasonable and answer my questions." He reverted to normal speech at the very end.

"I think not, halfblood." The man still talked with confidence, but Aleron could see in his eyes that what just occurred shook him a bit.

"There is no way for you to find any but me, even if you can read my thoughts. There are many who feel as I do, many powerful people, but I know not who they might be. I have no idea who gives me the instructions. I just receive them and the payment."

"So, you've done this sort of thing before, for these people?" Aleron asked.

"Not that sort of thing, no," the man answered. He was being more forthcoming since Aleron demonstrated the ability to enter his mind, despite his stating otherwise.

"I do various jobs for them, whatever needs doing."

"Who brings you your instructions and your payments?"

"I don't know the man; I never see him. He leaves me messages, and I leave my price."

"How did you and your employers come to connect, these men who share a common interest with you? It would be clearer if you were but a hired cutthroat, but you willingly undertook a suicide mission, for people you have never met, why?"

"I have a reputation for getting things done when others cannot. Many men hire me in just the same manner.

The only difference is the messages from these men were often just messages, not jobs. They shared the light of the Allfather with me these last months and kept me employed with honest tasks to support my family. This last job was to take care of my family for the rest of their lives, and I took it gladly because the task was just."

"Murdering me at my dinner table is a just cause?"

"The prophecies are clear; you will turn to darkness, and mankind will lose hope to fend off the Adversary. That is why you have to die, because the scourge of halfbloods is not natural to the world. You will hand us over to the darkness."

"Where is your family now?" Aleron asked, hoping for more leads to the ones acting behind the man sitting before him.

"Far away from you, halfblood," he replied. "I took the gold they paid me and sent them out of the kingdom. Even if you ruin my mind, you will not be able to touch them."

"Well, at least they paid you upfront. I would hate to think payment hinged on your success, leaving your family destitute with you dead. I have enough for now. Enjoy your stay."

Aleron stood and said, "Let's go, Barry; I think we've done all we can for today."

Barathol walked out ahead of him, and the palace guards fell in behind, as Aleron left the room.

"Take him back to his cell," he instructed the prison guards on the way out. "Thank you for your assistance."

"Yes, Your Grace," a guard replied, and Aleron and his group walked down the corridor to the guards stationed there.

Later, at the stewards' offices, Aleron recounted the interview to Gealton and Hadaras.

"He seemed pretty forthcoming about his motives, and I sensed his words as he said them. I felt no untruth in what he said."

"He likely does believe it wholeheartedly, but I do not," Gealton stated, unequivocally.

"My intelligence has given no indication of any sort of movement, clandestine or otherwise, religiously opposed to halfbloods in positions of power."

"There is indeed a general mistrust of sorcerers, these last couple of thousand years," Hadaras added, "due to their rarity since the Halfblood Caste dissolved, but I have never heard of any religious teachings against sorcery. It is possible that old mistrust could erupt in religious fervor, with Aleron's sudden appearance as a halfblood sorcerer and heir to the throne."

"Possible, but I don't think so. My eyes and ears would have picked up something. This was entirely too secretive for it to be anything widespread. I suspect, more likely, it was a plot among a few individuals at most, if not a single person. Whether what motivated those behind the plot was religion or not, I cannot say, but they found an individual, probably outspoken in his distrust of a halfblood ruling, and capitalized upon it. That is what I think is going on. We are thoroughly questioning every servant seeking reentry into palace service, asking what they know of your attacker."

"Are you finding anything out?" Aleron asked.

"Only that he was very new to the service, only a few weeks. The name he gave, Oberin, is probably an assumed one to hide a criminal record, and he came with excellent references from several prominent local establishments.

When we sent someone to check up on those references, we found all of the individuals he named, recently quit their jobs, or simply failed to come to work, for the past several days. One was found dead, in his room, and I'm sure we'll find more of those, before too long."

"Someone is covering their tracks," Hadaras observed.

"I would hazard to guess the shadow delivering Oberin's instructions and payment resides face-first in a ditch now."

"So it would appear," the Steward agreed.

"We will get to the bottom of this, Aleron, no matter how long it takes. Someone will let something slip, and one of my people will be there to hear it."

"Just how many spies do you have throughout the city and beyond, Lord Steward?" Aleron asked, beginning to comprehend that the position of Steward entailed being the spymaster for the palace.

"Exact numbers, I couldn't say for sure, Your Grace, but my network is quite extensive, I assure you."

"Very well, what would be an appropriate day for the trial and execution?"

"Trials and executions are traditionally conducted on Corballday," Gealton said. "That would make it one week from today, for the trial, on the twenty-first."

"The coronation is set for the thirtieth, right?"

"That is correct. It is the earliest a majority of lords and ladies can arrive at the capital.

Unfortunately, it will leave out my wife and brother-in-law, Damian, among others, but we cannot help that. We cannot afford to wait another six or seven months. Technically, you are still the crown prince until the official coronation."

"Then he will be tried and executed on the third day of the Hunger Moon. I will be king before he is tired and put to death. Have him moved to a more comfortable cell in the meantime. I won't have him dying of pneumonia before he gets to trial."

"A wise move," agreed Hadaras.

"It wouldn't do for you to appear heavy-handed by exercising too much authority prior to the official declaration of your rule."

"I was thinking more along the lines that I would have no authority to preside over either, before the coronation," Aleron replied.

"I want this to be my trial, not the steward's, no offence intended, Gealton. He tried to kill me at my own dinner table, and I'll not have anyone doing the dirty work for me."

"Do you intend to execute him yourself?" Gealton asked, with a hint of incredulousness in his voice.

"Considering it," he replied.

"It's not unheard of for the king to do the deed himself, in very serious cases, or for very high-ranking individuals, but it's been at least a thousand years since it ever happened."

"It's been over a thousand years since we had a king to do it."

"Be careful, Aleron," Hadaras advised.

"Is this what you wish for your first major act, as the king? The people might see it as vindictive."

"I will think it over, Grandfather, but I'm still leaning in that direction."

After leaving Gealton's office, Aleron stepped into his own offices, just off from the throne room and the Steward's office. The waiting area that he, Eilowyn, Hans, and Simeon occupied, after he first drew Andhanimwhid, connected both sets of offices to the throne room, though each had private doors to the throne room, as well.

A connecting hallway existed to allow passage between the offices, short of the outer corridor and the waiting area.

Lush blue and gold velvet seemed to be everywhere, and gold leaf adorned all the woodwork and furniture. Elaborate wall hangings, woven to depict significant scenes from Sudea's history, decorated most walls.

He unbuckled his belt and slipped the baldric and sword off from his shoulder, hanging them on a wall peg designed for that purpose. Pulling the sword from its scabbard, he carried it with him to the heavily padded chair behind the massive desk. Kicking off his boots, he sat in the chair and put his feet up on the desk.

SIGN OF THE WHITE RAVEN

With Andhanimwhid across his lap, he leaned his head back and closed his eyes, thinking about that day, over five years ago, when everything changed. He thought about Simeon, Hans, and where their faithful service brought them. Then he thought about his first day with Eilowyn, and his thoughts brightened. The sword glowed a soft blue as Aleron slipped off into a dream.

The summer sun is warm on my face as I ride across freshly harvested hayfields, just north of the city. Glancing down at my hands on the reins, they don't look quite right. To the right, I see Simeon ranging afield, and to my left is Eilowyn, a barely fifteen-year-old Eilowyn.

That explains the young-looking hands. I remembered this ride. It was the last time I visited Eilowyn before joining the Marines.

Looking back to my hands, they seem older now. I look up again to a place I do not recognize from my own life. Riding across unfamiliar green fields, I look to my left again. Riding beside me is a beautiful young elf maid, with jet-black hair and violet eyes. I recognize her now, as Lyssa, Crown Prince Aelwynn's younger cousin.

I am the first Aleron again, and this is my last time at Elvenholm. I am sixty now, and will soon return to Arundell, after five years at the elvish court, to take on more responsibility in running the kingdom. I will see Aelwynn again upon my return to the Sudean court. Lyssa, as well, is nearly sixty and barely out of childhood for an elf. I love her and have for a very long time, but we will never wed. It has become obvious lately that I am ageing much faster. Though I may live to three hundred, she should live past three thousand. I am an adult halfblood, while she is barely grown and not ready to wed for many years. We decided that I would return to Sudea and find a halfblood to be my queen and bear my heirs. Lyssa has no wish to watch me whither and fade while she lives on.

We round a copse, and Cyte comes into full view, the soaring minarets of the elvish palace dominating from its hilltop at the center of the city. We approach the gates…

Aleron woke from his dose, thinking, *now I can travel to Elvenholm.*

Chapter 32

Carpathday, Day 16, Allfather's Moon, 8766 Sudean Calendar

"It is very likely that the Adversary will break free of his bonds, in about three months from now," Aleron said to the gathered officials.

Generals Gershan, Twylin and Abershol from the Army, admirals Halger, Camar and Aeglun from the Navy, with General Corbak from the marines, as well as Gealton, Hadaras and the new Thallasian consul, Ambassador Ocaris, attended the lunchtime meeting, in the large conference room, off the Steward's offices.

"Zormat of Arkus has Zadehmal, and he is on his way back to Immin Bul with it. That is the reason for the blockade in the north, to cover his route to retrieve the axe. When he arrives at Immin Bul with Zadehmal, he will be able to free his father."

The generals and admirals broke into a heated discussion, immediately.

"Could the Sunjibis assist?"

"No, the Sunjibis are spread thin, as it is."

"Could Castia and Cop mount an offensive across Kolixtlan?"

"Can we call upon Ebareiza for assistance?"

"Are there enough ships in the north to break the blockade and head Zormat off?"

"No, there aren't enough ships, but how can we get more there, in time?"

"Can we move troops through dwarvish lands?"

And even, "Could we call upon the dwarves to invade the jungle?"

Their discussion ranged from brainstorming to bickering and back.

Only Ocaris seemed to have little to add to the discussion. The consul waited patiently for the discussion to die down before saying, "I believe that our current shortcomings pale in comparison with what's to come."

"What do you mean?" Camar demanded. All eyes in the room were upon the Thallasian now.

"According to a report I received just this morning, recent scouting expeditions into the northeast, five all told, have all failed to return. We have reason to suspect that the Arkan fleet is on its way."

After a few moments of silence, the discussion erupted anew. The addition of an Arkan fleet, crewed entirely by sorcerers, dashed any hopes of breaking the blockade. The discussion turned to land invasion and the likelihood that the Arkans would field ground troops into Kolixtlan and then on to Immin Bul.

General Twylin stated, "In all likelihood, they will field troops into Kolixtlan and on to Immin Bul to secure a clear route for their king, ahead of his arrival. We have little to answer even a small army of sorcerers. From what we know of the Arkan navy, one of their ships is a match for six of ours, even with Thallasian wizards aboard."

"What he says is true," Aeglun agreed. "Our usual tactic for the Arkans is avoidance, or fast disengagement. So far, we have identified only six of their ships, and we've only managed to sink one of them in over five years."

"I want to engage the dwarves," Aleron interjected, "as well as the Elmenians. They fought for us before, and I believe they will again if the cause is grave enough. I also mean to make inroads with Ebareiza. I know there is old bad blood between us, and I don't trust them, but I don't want them on the fence in this conflict."

"Your Grace, those would be useful resources in the upcoming fight," Gershan agreed, "but that fails to address our lack of sorcerers, to combat the Arkans."

"What of the Sudean Wizard's Guild?" Ocaris inquired. "I have heard that one exists, though renowned for its secrecy."

"The Sudean guild is very small, compared to yours," Hadaras answered.

"I'm afraid they will not make much of a difference in the grand scheme of things."

"I will reach out to our Wizard's Guild," Aleron stated.

"As a sorcerer myself, as well as their king, I hope to break them out of their shell.

After the coronation, I will issue an edict for all sorcerers to come out of hiding and offer their services in the upcoming conflict. I will offer them generous compensation and require their registration with the guild. Hopefully, that will sweeten the pot for the guild. I intend to offer state sponsorship to them as well. If I can reassure Sudean sorcerers of the safety in revealing themselves, they may come forward to lend their abilities to the cause."

"You will have centuries' worth of mistrust to contend with, on both sides of the magical coin," Gealton said.

"What will you offer to counter that?"

"Good pay, thorough combat training, and knighthood, if they successfully complete the training."

"Sudea hasn't had knights in over eight hundred years," Aeglun countered, "and no sorcerer knights for nearly four thousand.

Who would train these men? We have experienced trainers for conventional war, but we know nothing of arcane matters."

"Lord Marshal Hadaras?" Aleron posed the question to his grandfather.

"I believe I have sufficient experience in that respect," Hadaras answered. "I trained the halfblood knights for the last Great War. I think I can do it again for the next one if we can bring them out of hiding."

"That answers that question," Aleron said.

"Now I have another. Grandfather, can we convince the elves to deploy in force?"

"They will assist, to the best they are able, but the colonists will not leave their borders unattended. We cannot communicate directly with Elvenholm due to the wards protecting the homeland. It will take time for a ship from Wynn to reach Cyte, with a message requesting support. In that, it may be best for you to ask, in person."

"I thought the same, Grandfather, and I believe that I have a way to get there directly."

"How?" was all he asked.

Aleron projected the images from his dream yesterday into his grandfather's mind. "Do you recognize that place?"

"Yes, and lovely young Lyssa, as well," he admitted. "She is likely a thousand years dead now."

The men in the room, as a whole, looked utterly confused at what was going on between their king and the elf. Aleron chose to fill them in on a fact that only he and Hadaras knew.

"This sword," he said, standing to unsheathe it and lay it upon the table, "contains the spirit of my forebear, Aleron the First. He put it there, right before the Adversary cut him in two. I have seen the final battle, through his eyes, as I saw the aftermath of the massacre of Capar.

The most recent place he showed me was the gates of Cyte in Elvenholm, and if I have seen a place, I can travel there. That is how I came here from the central jungle where I was imprisoned."

Everyone remained stupefied, even Gealton, who should have been used to that sort of thing by then.

"The young king is full of surprises," the Thallasian Consul was the first to break the silence.

"Do these scenes come to you as visions, might I ask?"

"Usually, they come as dreams when I am close to the sword. I also see bits from every other king who ever held Andhanimwhid, but mostly from Aleron. This information must be held close. If the enemy discovers what I can do, they will think of a way to counter me."

"No offence intended, Your Grace, but I have trouble believing all this about a dead king inhabiting a magic sword," Abershol stated.

"I know that's a magic sword, but holding the spirit of our greatest king and your namesake. Moreover, this talk of traveling, I have never heard of anything like that, even among the elves. They speak over distance, but I've never heard of them traveling in that way."

Without a word, Aleron resheathed Andhanimwhid, and a break appeared in the air behind him, revealing a dimly lit library. He turned away and walked into Jacanda's study, letting the portal close behind him. After taking a few moments to check up on his grandmother and her servants through the crystal dome, he brought up an image of the meeting room.

Assuring himself that his end of the table was clear, he opened a portal into the floor, looking down on the table, and hopped into it. The table shook with the impact, and one of the pitchers of wine nearly tipped over. He reached down, took an apple from the basket of fruit, and tossed it into the air. He let the portal close, just as the apple reached it, and a cleanly sliced half fell back to his palm.

Hadaras and Gealton leaned back in their chairs, grinning, as the other men sat flabbergasted and speechless.

Aleron hopped off the table and handed a scroll to Gealton.

"Lord Steward, I think it would be good to have this copied, for posterity. Grandfather believed it to be one of the original copies, if perhaps not the original one."

Gealton unrolled the scroll and gasped in astonishment.

"This is the writ of independence for our kingdom, signed by King Balgare himself. Are you sure this is an original, Hadaras?"

"It certainly looks like my father's hand," Hadaras offered.

"If it is not original, it is a highly skilled forgery. Beside it, I saw ancient Coptian and Castian tablets, written in the old scripts of their tongues, from when the aelir first appeared to them."

"How is any of this possible?" Gealton asked.

"Nothing in Jacanda's realm ages or decays," Aleron answered, "and she has been there a very long time.

I think that she must have built it at about the same time as the first cities, if not before," he added.

"I would ask the same question, Your Grace," Admiral Camar said, "but let's expand it to the whole traveling question, let alone a whole realm that never ages.

How are you able to do this, something never known before? The military applications of such a talent go without saying."

"Grandfather, if you could help me, if I fail to explain properly," Aleron began.

"It is a skill the aelient have always had, and probably the aelir when they were here. They can enter the dream plane and travel there, covering great distances in a short time relative to time passing in the waking world."

"The place you just entered and returned from was some sort of dream?" Abershol asked.

"Not so much a dream as another plane of existence," Hadaras answered.

"The dream plane overlays the waking world. Mortals often enter it through dreams or visions, but normally only immortals enter there in the flesh."

"I have yet to pass into the actual world of dreams in the flesh," Aleron continued.

"The place I just visited is a sort of isolated bubble, a pocket built in the same manner as the dream world but constructed by an aelient for her own purposes. It follows her will, and she willed that no age or decay occur there. I don't believe that the dream plane acts in exactly the same way as her pocket."

"Different in what way?" Twylin asked.

"From what I understand of how aelient travel the dream paths," Hadaras recounted, "they must actually cross the physical distances involved. They may be able to cross the continent, leaving the waking world at one point and reentering at the other in seemingly no time at all, but they still must undergo the many months of travel to cover the distance involved. The way around this requirement is to build a bubble that connects to any and every point on Aertu, simultaneously."

"That is essentially what Jacanda, the aelient who had Shaggat abduct me, built so that she could see and travel to any place she desires," Aleron added.

"She taught me something of how to use it, and if I have seen a place, I can go to it directly from her abode. She has a sort of viewer that I can use to observe the place before I jump in. I'm not sure what would happen if someone was standing right where I open a doorway, but I can assume it would not be pleasant," he stated as he held up the neatly sliced apple, only just beginning to go brown, due to the cleanness of the cut.

"So, conceivably, you could move an army to any point on the globe, as long as you have seen the place before," Gershan ventured.

"How did you come to gain control of this aelient's private lair?"

"She hoped to sway me to the cause of the Adversary, and I played along until I knew enough of her secrets to escape. Then I subdued her and escaped back to here.

I have not yet tried to maintain two open gateways from Jacanda's lair, but it should be possible. I usually move through her library because that is where the viewer is located. For moving an army, I would use her courtyard or something similar."

"I think we are overlooking an important point in our excitement over this new possibility," Ocaris said.

"Your young king here claims to have subdued an immortal as if he were talking of roping an errant goat."

"Oh, aelient are not so difficult," Hadaras offered.

"They are very powerful, mind you, but at times they let that lull them into a sense of invincibility, and they are certainly not invincible. If you take them by surprise, which isn't difficult if they have become complacent or overconfident, they can be trapped and bound."

"Jacanda thought it enough to shield me from blue and red magic, not knowing I can wield the other colors."

Ocaris stared at him for several heartbeats and then asked, "What other colors? I have known only of red and blue wizards."

"There are two others," Hadaras replied, "and Aleron is the first mortal we know of who can wield all four.

Before him, we knew only the aelient and aelir to use the yellow and green. Yellow works for healing, and green for growth. He is also the first mortal of record to demonstrate an ability to physically enter the realm of dreams, but that may only apply to Jacanda's construct, not the real dream plane."

The room was silent for several moments, and then Aleron added, "I can combine the colors into different forms as well."

More stunned silence.

"I can combine them all and transform one thing to another. That's how I made myself a raven to travel to Kolixtlan."

"So what kind of wizard does that make you, Your Grace?" the Thallasian asked, after an interminably long pause.

"I guess, I'm a white wizard," Aleron offered as he took up the sliced apple again.

In a shimmer of white light, it became bright new silver, in the exact form of a sliced apple, down to the texture of the skin, the partly dried cut surface, and the exposed seeds. He needed to draw quite a bit of added material from the air about him, to bring up the mass of the fruit to that of silver, so there was a whistle of inrushing air to accompany the transformation.

He handed the piece to the astonished ambassador. "A token of our appreciation for your dedicated service to our alliance."

The generals and admirals around the table looked as astonished as the Thallasian consul did.

"Oh, it's pure silver, so it will dent easily," he added.

"I have no idea why the Allfather has seen fit to bless me with these abilities, but it must be for the battle to come. I will work toward using the ability to travel to our advantage.

After my coronation, I wish to travel to Elvenholm in order to enlist their aid, as well as to the dwarvish kingdoms. I know the two in the Blue Mountains, so I can go there directly.

As far as getting troops to anywhere useful, I will test the two-gateway idea. I know Kolixtlan, from recent memory, and Immin Bul, from one that's four thousand years old. If we move an army in that manner, I want to move it en masse through a pair of large portals, not in small groups to be slaughtered on the other side."

"How about ships?" Admiral Aeglun inquired.

"Ships will have to pass into the world of dreams and go the long route, if I learn to enter the actual dream world," Aleron said.

"So far, I know only how to enter Jacanda's creation, though she taught me something of the other. Unless I learn how to build a place like hers, over water, there will be no other way to bring in ships."

"But even by the long route, you could bring them around the world in a single day, correct?"

"I believe so," Aleron answered, "depending on my learning how it's done.

It's sort of like when you dream you've been at something for most of a day, only to wake and find you slept less than a bell. The crews will have sailed for months, even if no time passed in the waking world."

"And there are dangers on the dream plane that you will never face in the waking world," Hadaras informed them.

"Nightmares come to life there, as do your most pleasant dreams. Both may distract or even kill you. Aelient have the power to dispel the dreams of mortals, but there are things there that even they fear."

After much further discussion, deep into the afternoon, on how they might move troops and ships in time to make a difference in the face of the Arkan's efforts to free the Adversary, Aleron dismissed the officials.

Shortly afterward, Gealton dismissed himself, citing other pressing duties, not the least of which was checking up on the investigation of the assassination attempt, leaving Aleron alone with his grandfather.

"What do you think needs to happen?" Hadaras asked his grandson, the soon-to-be-crowned king.

"I think we can move troops straight to Immin Bul, ships to break the blockade, and we will probably do both of those things, but the Nameless One will still get free. Zormat will bring the axe to his father; it is meant to be, and I am meant to fight them. I will put our forces in the best position to fight that battle, not to vainly try to prevent it from happening."

"Are you certain there will be such a battle? The great war will not necessarily repeat itself."

"I'm not certain of anything, Grandfather, but I have to prepare for the worst case. I am sure that I will have to stand before the Nameless God and fight him. Whether that's at the head of an army, or alone, just him and me, I have no idea."

"Good, at least you're keeping reality in view," Hadaras granted.

"I think you are correct in thinking that fate will play a part. The prophecies seem to state as much, but all prophecies are like a coin, with two sides, one for dark and one for light. Unlike the coin, you have to do what you can to make it land on the side you want. If you rely totally on chance and fate, not putting any effort toward the outcome you desire, odds are good that the outcome will be the one that favors chaos and the Adversary's goals. Work your hardest to thwart his goals, and the rest should fall into place."

Chapter 33

Zorekday, Day 30, Allfather's Moon, 8766 Sudean Calendar

"Today is the day, my dear," Eilowyn said to Aleron, as he rolled out of bed.

The windows looked over a darkened courtyard, as the sun had yet to rise. Large oil lanterns hung from arched posts spaced along the walkways, illuminating the wisps of fine snow blowing across the paving stones.

Eilowyn padded around the rooms in a thick robe and slippers, lighting oil lamps from a candle.

"I've already called for a bath, and our breakfast will be served as soon as you get into your robe and slippers and make your way to the dining room."

Normally, they bathed in the evening and sat for breakfast after dressing, but today was different. Today was Aleron's coronation; dressing would take a bit longer than usual, and there would be no eating or drinking afterward, at least until after the ceremony.

"Gods, I wish this didn't have to be such a carnival attraction," Aleron stated, as he pushed his feet into his slippers. He dreaded the long, drawn-out dressing and primping he was about to be subject to.

More than three bells later, Aleron stood in his front room, dressed up like the prize peacock to which he so liked to refer. This time, he had no say in what he would wear. Vivid royal purple trousers, of thickly woven but fine silk, with a sharp crease and bright gold banding up the legs, bloused over mirror-polished knee-high black leather boots. Over a ruffled shirt of white silk, they placed a bright blue coat of heavy silk, with the gold scrollwork of a high lord on a backing of royal purple, the gold star of Sudea embroidered on the left breast, and bright gold epaulettes upon the shoulders. The purple leather baldric, newly dyed and polished to a high sheen, passed beneath the right epaulette, and the belt fastened with a new buckle of bright gold. For the final piece, Andhanimwhid rose above his right shoulder, the electrum and sapphires, meticulously polished and clean. His moustache and hair, freshly trimmed and brushed, shone golden brown in the morning sun. Aleron looked every inch a king from legend, and he despised every moment required to make him so.

Eilowyn stood before him, looking every inch a queen from the same legends. Aleron always thought her the most beautiful woman in the kingdom, but today, she nearly left him breathless. The delicately applied eye shadow set off her bright green eyes, while the judicious application of rouge accentuated her finely sculpted cheekbones and covered her faint freckles, remnants of the northern summer sun. She rarely wore makeup, so he was unused to seeing her so. They had her rich auburn hair elaborately coifed, as opposed to her usual braid, perfectly complemented by the large emerald studs in her earlobes. She wore a pleated gown of emerald-green silk, with a high collar of white lace. His betrothal gift hung round her neck on a new silver chain, and high green slippers of supple calfskin completed the ensemble.

"You look absolutely gorgeous, Eilowyn," he told her.

"I should for the amount of work they put into this, and you look lovely as well, Aleron," she chided.

"Like a prize peacock, I'm sure," he replied, wryly.

The royal dressing servants gazed upon their work with pride.

"You are a royal couple fit for a story book, Your Graces," Magda, the chief dresser, proclaimed. "I can hardly wait for the wedding in two weeks." Aleron groaned under his breath at the comment, and Eilowyn winked at him, amused at his discomfiture.

"Come now," she said. "We shouldn't keep the people waiting."

A squad of palace guards waited outside their quarters to escort the royal couple to the throne room. The men formed a square around them, and they made their way down corridors cleared of servants, down a gradually curving staircase to a large foyer, where Gealton and High Priest Dweilden waited.

Each carried their staff of office, the Steward's bearing the four-pointed Star of Sudea and the High Priest's bearing the figure of a white raven, symbolizing the Allfather.

The large double doors opened directly onto the raised dais where the throne sat. The Steward and the High Priest preceded them onto the dais and took their places at its head before the gathered nobles. Many common folk gathered behind the nobles as well, filling the expansive hall to overflowing.

Gealton announced to the crowd, "Lords and ladies, gentlefolk of Sudea, I present to you, Crown Prince Aleron, of House Sudea, the direct male-line descendant of the line of kings, heir to the throne of Sudea and Crown Princess Eilowyn, of the House of Stewards."

There was some murmuring among the lords and ladies. From his position at the front of the crowd, with Barathol, Feadra, Anjani, and Eilowyn's extended family, Geldun heard comments amounting to disapproval of Eilowyn taking part in the ceremony.

Common knowledge was that the couple was married, but many, not knowing the circumstances or not caring, disapproved of the arrangement. He noted Hadaras' momentary scowl, obviously overhearing similar comments.

He and Jessamine stood to the other side of the Steward's family, with Cladus, and Eilowyn's younger brother, Hameln. Jessamine appeared as an elf today, as did Hadaras, who no longer needed to conceal his true nature. Her beauty earned her many sidelong glances, if not outright stares, which earned several lords an elbow to the ribs from their ladies.

"They do make a stunning couple, do they not?" Jessamine said, a bit loudly, as Aleron and Eilowyn strode onto the dais and took a position between and slightly to the front of Gealton and Dweilden, while the palace guards fanned out to a semicircle, surrounding the four. These guards were mainly ceremonial, as guards were already in position at the steps to the dais and archers filled the balconies.

Aleron bowed low to the assembly, while Eilowyn curtseyed and took two steps back. Then, Aleron drew Andhanimwhid and set it point to the floor, as he genuflected behind it. The sword glowed blue in his hands, the power visible even to those not magically inclined. Streams of energy crackled over the backs of his hands, and his gray eyes shone blue.

I'd forgotten just how much raw energy is in that blade, Jessamine commented to Hadaras.

It's a wonder he didn't kill himself in Kolixtla, drawing upon its full power."

We have no idea what the lad can handle, either, Hadaras replied.

Don't forget that he took all that the red priests threw at him as well, and he hurled it all back at them, blended as purple. After that, he surprised one of your kind and subdued her. The only problem is that there is not any mortal who can teach him the limits of his power. He broke his bonds with yellow magic of all things.

Yes, my love, it requires a tremendous amount of yellow power to deal damage. With that being said, I believe that my people should take an active role in his training. I will seek trainers among my folk, but I am afraid that many are like my brother, and wish to avoid entanglement in the troubles of mortals.

Gealton opened the chest, atop a carved wood pedestal, and drew out the ancient crown of Sudea, a silver-framed spangenhelm, with electrum panels. A four-pointed star of gold emblazoned the brow, extending onto the nasal, and a raven about to take flight, worked in a dwarvish metal so white as to appear like ivory, formed the crest.

The steward held the crown high above his head and turned to Aleron.

He stepped forward and stated, "By my authority, as Lord Steward of the Kingdom of Sudea, Keeper of the Royal Tokens and the Record of Precedence, I name thee Aleron, King of Sudea, the second of that name, and lay upon your brow this crown, signifying your right to rule."

He lowered the helm onto Aleron's head and stepped back.

The High Priest stepped forward and said, raising his staff, "In the name of the Allfather, creator of all things, the beginning, and the end, I bless this, the raising of Aleron the Second, to be king over all of Sudea. May his reign be long and prosperous."

Aleron stood and sheathed the greatsword in one fluid motion.

"Lords and Ladies, people of Sudea, it is with a glad heart that I receive the great honor to lead your kingdom. For my first act, as your king, I wish for my wife, Crown Princess Eilowyn to come forward."

Eilowyn stepped up beside Aleron, took the hand he offered, and settled to her knees. Gealton returned to the chest and withdrew a circlet of intertwined silver and electrum knot work, fastened with ten wheeling white ravens of that same white dwarvish metal and a gold four-pointed star worked upon the brow.

He brought the crown to Aleron, who took it in both hands and held it high above his head.

"In the name of the most high, the Allfather, creator of all things, I name Eilowyn to be my consort, and queen over all of Sudea."

He placed the crown upon her head and then held out both hands; she took them, and he helped her to stand.

They turned to face the crowd, hand in hand, as Dweilden stepped forward again, to speak the words required of ritual. "In the name of the Allfather, creator of all things, the beginning, and the end, I bless this union and the raising of Eilowyn, to be queen over all of Sudea. May their union and her reign be long and prosperous."

As he raised his staff to complete the blessing, the ivory raven atop it erupted in a flash of white light, accompanied by the whooshing sound of incoming air.

A full-sized raven, white as the new snow outside, flew from the head of the staff and circled the royal couple three times before disappearing into the vaulted ceiling.

Somehow, the High Priest managed to maintain his composure, settling his now headless staff to the floor.

Many of the gathering stood slack jawed, to include Gealton and some of the guards for a moment. A lady in the front row fainted, caught by the lord beside her before she could hit the floor.

Hadaras looked to Aleron, with the obvious question in his eyes.

Was that you?

No, Grandfather, Aleron sent back.

Even if I thought of it, I wouldn't have done anything that audacious.

Well, that was definitely a sign, Jessamine sent to both.

Goodbye, Grandfather; it was nice to see you again, she projected out to the rafters, but received no reply.

Eilowyn stared at him, but he could only return her incredulous look with one of his own.

That was not me, he projected into her mind. Her look told him that she did not entirely believe him.

Gealton stepped to face the astonished crowd. "Lords and ladies, good people of Sudea, thank you for attending today's ceremony. The king will begin holding formal audiences at the first bell past noon. Thank you all again."

With that, they all turned and walked to the large double doors, which opened upon their approach.

The massive doors across the hall from the throne opened, and the crowd began to exit. The din of hundreds of people attempting to talk over one another filled the great hall and echoed into the rafters. Most were talking about what they had just witnessed, many proclaiming it a sign from the Allfather, some that it was the Allfather himself, while a few decried it as a work of dark sorcery.

Those last voices were the ones that worried Hadaras, as he and Jessamine worked their way toward a side door leading into the palace complex. Aleron's friends and Eilowyn's relatives made their way that direction as well, all set to gather in the large meeting room adjacent to the Steward's offices.

Back in the foyer, the tumult rose as Dweilden's composure began to crack. "What was that?" he cawed, staring at the headless staff.

The only part left of the carving was the crossbar that the ivory raven grasped as a perch. It was now smoothly polished ivory, devoid of any trace of the grasping feet once carved into its surface.

"Your Grace," he retained enough composure for the proper courtesies at least, "your coronation was not the time or place for magical trickery and stunts."

"Eilowyn looked to Aleron with studying eyes as he replied,

"High Priest Dweilden, I can assure you that was not my doing, and it was no trick anyone I know of could have done. Turning a dead statue into a living flying creature is beyond my abilities."

"My husband is telling the truth, Master Dweilden," Eilowyn assured him.

"Aleron is a terrible liar. I can assure you that he is telling the truth."

"Then who is responsible? That's what I want to know. It was in extremely poor taste."

"The Allfather was responsible," Jessamine answered. She and Hadaras had just entered the foyer from inside the palace.

"I told the others to wait for us, while we sorted things out," Hadaras followed.

"Preposterous!" Dweilden exclaimed.

"I know that you are elves, but the Allfather never appeared to you, any more than he appeared to us. All we know of him is through his children, the gods."

"I know my own grandfather when I see him," Jessamine proclaimed.

She let her guise shift from that of an elf to her preferred form, her green silk gown transforming into one of leaves and her dark hair entwined with thin vines. Her eyes became deep pools of purplish black, like the space between the stars or water too deep to fathom.

"My grandfather saw fit to bless this event in person, priest, take it for the blessing and wonder that it is."

She turned back to Hadaras and said, "My love, I must depart before the festivities. It weakens me greatly to be apart from my trees. Come to me when you are able."

She kissed him, turned away, and opened a portal, stepping into what looked to be the land around Arundell, only without the buildings.

As the portal snapped shut behind Jessamine, Aleron said, "I guess it's obvious now that Jessie is not really my cousin.

Anyhow," he turned to the once again dumbfounded high priest and said, "Perhaps I can help with your staff. I know it will be difficult to find an ivory carver to do it in time for the wedding."

He removed his crown and held it up, between them.

"Now, is this essentially the same pose and size, only in truesilver?" he asked.

"Y-yes, I...believe so," Dweilden answered.

Aleron reached out and grabbed the top of the staff at the ivory crossbar. He probed the ivory, gaining a sense of its structure and composition, and then willed it to grow into a copy of the white metal figure from the crown.

A misty white radiance arose at the head of the staff, and with a faint whistle of incoming air, the ivory raven once again held its place atop the High Priest's scepter.

"Will that work for you, Master Dweilden?"

"I...think that will do quite nicely, Your Grace. My thanks to you and your...family." Dweilden replied nervously, bowed, and walked out of the foyer into the palace beyond, obviously wishing to get away from all the strangeness that had just befallen him.

"Well, wasn't that exciting?" Gealton exclaimed.

"Now, we'd best get to the feast so you youngsters can get some food in you, before your first afternoon of petitioners.

They left the foyer and entered the area where the friends and family gathered.

"Are they nearly set up?" Gealton asked.

"Nearly so," Lord Anderly, Majori's husband, answered. The tables are out and set, and the food is coming out now.

As it turned out, many of the commoners, filling the back of the hall, were servants, waiting to set up for the feast. As soon as space became available behind the retreating throng, tables, chairs, and place settings came out from alcoves, hidden by hanging tapestries.

From a large set of double doors, leading directly to the kitchens, carts laden with food rolled in. The servants laid trenchers of roasted meat, fish, and winter vegetables upon each table. Soon, with the preparations complete, the guests began reentering the great hall.

"Looks ready," Barathol announced, peering through the gap between the doors.

"Let's get in there before they eat it all."

"Aw, listen to the poor starving child," Anjani chided him.

"See, his ribs are just sticking out, he's so hungry!" She latched onto him and dug her fingers hard into his ribs, just below the armpits. Barathol yelped and attempted to escape her tickling.

"Let's keep it together," Gealton announced.

"We can't walk out there acting like a bunch of hooligans. You will all go out now and take your places at the head table. I will announce the king and queen, and all will rise before I go to my seat on Aleron's right. Aleron will seat Eilowyn, I will seat Aleron, and then we may all sit."

After the choreographed seating, they got down to the business of eating. All the food tasted wonderful, and Aleron found himself eating more than he should have, washing it down with more wine than he should have.

By the time the feast ended, and it was time to prepare for the mostly ceremonial first petitioners, Aleron was ready for a nap, not to hold court. He considered healing himself from the effects of the alcohol, but was in too good a mood to want to sober out of it. He was glad nothing of real import would come before him today because he was not prepared to wield anything resembling true competence.

He sat upon the throne and hoped he could keep his eyes open for the entire thing. Eilowyn had an ornate, but still solid chair, set to the left of the throne.

Aleron was glad for her presence, to not only keep him awake, but also because she knew more about court politics, kingdom policies, and because she seemed far more awake than he did. Aleron braced himself as the first petitioner approached.

***

Jessamine ran, the long gown she sported earlier transformed into a short skirt. As an aelient, she did not tire and could run faster than a horse.

It would be easier to travel if she abandoned her physical form, but that had its own problems that she would rather not deal with, not the least of them being the necessity of taking a mortal's body to reconstitute oneself if one could not return to the original body, and a body was required to interact on the physical plane.

A disembodied aelient could always inhabit the body of a beast and undertake the laborious process of growing it into a form befitting an immortal, but that was a long process, and she would feel badly about even that sacrifice.

The unscrupulous of her brethren, Jacanda, for example, would simply take over the body of a sentient being. Most of her kind chose to simply travel the dream plane, however long it took to reach their destination.

She sprinted over the countryside west of Arundell, devoid of roads and with no human structures impeding her travel, only rocks, trees, and grass to contend with.

When she approached the spot where the bridge over the west fork of the Arun River existed in the waking world, she gathered herself and then leapt the chasm. The mix of vines and hair flowed up and behind her as she crested the arc and entered free fall, before landing deftly on the other side.

Daytime travel should be uneventful, but after nightfall, the potential for human nightmares come alive would be a real concern, and she would need to seek shelter.

She never understood how the day and night cycle here in the dream plane seemed to sync with that of the waking world, until one left the dream plane. Though she faced several days travel overland, she knew that she would arrive back at the farmstead only minutes after she left the ceremony.

Chapter 34

Corballday, Day 3, Hunger Moon, 8766 Sudean Calendar

"Today is the day, my dear," Aleron said to Eilowyn, as he rolled out of bed, sarcastically mirroring her greeting to him, three days earlier, "my very first trial as king, and a capital crime at that.

"You will do just fine, My Love," she replied. "You will have my father and the counselors to help guide you."

Traditionally, a Sudean court for a capital offense consists of the king and the steward when available, and enough members of the council of lords to make eleven.

The highest-ranking individual on the court, be he the king, steward, or the most senior lord, casts his vote only in the event of a tie among the other ten. The king, however, maintains the authority to pardon any ruling of guilt or lessen the penalty from death to fine or imprisonment.

"I'm not even required to go through with this, but it seems like the right thing to do. Are you ready to testify?"

"I'm ready," she replied. Eilowyn and the others present at the dinner, aside from Aleron and Gealton, would testify before the court today.

"I'm not looking forward to this at all, but it needs to be done. I guess I should get dressed now."

The court convened in the great hall, with Aleron seated upon the throne, crown upon his head, and Andhanimwhid across his knees. Five chairs fanned out on either side of the throne. Gealton sat directly right of the throne, while the heads of some of Sudea's most influential houses filled the other nine seats.

243

Aleron held responsibility for the majority of the speaking parts of the proceedings, with the council members and steward remaining silent to hear testimony. He would call the witnesses to speak, followed by the defendant who would speak last, on his own behalf.

There were no witnesses for the defense going into the trial, but anyone could volunteer to speak on the defendant's behalf before the senior member of the panel read the verdict.

After the verdict, there was no opportunity to appeal, as trials and executions occurred on the same day in accordance with Sudean law. The gallows waited on the parade ground, swept clean of snow, and with a freshly tied noose in anticipation of a guilty verdict.

Several hundred people stood among the columns of the great hall, leaving the center aisle clear for the procession to come.

When the bells chimed twelve, Aleron called out, "Bring forward the accused."

The great doors opened at the front of the hall, admitting the biting winter wind, along with six prison guards surrounding a lanky, dark-haired individual in irons, and a clean prison uniform of rough-spun linen.

They walked the long distance to the throne, the great hall being easily longer than the entire remainder of the palace, measured in any direction. They halted at the foot of the steps, and a servant brought forth a chair, placing it behind the prisoner.

The guards stepped to the sides, turning to face the accused as he sat.

"Oberin, you stand accused of attempted assassination against the Crown Prince of Sudea," Aleron announced to the accused and the audience. "How do you plead?"

"Not guilty, Your Grace," Oberin replied, his dark eyes conveying contempt.

"I tried to kill a filthy halfblood, pretending to be our king."

The crowd erupted in gasps and murmurs, the noise of which threatened to drown out the proceedings until Aleron put a stop to it.

"Silence in the hall!" he ordered, projecting his voice with a blend of red and blue power, overpowering the sound of the crowd.

When the noise abated, he continued. "So, you freely admit to trying to kill me?"

"Do you freely admit to pretending to our throne? That is who I intended to kill; was that you?"

"I hope you are aware that I am not required to proceed with this trial, having witnessed your crime myself. Would you prefer I dispense with this formality and order your execution straightaway?"

Oberin said nothing in answer, so Aleron continued. "You will now remain silent, Oberin, as the witnesses recall the events of the evening of the fourteenth day of the Allfather's Moon. I call forward the first witness for the crown."

Kaitelyn, the serving woman whose scream alerted the diners to Oberin's treachery, stepped up to the podium set up to the left of the throne, next to the last councilman's chair, and facing the accused. A small, plain-featured woman in her middle years, she wore her graying blonde hair in a severe bun and dressed in the uniform of the palace staff, a fine blue woolen gown.

"Please state your name, for the court," Aleron directed.

"My name is Kaitelyn, Your Grace," she answered.

"Do you pledge, by the grace of the Allfather, to testify truthfully, speaking no untruth, by word or omission?"

"I do, Your Grace."

"Were you present at the time of the alleged crime, and in what capacity were you present?"

"Yes, Your Grace, I was there. I'm the lead server to your Royal Highness's family, Your Grace, though that be a brand-new position."

"Do you know the accused who sits before you, and if so, for how long?"

She looked to the man shackled in the chair and replied, "I do know Oberin, Your Grace. He's been with our staff for a few weeks. He seemed a capable and trustworthy sort, up to that night."

"How did Oberin come to be working in the royal quarters, on the night the alleged crime is said to have occurred?" Aleron asked.

"I'm not sure how he came to be workin' with me, Your Grace. He showed up for the shift, claimin' to be replacin' Jonas, who was sick that night."

"What did you see on the night of the fourteenth, when the man before you served in the royal quarters?"

"Everything was going normally, Your Grace. We served several courses, and we were cleanin' up the plates an' cups at the end, when Oberin pulled a crossbow out, and pointed it at Your Highness."

She choked up a bit as she continued, "I screamed to warn you, but I was too late. He already loosed a bolt at you, but then it disappeared in a flash of blue flames, and Oberin went flying into the wall, ahead of a flash of purple light. The next I knew, he was hanging from the wall, by magic, I guess, and you ordered me to get the guards."

Oberin sat with an impassive expression upon his face as the woman stated his duplicity in plain terms. Outwardly, he seemed to harbor no ill will toward his former coworker but when his gaze turned to the king, it turned to cold malice.

"Thank you, Kaitelyn, for your honest testimony. You may go," Aleron said, releasing her to move on to the next witness.

They moved through several witnesses, Anjani, Feadra, Barathol, Geldun, Majori, and Eilowyn, all of whom corroborated Kaitelyn's testimony.

Finally, it came to Cladus, and as with all those previous, Aleron repeated, "Do you pledge, by the grace of the Allfather, to testify truthfully, speaking no untruth, by word or omission?"

"I do so pledge, Your Grace," the bard answered.

He stood tall and ruggedly handsome as he recounted the events of the evening with the eloquence of a true storyteller. The fawning expressions of several ladies in the audience hinted they were falling in love, or perhaps merely lust, much to the annoyance of their lords. However, when Cladus came to recount subduing the assassin, his words came out slowly and with some difficulty, breaking the spell he had over his audience.

"Is there some problem, Cladus?" Aleron asked, out of genuine concern.

"Your Grace," he conceded. "As you are well aware, not many are familiar with the fact that I am a halfblood and a sorcerer."

"Yes, of that I am aware. I'm afraid that your secret is out, old friend. Might you be the first to answer the call?"

"I am familiar with your edict, Your Grace, but I'm unsure if knighthood is for me. I'm an artist at heart."

Oberin glowered at the bard, realizing him to be of the minority he hated, and Aleron wondered at the source of that hatred. Growing up, halfbloods were more legend than real, and he recalled no true prejudice against them.

"The court requires no further witnesses," he announced to the assembly.

"Oberin, why is it that you hate halfbloods so?

My father was heir to this throne, though he knew it not. He was a simple woodsman and charcoal burner, but no halfblood.

I am halfblood because my mother was an elf. I had no choice in my parentage, so why do you hate me for it?

Until nigh on fifteen years of age, I thought myself a commoner, the simple son of a charcoal burner. Do you suppose I became suddenly evil upon learning of my parentage?

I apologize to the court, for these questions have no bearing upon the case at hand, only to my own curiosity."

Pausing a few moments to let the assassin digest his words, he continued, "Oberin, I now afford you the time to explain and defend your actions, as I choose to call no further witnesses. You are free to speak on your own behalf."

Oberin stood, looking a bit more thoughtful than before. He previously gave no thought of Aleron's origins, having assumed him raised for the throne in secret with full knowledge of his parentage.

"Your Grace," he began. It was the first time the assassin utilized the honorific, without a tone of contempt.

"It is true that I attempted to kill the crown prince, yourself at the time, on the night of the fourteenth. I was led to believe my cause was righteous by those who persuaded me to do the deed. At this time, I have second thoughts and questions for my employers.

Though I still distrust sorcerers, I have doubts now as to the righteousness of my actions. I throw myself upon the mercy of this court and hope that you will treat me fairly."

"Councilors and Steward, I await your decision on the matter," Aleron entreated, "Do you require time to deliberate?"

Gealton, looking younger than his sixty years with a full head of salt and pepper hair, turned to each councilor in turn. The councilors, all nine, in turn shook their heads in the negative and displayed their fists, thumbs-down to indicate a guilty verdict.

"The council is decided," Gealton announced.

"The defendant, known to us as Oberin, is guilty and will be sentenced to hang by the neck, this third day of the Hunger Moon of the year 8766."

The assassin looked somber but unsurprised, a major departure from the attitude he displayed upon his entry to the court, as the reality of his actions and the court's decision set in.

"Your Grace, if I may address the court one more time?" he entreated.

"You may," Aleron allowed.

"Your Grace, I would apologize for the inconvenience I have placed upon you and your family."

"From what I gathered, in our conversation prior to this trial, you value your family's welfare above all else, do you not, Oberin?"

"Yes, Your Grace. All of my misdeeds, my whole life was so that they could have better than I."

"I decree," Aleron announced to the gathering, "that the Crown of Sudea is not without mercy.

Oberin, you will not be executed this day, having shown genuine remorse for your actions. I sentence you to exile from the Kingdom of Sudea. A military escort will conduct you to the border of your choosing and allow you to leave our kingdom, never to return. Do you accept these terms?"

"Yes, Your Grace," Oberin replied, surprise and hope in his eyes.

"I gladly accept these terms, and would choose to seek my family in Ebareiza, though I deserve no such thing."

"I will arrange that. Fare thee well, Oberin."

Turning to the crowd, "I hope this serves as a message to those who unjustly manipulated this man that I hold thee more responsible than those perpetrators you bend to your designs.

If ever I find those who orchestrated this attack, or any like it, I will bring no such mercy, and there will be no hanging. I will take their heads with the blade of my office."

Andhanimwhid blazed bright blue as Aleron stood and raised it above his head. Azure lightning arced to the rafters, and blue radiance permeated his eyes.

"A true king may not shirk the duties of his office, no matter how unpleasant.

From here on, in regard to capital crimes against the Crown of Sudea, none other than the king may execute those so convicted, and the method shall be beheading with the symbol of his office, Andhanimwhid!"

The blue lightning turned to brilliant white, blinding all but Aleron.

As the crowd regained their composure, most blinking and some rubbing their eyes, Aleron announced, "This royal court is adjourned, and the sentence is final!"

Such a proclamation from the king left no room for controversy. Not even a subsequent king could ever overturn the ruling.

Later that evening, as they retired in their quarters, Eilowyn said, "I am happy that you showed mercy on that man, my love. He was manipulated by others in his thoughts and actions."

She let him assist her in undoing the laces of her bodice, and she slipped out of her gown, hanging it with care in their closet.

"I never intended to execute him after talking to him in the dungeon," he confided, as he shrugged out of his uniform.

He hung the coat on the back of a chair and slung his baldric overtop.

"Someone in a powerful position, with money, paid him to do what he did. I don't think he ever would have gone to the ends he did if they hadn't convinced him of the righteousness of it, as well as assuring his family's well-being.

Now, I want to assure there will be no retaliation against his wife and children. I will locate them, and if anyone moves against them, it will lead me to the perpetrators."

He kicked his trousers off to the side, leaving him in his undergarments.

Eilowyn undid the top laces to her shift, letting it fall to the floor, as she said, "You are a true king to these people, my love."

She moved to him and pulled his undershirt over his head.

"Now come to bed and make me your queen."

Chapter 35

Sildaenday, Day 5, Hunger Moon, 8766 Sudean Calendar

Aleron and Hadaras stood together in Jacanda's library, gazing upon a land Aleron knew only from a dream. To Hadaras, the scene was old and familiar. Aleron wore the full regalia of his office, to include the crown, and Hadaras wore the green dress uniform of a Sudean army lord marshal, the last official rank he held.

"It's not exactly as I remember it," Aleron commented, "but I suppose that's to be expected."

"Yes, my boy," Hadaras replied, "considering that memory is four millennia old. I find it's remarkably unchanged from how I remember it, disturbingly so."

"Why do you say that, Grandfather?"

"My people are somewhat resistant to change. I believe it to be our greatest flaw. The colonists are a bit better about it because they must be to survive on the continent. Elvenholm persists through the ages, neither changing nor growing. No strife or hardship befalls that land. I'm afraid that I won't find it much changed from my youth, when the aelir walked among us."

"Are you saying that stability and peace are a bad thing?"

"When they lead to stagnation? Yes. My nephew, Anglemar, is only our people's third king and has held the throne barely three hundred and nineteen years. Little changes in just three generations."

"Is that why you choose to live among us men, Grandfather? Jacanda said you were impatient and impulsive for an elf your age."

Hadaras gave his grandson a look that was somewhere between cross and amused.

"There is no elf "my age," as you say, and much as I value history, I value discovery more.

My people ceased discovering new things a very long time ago.

Look at the dwarves, with no magic for a crutch, and lives just long enough to pass knowledge down to three generations. They are proud of their history, and they build upon it, creating wonders of artisanship. I've heard rumors of flying engines seen over the White Mountains.

Elves would never invent such things, even less now than before. We are becoming old as a people, and it saddens me."

"You were supposed to be the second king of Elvenholm, weren't you, Grandfather?"

"Yes, you know that story already. Aelwynn was born more than forty-seven-hundred years after me, with our father nearing the end of his life. I thought I would not live much longer myself, as our father was only five-hundred and fifty years older than I, so I gave up my claim to the throne. Mostly, I did it because I had no desire to hold it."

"Why wouldn't you want to be king?" Aleron asked.

"I saw the stagnation beginning even then, and I felt I could do more good as high sorcerer than as king.

I studied with the dwarves for hundreds of years to learn the techniques required to forge that blade you now carry. Their methods, plus our magic, built things unheard of before, but few others among elves could be convinced to do the same. They preferred to learn from me rather than from the dwarves, whom they consider uncouth, limiting the flow of information to those few elves willing to work with other peoples."

"I guess I understand," Aleron replied.

"Are you ready to cross over now?"

"As ready as I'll ever be."

Aleron opened a portal onto the cobblestone roadway, leading up to the gates of Cyte, two hundred paces from the walls.

"We should be out of bowshot here."

"Yes, but only just," Hadaras replied. "I would suggest we wait here for an escort."

"Why do they have walls and guard towers if no invaders can come here?"

"We built them in response to the inevitable possibility that someone would find a way through, and here we are."

"Ten thousand years is a long time to wait to prove a suspicion."

"I told you, my boy, elves are resistant to change. They walk the walls because they have always walked the walls."

As they waited, a horn sounded a complex note, and soon after, the city's massive gates opened. A contingent of armored knights issued from the gate. Their silvered armor gleamed in the morning sun.

"And here comes the Royal Guard," Hadaras commented as they rode forth, the gates closing behind them.

"They recognized your uniform and sent the appropriate escort. The crown has likely heard of your nature and expected this eventuality."

"How is this specific to me?" Aleron asked.

The silvered armor implies a royal escort, my boy. Best you reply to them appropriately."

Aleron stood straight and awaited the escort.

"Who be you, to set foot in the sovereign territory of the kingdom of the Elves?" the leader of the escort asked, in a formal yet challenging tone.

"I am Aleron, King of Sudea, second of that name, and this is my most trusted advisor, Hadaras, known in the past as Goromir," Aleron answered, in the most severe tone he could muster.

"I am Kalmir, Captain of the Royal Guard. I see that the stories are true. A new king has arisen, and Goromir once again walks among the living.

I was but a youngling when Aleron the First sacrificed his life, and our greatest sorcerer Goromir vanished.

On behalf of King Anglemar, I welcome thee to Elvenholm. I am sure that he will have the same questions as I, in how you came to us, but on an elven vessel.

Please follow me, Your Grace. The king awaits you."

Kalmir wheeled his gray stallion about and then dismounted, out of respect. The other eight followed suit. As they approached the city gates, each elf led a near identical gray stallion.

"Quite a lot of consistency in the breeding of their horses," Aleron commented to his grandfather.

"Yes, they have had quite some time to get it straight. I used to crossbreed them purposely, to get the performance I wanted in a not so obvious package. Do you remember my old brown mare?"

"The one who could outrun the best racers in Swaincott? Yes, I remember her."

"She was half this breed, at least the colonial version of elvish destrier and half Sudean desert charger. It makes for a fast little package, with the stamina to run all day and still have strength for a fight."

"And she looked like a local cart horse. As I recall, most of those who bet against her were sadly disappointed."

"Yes, sadly so," Hadaras agreed, grinning, as they approached the golden gates of Cyte.

The gates actually consist of a steel core, overlaid with pure iron, and plated heavily with pure gold, making them virtually maintenance-free, aside from lubricating the hinges.

The trumpeter raised his instrument to his lips, blew a series of notes, and the massive gates swung open, with barely a whisper to belie the sheer amount of metal in motion.

As they drew near, Aleron saw each twisted octagonal bar to be as thick as a man's calf and spaced no more than to allow a child's head to pass through. The archway vaulted high above their heads as they passed through the white marble wall, nearly as thick as the one protecting Arundell.

"Very impressive masonry and smith work," Aleron commented.

"Yes, this dates to the time we were willing to learn of what the dwarves had to offer. I fear that their skill has now surpassed this tenfold," Hadaras replied.

"I dare say you're right, Grandfather," Aleron agreed, remembering the sheer scale of the breastworks at Dhargul and Nhargul.

Some of the escort looked askance at their commentary, though they maintained the discipline to keep their opinions to themselves. Elves are unaccustomed to admit learning anything from the "lesser" races.

The procession continued through the city with its white marble buildings and vaulted arches. Elevated walkways connected most buildings at the second and third stories, and sometimes higher, keeping most foot traffic off the roadway.

To Aleron, it reminded him of the colonial architecture, only in stone instead of wood, and he could easily see where some of Sudea's architectural traditions originated.

He also sensed blue magic all around, just as when he visited Wynn as a boy, only now his experience gave him a better gauge as to its magnitude. The local air felt positively thick with the stuff.

When they reached the palace gates proper, the trumpeter blew another complex series, and the great gilded doors swung inwards, once again with barely a sound.

Kalmir handed the reins off to his second and said, "Please follow me, Your Grace."

He led the way into the palace, straight up the corridor leading to the royal audience chamber. These doors stood open, and they stepped into the chamber.

He announced in Elvish, *"Your Majesty, I present to you the King of Sudea, Aleron the Second, and his advisor Hadaras, known formerly as Goromir."*

"Send our honored guests forward," said the herald standing off the left side of the throne.

King Anglemar sat straight upon his throne of carved pear wood, and another, in the robes of the High Sorcerer, stood at his right hand.

Kalmir stepped off to one side and said, "You may proceed, Your Grace."

"Thank you, Captain," Aleron answered.

He understood the exchange quite well, Elvish being the first language he learned after his native tongue, and not far removed from Sudean.

He and Hadaras walked forward, stopping three paces from the throne, whereupon Hadaras dropped to one knee, and Aleron bowed low, befitting one of equal station to the king.

"I greet thee, Anglemar, King of Elves, as king of the men of Sudea, and request audience with thee."

Aleron's Elvish was impeccable, an obvious surprise to the king and those attending him.

"May my Sudean be as good as your Elvish, dear Cousin," Anglemar replied.

"Please rise, Uncle. Though I have never had the pleasure of your company, my beloved father spoke much and highly of you."

Hadaras stood and replied, "I appreciate your sentiment, Your Majesty.

Your father was much beloved to me as well, and I deeply regret being unable to attend his funeral."

"That would have been awkward if you had, Uncle, considering you were presumed over three millennia dead yourself.

Now, if you do not mind telling me, how did you manage to enter our realm without the benefit of one of our ships? I realize you were our greatest sorcerer, but such a thing should not be possible."

"For that, you must ask my grandson, the king, for he brought me here, not the other way around."

Anglemar and his high sorcerer showed their surprise again, turning their attention to Aleron, incredulous looks on their faces.

"Oh, and greetings, Trafelgar. I'm happy to see you have come far. You were one of my most promising pupils."

"I thank thee, Goromir. From such as you, the praise is indeed flattering," the current high sorcerer responded before turning his attention back to Aleron.

"Your Grace, you appear nearly identical to your forebear, Aleron the First, though I daresay your hair is a bit darker."

"There has been talk that the great king of men has been reborn," Anglemar directed to Aleron, "but he was not known to be a great sorcerer.

What say you to this, Cousin?"

"Cousin," Aleron began, taking Anglemar's cue on dropping the formality between equals, "I am definitely my own person.

I am familiar with the spirit of my ancestor. His spirit is housed in the sword I carry upon my back. He has yet to rejoin the Allfather."

"You mean he is imprisoned in Andhanimwhid?"

"Yes, he placed it there just before the Adversary cut him asunder, rather than be imprisoned inside Zadehmal, Eater of Souls.

I believe it was his choice, though perhaps an unconscious one, but I feel it imperative to release his spirit once I determine how and when it will become possible.

I can definitely assure you that he is not me."

"How do you know this?"

"He speaks to me through my dreams. That is how I knew this place to travel to it."

"That only brings us back to how you accomplished that," Anglemar commented.

"I may be able to enter the realm of dreams, in the flesh," Aleron answered.

Trafelgar took a half step backwards at the revelation, his eyes going wide, while the elvish king continued to stare levelly at Aleron.

"You must be aware that aelient can travel to and from here at will, despite your wards protecting the physical plane."

"Yes, of this we are aware, but they have never brought minions of the Adversary to these shores.

The water is still something of a barrier to their physical travel, though I'm sure any could swim the distance if they desired, and some occasionally do.

Our resident aelient and our own sorcerers are prepared for any incursion of dark aelient. Of the light aelient, we mind not their coming and going."

"As far as I'm aware, the creatures of the Adversary may not pass through the world of dreams and live," Aleron agreed, "but the people of the Allfather may, though only the immortals possess the ability to open the gateway."

"Aside from you," Anglemar corrected.

"Yes, aside from me," Aleron agreed, "though I have yet to enter the actual dream plane with my physical body.

I gained control of a construct, created by an aelient, which allows me to enter our world at any point I choose."

"You say, 'gained control.' Was this given freely, or did you somehow wrest control from this aelient?"

"I wrested control from a dark aelient, who held me captive for a time."

"How were you able to overpower an immortal?" Trafelgar asked, still disbelieving what he was hearing.

"The aelient possess strength far exceeding ours."

"Yes, High Sorcerer, they do," Aleron agreed, "but surprise lends its own advantages."

"What the king is getting to," Hadaras interjected, "is that the aelient, Jacanda, smartly shielded him from red and blue energy, not knowing of which type he is adept, but she failed to shield the other colors.

Aleron can wield all colors equally."

The other elves in the hall took notice of the last statement, even more than to the claim of traveling the dream plane.

All elves wield magic, so the herald and the archers, as well as the king and high sorcerer, looked at Aleron with a combination of disbelief and more than a little fear.

"That is a rather spectacular statement, Uncle," said Anglemar.

"Do you corroborate your grandfather's claim, Cousin?"

"Perhaps, a demonstration would be more convincing," Hadaras offered.

"Might one of your archers spare a shaft?"

"Yes, of course," Anglemar responded.

"Oelwynn, please lend my cousin the king one of your arrows."

The closest of the archers broke from the formation, dropped to one knee, and offered Aleron the arrow he kept nocked at the ready.

"Many thanks to you," Aleron said, bowing slightly and taking the offering.

He twirled the yard-long shaft between his fingers and probed to get a sense of its composition.

Birch, he concluded.

He focused red energy at the steel bodkin point, heating it until it became a blob of white-hot metal, and then pressed it point-first to the floor. The cooling steel formed a stand, of sorts, and the arrow stuck point-first to the marble flagstone.

He could see the grim expressions on all faces, save for Hadaras', at witnessing red energy wielded in their homeland. He followed with precise lines of blue to slice free the fletching, the three goose feathers fluttering to the floor.

Now came the complicated part, to Aleron's mind. The wood lacked life, even before cutting the tree, as the life of a tree resides just below the bark. He focused all the colors and used white magic to build a layer of cambium and bark around the arrow shaft.

When the white glow faded, all could see the layer of golden papery bark, but the twig still lacked life, though it possessed all the necessary parts.

He mixed blue and yellow to form false-green, brought life to his construct, and then applied green energy to impart growth. He needed to wield white again, to pull enough moisture out of the air to feed the rapidly growing roots.

To the witnesses, the shaft grew into a small tree, in a shimmer of green radiance, sprouting from a pool of white mist.

Now finished with his demonstration, Aleron plucked up the perfectly formed sapling, with its splayed mass of roots, and walked forward to present it to Anglemar.

"This I offer, as proof to my grandfather's testimony," he stated, setting it before the elvish king, before stepping back again.

"Astounding," Anglemar exclaimed, "truly astounding."

He reached out to touch the plant.

"And I sense a truly living plant, from what was naught but dead wood. What do you make of it, Trafelgar?"

The sorcerer stepped forward to touch the tree.

"Yes, Sire, it is as you say, as well as the correct tree, from which our arrows are constructed."

"I think, Cousin, that perhaps we might retire to my private audience chamber to discuss what brings you here. I am now inclined to believe all the fanciful claims you and my uncle have made."

Instructing the herald, he said, "Halsfer, take this tree to the gardener and instruct him to plant it in a position to the front of my favorite bench, by the reflecting pool. I wish to observe its continued growth."

"Right away, Your Majesty," the herald replied.

"Come, my kin and honored guests. I suspect we have much of great import to discuss."

"I agree," Aleron replied.

"Please lead the way."

The king rose from his throne, and all in the hall dropped to one knee, save for Aleron, who bowed low.

Anglemar returned the bow, and they both straightened. He then turned to his left, motioned for all to rise, and strode off to a doorway in the back of the hall.

Aleron, Hadaras, and Trafelgar followed.

Chapter 36

Sildaenday, Day 5, Hunger Moon, 8766 Sudean Calendar

Seated around the heavy carved table of beech were three elves and a halfblood.

A serving maid set a flagon of mead before each of them, along with a large pitcher for refills. She looked upon Aleron with obvious interest before turning to leave the chamber.

Though quite young looking, Aleron guessed that she might be three times his age, as elves only just reached maturity at around age sixty. She appeared around the same age as Lyssa, from his dream.

"It is painfully obvious that you did not come here in the manner you did to merely exchange pleasantries," Anglemar began, after the serving maid left the room.

"I would think you might send word ahead to forewarn us, had you the leisure time available."

"Of that, Cousin, you are correct," Aleron agreed.

"There is no time to lose, and as yet, we are likely too late to change the initial outcome of the events recently past."

"And those events would be?"

"I'm sure you are familiar with the Arkans and their leader, Zormat?"

"Yes, of course. These apparently tainted elves from the east have been stirring up trouble for nearly six years now.

Their king, this Zormat, claims to be the actual son of the Adversary."

"That he claims in truth, I'm afraid, but it's what he recently accomplished that's our highest concern. He has recovered Zadehmal and now journeys to Immin Bul."

"That is grave news indeed," Anglemar stated.

"We believe this to be the primary reason for the recent blockade of the Wabani Inlet, to cover his passage to and from the northlands."

"You told me this would happen, Goromir, four thousand years ago you did," Trafelgar announced.

"Shortly before you disappeared, you told me it would not stay gone forever, and that the Nameless One would eventually break free. That time is upon us now."

"Yes, old friend," Hadaras agreed, "indeed it is."

"Aleron, My Cousin, how is it that you know so much of this event?" Anglemar inquired.

"And please call me by my name. The formality of the hall is unnecessary here."

"Anglemar," Aleron answered, "the aelient who held me showed me Zormat, leaving the mountains with the axe.

She showed me several things that she viewed through a device in her library, which I later discovered, and I believe what I see there is actually occurring in the present. Since that time, when I use it to travel, it shows me everything happening in the place I view, right before I go there."

"And you witnessed Zormat leaving what mountains?"

"Far to the north of Norwyyl, I saw him with five companions moving down a mountain path. Four of them carried a large container. Jacanda stated that the box held Zadehmal."

"When Aleron showed me the image from his mind, it did indeed appear to be the chest in which I interred the axe," Hadaras added.

Trafelgar asked, "Why would this dark aelient, Jacanda, show you these things? She demonstrated how to navigate her realm, did she not? Why would she show such things to an enemy?"

"I believe she felt secure in her power over me, not knowing of my abilities. She captured me in hopes of turning me to the Adversary's cause.

We are kin as it turns out, and among the aelient, kinship means control."

Aleron left the last statement hanging, and Hadaras looked to him with an expression of surprise that he would bring up that detail. Aleron saw the other elves' eyes widen at the revelation while he took a tug from his flagon of mead.

"How might you be kin to this creature?" Anglemar asked.

Aleron looked to Hadaras, seeking approval to proceed on a potentially embarrassing tack for his grandfather.

Hadaras nodded in affirmation, and Aleron proceeded, "Jacanda is my maternal grandmother. She is a demon, without a physical body of her own, and she possessed the body of my grandmother, Quiana, transforming it to her own purposes."

He waited for that part to sink in before proceeding.

"Since Jacanda is one of the Nameless One's actual children, with his consort Iselle, she is half-sister to Zormat, who is my cousin, in the same manner as your father would be my cousin. This also makes the Adversary my great-grandfather."

After a long pause, Anglemar inferred, "From what I gather, Jacanda expected her blood relation to exert influence over you. Is that correct?"

"Exactly," Aleron confirmed.

"It worked on my mother, who was half aelient. What she believed were revelations to seek out my father and bear the heir to the throne were, in fact, promptings from her mother.

I myself, being only a quarter aelient and half man, proved to be less tractable."

"Did she have any such power over you?"

"I did feel an innate desire to follow her directions and to please her, but the pull was not strong enough to overcome my reason and personal convictions. When I saw the opening, I did not hesitate to overpower her."

"That is good news," Anglemar agreed.

"But what of the Nameless One? What power might he have over you?"

"That is a fear of ours, as well," Aleron conceded.

"I know not how much power an aelir might have over his descendants. By all accounts, he brought every one of his own offspring into rebellion. I just hope the dilution might serve in our favor."

"Are you familiar with the Eltheri Prophecy?" Hadaras directed to the two elves.

"*Darkness shall envelope the world and the mighty shall fall to contain the nameless shadow,*" Trafelgar began in Elvish, continuing, "*Though the light shall seem victorious, it is but the start of the waning.*

The tree appears dead; yet one branch lives on, hidden among the weeds, and the fruit of the living branch shall be chosen above all others when the nameless shadow shall walk the world again.

The chosen will carry my power and might and shall be the only hope against the nameless shadow.

Should the shadow consume the fruit of the living branch, all is lost, but the chosen may turn the darkness to light."

Finished with the recital, the High Sorcerer switched back to Sudean.

"That prophecy is older even than you, Goromir."

"Yes, by one thousand and eleven years, and it predates the founding of this kingdom by one thousand and two.

It was preserved first orally, as it happened just before we learned our letters from the aelir, and only recorded after the raising of the temple.

At the time Elther uttered the words, no one knew what portents they held. Now, in this age, I believe the words are all too clear."

Hadaras expounded further on the words of the prophecy, while Aleron sat in silence, sipping his mead. He felt none too comfortable on the subject of the ninety-five-hundred-year-old prophecy, only recently learning of its existence.

Hadaras held doubts as to its applicability until Aleron returned from Jacanda with the revelations on his ancestry.

Anglemar broke into the discussion between the former and current High sorcerers, "It all seems very clear, in light of what we know now.

My young cousin obviously holds power never before afforded to a mortal.

But what of the last line, specifically the final part? It seems to imply our victory may not consist of simply defeating the Adversary, as you did four millennia past."

"The implication is there," Hadaras agreed, "as unlikely as it seems, for the Nameless One to return to the light."

"It may only apply to some of his minions," Aleron offered, "namely the hobgoblins, half-trolls, and Arkans."

"What brings you to that conclusion?" Trafelgar asked. Aleron could see the question in his grandfather's eyes, as well. He had yet to share this suspicion with anyone else.

"Jacanda believed that the creations of her father could not pass alive into the world of dreams. I brought a hobgoblin through with me.

Shaggat, a leader among his folk, captured me and brought me to Jacanda. She told him that he could not travel the path we were taking, and she left him to his own devices with my people closing fast. One of my captains captured him and put him on a ship to Arundell.

When I arrived via Jacanda's lair to bring my people to Arundell, I gave him the option of accompanying us or completing the journey by sea. Knowing the risk, he chose to accompany us and came through mostly unscathed."

"So these crossbred creatures can pass, where their purebred cousins cannot. What bearing does that have on the prophecy?"

"Not all of him passed through the barrier. A certain darkness within him that I assumed was part of his goblin heritage failed to make the passage.

Shaggat claimed to feel a wrenching sensation as he passed into Jacanda's realm. After the passage, his essence felt little different from a man's.

I think the process might kill an actual goblin or troll, but the crossed varieties seem able to weather the passage."

"That implies that the Arkans, especially, might be redeemable," Hadaras surmised.

"I'm unsure that any attempt to cleanse the half-trolls would bring any benefit. They are still little more than beasts. Nor would the hobgoblins comply willingly. They are already little different from the wild men who are untainted in that way.

The Arkans, however, are much more of a threat to us. If they might be turned in some way, it may give us a hope of victory."

"That does seem a more likely hope," Anglemar agreed, "than to turn the Nameless One back to the light, after eons of rebellion."

"Though this is all relevant to the situation at hand," Aleron interposed, "I believe it's still far in the future. I came here to ask for your help for a more immediate threat."

"Go on," Anglemar said.

"We have good reason to believe that the Arkan fleet is moving to the Wabani Inlet. The Thallasians have lost several patrols in the northeastern waters.

With the strength of the current blockade, we have no hope of moving enough ships to break it before Zormat completes his passage.

With the additional Arkan fleet, our hopes of ever controlling the North Sea will be for naught. For naught, unless we can field a comparable fleet."

"You wish for us to provide the comparable fleet?"

"There is little other option," Aleron replied.

"Our current tactic is avoidance when encountering an Arkan ship. We have not nearly enough sorcerers at our disposal to fend off the attack of an Arkan vessel, entirely crewed by sorcerers. The only answer is elvish crews."

"I understand what you ask, and why. I must ascertain whether this commitment will benefit our people or bring us harm."

"In my day, so to speak," Hadaras presented, "we returned to the continent, reestablished contact with our old colony in Sudea, and established new colonies when we learned of the Adversary's return to Aertu.

Now, Sudea asks for assistance, and you hesitate. The threat today is more critical than it ever was all those millennia ago. Will my people falter now that the time of truth is nigh, and the Nameless One returns with thoughts of vengeance?"

"Uncle, I can assure you that our people will not falter. We simply need time to assess the situation."

"My Nephew, do not spend too much time in deliberation. I fear that our people are fading to irrelevance in the upcoming age. The battle to come will occur with or without us. Let the elves be a force to be reckoned with, rather than a forgotten people looking on from the outside."

Anglemar said nothing for a time, staring between Aleron and Hadaras through steepled fingers. He looked to Trafelgar, who gave a barely perceptible nod.

"Uncle, the words you speak are strong ones. Aleron, you can count on my ships, for what they are worth. I have two hundred twenty warships at my disposal, fifty carrack class, seventy of the faster caravels, and one hundred assorted scout and support vessels.

"Are you committing all these ships?" Aleron asked.

"We can put our trading expeditions on hold at any time. Elvenholm is largely self-sufficient, and we can maintain indefinitely with no outside support. People will simply have to part with their luxuries for a brief period. We have dealt with it in the past, albeit before my time, and we will deal with it again."

"The brief period of which you speak may be five years, or more. Are you prepared for that?"

"What is five years to our people?" Anglemar retorted. "It is but one or two thousandths of our lives, merely a blink of the eye."

"Well then, I thank you and your people for the sacrifices you have committed to," Aleron responded.

"The sacrifice is negligible in the face of what the Adversary would bring to Aertu, were he victorious."

"The numbers you offer are substantial, but the greatest advantage will be the addition of elvish sorcerers to our combat strength. Two hundred twenty elvish crews, regardless of the ship type, will bring us into contention.

We still have no idea as to the extent of the Arkan fleet, but we must assume they spent years in preparation. All the Arkan ships we have so far encountered have been of the caravel class, curiously equipped for arctic travel. They may have larger warships en route, or not. We do not know."

"From our belief that they come from beyond the northern ice, their equipping is no surprise."

"They are from a cold place, without a doubt, one that we have yet to pinpoint.

I know from Jacanda that they are one-eighth goblin, seven-eighths elf, so they have essentially the same abilities as an elf but wield red magic. We have seen no indication that they can wield blue, so there may be a limitation there."

"But in truth, we know not their capabilities," Trafelgar stated.

"Judging from halfbloods, like you, a mixed-blood sorcerer should be capable of wielding either form."

"Yes," Hadaras agreed, "but they have yet to show any such capability.

We know not whether this is by choice, as with halfbloods, or if it is an innate limitation, as with ourselves."

"Will the deployment of our fleet have any hope of breaking the blockade before Zormat completes his passage?" Anglemar asked.

"We think not," Aleron replied.

"By the time your ships could reach the inlet, Zormat would have landed in Kolixtlan and be well on his way to Immin Bul."

"Therefore, you see no likelihood of preventing Zormat's success even with our help, and neither do I. This war will come, and we will fight it just as we did in ages past. Let it not result in the amount of bloodshed it did then.

Our long age of blissful peace is ending," Anglemar finished, with a look of sadness in his eyes.

His young face, framed in golden locks, seemed to age before their eyes. His High Sorcerer obviously held the greater sum of years, but for the moment, the difference between the two seemed less obvious. He took a long tug at his flagon and set it down, his smile returning.

"Now, we should probably get to the details."

Following a lengthy discussion of the numerous requirements contingent on Elvenholm fielding its entire navy, Aleron and Hadaras took their leave of the king and his high sorcerer.

They decided that the elves would transport additional troops to fortify the colonies and prepare for an overland campaign across the Central Jungle.

Afterward, the warships would proceed up the coast, along with Sudean vessels, to break the blockade and reopen the northern passage. Elvish supply ships would continue to ferry troops and supplies to the continent.

Aleron hoped to convince the Westland nations to assist in supplying the navy, and especially for Waban and Sunjib to garrison troops within striking distance of Kolixtlan. He planned to negotiate the same with Chebek and Talik, but primarily for supply and garrison services for Thallasian fighters, and to move against Adar.

When they finally stepped back into Aleron's private audience chamber, Hadaras commented, "Now, my boy, don't you have some wedding preparations to make? You really should stop stalling."

Aleron smirked and responded, "Indeed, I do, Grandfather, and if cementing allies to fight for the fate of Aertu is stalling, then so be it."

He continued for a moment before adding, "I do sincerely hope Ellie sees it the same way."

"Oh, I'm sure she will, my boy; I'm sure she will," Hadaras replied, with a grin, before leaving the chamber.

Chapter 37

Zorekday, Day 12, Hunger Moon, 8766 Sudean Calendar

*E*lvenholm's fleet will be underway within another week. Aleron thought, as the royal dressers applied his wedding uniform.

He wished he could think of nothing other than the upcoming nuptials, but the fact that he and Eilowyn had been married for months already made it all seem like a pointless charade. It was important to Eilowyn and to Sudea, so it needed to be important to him, but he couldn't help but worry about the pressing issues at hand.

She was already upset with the amount of time he devoted to matters of state in the weeks leading up to the ceremony.

How did I get to this point? I used to think only about doing my job and spending time with Ellie. Now, I worry about positioning the elvish fleet, or when I can get to Dhargul and Nhargul to speak with the dwarves. I never wanted it to be this way. I should be thinking about Ellie right now. Why did it ever have to come to this? I used to enjoy my life.

"Please hold still, Your Grace. We need to get you fitted properly," Hevril, the chief tailor, admonished him.

This fitting was beyond the scope of mere dressers, as the final stitching required the subject to wear the clothes.

"Sorry, I'll try to keep still."

He stood, with his arms outstretched, as they pinned and stitched his new white coat into place.

The traditional royal wedding clothes were worse than anything he had yet experienced. The stark white coat and trousers piped in purple-bordered gold

266

were designs taken from four-thousand-year-old texts and interpreted by modern sensibilities.

Aleron despised every inch of them. He wanted nothing more than a comfortable gambeson and chainmail, shaped for fighting, rather than this ridiculous and constricting monstrosity. He had no choice but to deal with it, as expected of the king.

The late winter ceremony defied tradition: historically, most kings married in the early summer, but Aleron was glad for the season. He was quite sure that he would die of heat stroke if made to wear his wedding clothes in the summer.

His groomsmen, Barathol, Geldun, and Hameln, Eilowyn's only brother, stayed with him for a while but eventually offered excuses for pressing duties elsewhere and left him to his fate. Aleron couldn't blame them for becoming bored; he was quite bored as well.

He tried to concentrate on the advantages today's ceremony would bring. It would legitimize him and Eilowyn as king and queen, quashing the rumors of infidelity for good, and give the nation something positive to focus upon.

Eilowyn thought that she might be pregnant already, and the timing was close enough that no one would suspect a child conceived out of wedlock.

Aleron thought the concern unwarranted, considering he and Eilowyn were married months prior, but he knew that not all accepted that explanation. Today's wedding would guarantee their child's legitimacy in the eyes of the people.

He believed that with the typical halfblood gestation of fifty weeks, as opposed to forty-seven weeks for unmixed humans, Eilowyn's pregnancy would likely land her at forty-eight or forty-nine weeks, to further dispel any perception of impropriety, as she could only be a few weeks along.

When he offered to check, Eilowyn declined, not wanting to risk learning the gender of their baby ahead of time.

More importantly, to Aleron's thinking, a married king held greater influence than an unmarried one, for he carried the weight of his wife's house as well. Considering he was marrying into House Arundell, the second most prominent house of Sudea, Aleron's union with Eilowyn carried more authority than any since Aleron the First, who also married a steward's daughter. House Sudea and House Arundell, united, held more weight than all other noble households combined.

All I ever wanted was to be a soldier and to have Ellie as my wife, but I always knew I couldn't have both, not since the day I met her and found out who I am. How did I ever expect it to turn out any different?

Aleron's thoughts continued to spin in circles as they applied the final touches to his uniform. Already tailored to fit him perfectly, the clothes still required extensive adjustments after the fact.

He wondered how Eilowyn was faring. She would be going through much the same process, though likely enjoying it more. He had not seen her since yesterday afternoon, when she moved back to the Steward's quarters to be with her mother and sisters.

Majori had been in Arundell for the past month, her estates being close to the city. Eilowyn's mother, Vetina, and her eldest sister Carwyn were away, visiting Vetina's ancestral estates, when Aleron and Eilowyn made their unexpected return.

They timed the wedding for this date to allow Eilowyn's family time to return. As well, the timing allowed other important Sudean lords and ladies time to travel from outlying estates. The date was a compromise between the need for immediate validation of their marriage before the people and allowance for travel. As a result, many dignitaries from the far-flung corners of the realm would be unable to attend, Eilowyn's uncle Damian being a case in point, as well as representatives from foreign royal houses. In the case of foreign nations, the consuls would have to do, and Aleron sincerely wished for no perceived insult to his neighboring kingdoms or his more remote vassals.

Eilowyn turned her head to see her side profile reflected in the full-length mirror. The white gown's bodice, seemingly made entirely from lace, pushed her bosom into a gravity-defying position, while squeezing her waist to the circumference it held when she was twelve.

Now I know why brides walk up the aisle so slowly. It's so they don't pass out. I can only manage half a breath in this thing.

It did look wonderful, she had to admit, with the modest bustle flowing into a ridiculously long train. She was thankful for the high lace collar. Considering where the bodice positioned certain parts of her anatomy, a low-cut neckline would have been downright scandalous.

Just wait until he sees me in this.

Vetina, Carwyn, and Majori watched on.

"You look lovely, Ellie," her mother praised.

"Every man in that hall will be wishing he were the groom."

Her sisters emphatically agreed.

I wish I could have looked as gorgeous at my wedding," Carwyn remarked.

"This cross-country trek of yours has certainly agreed with your figure."

"Indeed, you look as lithe as a teenager," Majori said, then adding, "Who would have guessed the young man you chose would end up as the king."

Who indeed? thought Eilowyn.

She reacted from long habit, as her older sister never approved of her choice of Aleron and was only now putting on a better face, since the revelation of his heritage.

"This is not my figure," she replied, straining to breathe deeply.

"I'm not sure what it belongs to, but I'm certain it isn't a live woman."

"Oh, you're exaggerating, Ellie, I mean, Your Grace," Damlyl, the Head Seamstress, admonished her, as Magda adjusted the lacing of the bodice.

"Every high-born bride puts up with the same trials as you."

The old woman worked in the palace nearly fifty years, knew Gealton as a boy and all Gealton and Vetina's children since birth, so one could expect a certain familiarity.

"Isn't that the truth?" Vetina agreed.

"After Damlyl cinched me into my gown, clutching my father's arm was the only thing that kept me upright."

Her older daughters laughed aloud.

Eilowyn managed only a stifled giggle that left her gasping for air, but then her mind took a serious tack.

Is this what I'm reduced to…an object to be admired and desired? I escaped captivity, trekked across half the continent, and killed a half-troll with a knife. Is this all that being queen holds in store, giggling and admiration of my looks? I think not. I will make a difference in the governance of this nation.

She held as still as she could, following a scowl from the seamstress at her giggle. The fit required absolute perfection, or Damlyl would consider the whole affair a failure and likely start over from the beginning. Eilowyn had no wish to start over from scratch.

I hope Aleron is having a better time than I am, she thought.

He must be. It has to be easier for men to get into their uniforms.

Meanwhile, Aleron endured the poking, prodding, and fitting of his wedding uniform.

I've had about enough of this, but if I don't let them get everything just perfect, I won't hear the end of it from Ellie. Nothing to do but deal with it.

"It looks as if we are finished here, Your Grace," Hevril announced.

"Just in time, too, the ceremony is only a bell away.

"That is wonderful news, Hevril," Aleron said.

"Yes, Your Grace," he agreed.

"As long as you remain standing and avoid any unnecessarily large movements, your uniform will look perfect. If it doesn't, that head seamstress will have my hide, I swear it."

Aleron laughed at that. He knew Damlyl to be Hevril's wife and that Hevril wasn't the only one in danger of a haranguing if things didn't look perfect.

"I promise to keep it pristine, to the best of my abilities, Hevril. Otherwise, the queen will have my hide."

Hevril chuckled and replied, as he packed his tools, "I suppose you are right, in that respect, Your Grace. Our queen was always a sweet girl, but her usual demeanor belies the sharp streak that comes with that hair color."

"It's buried deep, but it's surely there," Aleron agreed.

"Thank you so much for your effort. It must have been like dressing a goat. No amount of polish can hide that I'm a marine and a farm boy, but thank you for trying."

"On the contrary, Your Grace, you cut an impressive figure. One would swear you are truly Aleron reborn, judging from the statues and paintings.

You had best be going, or the high priest and steward will be in a tizzy."

"Right you are, Hevril, as usual. Once again, thank you."

"You are quite welcome, Your Grace."

Stepping out to the corridor, he found his groomsmen and a contingent of palace guards waiting to escort him to the royal hall.

"I seem to be finished and you all look ready to go. Shall we then?"

"Certainly, Your Grace," Geldun replied, with a flourishing bow.

"It is our most fortunate honor to escort Your Eminence to the ceremony." The guards looked tense when Barathol guffawed at Geldun's feigned veneration, and Hameln grinned."

"If I could belt you, I would, but it would likely rip these clothes, and I promised Hevril I wouldn't mess them up."

The guards relaxed visibly at Aleron's reaction, realizing Geldun's greeting was a jape, rather than a sincere adulation.

Aleron envied his groomsmen, wearing only their best dress uniforms and still capable of unrestrained movement.

"Let's get moving. I don't want Dweilden to lose his mind because I am late."

He led the way down the corridors to the royal hall, groomsmen and guards trailing behind.

"Do you realize they had to stitch me into this ridiculous costume? If I raise my arms, it's all over."

They entered the same room he used to stage for his coronation, Gealton and Dweilden waiting, as before.

"Thank the Allfather you've arrived, Your Grace," the high priest exclaimed. "We were worried."

"No, we weren't worried," Gealton emphasized the "we."

"He was worried. I know that the tailor and dressers know their business. Are you ready for this?"

"Considering we've been married for half the year, I think so," Aleron replied.

"This is a bigger affair than even the coronation," his father-in-law countered, "with easily twice as many nobles in attendance.

Everyone who could get here in a month's travel is here, plus some. The Coptian prince Sethotep and his bodyguards rode fifteen horses nearly to death to arrive here just this morning."

"The prince made it? That's impressive, considering the distance," Aleron said.

"I'm surprised they thought it that important."

"It is that important. Sudea has not seen a royal wedding in over a thousand years. In all reality, it is more important than the coronation, which was only a formality. Your pulling the sword was more significant than the coronation."

"But this wedding is the same, merely a renewal of the vows we already spoke."

"Not in the eyes of the people, the houses, and the other nations. All of them need a prominently visible ceremony to join you and Eilowyn as king and queen. It matters not that you tied the knot in a private ceremony. Indeed, that is more common than you might think. Sudea and the rest of the world need the spectacle."

"And please try to avoid the same spectacle as the coronation, Your Grace," Dweilden added.

"I assure you, once again, that was not my doing."

Aleron's assertion did little to reassure the High Priest, who maintained an air of suspicion, mumbling under his breath as he moved to his position to enter the hall.

The tower bells tolled for the eleventh hour past midnight, and the sentries pushed the great doors open.

Dweilden stepped out and took his position, center dais, facing the assembled crowd.

Gealton entered to take his position, three paces to Dweilden's front.

As the eleventh chime faded, he announced, "Lords and ladies, people of Sudea, I present to you your king, His Royal Highness, Aleron the Second!"

On cue, Aleron strode out to face the audience, immediately to the High Priest's front-right, his groomsmen fanning off to the right.

"Good people of Sudea," Gealton continued, "having an additional duty to attend to, I must leave you at this time."

The Steward stepped down from the dais, turned right, and walked across the first row of assembled dignitaries, exiting the hall through a small side door.

Several moments passed before the trumpets sounded and a large set of doors opened on the left side of the hall, between the nobles and the commoners.

The band played the traditional wedding march, and Gealton stepped out with Eilowyn on his left arm.

The bridesmaids, Eilowyn's sisters Carwyn and Majori, and her lady in waiting Feadra, followed behind, holding her long trail as Eilowyn turned the corner and glided up the aisle maintained between the assembled nobles.

She ascended the platform to Aleron, who took her hands in his. Gealton released his daughter's arm and turned to descend the steps, taking his place beside Vetina.

Aleron could not believe his eyes as he slowly guided his bride to his left, where they faced one another, between the High Priest and the audience.

I thought she was beautiful before, but this is ridiculous, he said to himself.

The bridesmaids arranged her train and took positions mirroring the groomsmen, who performed a sharp left face.

Dweilden stepped forward and repeated precisely the same words Bruji uttered months before.

"Do you, Aleron, pledge to take this woman, Eilowyn, to be your wife, to protect her and serve her, for all the days you live upon Aertu and for all of eternity beyond?"

"Yes, thusly I pledge my life and eternal spirit," Aleron answered.

"Do you, Eilowyn, pledge to take this man, Aleron, to be your husband, to comfort and serve him, for all the days you live upon Aertu and for all of eternity beyond?"

"Yes, thusly I pledge my life and eternal spirit," Eilowyn answered, smiling as if it were the first time she uttered the words.

They extended their right hands, palms down, she placing hers atop his. Dweilden produced an ornate silk ribbon and wrapped it six times around their hands, fastening it with a square knot on top, just as Bruji had.

"In the name of the one called Allfather, let this binding signify this man and this woman, bound to one another, in life and in spirit, for all of eternity."

They held each other's rings in their left hands again, as before.

272

"Let these rings of precious gold act as a visible sign, for all to see, of the never-ending nature of time and their commitment to one another, for all of eternity."

Steadily, this time, they placed the ring on the other's finger.

"Now, under the eyes of the Allfather, I name this once separate man and woman married, sealed to one another and their children to come, for all of eternity."

The crowd erupted in cheers, commoners and nobles alike. Eilowyn and Aleron looked out on the crowd to see faces, both familiar and unfamiliar. Gealton, Vetina, Vetina's sister-in-law Guenvair, Damian's wife, Hadaras, Jessamine, Cladus, and Anjani stood at the front of the throng, along with many of the lords and ladies Aleron met over the past weeks.

Eilowyn knew many more in the audience from her years at court.

Aleron recognized his generals and admirals, along with their ladies, in a tight knot to one side, with a couple faces he failed to recognize, generals only recently arrived in the city.

Black-skinned Prince Sethotep, with his consul and four bodyguards representing the oldest nation of men on Aertu, stood out in sharp contrast to the pale-skinned Sudean masses.

They noted the consuls of many other nations as well, holding positions of honor to the front of the assemblage.

"Prince Sethotep of Coptia," Aleron began, "esteemed Consuls, Lords and Ladies, Citizens of Sudea, I welcome you all and thank you for attending our wedding, signifying the binding of our eternal spirits, under the watchful eyes of the Allfather.

This act not only seals Eilowyn, our descendants, and me to one another, it once again binds House Sudea to House Arundell by royal decree, for three generations henceforth. For that period, our houses shall act as one house and shall marry only outside of either house. We will act in one another's interest, but always placing the interests of the kingdom above our own and only in the fourth generation, shall we again be considered separate houses."

He left those words, fully in keeping with ancient Sudean law, to sink in amongst the gathered nobles.

The rule, unenforced for a millennium, prevented weakening of the royal line from inbreeding, but more importantly, prevented houses from consolidating power through repeated intermarrying of close cousins. It forced closely linked houses to disperse their alliances through marriage to unrelated houses.

The law was difficult to enforce and mostly ignored, but the setting of a royal precedent would likely bring it back into fashion.

It was Eilowyn's idea to house it in an official decree, thus bringing it to the attention of all Sudeans.

"I now declare the proceedings closed, and on with the feasting!"

So ends Sign of the White Raven

the second volume of

The Chronicles of Aertu

Appendix A

Sudean Agricultural Calendar
Utilized for Daily Accounting in the Kingdom of Sudea

1	ALLFATHER'S MOON				
GURLACHDAY	SHILWEZDAY	CORBALLDAY	CARPATHDAY	SILDAENDAY	ZOREKDAY
1 NEW YEAR WINTER SOLSTICE	2	3	4	5	6
7	8	9	10	11	12
13	14	15	16	17	18
19	20	21	22	23	24
25	26	27	28	29	30

2	HUNGER MOON				
GURLACHDAY	SHILWEZDAY	CORBALLDAY	CARPATHDAY	SILDAENDAY	ZOREKDAY
1	2	3	4 FEAST OF FAELWE	5	6
7	8	9	10	11	12
13	14	15	16	17	18
19	20	21	22	23	24
25	26	27	28	29	30

3	BUDDING MOON				
GURLACHDAY	SHILWEZDAY	CORBALLDAY	CARPATHDAY	SILDAENDAY	ZOREKDAY
1	2	3	4	5 FEAST OF LILLANE	6
7	8	9	10	11	12
13	14	15	16	17	18
19	20	21	22	23	24
25	26	27	28	29	30

4	PLOWING MOON				
GURLACHDAY	SHILWEZDAY	CORBALLDAY	CARPATHDAY	SILDAENDAY	ZOREKDAY
1	2 SPRING EQUINOX	3	4	5	6
7	8	9	10	11	12
13	14	15	16	17	18
19	20	21	22	23	24
25	26	27	28	29	30

5	SOWING MOON				
GURLACHDAY	SHILWEZDAY	CORBALLDAY	CARPATHDAY	SILDAENDAY	ZOREKDAY
1	2 FEAST OF CERDAE	3	4	5	6
7	8	9	10	11	12
13	14	15	16	17	18
19	20	21	22	23	24
25	26	27	28	29	30

6	GROWING MOON				
GURLACHDAY	SHILWEZDAY	CORBALLDAY	CARPATHDAY	SILDAENDAY	ZOREKDAY
1	2	3	4	5	6 FEAST OF KORELLE
7	8	9	10	11	12
13	14	15	16	17	18
19	20	21	22	23	24
25	26	27	28	29	30

7	HAYMAKING MOON				
GURLACHDAY	SHILWEZDAY	CORBALLDAY	CARPATHDAY	SILDAENDAY	ZOREKDAY
1	2	3 ALERON'S BIRTHDAY YEAR 8745	4 SUMMER SOLSTICE	5	6
7	8	9	10	11	12
13	14	15	16	17	18
19	20	21	22	23	24
25	26	27	28	29	30

8	SQUASH MOON				
GURLACHDAY	SHILWEZDAY	CORBALLDAY	CARPATHDAY	SILDAENDAY	ZOREKDAY
1	2	3	4	5	6
7	8	9	10	11	12
13	14	15	16	17	18
19	20	21	22	23	24
25 SQUASH HARVEST FESTIVAL	26 SQUASH HARVEST FESTIVAL	27 SQUASH HARVEST FESTIVAL	28 SQUASH HARVEST FESTIVAL	29 SQUASH HARVEST FESTIVAL	30 SQUASH HARVEST FESTIVAL

9	HARVEST MOON				
GURLACHDAY	SHILWEZDAY	CORBALLDAY	CARPATHDAY	SILDAENDAY	ZOREKDAY
1	2	3	4	5	6
7	8	9	10	11	12
13	14	15	16	17	18
19	20	21	22	23	24
25 HARVEST FESTIVAL	26 HARVEST FESTIVAL	27 HARVEST FESTIVAL	28 HARVEST FESTIVAL	29 HARVEST FESTIVAL	30 HARVEST FESTIVAL

10	STORM MOON				
GURLACHDAY	SHILWEZDAY	CORBALLDAY	CARPATHDAY	SILDAENDAY	ZOREKDAY
1	2	3 FINAL BATTLE ANNIVERSARY	4	5 AUTUMN EQUINOX	6
7	8	9	10	11	12
13	14	15	16	17	18
19	20	21	22	23	24
25	26	27	28	29	30

11	FALLING LEAVES MOON				
GURLACHDAY	SHILWEZDAY	CORBALLDAY	CARPATHDAY	SILDAENDAY	ZOREKDAY
1	2	3 FEAST OF ANDULLE	4	5	6
7	8	9	10	11	12
13	14	15	16	17	18
19	20	21	22	23	24
25	26	27	28	29	30

12	ICE MOON				
GURLACHDAY	SHILWEZDAY	CORBALLDAY	CARPATHDAY	SILDAENDAY	ZOREKDAY
1	2	3	4	5	6
7 FEAST OF FINLE	8	9	10	11	12
13	14	15	16	17	18
19	20	21	22	23	24
25	26	27	28	29	30

YULE FESTIVAL WEEK					
ONEDAY	TWODAY	THREEDAY	FOURDAY	FIVEDAY	SIXDAY
1	2	3	4	5 FEAST OF ISELLE	6 ONCE EVERY FOUR YEARS

Appendix B

Comparative Timelines of Dwarves, Elves, Sudeans, and Arkans

MAJOR EVENT	ELVISH CALENDAR	SUDEAN CALENDAR	DWARVISH CALENDAR	ARKAN CALENDAR
CREATION OF THE WORLD.	BILLIONS OF YEARS BRH (Before Recorded History)			
ELVES CREATED.	~6000 BRH	~7255 BRH	~5830 BRH	~10635 BRH
MEN, WESTMEN AND DWARVES CREATED.	~5000 BRH	~6255 BRH	~4830 BRH	~9635 BRH
DWARVES BEGIN WRITTEN RECORDS.	170 BRH	1425 BRH	YEAR 0	~4805 BRH
GODS APPEAR TO ELVES	YEAR 0	1255 BRH	170	~4635 BRH
DWARVES MIGRATE TO BLUE MOUNTAINS.	971	624 BRH	1141	~3664 BRH
GODS LEAVE ELVES, APPEARING TO MEN, WESTMEN AND DWARVES.	1255	YEAR 0	1425	~3380 BRH
GODS DEPART WORLD.	1755	500	1925	~2880 BRH
DWARVES BEGIN TO COLONIZE GREEN AND WHITE MOUNTAINS.	1760	505	1930	~2875 BRH
ELVES REACH CONTINENT.	1867	612	2037	~2768 BRH
GREEN MOUNTAIN KINGDOM OF DWARVES ESTABLISHED.	1990	735	2160	~2645 BRH
WHITE MOUNTAIN KINGDOM OF DWARVES ESTABLISHED.	2032	777	2202	~2603 BRH
SUDEA DECLARES INDEPENDENCE. ELVES WITHDRAW FROM CONTINENT.	3886	2631	4056	~749 BRH
ADVERSARY RETURNS TO WORLD. ELVES RETURN TO CONTINENT.	4514	3259	4684	~121 BRH
ADVERSARY ESTABLISHES ARKUS	4635	3380	4805	YEAR 0
BEGIN THE GREAT WAR OF THE FREE PEOPLES AGAINST THE ADVERSARY.	6000	4745	6170	1365
THE ADVERSARY DEFEATED, ENDING THE GREAT WAR. DEATH OF ALERON I.	6004	4749	6174	1369
SECOND CLEANSING OF ARKUS	6115	4860	6285	1480
KING ALAGRIC IV OF SUDEA DIES WITH NO HEIR.	9000	7745	9170	4365
WRITING OF SUDEAN HISTORY: YEAR 8000 EDITION.	9255	8000	9425	4620
WRITING OF DWARVISH HISTORY: YEAR 10,000 EDITION.	9830	8575	10000	5195
WRITING OF ELVISH HISTORY: YEAR 10,000 EDITION. BIRTH OF ALERON II.	10,000	8745	10,170	5365

Appendix C

Myths, Legends, and Prophecies

The Allfather Creates Aertu and the Nameless One Rebels

According to the elves' recounting of their teachings from the aelir, at the beginning of time, the Allfather, creator of all things, begat the universe from incoherent matter. He created the multitude of stars in the night sky.

He beheld the beauty in what He had created from nothingness, but it gave him no comfort, for it still seemed cold and empty.

The Creator fashioned beings like unto Himself, in the forms of male and female, for He remembered His Sisters as well as His Brothers and wished to create a family like unto the one from whence He came.

These first children, the aelir, numbered fourteen in all and equally matched, consisting of seven male and seven female, not truly brothers and sisters, but intended to pair and multiply.

This celestial family coexisted happily for uncounted ages, with only the stars as companions. They traveled widely, marveling at their Father's creation.

The male and female of his children coupled and over the course of the ages begat untold thousands of offspring, the aelient, like unto themselves, but of lesser stature. This was the natural state for these beings, and they did just as their Father had, before coming of age in his Mother's universe.

These first children were not destined to stay forever in their Father's cosmos but would someday come of age and create their own to their own liking. Their offspring, however, begat of their Father's universe, would remain forever tied unto it.

As is the way of stars, some grew old and died. From their death were born new stars. It was at this age that the Allfather knew the time had arrived for the next stage of his creation. About one likely star, He congealed the formless gases into balls of matter, glowing hot like steel from the crucible, spinning around the star. He did the same about many other stars and left them to cool for eons untold.

One day, He returned, with his children and grandchildren in tow, and said, "See all of you the many worlds I have made here unto this star. Only one of them will be suitable for our purposes next."

He then led them to the third small rocky world from the star and said unto his children and grandchildren, "Behold that which is to be the fruit of my Creation."

His children did not yet understand, and one asked his Father, "Why this one Father, for there are much larger and more beautiful worlds further out than this one?

It is plain, dark, and uninteresting with its steaming pools and black rocks."

"Ah, my child, you do not yet understand our purpose. Though still rough yet, it will be as a jewel when we are finished.

Let us go down and shape this rough new world to our liking."

The Allfather proceeded to separate the land from the sea. He brewed monumental storms over the seas and used the rain and winds to carve the highest mountains, wearing them flat and then raising new mountains in their place. Thus was barren rock turned to soil over the course of untold ages.

When at last it was ready, He said, "Come, my children, let us bring life unto this fertile world we have before us."

"What is life, oh Father?" they asked in unison.

"I will show you now," He told them, as He took up water from the sea and bent His will to it.

The first life sprang forth in His cupped palms.

His children saw and were amazed, and He was glad for that, but then admonished them, "My children, do not attempt to bring forth beings like unto yourselves into this world, for that is my prerogative.

Make all forms of plant and beast, but save for me the beings who will rule over them.

My grandchildren, do not attempt to bring forth life as your parents do, for if you succeed, your creations will be flawed. Instead, it is your destiny to inhabit this world and others that we build, so that you may watch over them as caretakers."

With that instruction, the children of the Creator made all the life in the seas, then they made all the life on land. What had been barren rock and steaming pools became green hills and valleys, white-capped mountains, and crystal blue waters. The world had indeed become like unto a jewel.

At the point where the world had been populated with all manner of life, one of the children became so enamored of their handiwork that he begged of the Creator, "Father, please, may I have this world as my own? I love it so and wish to watch over it and care for it for all the ages that are yet to be."

The Creator knew that this could not be so and saw through his son's plea to the covetousness that lay beneath the request.

"Do not ask this of me, as it cannot be so. Your purpose is to create a universe of your own when you are grown. In due time, you will be able to create worlds and populate them, just as I have done. Do not thwart your own destiny, just to possess a portion of mine."

The errant child, much chagrined by his Father's reprimand, grumbled loudly to his brethren and their children over the unfairness of the Creator's decision.

His brethren rebuked him as well for his disobedience to their Father; however, he swayed many of the grandchildren with his words, and they became his followers.

Secretly, he preached to his following of the unfairness of the Creator's prohibition on them to create living things. He taught to them the way to accomplish it, and together they created all manner of despicable creatures, for it was true, as the Creator had said, that the creations of the grandchildren would be imperfect and flawed.

Soon enough, the others discovered that the beautiful world they had created was beset with foul creatures that crawled in dark places. The beasts were beset upon by biting things, parasites, and disease. The plants died from fungus, rot, and ravenous creatures.

The Creator was not pleased with what He beheld and asked of His children, "Who among you is responsible for these foul creatures? They are a disgrace and a disfigurement upon our beautiful world."

None spoke up to own to the wrongdoing.

The Creator looked into the hearts of his children, and when He came to the one who had disobeyed Him said, "Do you think you can hide the truth from me, my disobedient son?"

"It was not I who disobeyed you, Father. I have always been your faithful servant," the son lied.

"Do you think I cannot look into your heart and see the truth? You add lies as well to your treason. I have seen now what you have done, and that you have drawn my children's children into your disobedience. Get thee gone from my sight, never to return, and those of your following who refuse to repent."

The disobedient son left the presence of his Father and his brethren, taking with him the grandchildren who would follow.

Though many rebellious grandchildren repented, begged for forgiveness, and returned to the fold, most did not and followed the disobedient son. All told, he brought one-third of the grandchildren with him into exile.

The other children then proclaimed, "Father, we must rid this world of all the vile things our brother has brought into being."

"That cannot be so," the Creator replied.

"That which has been brought into being must not be destroyed out of hand and must be allowed to follow its natural course. We will give our creatures a means to defend against the creatures of your brother, who will not be named. Now our beautiful world will be marked by strife forevermore."

Soon after, the Allfather discovered that the one who would not be named had done that which was unthinkable. He had created creatures after his own likeness, as was to be the sole prerogative of his Father. Like the creatures of his followers, these were fraught with imperfection, and he made many attempts, failing each time. Now, gruesome creatures of dim intelligence and evil disposition stalked the dark places of the world, wreaking havoc among the beauty of creation.

Eltheri Prophesy

Darkness shall envelope the world, and the mighty shall fall to contain the nameless shadow.

Though the light shall seem victorious, it is but the start of the waning.

The tree appears dead; yet one branch lives on, hidden among the weeds, and the fruit of the living branch shall be chosen above all others when the nameless shadow shall walk the world again.

The chosen will carry my power and might and shall be the only hope against the nameless shadow.

Should the shadow consume the fruit of the living branch, all is lost, but the chosen may turn the darkness to light.

> -Elther the Enlightened
> Roughly two years before the arrival of the aelir
> Recorded at the High Temple of Cyte
> Year 500, Elvish Calendar

Halfblood Prophecy

The strength of the halfbloods fails; the line of kings dies.

The might of the halfbloods is but a distant memory.

Millennia shall pass before another comes to reclaim past glory.

From the weeds, a hidden seed sprouts; the tree grows anew.

The glory of the halfbloods comes at great cost.

Darkness seeks to swallow light at every turn.

-Duran the Mad Hermit
Recorded by Ethelred
Scribe of the Great Temple of Iesenholdt
Year 3254, Sudean Calendar

Arkan Prophecy

The One True God needs no other name; no other gods shall come before Him.

He is the beginning and the end; all the world is His dominion.

You, my offspring, His chosen people, shall rule this world and all that inhabits it, in His name.

Always, shall you follow His commandments, for should you fail Him in that, a new people shall be chosen to rule in His name and a new champion shall lead them to glory.

-Ghizmuk the Last Quarter-goblin
First Seer and Revelator to the Arkans
Recorded at the Executioner's Block
The Second Cleansing
Year 1480 Arkan Calendar

Appendix D

Sentient Beings of Aertu

Immortals

THE ALLFATHER

Creator of the universe

THE AELIR

First children of the Allfather, each was destined to create a new universe upon maturity. Numbering fourteen, seven male and seven female, they pair-bonded prior to maturity, producing offspring known as aelient. Men commonly venerate them as gods and goddesses. Sent by the Allfather, the aelir came to elves and men as teachers, assisting them in building complex societies and advancing knowledge.

Gurlach: God of the Forge/Metalworking
Finle: Goddess of the Loom/Weaving

Shilwez: God of Husbandry/Livestock
Cerdae: Goddess of Agriculture/Crops

Corball: God of the Sword/Law
Andulle: Goddess of the Bow/Government

Carpath: God of Numbers/Mathematics
Faelwe: Goddess of Scrolls/Writing

Sildaen: God of Stone/Engineering
Lillane: Goddess of the Hearth/Cities

Zorek: God of the Sea/Fishing
Korelle: Goddess of Wind/Sailing

Nameless One: God of Evil/Adversary (Intended God of Philosophy)
Iselle: Goddess of Mercy/Medicine

THE AELIENT

The offspring resulting from the pairings of male and female aelir, produced during the period preceding the creation of worlds, to serve as caretakers of the finished worlds after the departure of the Allfather and aelir. Numbering in the thousands, they manifest as various nature spirits, often forming attachments to land and water features. They taught elves and men to live in the wild, before the arrival of the aelir. Fully one-third of the aelient followed the Adversary into rebellion against the Allfather and remain under his sway.

Mortal Peoples of the Allfather

ELVES

NATIVE TO: Elvenholm (The Western Isle)

LIFESPAN: 3000+ years

ATTRIBUTES: Elves range from five and one half to six and one half-feet-tall and weigh 100 to 200 pounds. They are generally human-like in appearance, with a slight pointed shape to the ears; clear fair skin color, never freckled; hair color white through black, but never red, located head and groin region only, always straight, with males beardless. Very quick and lightweight for their size, they are omnivorous, with fair night vision.

NOTES: Elves are not immortal, but extremely long-lived, with some individuals greatly exceeding the minimum life span of 3000 years. All elves possess some degree of ability for sorcery.

MEN

NATIVE TO: Northeast and South of Continent

LIFESPAN: 50+ years

ATTRIBUTES: Men range in height from five to seven feet tall, weighing 100 to 250 pounds. Heavier than elves of similar size, but not significantly stronger, men appear clumsy in comparison. They are regionally variable in size and appearance, with skin color ranging from fair, sometimes freckled, to dark brown, approaching black; hair color ranges from pale blond, through browns and red, to black, texture from straight to tightly curled, males usually bearded, and body hair distribution is highly variable. They are omnivorous, with poor night vision.

NOTES: According to historical records, pale skin and hair colors other than dark brown through black did not exist in men prior to their contact and intermingling with elves, and are most common within the historical borders of the Sudean Kingdom. Lighter shades of brown skin, with straight black hair, are natural to northeastern populations, while a similar, though darker-skinned, physical type is native to Kolixtlan and the central jungle. Populations south of the inland sea and the Blue Mountains were originally dark brown-skinned, with curly hair, prior to elvish colonization. Sudean populations assimilated many of the outward physical traits of the elves, while the traits of longevity and sorcerous ability consistently passed on only in populations maintaining greater than 50% elvish ancestry.

WESTMEN

NATIVE TO: Northwest of Continent
LIFESPAN: 50+ years
ATTRIBUTES: Westmen range in height from five to six feet tall and weigh 150 to 250 pounds. They are extremely heavy boned and muscular, far more powerful than men or elves, great sprinters, but poor distance runners. Their skin color is fair, sometimes freckled; hair color ranges from blond, through browns and red, to black, texture straight to wavy, males bearded, and body hair distribution varies. Heavy brow ridges, large noses, large teeth, and chinless jaws characterize their facial features. They are omnivorous, with poor night vision.
NOTES: Considered by elves to be a variety of men, there has been little to no intermingling of their populations with those of other men for over 10,000 years. According to the dwarves, whose records extend that far, their immense strength is due to their method of hunting large game by ambush, prior to becoming civilized.

DWARVES

NATIVE TO: Iron Hills, Northwest of Continent; migrated to Blue, Green, and White Mountain ranges
LIFESPAN: 80+ years
ATTRIBUTES: Dwarves range in height from four and one-half to five feet, weighing 150 to 250 pounds. Their skin color is fair to brown, sometimes

freckled, hair color ranges from blond, through browns and red, to black, texture straight to curly, males heavily bearded, with heavy body hair. Heavy brow ridges, large noses, large teeth, and prominent chins characterize their facial features. They are omnivorous, with fair night vision.

NOTES: Dwarves may have originated from an intermingling of westmen and men, in prehistoric times, or as an independent branch of the family. By appearance, they seem more closely related to westmen, who were their close neighbors in prehistoric times. Their short stature may be an adaptation to their inclination for underground habitation. They shelter exclusively in caverns, often enlarging them substantially through mining. Dwarves were the first race to develop writing and forge metals, preceding Elves in those respects, and are the most skilled in metal and stonework of all peoples.

Mortal Creatures of the Adversary

TROLLS

NATIVE TO: All mountain ranges of Continent
LIFESPAN: 300+ years
ATTRIBUTES: Trolls are seven to ten-foot-tall bipeds with short tails, weighing 500 to 1000 pounds. Thick fur covers their bodies, with small areas of exposed skin on the face and hands, reptilian in appearance, and mouths filled with sharp reptilian teeth.
NOTES: Usually solitary, sheltering in caves and overhangs in mountainous areas, individuals native to higher latitudes and elevations are larger and lighter colored than those from lower latitudes and elevations. They practice primitive stone tool making, to include thrusting spears, clubs, and hand axes, but no known use of fire. Trolls are carnivorous, with excellent night vision.

HALF-TROLLS

NATIVE TO: North foothills, Blue Mountains; Castia, Kolixtlan, Elven Colony, and Central Jungle
LIFESPAN: 200+ years
ATTRIBUTES: Six to eight-foot-tall humanoids, with a vestigial tail, half-trolls weigh 250 to 400 pounds. Their skin, dark green to black in color, appears reptilian overall, with hair only on head and groin region. They have humanlike teeth, with prominent canines, and are omnivorous, with excellent night vision.

NOTES: Believed to derive from the crossbreeding of smaller varieties of trolls to westmen, half-trolls appear much more humanlike in behavior than trolls. They engage in advanced tool making, to include ironworking, use fire, build shelters, fabricate crude clothing, and congregate in small bands.

GOBLINS

NATIVE TO: All forested regions of Continent
LIFESPAN: 60+ years
ATTRIBUTES: These four to five-foot-tall humanoids weigh 100 to 150 pounds, with greenish-black, smooth, hairless skin, a slightly stooped posture, with apelike gait, and an apelike face, with prominent canines. They are omnivorous, with excellent night vision.
NOTES: Goblins are semi-arboreal, though known to shelter in caverns where available. They employ advanced tool making, to include ironworking, use fire, fabricate crude clothing, build shelters, often occupying caves as well, and congregate in large bands.

HOBGOBLINS

NATIVE TO: Kolixtlan and Central Jungle
LIFESPAN: 70+ years
ATTRIBUTES: Five to six-foot-tall humanoid, hobgoblins weigh 100 to 200 pounds, having light to dark brown skin with a greenish tinge, straight black hair on head and groin region, a fully upright posture, and a humanlike face, with prominent canines. They are omnivorous, with excellent night vision.
NOTES: Believed to derive from the crossbreeding of goblins to men, hobgoblins are much more humanlike in behavior than goblins. They are excellent climbers, though not as arboreal as goblins. Practicing advanced tool making, to include ironworking, they fabricate advanced clothing, use fire, build shelters, often occupying caves as well, and congregate in groups to the extent of small villages.

ARKANS

NATIVE TO: Arkus; (The Northern Isle)
LIFESPAN: 3000+ years
ATTRIBUTES: Arkans range from five and one half to six and one half-feet-tall, weighing 100 to 200 pounds. Generally human in appearance, with a slight

pointed shape to the ears; light tan skin color; hair color dark brown through black, never red or blond, suspected to turn white in older individuals though none have been witnessed, located head and groin region only, always straight, with males beardless. Very quick and lightweight for their size, they are omnivorous, with good night vision.

NOTES: Arkans are 88% descended from elves abducted by the Adversary, during their second colonization of the continent, crossed with goblins for night vision and to instill affinity for dark sorcery. Just as with elves, they are not immortal, but extremely long-lived, with some individuals greatly exceeding the minimum life span. All possess some degree of ability for sorcery. Arkans are not inherently evil, but culturally indoctrinated to venerate the Adversary, believing him to be the creator of the world. They refer to the Nameless One as "The One True God" and claim that he needs no name to distinguish him from the false gods.

DRAGONS

NATIVE TO: Desolate areas of Continent

LIFESPAN: 3000+ years

ATTRIBUTES: Dragons are large reptiles, up to forty feet long from nose to tail, having slim, sinuous bodies, with the exception of a deeply keeled chest for anchoring of flight muscles, bird-like legs ending in clawed grasping toes, wide leathery bat-like wings, with wingspan exceeding length of body, and a long snout with numerous sharp reptilian teeth. They possess lung-like organs that concentrate a flammable gas and an oxidizing gas, which, upon combining in the nostrils, burst into flame. They come in several different varieties, some preferring mountains, some deserts, and others, like the water wyrm, gravitating to low wet areas. They are carnivorous, with excellent night vision.

NOTES: One of the Adversary's earliest attempts at intelligent life, dragons are notable in that they seem to be indifferent, rather than truly evil.

Numerous reports exist of compassion and restraint on their part. Solitary by nature, they are slow to reproduce and have never been numerous. Dragons are notoriously difficult to kill, but a well-placed spear, puncturing both flame organs, causes immediate death by incineration.

OTHER MONSTERS

Other monsters exist throughout the Continent, with highly variable lifespans and intelligence ranging from nearly non-existent to advanced. They exist as small populations overall, lacking reproductive viability, but intelligent forms are extremely long-lived, with some individuals surviving from the creation period. Intelligent specimens, like dragons, were early attempts by the Adversary, before his creation of trolls and goblins, while non-sentient forms are the creations of renegade aelient.

Appendix E

Magical System of the Allfather's Universe

Magic of Aertu

Upon creating his universe, the Allfather established physical laws to his liking and chose a system of magic based upon colors visible to the sentient peoples he created.

His Mother's universe had no such magical system, and physical laws very different from those chosen by the Allfather.

Of the myriad universes created by his kind, the Allfather's is unique in its combination of physical laws and magical system.

The various forms of magic existing on Aertu manifest themselves as colors to practitioners and occasionally, at high intensities, non-gifted onlookers. Listed below are the various colors and their attributes.

PURE COLOR	PROPERTIES	SOURCE
BLUE	ORDER, PRECISION	LIFE
GREEN	GROWTH, FERTILITY	SUN
YELLOW	HEALING, HEALTH	LAND
RED	DISORDER, DESTRUCTION	DEATH

Blue is the only strain of magic available to elves. Blue and red are available to men and Arkans, though Arkans are only trained to practice red magic, and may be completely unaware of their ability for blue. Men of good character tend to choose blue, while evil men gravitate to red, though there are occasional exceptions.

Immortals are the only known practitioners of green and yellow magic. The Allfather and the aelir are able to combine pure strains into new forms, while the aelient are capable of using pure strains singly.

SIGN OF THE WHITE RAVEN

All forms of magic may be used to manipulate objects in the natural world. Blue can be used as a destructive weapon, for example, while red can affect rudimentary healing if needed. The basic attributes remain, so that blue makes for a very precise implement, while red lends itself to powerful, yet imprecise applications. Red requires a practitioner with a high degree of control for anything non-destructive, while blue requires the ability to channel large volumes of power to attain destructive force. As only immortals can harness all forms of magic as required, there is little documentation for yellow and green used for anything other than healing and growth.

The Allfather was the only being known to combine all four pure strains of magic to form the white magic of transformation, though it is suspected that the aelir were capable of it, though they rarely used it.

COMBINATION	RESULT	PROPERTIES
BLUE/GREEN	TURQUOIS	CONTROLLED GROWTH
BLUE/YELLOW	GREEN	RESTORATION OF LIFE
BLUE/RED	PURPLE	CONTROLLED POWER, MOVEMENT
GREEN/YELLOW	CHARTRUSE	REGENERATIVE HEALING
GREEN/RED	YELLOW	LIFELESS STASIS
YELLOW/RED	ORANGE	INSTANT DEATH WITHOUT DAMAGE
B/G/Y/R	WHITE	TRANSFORMATION

For reasons yet to be determined, Aleron possesses the ability to wield magic in combination, to include the white magic formerly ascribed only to the Allfather.

www.ingramcontent.com/pod-product-compliance
Lightning Source LLC
Chambersburg PA
CBHW022138170626
46807CB00005B/1991